# About th

They say that you cannot teach an old dog new tricks... well, thank goodness I am not an old dog...

So, why write this story now, well, ten years ago, at the age of fifty-three, my wife, Sheila, got early onset dementia, Alzheimer's disease.

Then, a motorbike accident broke my arm and collar bone.

So, at the age of sixty-three, I finally sat down, and with one finger I tapped at the keyboard.

Writing has now become my therapy; it got me over the bad thoughts, an escapism from the illness that my wife is going through.

When I am writing, there is no real world, just the ones I am in with my characters.

GOLD WAR

# Terry Dee

## GOLD WAR

Vanguard Press

VANGUARD PAPERBACK

© Copyright 2021
**Terry Dee**

A CIP catalogue record for this title is
available from the British Library.

ISBN 978 1 784659 32 5

*Vanguard Press is an imprint of
Pegasus Elliot MacKenzie Publishers Ltd.*
www.pegasuspublishers.com

First Published in 2021

**Vanguard Press
Sheraton House Castle Park
Cambridge England**

Printed & Bound in Great Britain

# Dedication

To Sheila, my wife. I miss you so much.

# Acknowledgements

Colette Haseldine, for talking me into writing my first book after a motorbike accident; Stuart Atlee, for his wit, humour and letting me bounce ideas off of him, as well as putting up with me talking about it for the last year; to Sylvie and Trev for an afternoon of dinner, red wine and a lot of rugby talk; Colin Franklin for his constant encouragement and avidity; and finally, to Ellie Haseldine for her enthusiasm, as well as a lot of help with German and French.

A special thank you to my wonderful friend and companion, Fee Bourouba-Poole, for introducing me to her family and showing me a part of the world, I would never have otherwise seen.

# To the reader

With 7.7 billion people on the planet, I do apologise if I have used your name; the chances are, with that many people, I will have used someone's.

This is a work of fiction. Names, characters, businesses, places, events and incidents are either the products of the author's imagination or used in a fictitious manner. Any resemblance to actual persons, living or dead, or actual events is purely coincidental.

All historical place names used in this book are true, I have written a fictional story around those places.

# Prologue
## The Mobile Phone Video
## Summer Present-day

"Stop it, stop it *now* you two!" screamed the woman's voice.

The image on the mobile phone showed a boat; it had stopped, drifting, but with the engine ticking over, the deep droning thm, thm, thm of the engine could be heard, background noise as it ticked over, idling, just a slight sway as it floated, but no movement.

It was in the middle of a sea, presumed to be the Mediterranean. The boat, motionless, but with an almost calm sea, it rocked very gently.

"You bastard. You thought *you* were getting it!" snarled the taller, dark-haired man in the video.

The taller man, strong and handsome, his combed back hair, dark brown, collar-length and slightly wavy, a small beard, narrow piercing eyes and tanned complexion, his clothes smart, he appeared to have expensive tastes.

His fists clenched tight, he punched the slightly smaller, fair-haired man, who fell back, half on the seat and half off, holding his chin where the blow had just hit.

"What the hell are you doing?" said the smaller man as he started to get back up from the seat.

While he was still dazed and getting back to his

feet, the taller man rushed in, grabbed him by the collar and landed two more blows on his chin and eye socket.

Still only half up, the smaller man kicked out with his legs into the taller man's stomach, sending the dark-haired man stumbling backwards. As he fell, the smaller man jumped up quickly, rushed at the taller man, who was now back on his feet.

The smaller man lowered his body and rugby tackled the dark-haired man, his shoulder hitting the taller man in the chest, their momentum crashing both of them into the helm seat on the opposite side of the boat.

The video moved from side to side, following the action around as the fight moved about the deck.

The woman again screamed at the two fighting men.

"Bastian... Tom, stop it for crying out loud, before someone gets hurt!" she shrieked.

The taller man putting his feet into the stomach of the fair-haired man, thrust him back to the other side of the boat, fair-hair landing on the deck, he slid into the seat, his head catching the corner of the table; the taller man jumped up, lunging at the man sprawled out on the deck, fiercely kicking him in the ribs, sending him further across the deck, his lungs exhaling air from the blow.

The taller man bringing his foot back for a second kick at the same ribs.

The man on the deck grabbing a fire extinguisher, quickly holding it in front of his body, the leg heading towards him kicking the fire extinguisher with a clang. As the taller man's foot dropped to the deck, the fire extinguisher followed through, coming down on his toes with a dull and painful thud.

"Aye, *you* FUCKER!" shouted the standing man as he jumped back.

The camera continued to follow the fight as the two men grappled; a blow to the temple from the bigger man, threw the man with fair hair backwards over a small table, which sat in front of the boats white leather seats.

As the smaller man toppled over the back of the table; glasses and a bottle of wine smash and crash onto the floor, wine spilling from the bottle, running onto the deck; the larger man jumped on top of the smaller man, grabbing the fair-haired man by the throat, his fingers tight around his neck, the man below pushing up at the man on top, desperate to force him away.

The fair-haired man's left hand on the chin of the man above, he pushed upwards, his right hand swinging around at his head, aiming to punch the dark-haired man.

The man on top getting the upper hand, as the lower man fought for breath, after several punches that got weaker and weaker, he struggled for air.

The fair-haired man's hand moved down, onto the table, feeling for anything that could help him. His hand coming to rest on a broken wine glass, running his fingers around it, he grabbed the glass by the base; he could feel that the top had gone, all that was left, was the base and stem.

He thrusted the glass into the side of the larger man, the stem piercing the skin in the kidney area, the taller man's face cringing with pain. The man below pulling the glass out, lunged again, puncturing the man on tops flesh just below the ribs.

"Fuck you! FUCK YOU!" shouted the dark-haired man.

He let go of the fair-man's throat with one hand as he punched the man below.

"Bastian, stop it. Bastian, you'll kill him. Stop it!" came a voice from behind the camera.

With a huge punch from the fair man, the darker man fell to one side, but was quickly back on his feet, as was the fair man. Punch after punch they threw at each other; there seemed no stopping.

The taller man, blood pouring from the wound in his side; the blood running down his white Fred Perry T-shirt and onto his light beige trousers, blood covering his top where the glass had stabbed, now mixed with wine from the broken bottles.

The dark-haired man picked up the broken wine bottle by its neck, jumping towards the smaller man, he thrashed the bottle from side to side, catching the fair-haired man's upper arm.

With a shout from the smaller man.

"Hey, what are you doing, just stop will you!"

The video stopped.

As the next video taken on the mobile phone started, the picture was in one place, as if on a tripod or a mobile phone bracket; the sound in the background was of fighting, punching and crashing; but as the hand of the person who had pressed the start button moved away from the lens, the picture was the face of a beautiful young woman, fair complexion, dark eyebrows and eyeliner surrounding her dark brown eyes. Her hair was straight but with a slight wave, long and light brown. She had high, lightly flushed cheekbones tapering to a narrow chin.

As she moved back from the camera, she was wearing a light cotton mini dress, multicoloured, as if a paintbrush from every tin in a paint shop had been used to add its own unique colour.

She had bare arms, shoulders and neck apart from the straps of the dress, thin over her shoulders, the front of the dress open, down to her stomach, with black lace zig-zagging its way to just above her breasts where it had a simple knot.

The skin of her arms, legs, chest and face had a slight tan, as if she had been somewhere warm and sunny; she was still taking up most of the frame of the video as she turned to face the two fighting men.

"Bastian... Tom... stop it!" she cried loudly.

Suddenly jumping out of the way as the two men, arms around each other's necks, the fair-haired man having hold of the taller man's hair from behind, forcing his head backwards, came crashing down where she had just been standing.

The dark-haired man pushing his arms up, between his and the smaller man's chest, his hand reaching the chin of the fair-haired man.

He pushed up hard as he slammed the back of the fair-haired man's head against the glass window to the starboard side of the boat, the left-hand side of the video; two, three, four times his head banged hard against the glass; the fair man's face bruised and cut, he quickly twisted his body, escaping the hold of the dark-haired man.

The taller man, caught off balance, they both stumble down the step to the outer deck, the sun shining on their bloodied bodies; the shorter man's orange baggy T-shirt torn, his baggy worn-out camel-coloured long shorts splattered with blood, his bare feet cut from the broken glass on the cockpit deck.

Although he was slightly shorter than the other man, he looked physically fit, strong and tough. He was good looking, with a short beard and tanned skin, but his facial features and attitude were that of a man of fair play, of humanity.

The woman rushed back into the picture as she climbed onto the white leather seats to the right-hand side of the video. She rested her knees on the soft leather, her body hanging over the back of the transom as she watched the fight continue, her hands resting on the top of the ship's hull; three heavy blows from the smaller man sent the larger man to the floor of the lower cockpit, hitting his back on the transom as he went down.

The woman moving her head out of the way to avoid being hit.

The bigger man lashed out with his legs, still wearing his light brown expensive-looking deck shoes. He caught the heel of the fair man, the smaller man's legs disappearing from under him. He crashed onto the side rail of the boat, just managing to grab the handrail as he stumbled backwards, half over the side.

Dark hair jumping to his feet, quickly rushing towards the fair-haired man who was still off-balanced, he punched hard into the stomach of the smaller man, whose body was now bent backwards over the side of the ship, trying desperately not to fall overboard.

The fair man quickly sending his foot upwards catching 'dark hair' in the groin. The taller man's body bent double, he fell backwards.

"Stop it!" snapped the woman, hanging over the back of the seat.

Fair hair pulling himself back onto the boat as dark hair picked up a lifebuoy that had been knocked onto the deck. He swung the lifebuoy, aiming at the head of fair hair, just missing his face, then quickly swinging it back the other way; fair hair taking an opportunity, landing a punch onto dark hair's face. Dark hair staggered back, losing hold of the lifebuoy as it fell over the side of the boat.

They rushed at each other, dark hair's arm around the back of fair hair, fair hair's arm around the back of dark hair, each having the palm of their free hand under the chin of the other, pushing each other's heads backwards. They pushed and shoved, anger and aggression finding its way onto both their faces, red and sweaty in the heat and high sun.

They crashed back to the upper cockpit, the woman watching as they fell up the step, clattering to the deck, they rolled around the wine-soaked floor, fragments of broken glass digging painfully into their flesh.

Fair hair on top, he punched down into dark-hair's face... once, twice... just as the third blow was about to come crashing down onto his bruised and battered face.

A sudden plea from dark-hair.

"Whoa, whoa, whoa!"

Fair hair stopped the last punch from hitting the taller man underneath him. Dark hair holding up his hand, his palm facing the fair-haired man, a signal to stop, at the same time stopping his aggression towards the fair man.

Both men breathing heavily, the exertion of the fight.

The woman, still kneeling on the white leather, looked around at the video, then at the two men, now motionless, apart from their panting caused by the struggle.

The hand of the lower man still up, facing the man on top, the smaller man's arm still back, his fist clenched about to land the last blow.

The women again looked back at the camera.

The fair-haired man started to lift his body upwards. Tentatively, the smaller man on top raising himself off of the man beneath him. The man who only seconds ago he was aggressively defending himself against.

Slowly the fair man rose, he felt a reluctant truce was being offered, and he wished to take it.

Finally, on his feet, the fair-haired man bent down towards the dark-haired man still lying on the deck, he lowered his hand in a gesture to help him up; the darker man took his hand; holding each other's wrists, the fair-haired man rises back to his full height, lifting the dark-haired man from the floor of the boat's upper cockpit.

They both stand facing each other, their bruised and bloodied bodies directly in front of the camera. Their hands part as they look over to the seat.

Debris, red wine, blood and glass covered the deck.

The woman looking up at them both as fair hair turned and limped towards the seat, in need of a rest. He was now battered, bruised and exhausted.

Suddenly, a crushing blow to the back of his head from dark hair sent him flying towards the woman still kneeling on the seat.

"You FUCKING stupid, FUCKING moron!" dark hair screamed at the smaller man through gritted teeth.

The woman quickly jumped from her kneeling position on the white leather seat, rushing around the back of dark hair, to the left side of the video picture.

The punch to the back of fair hair's head was so hard, that dark hair's middle finger bent back, into what looked like a broken bone. Dark hair held the hand to his chest in agony; fair hair landed on the white leather seat head first.

Dark hair grabbed fair hair's shorts and T-shirt from the back, throwing him forcefully towards the rear of the boat; fair hair hit the transom, crashing over the top to land in a heap on the lower cockpit below.

Dark hair bounded onto the leather seats. With one hand on the rail of the transom, he jumped over to disappear out of sight behind the transom wall; the woman leaving her position on the starboard, she moved back to the seat, from here to view the fight as she cried out again.

"Stop it... stop it now!"

Dark hair appeared again above the transom. Bending quickly, a second later having an oar in his hands, he thumped it down towards the lower deck; fair hair jumping back to his feet, holding a second oar; dark hair lifting his oar above his head, then with force, he chopped it towards fair hair's head. Fair hair putting the oar he was holding in two hands across the top of his head, defence, to stop the blow from dark hairs oar from hitting him. The force of the strike knocking him back. Dark hair lifted his oar once more and again thrashed it towards fair hairs head; fair hair taking the impact of the second blow, knocking him back further; a third chop from the oar of dark hair and fair hair tripped, falling onto the swim platform at the stern of the boat, but managing to stay on his feet.

Dark hair jumped down to the swim platform, the woman left the white leather seats, rounding the transom, she stepped onto the lower cockpit, from here she looked down onto the swim platform.

As she stepped down to the lower cockpit, she looked back at the camera.

One last crushing blow from the oar of dark hair and fair hair splashed into the water just below the swim platform.

The woman screaming once more.

"Bastian, no! Bastian, no!"

Fair hair now in the water, still holding the oar above his head as the taller man, standing on the edge of the swim platform, continued swinging his oar at the man in the water.

The woman rushed down the steps to the swim platform. Disappearing from sight, behind the transom.

Then, a splash as the dark-haired man hit the water; he swam towards the fair man, grabbing his hair, pushing him under.

The woman screaming to stop, looked back at the camera.

The two men still fighting in the water; she stepped up from the swim platform, through the lower cockpit, up the step into the upper cockpit as she swiftly walked towards the camera, broken glass cracking underfoot, her right-hand raises as her index finger moved forward, getting closer and closer... the mobile phone's screen... went black.

# Eight Weeks Earlier

# Chapter 1
## Sebastian Plant's Wharf
## Late Spring Present-day

The high buildings and skyscrapers of Docklands, glass and chrome reflecting in the late morning sunlight, wealth and money oozing from every edifice.

From Westferry Circus, we head east, into the glossy labyrinth of Canary Wharf, the cathedrals in praise of glorious riches; down West India Avenue towards Cabot Place, there to see the office workers grabbing a late breakfast coffee or an early lunch sandwich, all mingling with the building workers and sightseers craning their necks as they look up at César Pelli's gleaming, 1 Canada Square or the HSBC building or the magnificent Balfour Beatty building.

Past Canada Square and half way around Churchill Place, we head for Blackwell Basin, around Cartier Circus and onto Harbour Quay.

A Harris hawk flying over as it chases pigeons for its lunch. The bird's handler watching as the hawk swoops, dives and weaves, the bird of prey going about its duties.

Here we find the building of Milstone-Hanks Finance, the twenty-storey building for hedge fund management, the black windows, rounded corners and roof overlooking the South Dock, as if it were a polished onyx gem, reflecting sunshine against the blue sky, rainbow effects on the black glass.

Through the windows of the eleventh floor, we enter the office of Howard Hart, medium height, slim, with a shaven head. Howard, early fifties, wearing fashionable glasses, black shoes and a dark blue suit, of which he would take the jacket off while in the office, a white shirt with a thin dark blue stripe, the sleeves rolled up, tie loosened and the collar undone.

He was talking to Kamil Dudek from the floor above when he heard a strange and distant chanting, looking down at his clock, he wondered what the noise could be at this time of day.

"Bastian, Bastian, Bastian!"

The sound, muffled against the glass walls and doors of his office. Again, he hears it.

"Bastian, Bastian, Bastian!"

"Ha… Hang on a moment Kamil, there's something going on… in the office. I'm going to have to hang up. I'll get back to you as soon as I can… Okay, speak soon… Okay, ciao."

Looking down at the clock on his desk as he put the phone down, this time taking in what he saw… 10:58 a.m. "What the hell is going on?" he mumbled to himself.

Closing the lid on his laptop, watching as the screen turned black; he looked up.

The offices of the eleventh floor were open-plan, that is, unless you have risen above chasing the next jackpot, settling into a routine that you are happy with, your knowledge being your next step… you are moved behind the glass, to be a manager of the floor.

Howard's office was at the far end of the floor, the opposite end of the room from the entrance door, and roughly in the middle of the front and back wall, the view from his window looking south towards Deptford, Greenwich and the *Cutty Sark*; next to his office, were more offices, for secretaries, meeting rooms and stationeries.

The open-plan office was filled with tables, chairs, computers, printers, keyboards and paper, lots of bits of paper. Men and women all in dark blue, dark grey suits, skirts, black shoes, white or light blue shirts, young, middle-aged; no one seemed to be old, except the cleaner.

Computers sitting on desks, all filled with graphs, bar charts, pie charts, column charts, doughnut charts, you name it, there was a chart to reference it on at least one PC in the office.

"Bastian, Bastian, Bastian!" The muffled sound continued.

Howard stood up, walked towards the glass door. As he did, he could see a crowd gathering at one of the desks. Grabbing the handle of his door, he pulled. As it opened, noise from the chanting increased.

"Bastian, Bastian, Bastian!"

The door fully open; he braced himself for what he might see, how he might deal with it. Sebastian, he thought, was a bit wayward, a bit of a handful, a bit of a maverick, but you had to hand it to him, he was great at what he did... and that was, he made lots of money, and for a company that existed and thrived on money, he didn't want to rock the boat of one of the main contributors to the necessary growth in Milstone-Hanks' global wealth.

He once again looked back at his clock; now 10:59 a.m. The office, pulsating with the chanting, was now starting to clap.

"Bastian, Bastian, Bastian!"

Howard, leaving the safety of his office, walked towards the crowd on the east side of the office. The crowd chanting; Howard reaching the back of Sebastian Plant's desk.

Nothing seemed immediately different, Sebastian sitting on his chair at his desk, the computer in front of him, the usual signs of work in the office, the screen, filled with a chart, in this case, a line graph, a box below the graph giving a pound symbol, with numbers that were constantly rising, the heading at the top of the screen reading 'Fee-Friday Media'.

Howard knew about Fee-Friday Media; Sebastian had been into his office recently, having spoken about the latest contract that he was dealing with.

Sebastian Plant was a hedge fund manager, early thirties, tall, slim but muscular and very good looking, his mid-length hair having a slight wave, combed back; he had a short beard and narrow piercing eyes, covered with black-rimmed glasses.

The crowd parted as Howard moved up behind Sebastian's chair. He stopped, looking over his shoulder; there seemed to be nothing different to what he would expect, except: the crowd chanting; Sebastian's hand hovering over the sell button.

To the bottom right of the screen, a clock read 11:01 and 33 seconds, the line on the chart was straight, if slightly zig-zaggy, at 45 degrees towards the top right-hand side of the screen — so far, so good.

"Now, now, now!" shouted Harry Chang standing beside Sebastian.

Harry Chang was Sebastian's best mate.

"For fuck's sake, Baz, hit that fucking button!" Harry continued, frustratedly.

"Not yet," said Sebastian calmly staring at the screen. "Not long now though."

"Bastian, Bastian, Bastian!" the crowd continued.

Howard nervously looking on.

"I trust you know what you are doing Sebastian," he said.

Sebastian concentrating on the screen, the crowd chanting, Harry Chang urging him on. The clock now reading 11:02 and 25 seconds. Sebastian sat up straight in his chair, the crowd's excitement growing higher with anticipation.

Sebastian's hand hovering. "Ready?" he beamed.

The noise growing louder still.

11:02 and 47 seconds, the graph still rising, the share price growing by the second.

Sebastian having persuaded Howard this was a good deal, he knew it would be a certain winner, Howard agreed. He had to. He didn't know how Sebastian seemed to manage it, luck, intuition maybe, but he always seemed to get the big deals right. 11:02 and 54 seconds.

"Now!" cried Sebastian as his hand came crashing down onto his keyboard with a thud, his finger stabbing at the 'SELL' button.

Sebastian stopped still, both hands hovering, shimmering just above the keyboard as if it were a crystal ball that he was waiting for the mists to clear.

From the moment Sebastian's hand hit the keyboard, the crowd hushed, just a low hum of anticipation, the room was silent, not a sound... then 'Ping' went the computer, the rising line on the Fee-Friday Media screen went into a sudden and dramatic nosedive, from a steady and continuous growth, the line now going into a direct line down. The crowd erupted. Sebastian had done it again. The office whooping, whistling, cheering... Sebastian's hands slowly moved from hovering over the keyboard, his arms rising, rising and rising further, until they stop directly up in the air above his head, the crowd cheering. Howard's hands going skywards.

Sebastian slowly rising from his chair, his arms still raised, his fingers bent except for his index fingers, which were pointing towards the ceiling.

Standing to his full height, slowly turning but not looking at the crowd around him, his eyes in a daze, looking beyond everyone there; this was Sebastian's winning goal at Wembley, his hitting the ball for six at the Oval, his crossing the line first for Olympic gold.

The crowd pushing towards him, each and every person in the crowd giving him a high-five, a pat on the back, laying their hands on him, hoping that by touching this man, a little piece of his magic would rub off on them. He stopped, standing face to face with a smiling Howard, both being buffeted by the crowd congratulating Sebastian. Howard grabbing Sebastian's shirt either side of his chest, shaking it excitedly.

"YES, YES, YES!" he shouted.

Sebastian had bought the shares for Fee-Friday Media for $4.88, he had arranged with Howard that there would be 500,000 shares, a total of $2,440,000. For anyone else this would not have happened, but for Sebastian, he was sure of a return. The shares sold for $36.65, a total value of $18,325,000, giving Milstone-Hanks a profit of well over 15 million Dollars. Sebastian's arrangement was to get 0.5 percent for himself, £79,425.

Of course, Sebastian's timing had to be perfect; Fee-Friday he knew were not in a good position. Fee-Friday talked a good talk, they said all the right things. Fee-Friday Media was in the business to expand, they had set their sights on a rival interest and planned a takeover. To some, this looked like being a good investment for the future, others could see chinks in the sums on offer. Sebastian's task was to get the timing right. As the excitement subsided, Howard turned to the crowd.

"Okay, you lot, excitement's over, get back to work now, and let's see if we can have some more of them."

The crowd moving away, Howard took Sebastian by the hand.

"Well done Bastian!" he said, turning, heading

back to his office behind the glass.

Sebastian turned to face Harry, both their faces beaming. Wrapping their arms around each other, enthusiastically patting each other on the back. Harry moved back a pace as they did a double fist bump with exploding fingers, then stamping their feet as if excitedly running on the spot.

"Well, looks like the drinks are on you, my old mate," said Harry.

"Sounds good to me," replied Sebastian. "But it's going to have to wait, isn't it? "You're off to New York this evening, don't forget."

"No, I haven't forgotten, a couple of little deals in America and that will be my earner, can't wait."

"Then Queenie's next week?"

"Wouldn't miss it for the world!" replied Harry excitedly.

"And you're picking me up?"

"Of course, don't fret. I'll be there don't you worry."

By the early part of the afternoon, Harry was off to get his flight; Sebastian had made enough money for the day, so decided to head off out with Harry.

Sebastian and Harry had been best friends as far back as they could remember, getting into trouble as kids, doing up cars as teenagers, Harry was best man at Sebastian's wedding. Even jobs, they changed together and stayed together, and at Milstone-Hanks they fitted in perfectly. "Make fast money and spend money fast" was their motto.

Leaving Onyx House, the London head office of the investment group, they head north, up Harbour

Quay then left towards the docks; Harry making his way to the TFL station; heading east. Sebastian continued up South Colonnade, reaching the DLR station and north towards his home in Stratford. Under the railway bridge, up the steps, flashing his Oyster card at the terminal on the barrier; a fraction of a second later the barrier opened.

Onto the platform; the train, bright red with a sea blue wavy stripe down the side was already waiting at the station, doors open; with a self-satisfied saunter he stepped on board.

"Hello, Mr Sebastian, sir," said a voice from his left-hand side.

"Hello, Isaac," he replied, turning his head to greet him.

"And how are you today, sir?" said Isaac in his gruff Ghanaian voice.

Isaac Bahdoo worked for DLR; Sebastian would regularly stop and chat. Isaac's stories of his life and family, a million miles from his own. Isaac had moved to the UK some twenty-five years earlier, with his wife; they had three children born in England and were extremely happy with their lives. Then his wife got cancer. Isaac continued to work and bring the children up; struggling to make ends meet. But to look at him, you would not believe he had a problem in the world. Short and slightly plump, his big beaming infectious smile and large bright eyes seemed to exude happiness.

His job for DLR was: captain of the train. His role, to make sure everyone was happy, that their journeys are safe and enjoyable. He proudly strutted up and down the train in his Cobalt blue jacket and battleship grey trousers, white shirt with a blue and white diagonally striped tie. Sebastian knew all about Isaac Bahdoo. Sebastian's home being eight stations from Canary Wharf, he was a regular traveller.

"How are the kids, Isaac?"

"Oh, they are great Mr Sebastian. I have got rid of all three of them now, all at university."

"Which ones?"

"The two older boys, one is at Oxford and the other at Durham, the youngest, my girl, sir, she is at Canterbury," he proudly boasted.

With that, an announcement on the Tannoy said "This train is ready to depart, please stand clear of the closing doors!'" two or three seconds and the doors close, the train pulled away.

"I hope to see you again soon, Mr Sebastian."

"Me too, Isaac."

The train pulling out of the semi-dark domes of the station, he took his seat; the bright sunshine of the early afternoon bursting in through the windows. The train clattering as it crossed a track junction. It was not long before it arrived at West India Quay, this regular journey having no interest for Sebastian. He sat happily, content with his day's work and looking forward to next week and Queenie's.

The stations of Poplar, All Saints and Langdon Park pass as he blankly looked out of the window, Bow Church and Pudding Mill Lane before he jerked from his dreamlike state to see the tell-tale signs of nearing home: Queen Elizabeth Olympic Park to his left, the stadium now plastered in West Ham United colours, and finally the announcement over the Tannoy that the train was about to stop at Stratford. "This is Stratford"; Sebastian's home to the right and a weekend to himself.

*** 

After a two-minute walk from the station to his 36 storey-high home, through Stratosphere Towers main door, crossing the floor towards the lift, with a "Good afternoon!" from the concierge. With murals on the walls and chairs dotted about the ground floor, it had the look of a hotel. "Ding!" the lift arrived, the doors open, three steps into the lift, he turned, pressing the button to his floor. With a quiet whirring, the lift ascended the building to another "ding!"

Sebastian leaving the elevator, made his way up the short corridor, reaching the door of his flat. Walking through, he turned, pushing it too.

Making his way over to the window, throwing his jacket on the white leather settee as he passed. The window was the width and height of the room; facing south, sunshine beaming into the room.

Sebastian's flat, about halfway up Stratosphere Tower; from here he could view his world, his domain, the vista giving him a slight shiver, smiling, he gazed across the London skyline.

The skyscrapers of Canary Wharf and Docklands, at the trains and cars and people.

He stood, his feet slightly apart, his body

upright, his head looking up as a surge of emotion thundered through his body; shuddering as if he had just had an orgasm. Money and power, that was Sebastian's love.

Turning, he looked around his room, the oak wood floor, the white leather furniture, a small jet-black corner desk outside the bedroom. The minimalist look you would call it; every wall, white, being broken by two large paintings. Immediately behind him as he stood at the window was 'Masturbating in Red', a painting of about 100cm by 140cm.

A young woman in her early twenties, naked on a white armchair, similar to the ones in Sebastian's flat, the top half of the painting in a deep crimson red, the armchair having rounded arms highlighted in black, the chair at a slight angle to the front of the picture, the girl's head with long ginger hair at the top right-hand side of the picture, her hair flowing over her right shoulder and across the Caucasian flesh of her bosom, her feet on tiptoes on the seat with her legs open and her knees up in the air, her left hand on her left knee. Her eyes, slightly shut, looking down at her right hand, the corners of her mouth turned up, a slight smile on her face showing her pleasure as her right-hand middle finger gently strokes her clitoris.

The other painting was on the wall between the two main windows, a painting of 'Girl Stretching with Head Back', the background of the painting being various shades of red with blotches of black mixed in, the girl's body being transparent on the red and black blotches.

The bottom of the frame starting at the girl's thighs, around her naked bottom, with her stomach pushed out, leading up to her bare chest. The shape of her body being painted in white, as if showing only light hitting her torso, starting at her vagina, leading up past her navel and around her breasts, showing her erect nipples. Her arms to the elbows facing skywards, her head looking up allowing her long ginger hair to fall across her back and down to her bottom, both of her hands on her face and her body at a forty-five-degree angle to the front of the picture.

In the middle of the room was a three-seater white leather settee and a single white leather armchair. In front of the settee, a jet-black coffee table; above the coffee table, a large flat screen TV on the wall. The other side of the room had a small kitchen and cooking area. Pouring himself a glass of water, taking two large swigs, he laid the glass onto the worktop, then made his way to the bedroom.

The bedroom keeping the same minimalist style of white, including all-white bedding, broken on the walls by one wall having a Manga painting of eleven naked women standing in a line across the canvas, each a different look, a different nationality, a different posture: some large breasts, some small, some shaven, and some not, some with long hair, some with short, blond, dark and redhead, the Manga painting above his bed, 70cm high and 130cm wide.

The other wall had a painting of an American

Banknote featuring Benjamin Franklin on a $100 bill. His line-drawn face in the centre of the picture, his eyes looking directly to the front. Either side of Franklin being painted with pastel reds, greens, blues, oranges and yellows.

Sebastian changed from his work clothes into a tracksuit and headed for Stratosphere gym.

# Chapter 2
## Queenie Slocum's House Party
## Late Spring Present-day

'Cha-Ching!' went the sound of a cash register. Clink, clink, clink was the sound of coins being poured, the tell-tale sign that Sebastian's mobile phone was starting to ring. Bm Ba Ba Bm, ♫, Bmm Bm, ♪♫♪ Ba Bm, as Pink Floyd's *Money*, rang out from his phone. Bm Ba Ba.

"Hello," said Sebastian urgently, picking up his phone.

"Baz, it's me," said Harry, on the speakerphone of his car.

"You're late!" Sebastian said, abruptly.

"Sorry, mate, it's a long story. I'll tell you all about it on the way… be there in about ten minutes."

"I'll be in the lobby. See you soon."

The time was six-thirty. Harry was supposed to have picked him up at six. Sebastian had been all day getting ready for the night ahead, both his and Harry's three-monthly trip to see Her Majesty, the Queen herself, that is Queenie herself.

Queenie Slocum, former 'model', 'actress' and party girl. Queenie had been running parties for the rich, famous and powerful for some forty years, and never seemed to fail in her duties as the perfect hostess. She would have everything ready for her guests including the best drinks. With each guest came their own personal attendant; the best drugs, with all personal attendants trained in how to get the best from the experience; and their own personal bed. Your personal assistant will help in every way, two or more personal assistants should you require, and can afford it. Queenie's parties were not cheap, but you always went home looking forward to the next Queenie party.

Sebastian picked his jacket up, royal blue with a thin silver crisscross pattern, dropped his mobile phone into the pocket and headed for the door out of his flat.

Leaving his apartment, checking the door before he walked towards the lift. It soon arrived, descending towards the lobby.

He nodded to the concierge as he walked over to the main entrance door where he waited for Harry to arrive.

Taking a quick look at his reflection in the glass, beige trousers, sky blue Fred Perry Polo T-shirt and royal blue deck shoes, his jacket slung over his shoulder.

Two minutes later, Harry's car pulled up outside.

Sebastian left Stratosphere Tower and walked towards the awaiting vehicle: an Ara Blue Audi R8 Spyder V10 with the top up, as polished and shiny as both Harry and Sebastian.

Sebastian opened the door and jumped in.

"So, what's happened?" said Sebastian, getting straight to the point.

"You wouldn't believe me."

"Try me."

Harry put the car into drive and it sped away from Stratford with a throaty roar, satnav set for Twickenham.

"Well, you know when I left work last Friday, I was heading off for New York... business there on Saturday, flew back on Sunday?"

"That's right, I remember."

"Then flew out there again on Monday, to see the board."

"Yeh," agreed Sebastian.

"So, back on Tuesday," continued Harry, "barely caught my breath and another meeting at Aguila-Davis in Chicago on Thursday."

"Hey, sounds like you're doing alright for Airmiles," laughed Sebastian

"Was I in a panic, left O'Hare International at 11:30 their time, got into Heathrow at quarter past one Friday afternoon. I thought, great, I'll pop into the office for a chat with you about Queenie's, plenty of time."

Harry got onto an open stretch of road and put his foot down, straight up to 80mph, between speed cameras.

"No," he continued. "Fucking two hours at Heathrow, fucking two hours... fucking 'Green' protesters, fucked me right up. Glued themselves to the fucking baggage carousel, for fuck's sake, fucked everyone up!" He drove more erratically as he got angrier. "Everyone was saying, just chop their fucking hands off, that'll teach 'em. I mean, in the old days, they just used to go and hug a tree, why can't they still do that? Let us get on with making money, you know, we're keeping this country rich after all."

"So, you didn't get to the office?" asked Sebastian

"No," said Harry. "In the end, I was so late, I went straight home, slept for hours. I wanted to be ready for this evening."

They drove through Bow, Mile End and Old Street, getting up to 50mph on the short sections of road where he could, having to slow through the busier parts of the city. The heavier traffic just got Harry more frustrated, revving his engine trying to show the other road users that he had a fast car; they were just getting in his way. A night of pure unadulterated pleasure awaited; Harry couldn't get there quickly enough. Past Pentonville and St Pancras, Euston Road he could get a bit faster, Marylebone Road; then he was onto the Westway and time to really put his foot down. The car had a top speed of over 200mph, and he wanted to give it as much as he could. Flashing drivers doing the correct speed to get out of his way, he passed them as if they were not moving. Seemingly, he knew every speed camera along the way: as he reached a camera, he would brake hard, slowing down to 55 or 60mph, but only while he passed them; this, to the annoyance of all of the other drivers behind him doing the correct speed for the road and now finding themselves having to brake and slow down. Once past the camera, the right foot went down once again, the engine roared and he was soon back up to 130mph.

"Rumour has it, you are going away next week as well, is that right?" said Sebastian.

"Yes, Munich," he replied, concentrating hard on the road, which was speeding by very quickly. "It's some ecology thing Milstone-Hanks are involved in. They want to show the shareholders that we are caring for the planet, so they want me to show my face."

"While you are there, you must have a Zweibelrostbratten. Believe me, Haitch, it's to die for, you will not regret it, it will be the best thing you will ever have," enthused Sebastian.

"Zweibil... what?"

"Zweibelrostbratten!"

"What is it?" enquired Harry. "Some sort of blow job?"

Reaching Hammersmith and turning onto the Great West Road, their destination within striking distance, they ran parallel with the Thames, the bend of the river taking them towards Queenie's House. The miles being eaten up at the same speed as the fuel in Harry's car.

"Guess who I heard from this morning?" said Sebastian.

"Err, don't know," replied Harry. "I'll take a guess at Trump."

"Close," said Sebastian. "But no... do you remember when I got married?"

"Of course, I do," interrupted Harry. "I was the best man!"

"Yes, well you remember that wimpy guy I introduced to you, the one I thought might be useful

43

to us, so I got him to come on the stag do, you remember, five days in Bulgaria?"

"Oh wow, do I remember five days in Bulgaria... well, I remember two days in Bulgaria, I somehow lost the other three in a drunken stupor."

"Yeh, anyway, Modino Graziano, called me this morning, wants to meet up with the two of us, says he has a proposal that will be financially beneficial to us both."

"Oh yes, 'Modino Graziano'. Oh god, that was embarrassing, when you told me his name," said Harry sheepishly. "I said to him 'Hello Modino', that's an interesting name, what part of Italy are you from, and he said, with a plum in his mouth 'I'm not from Italy, I'm from Norfolk'."

"That's the one, and we were only in Bulgaria for two days and he got homesick, phoned his dad."

"Oh yea!" laughed Harry. "His dad flew out to Bulgaria and took him home!"

At that, they both fell about laughing.

Past Kew and now on the outskirts of Twickenham, ten more minutes and they reach their destination; Harry, quietly pleased with that, the twenty-one-mile journey in about fifty minutes, wasn't bad he thought.

Queenie's house was set in the quiet suburbs of Twickenham, one of the leafy green areas, places where house prices had many noughts attached. Following the Twickenham Road and St Margaret's Road, take the Richmond Road and you reach a small turn off to Queenie's called 'Game Lane', it was a short lane, with a single house, Queenie's house,

'Game House'. Built in the mid-nineteen-thirties, a seven-bedroom building, the bedrooms being of various sizes, small one-bed rooms, to rooms large enough for two king-size beds.

The ground floor had an entrance hall leading to the main reception, the bar room, a dining room and Queenie's office, as well as the guests' changing area. Beyond the dining room were the toilets, utility room and large kitchen. From the bar and dining room, both would lead to a garden room filled with soft furnishings, low glass tables and plants of various types. In the middle of the garden room were two large square green baize tables for playing cards, at each table were eight chairs. The glass roof and front having a low brick wall. The south-facing room, lit up with sunshine.

An extensive garden, surrounded by trees, shrubs and bushes, these covering a high fence beyond them. The garden had a grass area, plants, flowers, bushes and ornaments laid out on the patio and seating areas. Beyond the patio was a flat grass area, which had three large yurts set up on wooden platforms, the platform going all the way around the yurt, having patio tables and chairs, a wooden handrail following the platform with two steps up from the grass.

Viewed from the main patio, the first yurt was to the right-hand side of the grass area, the second yurt to the left and a little further away than the first, the third yurt being roughly in the middle and a little further back than the second.

Further into the garden led to trees, footpaths,

wooden carvings, as well as ornate huts that wouldn't look out of place as a Hobbit's home, interspersed with shepherd's huts of bottle green or crimson red, all covered in cream-coloured lines and murals of the sexual fantasies to be found within. The Hobbits huts containing various items, that is, those required to inspire some of the most exotic pleasures.

To the left-hand side of the garden, behind a tall hedge, a row of wooden buildings for the guests who wished to stay overnight, through the next day or longer should they require.

Harry turned his car east into Game Lane, after about two hundred metres he reached a set of gates on the right, which were open. He pulled through the gates and almost immediately stopped at the drop off point.

The 'meet and greet organiser' wandered over to his car as Harry wound his window down.

Queenies 'meet and greet organiser' was medium height, of a pale complexion, slim and in his fifties, with short hair and a small moustache. He was wearing black trousers and waistcoat, black polished shoes, a white shirt with long sleeves, the sleeves held up by sleeve garters, a black bow tie and a name tag pinned to the waistcoat giving his name as Gary.

"Good evening, gentlemen. How good it is to see you," said Gary. "If you would like to leave your keys with me, sir, you can make your way to the entrance where you will be met by Siobhan... a driver will put your car in the parking area for the evening."

Harry and Sebastian stepped from the car.

Sebastian walking around the back of the car and towards the house; Harry reluctantly handing his keys to the 'meet and greet organiser', Gary.

"Be careful with that car!" said Harry. "It cost me a lot of money!"

"There are many cars of a similar price range in this evening, sir." Gary smiled. "We make sure that each and every one of them is kept and looked after to a very high standard."

Harry held the keys up. Gary held out his hand as Harry dropped them into his palm.

"Thank you, sir," Gary said with a nod. "Siobhan will be waiting inside."

Harry looked over to Sebastian, who was already heading for the front door. Sebastian looking towards Harry, with a movement of his head, which said, hurry up we're nearly there, Harry put a spurt on to catch up.

As they reached the main door, it slowly opened. On the other side of the door was a beautiful woman, medium height, long blonde hair and in her mid-thirties with very little makeup.

She was wearing white comfortable shoes and a white thin cotton loose-fitting mini dress. It had wide straps over the shoulders, a rounded neckline that covered her upper chest and was sleeveless. The white cotton material was covered in many large red polka dots, each dot about the size of a cricket ball. This was all she wore, well, except for a beaming smile and a badge that read 'Siobhan'.

"Good evening," she said. "Please walk this way, we shall sign you in."

Sebastian and Harry stepped into the hallway, which immediately turned left, heading in the direction that Siobhan's hand was gesturing.

A few paces up the hall to a door on the left, a sign on the door saying 'Reception', which they enter.

Siobhan shutting the front door, followed them into the reception room.

"It's good to see you again Siobhan," said Sebastian. "I always wonder if it will all end, the last time we meet."

"It's wonderful to see you too, Sebastian... and you Harry. Oh, don't worry about me, I'll be here for a long time yet."

"Is her majesty in tonight?" said Harry

"She most certainly is," smiled Siobhan. "She said to me she is looking forward to catching up with you both after you are changed."

"Excellent!" said Sebastian "Let's hurry and get ready."

"Not a problem," said Siobhan. "If I could have both your signatures in the book please. Oh, and don't forget, first names only."

Sebastian taking the pen that Siobhan held up for him. She then pointed at the page in the book, which was open. There were many first names, followed by a reference number, then the blank area for a signature.

Queenie set the rules of the parties many years ago that only first names were ever used, that everyone was to only use their real first name. If a surname was used by anyone at any time, regardless of however rich or famous, they would no longer receive one of Queenie's 'by Royal Invitations'. They would no longer be welcome.

Of course, this was not the only rule. Over the decades, Queenie had learnt her trade well. She knew what people liked and disliked. Her aim was to please as many as she could; she knew they would then want to return. But for a few, over those decades, they had abused that privilege, got too drunk, got too lairy and mistreated the girls or boys.

Queenie eventually, set a committee of regulars and trusted guests to run the 'invitation lists'.

To get onto the list, you had to be recommended by a regular at the main 'Game House' parties, then to sit before the committee to prove you were a suitable person to be eligible to be put on the list.

Queenie started her parties in the late nineteen seventies; at the time, gaining popularity with film and TV stars, musicians, singers and artists. As they grew, she would see politicians, business people, lords... and ladies, civil servants and the clergy, as well as drug barons and senior police officers. Not all at the same party, of course. Queenie, on the whole, kept the conflicting groups separate, unless, of course, there was some gain for her or the individual.

The parties, of course, had young women, young men, drink and drugs. And when you have parties like that, however good they are, it is worth having something you can use as a leverage.

Sebastian and Harry's invites came through a friend of Sebastian's dad. His dad having a few friends in the criminal fraternity, they had their names put forward to the committee.

Once accepted, you would be invited to a 'half way' party, not as good as the Game House, but to make sure you were of a suitable character.

As Harry finished signing his name, they heard a dark brown sexy voice from the doorway behind them.

"If you would like to follow me now gentleman."

Sebastian and Harry turned towards the door to see a tall dark-skinned woman in her late twenties, wearing white sensible shoes, a white basque with medium-sized red polka dots, the dots about the size of a golf ball, with her shoulders bare showing her silky black skin, her beautiful face framed by her afro hair.

The straps on the lower part of the basque, holding up white stockings, she wore nothing else, the curve from just below her navel as it fell to her shaven pudendum, then to the parting of her vaginal lips, the skin as equally wonderful as on the rest of her body. She stood tall and proud, with a beaming smile and a badge that read 'Rusty'.

"I will follow you anywhere Rusty!" drooled Harry.

She reversed from the doorway, walking back along the hallway, to a door behind the front door. Opening it, she walked through to a large room with lockers, showers, sinks, toilets and seating.

Walking behind the chest-high desk to her left, Sebastian and Harry following her through the door, stopping at the desk.

"There are your gowns for the evening

gentlemen," she said, handing over two folded and neatly ironed white gowns, placing two pairs of soft sandals on the top.

Sebastian took the items, handing one set to Harry.

"Everything is perfectly safe in this room." she said, "Once you have changed and your clothes put in the locker, if you would hand me the key, I will put it in the safe, of which only two of us and Queenie have the combination."

"Sure, will do," said Harry.

Sebastian and Harry sauntered over to the lockers that Rusty had pointed at, removed all of their outside clothes, putting on the gowns and sandals.

The gowns giving the impression more of a toga. The white loose cotton material coming below the knees, having a wide rounded hole for their head. It covered the shoulders and was loose down the arm, finishing wide at the elbow.

Locking their lockers, they strolled back over to Rusty waiting at the desk close to the doorway.

"Thank you, gentlemen," she said as they handed their keys to her. "If you would both like to make your way to the bar, there will be a glass of wine waiting for you... Her Majesty will meet you there shortly!"

"Thank you," they both said as they made their way from the changing area.

Through the hallway and past the stairs lay a door on their right with the word 'BAR', Harry pushing the door, which opened into a room filled with mood lighting, low glass tables and soft low chairs. To their right was the bar; behind the bar was a tall West Indian barman with a beaming smile. He had short dark hair and round glasses.

Having just finished serving two previous customers who were moving away to one of the round glass tables, he looked towards Sebastian and Harry, speaking to them in a soft, deep voice with a gentle Jamaican accent.

"Good evening gentleman... there are two glasses of wine for you both here." He gave a sideways nod down to the bar.

The barman wore comfortable white shoes, white trousers with a neat crease on the front and back, a white shirt being covered by a white waistcoat, above that a white bow tie. The waistcoat and bow tie, covered in medium-sized red polka dots, a badge on his waistcoat gave his name as 'Carl'.

Sebastian and Harry thanked Carl, picked up their drinks and sat at one of the round tables. Only being there for a moment, when in from the garden room flounced Queenie, her deep lilac flowing silk robes waving in the turbulence of her movement as she walked towards their table.

Sebastian and Harry, seeing her coming through the door, stood up to greet her.

"Sebastian, Harry, how wonderful it is to see you both," she said, as she kissed Sebastian and then Harry on both cheeks.

"And good evening to you too, Your Majesty," said Sebastian as they all sat down. "Four times a year certainly isn't enough."

"Harry, how's that cock of yours… going to see some action tonight?" she said, mockingly

"We shall have to wait and see Your Majesty, there are so many other ways to enjoy ourselves here, I may just end up in a yurt for the night!"

"Ah," said Queenie. "You say all the right things Harry, and, of course, you are right, there are many pleasures that can be had here. In fact, I liken it to a theme park, well, an 'adults-only theme park', a different ride, a different entertainment wherever you look."

Queenie had had many years of holding parties, she, for a long time, had known how to throw the best party, and she certainly knew the best people to invite.

She had a party every two weeks and would invite like-minded guests. This evening, for example, was business men and women, those who not only liked the pleasures that Queenie's parties had to offer, but while there, acquaintances could be made, friends made, deals struck; and as Queenie had once said, "If you're going to strike a deal, do so with a smile on your face!"

Queenie planned on continuing to run her parties for many years to come. She was now in her early sixties, her long silver-grey hair, parted down the middle, one half over her left shoulder, the other half over her right. She was medium height, slim but not thin and extremely good looking for her age. She wore very little makeup, and this is how she liked her staff to be, very little or no makeup was best, she thought, let the air and the sun to your body and skin.

She would encourage her staff to eat healthily, drink healthily and enjoy sex. It too, she would say, is healthy.

Queenie's staff were called 'Qucummers', that is QUeenie sloCUMmers, but guests would affectionately call them Qucums; Qucums could be a boy, or girl, gay or straight, and would all wear white clothes to show they were a Qucum. They would then have a different polka dot depending on their experience or position.

New Qucums would have a small polka dot, the dot being about the size of a wine bottle top; if they had been working for Queenie for a while, a medium-sized polka dot and experienced staff a large polka dot, baseball size.

If the Qucum were a personal attendant to a guest, the polka dot would be multi-coloured, administrators a red only polka dot, cleaners and domestics a blue polka dot.

"I have two lovely girls for you both for this evening," Queenie continued, "For you Harry, I have Patricia, blonde with nice curves on her, just how you like your woman, is that right?"

"Sounds good to me, Your Majesty."

"And for you Sebastian, I have Stephanie, tall, slim, dark hair... very sophisticated!" said Queenie "They are both new girls."

"I look forward to meeting her, Your Majesty."

"Good... I will just go and send them in to you... I will catch up with you both later. Oh, and by the way, you must try the Fire OG in the Marijuana yurt, it is superb"

"Thank you, Your Majesty, we will make that our first date." said Harry

"And remember, the Qucummers don't participate."

"Noted," said Harry.

Queenie stood up and left the table, nodding and welcoming the couple on the table next to the door as she passed, her deep lilac silk gown flapping as she walked, like a purple butterfly.

She disappeared through the door.

Almost immediately, the door reopened and in strolled two Qucums. The leading girl was big of bosom and hips, not fat, but a beautiful hourglass shape, a very pretty face, with full lips and a cheeky, bubbly smile, long blonde hair combed back into a ponytail, held in place with a white band. The second girl was altogether different, tall, slim, her features sharp on a small face, long legs and a small bosom, her hair cut into a bob.

Both girls wore white shoes, a white light cotton mini dress, both being covered in small multi-coloured polka dots.

Having name badges on their dresses; the blonde girl was 'Patricia' and the tall girl 'Stephanie'.

Both wore nothing underneath.

"Harry," said the blonde girl as she walked towards him. "My name is Patricia. I am your date for this evening."

Harry's eyes lit up; his face beamed a huge smile.

"Hello Sebastian," said the tall girl with a very

posh voice. "What a pleasure it is to meet you. Her Majesty has spoken so much about you."

"Thank you, Stephanie," said Sebastian. "That's nice to hear."

"Would you like to stay here for a while and finish your drinks?" said Stephanie. "Or we could make our way out to one of the yurts?"

"Oh, Harry," said Patricia. "You should see the yurts; Her Majesty has had them refurbished. They are looking fantastic in this late evening sun."

"Yurt sounds good to me, Patricia," said Harry. "You coming too Baz?"

"I'm right behind you Haitch, but I think I might have a stroll around the grounds first," he said, as he looked up at Stephanie.

"A stroll it is then," she said.

"We'll be heading for the Marijuana yurt, so see you in there," said Harry.

"Okay, see you there!"

Harry stood up quickly, getting as close to his date as fast as he could, smiling in her direction the whole time. As he moved close to her, she smiled up at him, kissed him on the cheek, then took his arm as they started to move off towards the garden room.

Sebastian was slower getting up, grabbing his glass as he did so. Watching Harry as he left the bar, looked around at his date who was almost as tall as him; with a half-hearted smile from both of them, she took his arm.

Moving into the garden room, there were men and a couple of women guests on the soft easy chairs dotted around the room. The guests wearing white cotton togas, the Qucums in their multi-coloured polka dots, the boy Qucums wearing white loose-fitting cotton shirts and trousers; all watching the games being played at the two beige tables.

As Sebastian and Stephanie were passing the tables on their way towards the garden, he looked over to see how the games were going; on the nearest table, were four male guests, all wearing togas. The games being played were strip poker, but the strippers were the Qucums sitting next to their guest at the table; as the game started, each Qucum wore ten items, as their designated guest lost a round, so the Qucum removed an item of clothing. Quite clearly, thought Sebastian, one of the players on this first table were not good poker players, as three Qucums were still almost fully dressed, but one of the girl Qucums, now being down to just bra and panties.

The second table had three male and one female guest, the three female Qucums and one male Qucum being evenly matched, with them all still wearing underwear and T-shirts.

Sebastian and Stephanie left the garden room, strolling through French windows towards the garden as a cheer went up from the first table.

In the warm late spring evening, the sky turning to dusk, lamps and lanterns twinkling in the well-kept gardens.

They walked down through the patio with its plants and grasses, wonderful aromas of spring flowers in the air, then to the right as they walked behind the Marijuana yurt, towards the trees and statues.

"What do you do, Sebastian?" said Stephanie. "I mean, what is your job?"

"Me, I work in the financial district, in London."

"Is it a good job?"

"It pays the bills."

There was a short silence.

"I wanted to be a teacher," said Stephanie. "I don't really think I was cut out for it though."

"No?" said Sebastian abruptly.

"Do you drive?"

"Look, what is this?" said Sebastian, irritated. "The inquisition?"

"Oh, I am sorry," said Stephanie, genuinely upset.

They continued to walk the garden in silence, past the third yurt, through the trees, past the shepherd's huts and the hobbits' houses, following the path that would lead them back to the patio in front of the main house.

Passing the MDMA and Psilocybin yurts, they head towards the Marijuana yurt.

Up the two steps to the platform, pulling the curtained door back, they step inside.

There were two wood-burning fires, one to the left and one to the right. The smell of burning wood giving a pleasure and warmth to the orange glow of the lamps which hung around the outer wall of the yurt.

The wall itself was made from criss-cross trellis and canvas. The roof having beams from the outer wall, up to a centre point in the middle of the room.

The floor, oakwood; settees and armchairs following the curve of the yurts round outer wall.

In the centre of the room was a low table; in the centre of the table, a bong, the bong having a series of pipes leading from it.

Around the outside of the table were several round and very comfortable-looking settees, the settees being the same distance from the bong, wherever you sat, having soft raised arms, each settee big enough for two people: a Qucum and a guest.

Sebastian quickly looking around the room as he walked in, mainly to see if there was anyone he knew apart from Harry.

There was no one, but Sebastian's eye catching one guest who was on his own, a small man with short greying hair and a short goatee beard, making notes on a light green pad.

Sebastian seeing Harry and Patricia at the centre round settee; he and Stephanie headed towards them.

As they sat, Stephanie leaned forward, picking up a new clean mouthpiece, handed it to Sebastian. Taking it from its wrapper, he plugged it into the pipe leading from the bong.

"This," said Stephanie, as Sebastian was about to suck on the pipe, "is Fire OG... the leaves look like they have spikes of fire."

Sebastian drew a deep breath.

"It has a lemony smell," she continued.

As he sucked, Stephanie rubbed her hand across his thigh, up across his groin till she reached his chest where she gently eased him back into a semi-lying position on the settee.

"Relax," she said.

Sebastian took a second lungful as he looked towards Harry. Harry was well chilled, pipe in his left hand, his eyes shut, his head back against the settee, his right arm out to the side as Patricia lay against his chest, her right hand up under his toga as she fondled his cock.

An hour later, Sebastian and Harry chilled, Stephanie and Patricia lead their guests from the yurt back to the main house, the sky now dark, with just the house and the lanterns to light the way.

They strolled across the cool patio, into the garden room, through the dining room, into the hallway and up the stairs towards the bedrooms.

Reaching the first floor, Patricia and Stephanie look into the five rooms, they were all full, so continued up to the second floor, the left-hand room was free.

Patricia taking Harry's hand, pulling him into the room, pushing him down onto the big comfortable settee on the far side from the door, pulling off his toga at the same time.

Sebastian walking in, followed by Stephanie, they head towards the double bed behind the door. Still wearing his toga, he sat on the bed, Stephanie rounds the door, standing between his legs, bending down she kisses him on the lips as she slowly eased him backwards.

Climbing slowly onto the bed, over him, pulling off her polka dot dress, naked, she kissed him once more.

Sebastian, lying still on the bed.

Taking the bottom of his toga, she slowly pulled it up. As she reached his hips, she ran her hands under the toga, stroking her fingers across his stomach, brushing over his cock.

Grabbing the toga once more, she pulled it further up his body, again letting her hand stroke between his legs, around his balls, the toga crossing his chest, Stephanie finally pulling it over his head as she threw it across the room to a chair in the corner of the chamber.

Once again, she kissed his lips, slowly moving down to his chest. Kissing his nipples, his stomach; reaching the pubic hair, she brushed her cheek against his semi-erect penis, her lips and face making a circle around the manhood as it flopped from side to side. Finally, her lips parting as the semi-erect phallus entered her mouth, twirling her tongue around the top as she sucked the shaft deeper into the warm moist hole.

"Argh!" Sebastian suddenly winced "What are you doing?"

"I'm sorry, am I not pleasing you?"

"For fuck's sake!"

Stephanie taking Sebastian's cock in her hand, gently rubbed, smoothing out any trouble; Sebastian settled, she again putting her mouth over his manhood.

"That's it, for fuck's sake!" shouted Sebastian. "You're fucking useless!"

Stephanie jumping up from the bed, grabbing

her polka dot dress as she quickly ran from the room holding it to her face, tears in her eyes.

"I'm sorry," she cried.

Sebastian lay back on the bed, he looked over to Harry.

"Are you all right mate?" said Harry, lying back on the settee, Patricia sitting on top of him.

"I've had better times."

A few seconds later, Queenie entered the room.

"I'm sorry Harry," she whispered towards Harry and Patricia. "Carry on you two, you look like you are enjoying yourselves."

She turned to Sebastian on the bed, sat down on the edge and looked down at him, running her hand up his thigh, stroking his limp penis.

"Are you all right my young friend?" she said, calmly.

"Thank you, Queenie. I'm sure all will be okay."

"Now listen, young man, a word of advice. I have over the years seen many young men like you come and go, overdoing the lifestyle, wildly spending money and burning themselves out... I wouldn't like to see this happen to you. Take my advice, have a break. You are overflowing with runaway hedonism... Now, you need a break, or it will be the death of you!"

"Okay Your Majesty, I will take that on board. I'm taking my son to see his nan and grandad tomorrow. That can only be to the good... right?"

"I believe it can Sebastian. I believe it can."

Queenie stood up, blew him a kiss, turned and started to leave the room.

"Oh," she said. "I hear there's a friend of yours on her way here now, she should be here soon."

Her deep lilac dress drifted along behind her as she went through the door.

Suddenly stopping she spoke to someone in the next room.

"Now c'mon Donald," she said softly. "Please try and make it to the toilet. Don't throw up on the carpet there. It's very expensive to clean."

The words of Queenie *'overflowing with runaway hedonism'* and *'you need a break, or it will be the death of you'* still going around his head as he lay on the bed.

The door to the bedroom which he and Harry were in, had been open all evening. It had at one time or another had a head poke around the corner to see who, or what was happening in that particular room, only this time the head poking around the corner was a friend.

Suki Watanabe looked over to the bed where Sebastian lay; she had already guessed he would be there. She could see Harry spread across the settee on the other side of the room; the young blonde Qucum, lying between his legs, his now semi-limp cock in her mouth.

Suki entered the room, naked, with a pretty young petite girl of about twenty on her arm. The young girl was slim, with beautiful features and light olive skin; she had short hair coloured a plum red. She was a bit shorter than Suki.

Suki was herself not very tall. She was slim and extremely attractive, her hair long, straight and very dark, her skin pale and glowing on her oriental features. She was twenty-eight years old and overflowing with confidence.

They walked arm in arm towards the bottom of Sebastian's bed.

"Hello," she said to Sebastian. "I thought I might find you here."

"Ah Suki," replied Sebastian, a little bleary from the drugs and drink. "I was just thinking about you."

"Well," said Suki. "It can't have been very good thoughts; you haven't even got a hard-on!"

Suki reaching the bottom of the bed, turned the young girl she had on her arm towards her, put one arm over her shoulder, her other arm around her lower back, pulling her close, their naked bodies squeezing tight together as their lips met. Suki's hand caressing the young girls back, her fingers stroking across her bottom; the young girl's fingers stroking gently up the sides of Suki's chest, then down to her hips.

Suki slowly pulling her lips away from their passionate embrace, she turned to Sebastian.

"Do you mind if I lay down next to you?" she said.

"It would be my pleasure," smiled Sebastian.

"I think it might be," said Suki. "Both now and later."

Suki lowered herself onto the bed next to Sebastian, crawling on her hands and knees to the top of the bed, her face moving closer to Sebastian's face, her lips onto his lips as she gave him a slow lingering kiss.

"It sure is good to see you again," she said as

their lips parted.

Suki rolled over onto her back, looking up at the young Qucum she had walked into the bedroom with; Suki relaxing her body, her arms by her side as she lay on the blue silk bedding; opening her legs to reveal the slit of her vagina, the short soft black hair covering the mound of her crouch. The young girl moving to the foot of the bed, bending down to her knees as her upper body slid up the bed.

"How's your dad?" asked Sebastian as he rolled his body over to face his friend.

"He's good," said Suki. "You'll have to come over for dinner again sometime... soon I hope."

"Love to."

Suki's father, Takumi Watanabe, moved from Japan to London many years ago, as a lecturer at the London School of Economics. Suki, born in England, grew up with a love of numbers and finances. She went on to work for Eliane-SuCol (Swiss) Investments.

The young girl eased her face up between Suki's open legs, closer to Suki's moistening womanhood. Her hands gently stroking Suki's hips, they slowly moved towards her tummy, then back to her sides.

"Do you remember when you came over last time...? oh, oh... that's good!" Suki oozed as her mind suddenly switched from Sebastian to the tongue twisting around her clitoris.

Sebastian watching Suki's beautiful face as the middle of her body rose in the air, her arms either side of her, pushing into the bed, her head going back as her face disappeared into her long black hair. Her fists clenching the silk sheets, as the thrill of the young girls' mouth on her labia tingling every nerve ending in her body.

"Ooh, she's good Bastian," Suki shuddered.

The Qucum's tongue flicked up and down, Suki, unable to speak as she squirmed in the bed, the young lips sucking at her clitoris. The Qucum's tongue pushing deep inside her, Suki's hands lifting from the bed, gently holding the back of the Qucum's head, pulling her face into her increasingly wet genitals.

"Ooh Qucum, you are very good," said Suki. "What's your name again? I'm having you next time I get to one of these parties."

"Melanie, miss."

"Melanie ay?" said Suki "Are you as good with cocks as you are with clits...? see if you can do anything with Bastian's. I will say though, Bastian, it looks a bit dead to me."

"Oh, it's okay, couldn't get on with the Qucum earlier," he said.

Melanie's head moving away from Suki's vagina as she shifted her body towards Sebastian, getting between his legs, lowering her body.

"She couldn't suck the skin off a warm bowl of custard!" he continued. "Ooohhh!"

Melanie's mouth taking in Sebastian's cock, she sucked, it started to get harder.

"Now that looks better," said Suki.

"Ooommm!" said Sebastian.

"Now, I want you to listen to me, and listen hard!"

"Mmmmoooh."

"Was that a good call on the Fee-Friday deal… no, you don't have to answer that; I know it was. Now, I got that from the horse's mouth, and just for you. I have another, this time a telecommunications company. They are doing the same trick. You know what these rich companies are like. Why make a dollar when you can make five?"

"Ooooohhh!"

"Now can I have Melanie back please; I think that prick of yours looks hard enough now… I will text you in a few days… give you more details."

Melanie lifted her mouth away from Sebastian's cock, shifting her body back across the bed, like a limpet, attaching it to Suki's expectant womanhood. Suki's eyes close as the pleasure returns to *her* body.

Sebastian slid down the bed till his feet touched the floor at the bottom of the bed. Standing up, he looked toward Suki as he moved to the back of Melanie.

Melanie's head between Suki's legs, her tongue flicking her clit, he pulled Melanie's bottom towards him, slowly working his erection into Melanie's vulva; Sebastian looking down at Suki's beautiful body, dreaming that it was his tongue pushing into his beautiful friend's moist hole.

# Chapter 3
## Russell and Elizabeth Plant
## Late Spring Present-day

Bing, bong... bing bong... bing bong... bing bong bing bong bing bong... The impatient Sebastian rang the bell of his parents' house... bing, bing, bing... he kept pushing the bell now until the door was answered.

Hang on one minute," said the happy voice on the other side of the door.

Bing bing bing...

"Just comin'!"

Several locks clattered from their hasp till, finally, the door swung open.

"Oooh myyy godddd!" said the extortionately happy woman who opened the door.

"Hello, Mum!" said Sebastian, offhandedly, as he stepped across the threshold and walked past her.

"Just looook who we haaaave heere!"

Sebastian's mum was looking beyond Sebastian, as behind him stood her one and only grandson, Samuel.

"Good afternoon, Grandmother!" said Samuel in a posh public-school voice.

"Samuel... Samuel... Samuel... Samuel... my beautiful, beautiful grandson, oh how lovely it is to see you!" said Mrs Plant in a gooey high-pitched childish voice.

"How lovely it is to see you equally, Grandmother."

Mrs Plant stood back in the doorway, the boy still outside on the step. Mrs Plant was a large woman, to say the least, in a loose-fitting bright blue polyester-cotton-mix dress with 'V' shape from the neck down, open to the middle of her overly large bosoms.

Her arms open wide, her head tipped to one side. Her hands open as her fingers at first wide, gestured inwards, that the boy should 'come to momma'. The boy looking either side of his nan, seeking a way through that would avoid the overwhelmingly emotional attentions of this woman.

Samuel stood upright, his public-schooling, he told to himself, would not allow for such 'working class-ness' to distract from the aim, the aim that he and his father Sebastian had set themselves. Which was the four times a year trip to see the family; but then... suddenly, his grandmother leaned to one side, he thought he could see a way through. He took a deep breath and went for it... he misjudged his approach, he hesitated too long. As he stepped over the threshold, his grandmother's arms came from the side and now her hands were heading towards his face, Samuel stopped... a bad move he thought, he should have kept going he told himself. No... Mrs Plant's hands rounded on him, her fingers twitched with excitement as they closed in on his cheeks.

Her hands either side of his face, her index fingers and thumbs grabbing the skin behind his mouth... as they tweaked and twiddled.

"Oh, my beautiful baby boy!"

"But Grandmother... I am twelve years old!" he pleaded

She stood back again, the rounded features of her face beaming with pleasure.

"Now c'mon," she said, as her arms opened wide once more. "Come and give your nan a big, Big, BIG hug!"

"I'd rather not, Grandmother."

"Come on, come on... come to Nanny Plant."

"But Grandmother... please?" he begged.

Too late, his eyes bulged as his left cheek plunged into the gap between her right and left womanliness.

Her arms wrapped around his head as she squeezed it deep into the bare flesh of her extensive cleavage, she shook her body from side to side with excitement, her head facing upwards with Grandmotherly delight.

Elizabeth Plant was in her mid-fifties, a onetime stripper working in the night clubs of the East End of London; her loves these days being a snow-white poodle called Tinkle, red wine, luminous pink and luminous blue, gaudy ornaments, even more luminous pink... and her grandson, Samuel.

Samuel was a creation emanating from a six-month marriage between Sebastian and Samuel's mother, Amelia.

Elizabeth Plant had no time for her, a stuck-up rich bitch she would call her, that was to her face as well. The truth be known though, she really was a stuck-up bitch.

Having Samuel was, for Amelia, a step into a comfortable life, only the best for her boy, and in her mind that included public school.

Samuel was wearing his Sunday best to visit his grandparents. White trousers, white shirt with a navy-blue bow tie, a crimson red jacket, with double white vertical stripes all the way around the jacket. He looked as if he had just arrived from punting on the Thames.

Tinkle was bouncing with excitement behind Elizabeth, waiting for his opportunity to get fussed over. Jumping up and down, tail wagging, mouth open, a pink bow around his head.

"Now," said, Nanny Plant. "I've made some chocolate-covered Rice Crispy cakes this morning, especially for you. Come through to the kitchen and you can have one."

"I'm sorry, Grandmother," said a worried Samuel. "Don't you remember the last time I had chocolate here, I had an allergic reaction? I came out in all those blotches."

"Oh, don't you not, no, never mind about silly things like that. I'm sure *one* will be okay."

"But mother said, I really shouldn't. In fact, because I reacted to the chocolate, she won't allow chocolate in our house."

"What a load of rubbish!" interrupted Nanny Plant. "Children and chocolate go together."

"But I have forgotten to bring my EpiPen with me, in case something should happen."

"Epi... pen?" said Mrs Plant turning around to look at him, suddenly realising something, a smile creeping onto her face "I've got pens here… all sorts of colours, have a cake first and we will find some paper for you to draw."

***

"Hello, Dad," said Sebastian as he entered the lounge.

Sebastian's father, Russell, was sitting on a large red reclining armchair with a glass of beer, in a beer holding tray, attached to the side of the chair.

"Hello son," he replied. "How's tricks?"

"Ah, it's fine."

"Work okay?"

"Getting by."

Apart from Russell Plant's armchair, the rest of the room was the creation of Elizabeth; sky blue walls, bright chrome chandelier, silver settee and single armchair with large sky-blue cushions. Bright pink coffee table, bright pink sideboard and TV stand, all on a pink carpet.

Dotted around the room were ornaments from Spanish holidays: a donkey, a Porron Sangria wine pitcher with a leather cover, featuring a picture of a bullfight. Also in the room were two black Spanish fans with an overly colourful print of Spanish dancers. Both fans sitting in open castanets.

Russell was watching the TV.

"Horses, Dad?" said Sebastian.

"Yeah, the race I want is in about ten minutes."

Russell Plant was tall and strong for his age, but now in his mid-fifties, he was putting on a bit of midlife spread.

In his younger years, he was tall and handsome, from the Essex — London border. He worked for, and with, the East End mobs, running errands, managing some of their interests, which included strip joints where he met Elizabeth.

He kept himself fit and was an amateur boxer.

He still kept his hand in, helping the local and London mobsters. A bit of driving, a bit of fetching and carrying and a bit of standing in the background in a black suit and dark glasses looking 'hard'.

These days though, he was more than pleased to just be sitting, having a flutter, watching the horses on the telly.

Today was different though, he had heard from one of his mob friends that in the three o'clock on the telly, was a 'dead cert'.

It was the horse of one of the country's most notorious 'Dons'. This horse, so Russell had been informed, would not lose. No one, according to the informant, would dare to get in front of it.

Of course, bookmakers were not taking such things into account when giving the odds.

The other horse owners though, did not want their favourite steeds' heads to join them in bed, so took no chances.

"What's the horse called then, Dad?"

"It's called 'Edinabed' son."

Sebastian was not aware of the mob connections.

"We'll have to see how it gets on."

Samuel walked in from the kitchen, his jacket and bow tie now off, chocolate on his shirt and around his face, blotches on his neck.

"Hello Grandpapa, and how are you today?" he bounced.

"Hello, Sam… oh, I'm fine."

"Samuel, sir!"

"Oh yeah, of course."

"Ah, I see you have horse racing on the television."

"Yes Sam, I've got a bet on."

"Samuel, sir!"

"Of course,"

"May I watch with you, Grandpapa?"

"Of course, you can Sam… b… b… uel," stuttered Russell.

"I have some friends who own horses, sir," said Samuel politely. "Sometimes they win."

"My friends own horses too, Samuel," said Russell. "They are guaranteed to win!"

Samuel went over to the side of the pink cabinet, where he pulled out a pink stool. Picked it up, then dropping it beside Russell's chair.

"Who are we cheering for. Grandpapa?" asked Samuel.

"That one there," said Russell pointing at the TV.

"The blue one, Grandpapa?"

"No," said Russell. "The one in the blood-red colours, number 6."

"Oh, I see," replied Samuel.

The horses in the starting gate, one or two jumping and agitated.

"They're off!" called the commentator.

"Here we go," said Russell "Money coming my

way."

"What's the odds then, Dad?" asked Sebastian.

"It's a cockle son," Russell replied.

"A cockle Grandpapa?"

"Yes Sam, it means the odds are 10 to 1."

"Is that good then?"

"If you win, yes, it is good."

There were ten horses running in this two-mile flat race; with the race about a third of the way in. The leading horse at this early stage being Life in Space, closely followed by Rocket up the Backside, with Balls of Steel third. Edinabed about half-way back in the running order.

At the halfway point, the lead had changed to Rocket up the Backside, Life in Space second.

"Would you like a cup of tea Sebastian?" called Elizabeth from the kitchen

"Yes please, Mum," he replied.

"C'mon... c'mon!" exclaimed Russell, through gritted teeth, getting excited at the television.

"How much you put on it then, Dad?" asked Sebastian.

"A grilla," said Russell.

"A grilla?" repeated Sebastian. "Are you sure? It looks like a nag to me."

"I'm sorry, sir," said Samuel politely to his grandfather. "What is a grilla?"

"It's two monkeys," he said, like Samuel should know.

The race, two thirds over, Life in Space, had dropped back, Edinabed up to third place, Rocket up the Backside, in second, and Balls of Steel, out in front; five furlongs to go.

"Two monkeys being?" enquired Samuel.

"A thousand pounds," said Russell. "A monkey is five hundred pounds."

"A monkey, sir? I still don't understand what a monkey has to do with horses," Samuel continued.

Four furlongs to go, Edinabed eased into second place, just in front of Rocket up the Backside, but Balls of Steel, had a four-length advantage. There's no way Edinabed will make up the gap.

"A monkey," Russell said, while his eyes were fixed on the television. "It comes from the five hundred Rupee note they have in India. The note had the picture of a monkey on the front, so we here, now call five hundred pounds, a monkey"

"Oh, I see… thank you, sir."

Three furlongs to go, Balls of Steel with a commanding four length advantage, there was no way it could lose.

"C'mon… c'mon!" Russell shouted at the television, Samuel joining in, copying his grandfather.

"I hope you're right about this, Dad, that's a lot of money to lose," said Sebastian.

"C'mon Edinabed… c'mon Edinabed!" shouted Russell, jumping up and down in his red armchair.

Two furlongs from the finish line, "It's Balls of Steel," the commentator excitedly announced from the television, "Balls of Steel followed by Edinabed… Rocket up the Backside in third."

Balls of Steel's jockey looking back over his shoulder, he can see Edinabed behind, too far behind, he looked forward again. Looking back once more… Balls of Steel in first place, his jockey looking towards the stand, towards the horse's owner… Suddenly, with a furlong to go, he slowly pulled the horse to a trot. The jockey's body raises from his racing position to sit upright, gesturing to the stand with hand signals.

Pointing down to the horse's rear leg, then poked his own leg. His clenched hands coming together then parting, mouthing "Pulled a muscle", then gestured that he is stopping, with his palm down, his hand making an up and down movement.

Edinabed sailing past Balls of Steel with just fifty metres to go. Russell was ecstatic as Edinabed crossed the finish line. Jumping up from his chair, grabbing the hands of young Samuel, they danced around the room.

"There's your tea, Sebastian," Elizabeth said, as she walked into the lounge, completely ignoring the shouting and dancing of Russell and Samuel.

***

Elizabeth was doing the washing up. Samuel a 500-piece jigsaw puzzle of 'The Simpsons' in the lounge. Russell and Sebastian sat in the back garden with a beer each.

"I've done very well for myself, I think Bastian," said Russell. "I've done a lot of risky things when I was young, got into some very nasty scrapes. I look back and think, how did I get away with that?"

"What's that, back in the mob days, Dad?"

"Yeah, it was good though, the clothes, the suits, the women!" continued Russell.

"You're still doing okay now though, aren't you? I mean, look at you, nice house, lovely garden, perfect area. I mean, what more can you want?" said Sebastian.

"Yeah, I know, time moves on, things change. Life has a past, which we know about, it's happened. It has a future, but what does that hold…? I don't know, I guess I am thinking, Mum and I will not be around forever."

"You have Samuel, we have Samuel, he is our future, is he not?"

"Yeah… no… oh, I guess I'm just going over this 'coz I'm thinking about Samuel… you know, he'll be thirteen soon. That it's about time he got more involved with the family… found out more about our past… you know?"

"Yes, Dad, I know exactly what you mean. Look, I'll tell you what, if it's okay with you, we'll go and have a rummage around the loft, see what we can find; old pictures, jobs the family used to do. I'll put it to one side, then the next time we come over, we'll get him to sort it out, let him know where he has come from. It'll be good for me too; it's been a long time since I've seen all the family stuff."

"And don't forget to tell him about his Great-Great-Grandfather Plant, Samuel Plant, the sergeant in the war," said Russell.

"Remind me again!" asked Sebastian.

"Two years after the war, he got shot in that pub in the East End, not far from where you live now," explained Russell.

With a nod to his father, Sebastian drank down his beer, got up from his garden chair and headed for the house.

Walking through the patio door and into the lounge.

"Samuel, how are you getting on with that puzzle?" asked Sebastian.

"Three more pieces to go, Father," he replied, putting them into the puzzle, Sebastian looking over Samuel's shoulder.

"Good," said Sebastian. "Come with me, we are going to look for some old photographs."

"Where will they be, Father?"

"In the loft, there's a box up there with a history of the family, we need to sort it out. Come with me."

Sebastian wearing his Nudie jeans, Ralph Lauren pink Polo shirt and Burberry trainers didn't seem to worry about getting into the loft. Samuel was far more worried about getting dirty, although his white shirt and white trousers already had chocolate stains.

Sebastian found the extending ladder, propping it up under the loft hatch, climbed two steps till he could push at the hinged hatch. It opened backwards, till it just went over its top position and stayed open. He climbed up the remaining steps of the ladder until he was in the loft. He then attached a hook to the loft hatch, making sure it didn't get knocked closed. Sebastian felt up for the light switch as Samuel made his way up the rungs. Sebastian found the pull cord, clic-click as the loft burst into light. Samuel's head just reaching the loft opening as the light came on.

"Oh… wow!" exclaimed Samuel. "Look at all this."

The loft was full of toys, boxes, shelves with smaller boxes on, marked up as 'watches' and 'jewellery' and 'cash'; things that, at one time or another Russell had been asked to 'take care of' from his gangland friends, but had slipped everyone's memories over the years.

Sebastian started to head for the back of the loft, towards two big suitcases filled with heirlooms; Samuel stepped into the loft.

As Samuel followed Sebastian, his eye caught the sight of a half-opened box with the word 'toys' on the side. He gingerly opened the lid further, peering inside.

"Father, look at this, are these your old things?"

"Yes, from when I was a boy."

As Samuel peered inside. He lifted up the first things he could see: a Mega Drive with an Aladdin case, Loopin' Louie. Below these, were models and boxes of Thundercats, Toxic Crusaders, Hungry Hippos and Mr Frosty.

"In another thirty years Samuel," said Sebastian, "it'll be just as fascinating to you to see what your old toy box will hold."

"I look forward to that, Father."

"Now, it's time for us to look backwards," said Sebastian, as he lifted the lid on one of the cases. "These two cases here hold our family's history. It's just as important to look back on how *they* lived, as it will be in thirty years' time, for you to look back on your life."

"I understand, Father."

"Okay then, come and give me a hand here."

Inside, the case was piled with bits of paper, document wallets and folders, as well as an old biscuit tin filled with photographs.

Samuel picked up the tin and flicked off the lid. Sebastian rummaging through papers, wedding certificates, old wage slips, drawings done by him and Samuel.

Samuel grabbing a handful of photographs, looked at the first one: a tall good-looking young man in his late teens, slim but big built, his hair cut into what Sebastian had pointed out was a mullet, long at the back and short on top. He wore baggy black jeans, a white T-shirt and on top of that, a black shiny plasticky-looking bomber jacket, with a brown fur collar. On his feet, he had white socks and white tennis shoes.

"Is this Grandpapa?" Samuel asked Sebastian.

"It certainly is, that would have been in the nineteen-eighties."

The next picture Samuel looked at had 'Grandpapa' standing in front of the doors to a night club. He had on a large white baggy cotton long-sleeved shirt, white jeans and tennis shoes. This picture had a slim young lady with her arm through his; she was shorter than the man in the picture. She wore white tennis shoes with short white socks, black fishnet tights that came down to just below the knee, her legs bare from the knee to the socks. Over the tights she had on a white tutu and above that a mauve basque. The basques stocking clips, hanging down over the tutu. Over the basque, she had a light-weight cotton waistcoat, with a light blue and pink crisscross pattern, pink sweatbands on her wrists, long white beads hanging around her neck coming down to her middle. She had shoulder-length, slightly curly, blond hair, with darker roots. Dark eye shadow and bright red lips.

Over her shoulder, was a bright pink bag.

"And this, Father," Samuel continued disbelievingly. "Is this Grandmother?"

"Yes," agreed Sebastian.

"Oh my," said Samuel. "She doesn't look like Grandmother now."

"Time," said Sebastian, "is not on any of our sides Samuel, you will find. You get what you can, when you can. You make the most of every opportunity!"

"Okay, Father." Samuel thought he understood.

Having spent some time going through the case, they talked about where they had come from, who made them, what they were, Russell and his East End past, Elizabeth and her family.

Sebastian closed the lid on the first case. The time getting late, he opened the second case.

"I don't remember much about this case," he said, picking up a couple of items from it. "What I do know about this case is, your Great, Great, Grandfather is mentioned a lot in here."

"Was he famous then?" enquired Samuel.

"Famous only in the fact that he was shot dead in a pub in London!"

"Why was that?"

"Oh, it's a long story, and as it's getting late, I think we should leave this case until next time."

While Sebastian was telling Samuel about the case, he was picking up odd bits of paper, looking over them then dropping them back into the case.

He suddenly stopped. A curious piece of paper, 'Why should this be here?' he thought to himself. It seemed out of place, why in with Great Grandfather Samuel Plant's things? The piece of paper was handwritten, with magnificent pencraft. The letters bold and clear, scribed by someone clearly knowing what they want. The problem was it was all in a foreign language.

"What do you think this is Samuel?" asked Sebastian.

"Not sure sir, I believe the top part may be German, not sure about lower down, Indian, African… Arabic maybe?"

"Mmmm," Sebastian thought, then said. "Well, let's put it all away, when we come next time, we can relook at this one, see if we can find out any more about this!"

Sebastian threw the bits of paper, photos and documents back into the case, the German writing on the top. He started to close the lid, when a word caught his eye: Barren; Barren, if it is German, is a gold ingot. A word he would occasionally come across in his job, so why should this paper relating to his Great Grandfather's time during the war-years, be mentioning gold ingots?

Curiosity got the better of him, partly opening

the lid, took the paper then dropped the lid shut again, folded it and put it in his back pocket. He stood up and turned to face Samuel, who was still scratching at the red blotches on his neck.

"Okay Samuel, time we were going."

"Yes, Father."

"Are you two nearly finished up there?" came the voice of Elizabeth from below the loft hatch.

"Yes, be down in a few minutes," Sebastian called back.

"Well, you be very careful comin' down these steps, Samuel," she urged.

Down the steps, Sebastian switched off the loft light, lowered the loft hatch, while Samuel rushed off to see Russell and Elizabeth, excited to tell them of the photographs he had seen of them in the first case. And how funny they looked, how much they had changed, and that they hadn't really started on the second case but, had planned to do so during their next visit.

Sebastian put the ladder away then made his way to the lounge.

"Well, this has been a good day," said Russell happily. "A win on the horses and finding them old pictures of me and your grandmother."

"We need to see more of you- young man!" said Elizabeth to Samuel.

"And I can't wait till next time, Grandmother," Samuel replied. "The second case looks really interesting."

"Come on then, Samuel, time to go," Sebastian announced.

Samuel got up from the stool he was sitting on next to Russell. Walked over to Sebastian. Russell rose from his armchair as they all headed for the front door.

As Sebastian and Samuel stepped out of the door, Elizabeth suddenly cried out.

"Oh, wait one moment!" as she went back into the kitchen, returning a few seconds later she said to Samuel, "Put your hand out." Which he did. "Here's some cream for that nasty rash on your neck!"

\*\*\*

By the time they had arrived back at Stratosphere Tower, the evening was getting late. Sebastian told Samuel to get himself ready for bed, once done, to go to bed and he will see him in the morning, when he will take him back to his mum, Amelia.

Sebastian sat at the dining table, getting the note from his back pocket, he opened it up.

As he studied the paper, thinking to himself, *what can it be?* A hand-written note, signed by his Great, Grandfather, and what looked like a German name, *and* dated during the war.

And this other wording, what can it mean?

Sebastian didn't speak German, or any other language, but he felt this was not something he wanted to share with anyone else. Well, not until he knew more about it, not until he had more information, until he understood exactly what the wording meant and what the other writing or language was.

The note read:

*EIN VERTRAG zwischen*
*Samuel Plant und Wilhelm Schick*
*Die Boxen enthalten Barren, die gehören zu den Namen oben*
*gedruckt, des finanziellen Gewinns aus den Blöcken zwischen den*
*oben genannten Namen zu gleichen Teilen getragen. Die Schachteln*
*dürfen erst im Herbst 1947 angefasst werden, bis ein Zeitraum von*
*etwa zwei Jahren nach dem Krieg, wenn wir einender kontaktieren*
*und der Erlös zwischen uns geteilt. Bis zu diesem Zeitpunkt wird*
*es in gehalten und von den Namen und Ort unten betreut.*

*Wilhelm Schick*               *Samuel Plant*
*24ᵗʰ Februar 1945*            *24ᵗ February 1945*

عائلة بن دي و عدت أن تـعتنـي بـألـسنـا ديـق و تـحافظ
عـليـهم آمنة في قبو مـنزلـهـا حتى يتم جمعها

كما أن الله هو شهادتي

سيلستين بورغوان

مصطفى بن دي

86

Sebastian sat at the table and thought to himself, I must find out what he was doing at the end of February 1945. I have got to work this out.

What was the old bugger up to?

Archives, they will know, that's the answer. As soon as I can, I must go to the archives.

# Chapter 4
## Rugby Union
## Late Spring Present-day

Tom Paige stood tall; his right hand coming up to his mouth, pushing his gum shield from underneath into his upper set of teeth.

His arms raising either side of his body as he stood statuesque, as if about to be nailed to a crucifix. 'Ora et Labora' was their badge. 'Prey and Labour' was about to happen; as he readies himself for the scrummage.

A last-second straighten of his red and white scrum cap.

From his left and right came the Loosehead Prop, Marcus Deveraux and Tighthead Prop Steve Duxford. Both big men, 195cm (six feet five inches) tall and weighing over 105 kilos. Tucking their heads under Tom's arms, into each side of his chest. Moving forward, standing next to each other, side by side, Tom's arms drop, he grips their shoulders.

The referee, having marked the spot of the scrum with his heel, the left side of the field of play as Tom's team, the Dartfordians attack, and just over the ten-metre line of the opponent's half; the ref retreats backwards, reaching the outside of the pack.

Tom looking down, as the heads of the two second-row pop in either side his body, between him and the props.

Tom's team, in deep red and sun yellow stripes, with two diagonal stripes across the front, black shorts, red and yellow socks.

In front of them... the enemy, Sevenoaks RFC, the anti-heroes, the challengers, dressed in midnight blue with yellow horizontal stripes, blue shorts and blue and yellow socks, were themselves to enter the scrum.

"Crouch," called the referee.

In the second row, Martin James and Ewen McAlister, behind them the loose forward Chowey Dong. The two opposing teams facing each other, still with a metre gap between them.

Tom was at the head of his pack. The raw power of the large and powerful players behind him. The urgency to come together, ready to challenge for the ball, like fitting a dragster engine to a moped, a huge amount of energy ready to burst into motion on the lighter weight of Tom.

"Bind!" the referee signalled, as the crowd on the touchline shout the name of their team.

The front row's arms went out, grabbing the opposing team's forearm shirt sleeves.

The Scrum-Half for Dartfordians, Clive Shorter, picking up the ball, walking to the side of the scrum as both sides came together; they ready themselves to push.

The referee standing behind the number nine.

"Set."

Shorter holding the oval ball, threw it into the melee of legs with both hands, as both teams pushed; aiming to gain the advantage.

Tom's legs shooting forward first, his boot catching the ball, it diverted into the mass of legs of his team. Still, both teams pushing forward, the ball slowly working its way to the back of the Dartfordian's side of the scrum.

Under McAlister's legs; Shorter working his way to the rear of the scrum, he tapped the back of Chowey Dong, letting him know he was there and ready to receive the ball. One last tap of the ball from the heel of Dong and the ball left the pack.

Shorter was quickly down, ball in hands as the Sevenoaks players descend on him. The pass to number ten; Trevor Becks, ball in his arms, takes three strides forward. George Ghost of Sevenoaks thundering towards Becks; with a swift flick, the ball then travelled off to his right, missing Bryn Cook. The ball reaching number thirteen, Jamie Jackson. In the meantime, Becks the Fly-Half, was making a loop move, coming around the back of his own team.

Jamie Jackson, just in the Dartfordians' half, was caught by Robert Banks of Sevenoaks. Sending Jackson crashing to the ground. Quickly, in behind him came Cook.

Cook scooping up the loose ball, seeing Becks move into an open position to the right-hand side of the Dartfordians field of play and between the ten and twenty-two metre line of their own half, the ball sailed to Becks.

The scrum having dispersed onto the field of play, a gap opened up where the scrum had been. Becks dropped the ball, with a huge kick, aiming the ball towards the now open space.

Knowing most of his team in front of him would be offside, he ran in the direction of the airborne object.

Number eleven, Ivan Love, predicting what Becks was about to do, and being in an onside position at the time of the kick, started running towards the open space also, up the left-hand side of the field, and in the direction the ball was heading.

Becks starting on the right-hand side of the field, heading diagonally to the left.

For Sevenoaks, George Ghost and Robert Banks making their way back into position as fast as they could. Sevenoaks defenders Harrington and Smyth head to cover the centre-ground, French to intercept the airborne ball.

Tom Paige, stationary as he was in an offside position, waiting for Becks to pass him. Once passed, he ran to the centre of the Sevenoaks half, tucking in behind Becks' right-hand side. The ball losing height, Ivan Love's eyes fixed on the ball, judging its dropping position; Sevenoaks' French running for the same ball.

The two teams piling back into the Sevenoaks half; Love catching the falling ball from the air.

"Right behind you Ive!" called Becks to Love's right.

Love immediately, and without looking, throwing the ball slightly behind and to his right. The ball released the ninety-five kilogrammes of Dave French crashing into Love as they both hit the ground.

The ball with Becks, he crossed the Sevenoaks'

twenty-two metre line; in the centre of the field, Harrington and Smyth rushing to cover his path to goal.

"Trev, to the right!" Paige shouted.

Harrington, seeing the danger from Paige, left the defence of the Becks' run to Smyth.

Becks releasing the ball, throwing it to his right, it reached Tom Paige who caught cleanly, the ball tucked under his right arm, tight against his chest.

Only Harrington in Tom's way, Harrington *had* to stop Paige from reaching the goal.

Paige stepped left, Harrington followed. Paige's weight immediately changed to his right, the swerve of his body, wrong-footing Harrington.

Tom passing the stricken Sevenoaks' defender as he ran towards the far-right corner flag. With just ten metres to the try line, he turned in, towards the centre of the field and behind the goalposts.

Crossing the line, Sevenoaks players still rushing back to stop him placing the ball down.

But too late.

Five metres from the right-hand post, he touched the ball to the ground, quickly bending back to his full height, he threw the ball straight up into the air.

The Sevenoaks players slowing down as Dartfordians ran past them, catching up with Paige, shouting and cheering as they reached him, hugging, and patting his back and scrum cap.

His arms went up in pleasure as he panted, trying to get his breath back.

"Yeeeah!" he shouted at the sky, as the crowd on the touchline shout and scream in joy.

Five points to Dartfordians, the score now ten, to Sevenoaks' five, and from the try, now came the kick.

Tom Paige picked up the ball, looking over to the referee who was pointing to the spot that the kick could be taken from. Walking to the position he thought would be the ideal spot to take the kick.

"Okay here, sir?" Paige called to the referee.

"Yes, that is fine there," replied the ref.

Tom Paige stopped, turning he looked up the two tall posts in front of him, taking a deep breath, he placed the kicking tee onto the grass, pushing it firmly into the soil; then brushed a small amount of loose grass away from behind it.

The kick to be taken a little to the right of the right-hand post, and on the twenty-two-metre line.

Bending, he placed the ball end on into the tee, the ball upright and slightly leaning back towards him; he stood back upright, putting his left foot to the left side of the ball, his right foot behind it.

Looking up at the posts, his breath shortening, everyone quiet, they watch his every move.

The home team and crowd willing him to score, everyone on the opposing team, hoping he misses.

Tom took one, two, three, four steps back and stopped. With one last quick look up at the posts, then back to the ball; his body leaned forward as his centre of gravity took him towards the ball, his eyes fixed on the turquoise and yellow object.

Three paces, his boot hit the ball; it took to the air and within seconds sailed directly between the posts of the Sevenoaks team's goal.

The referee standing behind the posts, watched

as the ball passed over his head, he pointed up the field blowing his whistle; goal.

Dartfordians had two more points.

The game played on for ten more minutes with no more score, twelve, five to Dartfordians.

The referee blowing his whistle, on what was both team's last game of the season, and a great season they had both had. The players from both teams wearily making their way back to the clubhouse.

Tom Paige, about half way to the changing room, his teammates around him, excitedly chatting about the game they had just finished, when a call came from one of the Sevenoaks players behind him.

"Tom, you pussy, why are you still wearing those jockstraps on your head?"

Tom's team, insulted that one of their side should be shouted at in this way, turn and start to walk towards the player shouting the comments.

Paige turned, recognising it was the voice of George Ghost, a Sevenoaks player and an old friend.

"Hang on lads." Tom said to his teammates.

"George, great to see you, how come we only meet like this?" Tom's arms went out, they hug with a manly back slap.

George Ghost and Tom Paige were very old college friends. George was slightly smaller than Tom, and very good looking.

George had come originally from Australia to study at Oxford University, Tom starting at Oxford the same year to study Languages. Both looking for an outside interest, they joined the local rugby football team, where they became the best of friends, partying, drinking and political rallying.

At the end of university, their lives took a different course. George, going into medicine management, had met and married Lisa, moved to Kent and settled down.

"Hey, Tom. I've got the missus and the kids here today, come and say hello."

"Love to!" replied Tom. "And I mean it, we don't get together half as much as we should."

"I know mate," said George. "Work and family, you know what it's like... anyway, have you met the latest edition to the family?"

"I have heard there was a third."

"Yeah, here they are."

Lisa was about 160cm (five feet three inches) tall, thirty; the same age as George, slim, her long brown hair having a copper-coloured tint, tied back in a ponytail; she was wearing jeans, a lightweight lilac/grey jacket and a grey roll neck jumper underneath.

"Hi Lisa," said Tom, kissing her on both cheeks.

"Tom, it's great to see you, we don't see you enough... George is always saying that."

"Well, it's been a good spring so far, maybe we can get together over the summer. How about that?" Tom suggested.

"Sounds great!"

"Now let's say hello to the Ghost family!" Tom said, bending down onto his knees, making himself the same height as the children.

"Don't tell me?" he said to Zak. "You are John?"

"No!" said Zak.

"Brian then?" Tom continued.

"No!"

"Hang on then… I know… yes, I know… it's Fred!"

"It's Zak," said the four-year-old, excitedly.

"Of course, it is," said Tom "And you," he said, as he turned to the next boy, "are, if I am not mistaken… Bert?"

"My name is Max," the three-year-old said politely.

Tom stood back up, then leaning towards the pushchair.

"And this is?" he said to Lisa

"This is Phoebe," she replied.

"Hello young Phoebe," said Tom looking at the young girl in the pushchair. "If your mum, dad and I can get ourselves a little more organised this summer, I might get to see more of you and your brothers, what do you say?"

Tom turned to look at George.

"Fancy going down into Bexley for a drink before you make your way home?"

"Sounds great, somewhere with a garden, get the kids to burn their energy off."

"I know the place," Tom said with a smile. "Just follow me!"

After showering and changing, George went over to his car, opened the door, then jumped into the passenger seat.

"He's just on his way," he said to Lisa.

Ching, ching, pop, ching pop, pop came the

sound of a Vespa Scooter; black and white checked, like a chess board, black front leg cover and mudguard, with a white front steering column and headlight, red handle grips and seat. Pulling up alongside George and Lisa's car, the black and white checked crash helmet looked down into the car, the visor went up as the face said,

"Follow me."

The visor back down, the scooter pulled away, the car following.

A few minutes later, they were all in the pubs garden, the kids on a climbing frame, Lisa organising the chaos.

George and Tom at a bench with a pint of the local Shepherd Neame's best. Tom's years at Uni had been studying languages, German, French and Polish, but he seemed to have a flair for all languages, he picked up most, with ease.

He was tall, shoulder-length fair hair, good looking, having a short beard and a strong physique.

Tom had a presence of fairness and humanity.

He was wearing cream corduroy trousers and red Airwair boots, a thick knitted grey coat with wide sleeves, a dark red Aztec marking around the body and ends of sleeves, a dark orange scarf wrapped several times around his neck. On his head he had changed the crash helmet for a dark red slouch beanie.

"How have the years been treating you then, George?" asked Tom.

"Fantastic Tom!" George replied with a smile. "You can't beat working for the NHS, the atmosphere, the people, you know. Working with people who are going to get better or die, really gives you a grip on life, a reality!"

"What about your mum and dad, do you get to see much of them?"

"Lisa, the kids and I make a pilgrimage back to 'Aus' once a year. We are going back there again soon, see the old folks."

"You ever thought about moving back out there?" asked Tom.

"Oh, regularly," answered George. "Especially with what's happening here at the moment, uncertainty and all that."

"So, what's the holdup?" enquired Tom.

Lisa wandered back over to the bench and took a swig of her orange juice, as one of the kids fell and she rushed back over to them.

"Well, to be honest with you Tom," said George with a tight grin on his face, "I think it may happen soon, Lisa seems up for it now, the kids are at the right age… and for me the rugby is soon going to be over, too old. I am thirty you know; I can't play forever!"

"Soon?" spluttered Tom.

"Yeah, we are talking; going to see the oldens this autumn. We may look for jobs and at the housing situation while out there."

"Well, we had better make the most of this summer's get together then!" grinned Tom.

They both picked up their glasses and took a gulp.

"You and Lisa are looking happy," continued

Tom.

"Extremely," replied George. "Life could not be better, and the kids, fantastic."

"Just thinking back to when you two got together," said Tom. "That was towards the end of Oxford, wasn't it?"

"Yeah, married the following year," agreed George.

"D'you still see that guy who was at the stag do, oh, that was funny... what's his name now... Mick... Micky?" asked Tom.

"Micky, yeah, I still hear from him now and then. Micky Ringer, he works in a hospital up north."

"Micky Ringer, that's the one!" Tom laughed "The stag-do in Brighton!"

"Oh, I will never forget that weekend," George shuddered. "Arrived on Friday, came home on Monday!"

"And the Sunday morning, Micky Ringer was so drunk, he rang his dad to come and get him, he was so ill."

"That's right," agreed George.

"His dad told him to 'Fuck off out of it, you fucking wimp, make your own fucking way home!'" Tom chuckled.

"Oh, bloody hell!" George smiled. "I know, we couldn't believe it, that sort of language coming from a man of the cloth... a priest, you would never have thought it!"

They both fell about laughing. Lisa walked over with the kids.

"We had better be going now George, got to get

this lot to bed," said Lisa.

"No problem my dear," he replied.

They all finished their drinks, then laid their empty glasses back on the table. Lisa putting coats on the three little ones.

"George," said Tom, hesitantly.

"Yes?" replied George uncertain of what Tom wanted.

"Well, it's been years now, and you still haven't told me," said Tom, sheepishly. "And if we can't get together in the summer, I might not ever get to see you again, you know."

"Yes?" came another uncertainty from George.

"George T. Ghost, your name, you have never told me what the T. stands for."

"Ah, now come on, Tom," laughed George. "You should know I can't tell you!"

"For years I've been asking."

"And you will be asking for years to come, now I will tell you the same as I tell you every time... it doesn't stand for Tiberius, even though I know you want it to!"

***

The time had just gone seven-thirty in the evening as Tom rode through Deptford heading home, along Creek Road, as it turned into Evelyn Street.

The late spring warmth in the air and the light evenings adding to the joy of being on his scooter.

Crossing the roundabout at the Coral Bookmakers, he continued till he reached the junction into Grove Street.

A pleasant ride on a Sunday evening, well at any time other than rush hour.

Passing Sayes Court Park on his right, a gratifying landmark, letting him know he was nearly home.

At the end of Grove Street, he turned right into Plough Way, past Windsock Close, reaching the end, turning left into Calypso Way.

The scooter's revs drop as he pulled to a halt close to a railing, dragging at a heavy chain he had left there, he wrapped it around the scooter, then covered it over with a tarpaulin.

Taking a deep breath, he looked up.

The calm water reflecting the blue sky and the flats opposite, the air filled with the moist atmosphere of South Dock.

Tom thinking to himself; he loves Rotherhithe and the Docks; life can't get any better than this.

His houseboat was down a floating walkway and on the right. White and blue, glass panels around the top, more in the middle, three small portholes on each side of the hull.

Tom stepping on board, an imaginary whistle in his head; checking his pot plants around the edge of the boat, he pulled out the door key; pushing the door open: a solid pine wood door with a small round window.

Ducking under the roof of the boat, he stepped through the door, down two steps to the living area. Laying his crash helmet on the floor by the door and throwing his bag onto the armchair that was to one side of the boat.

He walked across the small living area and down the next couple of steps to the galley where he flicked on the switch to the kettle.

The houseboat was about eight metres long and three metres wide; and perfect for Tom.

The floor, a mixture of light wood and cream carpet; the walls, cupboards and cabins, filled with natural pine wood tongue and groove panels and doors. Tom's love of the natural world of water, trees and fresh air were in this one small area of London, when outside could be filled with the hustle and bustle of Metropolitan life.

His tea ready, he picked up his Greenpeace mug, turned, putting it down onto a small dining table behind him, plonking himself down on the built-in soft green bench chair next to the small table, he kicked off his boots and put his feet up on the chair opposite.

Taking a sip of his tea, then putting the cup back down, he lifted his mobile phone, pressed a few buttons, it started to ring.

"Hi, Tom, how are you?" said the voice with a Dutch accent on the other end of the phone.

"Hey Kristina, what's the news?" asked Tom.

"Just on the move Tom," said Kristina. "I left the *Esperanza* this morning. They want me to head over to Colombia, seems there is talk of a hotel chain wanting to build an offshore island, hotels and holiday resort, close to a beach used by turtles for egg-laying. What about you?"

"Really good. Rugby this afternoon. I scored the

winning try and the conversion, it was a fantastic game, really enjoyed it… and guess who was there?"

"Go on!"

"George Ghost!"

"Oh, excellent… how was he?"

"Great, Lisa was there too, and all the kids, Zak, Max and Phoebe. It was wonderful to see them all."

"Oh, you met Phoebe, oh how lovely. I had spoken to Lisa, but not had a chance to go and visit. We'll have to do that when I get back."

"Yes, I had said more or less the same. We haven't seen them for such a long time."

"As soon as I get back… okay?"

Tom, Kristina, Lisa and George had all been at university together, all being part of the politics group; George and Lisa studying the management side of medicine, Kristina studying the environment and biology.

"I saw your pictures from the Dirty Palm oil trip. It got some good feedback," said Tom.

"So I see," answered Kristina. "Still didn't stop them though!"

"No, there is still a way to go. Hopefully, one day, common sense will prevail."

"And let's hope it's not too late," said Kristina exasperatedly.

"How long will you be in Colombia?" asked Tom.

"Not sure," said Kristina. "Not long I would think, I will be talking to the locals, the environmentalists and the papers. I will have to dive at the proposed hotel zone, get some photographs of the area."

"You stay safe!"

"Will do. I should be in Bogota in a couple of days. I will call you as soon as I can. Can't wait to be back in the houseboat with you Tom."

"Me too Kristina," said Tom. "Speak to you in a couple of days!"

"Bye, Tom."

## Chapter 5
## WFR Evelyn Street
## Late Spring Present-day

Tom woke up on the Monday morning, seven-thirty, drew back the curtains and peeped out of the porthole.

Looked pleasant enough he thought to himself, though it had been raining overnight, and the forecast was to rain later in the day, but for now, it looked like he was going to work and not get wet on the way.

He slid down the bed till he sat at the bottom, where he picked up a pair of underwear. They looked clean enough, he said to himself, gave them a sniff and put them on.

He chucked a pair of long baggy camel-coloured shorts into a rucksack, along with a T-shirt and cardigan; then he put on a running shirt and shorts, followed by a pair of trainers.

Making his way to the galley where he flicked on the kettle, two slices of bread in the toaster, then turned on the television. He was hoping to see if there was any news on Kristina and her visit to Colombia and Turtle Beach.

He made himself toast and marmalade, a coffee, then sat next to the little table, putting his feet up, munching on the toast and slurping coffee, while he caught up on the world's events.

Eight o'clock and he was up and ready to leave, rucksack on his back, out of the boathouse, around the wooden walkway, till he reached the bank.

Tom ran this way to work every day, two kilometres. Starting at Windsock Close into Plough Way, he turned left into Grove Street, following this to the end where he turned right into Evelyn Street, from here, eight hundred metres to the office.

There were three shops in a row, on the corner of a small side street. Tom turned into the side street, through the gate that led to the back of the shops. In the garden at the rear of the first shop, a black painted and very rusty set of cast iron steps that ran up to the first and second floors.

He reached the first-floor landing, to a maroon painted door with patterned glass panes on the top half. The door itself looked in need of repainting and repair. The door knob was wobbly and the hinges creaked.

Tom opened the door and stepped inside.

On his right was a small galley kitchen, no more than a small worktop, with a kettle, sink and draining board, a free-standing oven and hob.

To his left, a living room with a single bed in the corner; a couple of old wooden chairs tucked under a wooden table.

Ahead of him, was the door to the office.

This was the office of Professor Wise of Wise Find and Return, set up in the nineteen-eighties.

Professor Wise, a lecturer at Newcastle University, became aware of the injustices that occurred during the Second World War, items stolen to fund the war or to appease some leader or politician somewhere.

Although not Jewish, Professor Wise felt he needed to right this wrong. To search for the missing or stolen gold, jewellery, paintings or cash, to then find the owner of these items, if still alive, or the families of the stolen things, to return to their rightful owner.

"Good morning, Professor," said Tom, slightly out of breath.

"Good morning, Tom," replied Professor Wise. "And how are you today?"

The office was one room, about three metres by four metres. A large window looked out onto the street below. Professor Wise was sitting at the desk against the left-hand wall, the desk pilled with hundreds of bits of paper, maps files and folders, all surrounding a single very old computer. The walls above Professor Wise's desk having four shelves, filled with books, file boxes, pens and pencils.

On the wall to the window, were picture frames. In the frames were certificates given to Professor Wise in praise of the work he was doing, articles cut out from newspapers and another frame, with the details of the charity that ran from the office: WFR, Wise Find and Return, Evelyn Street, London.

Tom's desk was behind the door, to the back wall, it too, covered in paper and files.

Tom, after changing from his running clothes to his baggy shorts and T-shirt, sat down at his desk, pressed the 'On' button on the old computer and waited for it to warm up.

"Have you had any leads lately?" the Professor asked.

"No," replied Tom. "It's very quiet at the moment... the only thing I am dealing with is a painting that has been put up for auction in Italy. A name came up on the previous owners' list that might be of interest to us... I am waiting for the certificate of ownership to arrive; we can cast our eyes over!"

"That sounds very interesting Tom," agreed the Professor.

"And you, Professor?"

"Well Tom, I am waiting for a box to arrive, so I hope to be able to tell you more once it is here. It seems there was a fire in a house in Germany. When they cleared the house after the fire, they found a secret hole in the wall, all sorts of papers and documents, many in code or meaningless to the owners of the house. Seems someone suggested sending it to us to look at, but in the meantime, I had been doing some finding out about the owner during the war: a business man... When they contacted me, there were a couple of names mentioned, people that had fled to Russia as the Germans entered Poland. It seems there is a great-granddaughter living in America. I have had a couple of emails from her, just making sure she is the right person before I go into too much detail with her."

"And what do you hope to get from the box?" enquired Tom.

"Not really sure, the message I got was, the box has had some damage from the fire, some of the papers are burnt and singed, so let's wait and see, shall we?"

"I look forward to that."

Tom turned back to his desk, picked up some papers he had received; the painting, an early work with the name Leonardo di ser Piero at the bottom, had part of its history without an owner. Having been owned by a French, Jewish family in Paris, at the outbreak of the Second World War, it had disappeared for many years. An Italian family finding it in the loft of the house they had just bought, thought it had been left by accident. They mentioned it to an art dealer friend of theirs.

Many items like this turn up, still now, all these years after the war. It was Tom and the Professor's job to find the rightful owner.

Late morning in the office, Tom stretches his arms.

"Would you like a cup of coffee, Professor?" asked Tom.

"I would love one, thank you, Tom."

Tom turned on his chair, stood up stretching his legs, walked into the kitchen, filling the kettle then putting it onto the kettle base, flicking the 'on' switch.

He took two cups from the mug tree, looking inside; picking up a tea towel he wiped the cup over, placing the mugs onto the work surface, coffee and three spoons of sugar for the Professor, none for himself.

Coffees made, he walked back into the office.

"There you are Professor."

"I am very grateful, Tom."

As Tom sat back down, ready to carry on with his work... ding dong... went the doorbell. Tom and the Professor looked at each other.

"The post?" said Tom.

"I hope," answered the Professor.

"Shall I go?" asked Tom.

"Yes... I think so... yes, you go."

Tom got up, walked back through the kitchen to the entrance door.

The bell to the office was at the bottom of the steps, in case there should be a disabled visitor.

Tom stepped out, looked over the side of the handrail, there stood the postie.

"Hi!" Tom called down.

"Hello, sir," the postie called back.

The postie was holding a package and several letters.

"Are all of those for us?" Tom asked.

"Yes, sir," answered the postie. "A box and few letters."

"I'll be right down."

Tom made his way down the iron stairs till he reached the postie at the bottom, a light drizzle in the air.

"The package has to be signed for, sir!"

"Oh, right, of course... not a problem," agreed Tom.

The postie held out the electronic signature pad, Tom squiggled on the screen and the postie handed the parcel over.

Back in the office, the Professor was eagerly

waiting as Tom walked through the door.

"Is this the one you are waiting for, Professor?"

"I certainly hope so Tom... where's the postmark say it's from?"

Tom looked down at the package.

"Yes, it's Germany!"

Tom walked into the room, the Professor jumping up from his chair, swiftly making his way to the table below the window, pushing papers that were laying on the table to one side.

Tom slowly walking over to the table, both hands under the box, carefully making his way across the room with the parcel, as if it were a birthday cake or a bomb. The Professor watching every movement of the parcel, ready to catch it should it fall from his hands.

The package slowly lowering towards the table top, the Professor's eyes unblinking as it came to rest. Tom's hands slowly pulling out from beneath it to... silence.

The Professor looked up at Tom, Tom looked down at the Professor.

"Well," said Tom, excitedly. "Aren't you going to open it?"

"All in good time," said the Professor. "I have a feeling Tom, that this is what I opened this place for in the first place... I feel it Tom, I feel that this is the one that will put us on the map!"

"That would be fantastic Professor, but what about opening it?"

"Patience, young Tom... let's not rush into this... slowly, slowly... catchy monkey," said the Professor, calmly. "Now, first of all, let's open the post."

"Post?" said Tom.

"I am going to savour this moment, everyone will want us to help after this, let's just savour it..." he said, serenely. "Now first, let's look at the post."

The Professor picked up the first letter sitting on the box.

"A bill."

He held the letter in between his finger and thumb, moved it over the bin and let go, in the bin it landed. He then picked up the second letter.

"Bill," he said again,

Dropping once more into the bin, then picking up the next letter. He lifted it to eye level, looking at it through the light from the window, he then held it at each end, put the top edge to his nose, sniffing it as he ran the envelope under his nostrils to and fro.

"I think this is money," he chirpily announced.

Folding the envelope in half, he pushed it into his back pocket.

"And the box?" beamed Tom.

"Look... I'll tell you what we will do with the box," announced the Professor. "I will rush over to the shops up the road, I am going to get us a couple of cakes, and a bottle of wine... this is going to be a celebration."

"A celebration it is then." Tom accepted.

Tom went back to his desk, carrying on with his work, his mind firmly on the contents of the package.

The Professor, pulled his worn-out coat on, walked over to the door.

"I won't be long Tom; you just wait and see, this

will be the making of us!"

The Professor left the office, Tom heard the main door close as the sound of footsteps clanged down the iron steps.

Tom stood up, searched along the shelves till he found the book titled *Italian Painters*, laid the book down on the space he had made on his desk, thumbed through to the index where he found di ser Pier... Screech... Bang!

Tom quickly looking up from the book, a car accident by the sounds of it, he thought to himself.

Standing up quickly, he rushed over to the window to see what had happened. *No.*

"Professor," he called. "*No*, that's the Professor!"

In the middle of the road, in a crumpled heap, lay the Professor. Kneeling down beside him, was a large, slightly tanned man with short-cropped hair and wearing a dark suit. Behind the pair of them a large black car.

"Professor!" shouted Tom, banging on the window.

The man kneeling beside the Professor, had a quick look around, standing up, he hastily walked back to his car, jumped into the driver's seat and with a roar, raced away down the road.

"Professor!"

Tom's voice choking up as he continued to call for his friend.

Tom rushed out of the building, down the steps and around the corner.

He ran as fast as he could until he had reached his mentor.

Tom quickly stopping beside the Professor, a shallow breath wheezing from the Professor's mouth.

A crowd started to gather on the curb, as in the distance the sound of police and ambulance sirens could be heard.

"Hang on, Professor," implored Tom. "Just hang on. Help is on its way!"

# Late Autumn 1941

Petrykozy, Lodz district
Poland

# Chapter 6
## Commander Schick
## Late Autumn 1941

A cold wind blew through the trees and copses, the clouds dark and gloomy. There was a thick and heavy greyness to fields and forests. The trees, bare of leaves, bare of animals and wildlife. Shadows, blacker than normal, as the days grew shorter. Death in the air; air so cold you felt it would stop the blood flowing, not yet cold enough to freeze. But a piercing north wind making life very uncomfortable for those forced to bear it.

Along the narrow dark leafless tree-lined road that led to the little village of Petrykozy, fifteen kilometres south-west of Lodz, drove two vehicles, a black Mercedes-Benz 770 Series II, Swastika flags mounted on each front wheel arch. The dark gloominess emanating from inside the car as well as the blackness outside; the driver in a grey-green Feldgrau uniform, buttoned up to the top, his collar having a Litzen insignia on each lapel.

He wore an M34 field cap, Nazi Eagle above a black, white and red circle; he sat comfortably in the front of the warm car, slowly driving along the damp road, the headlights of the car on.

In the rear, a Nazi officer looked steely-eyed out of the window. His face only just visible in the murkiness. He despises being in the sparse ugly countryside. A menacing hatred of the place etched on his face as he glared into the gloom. Following behind the black staff car, a Krupp-Protze L 2 H 43 truck, carrying a driver and three Nazi troopers. Field grey uniforms, all with a dark green collar. Litzen markings on each lapel, high black boots, muddied from the dampness on the ground. Thick jackets to keep out the cold; over the jacket a belt for spare rounds of ammunition; on the top right of the jacket, a Nazi eagle badge. All four soldiers wore steel helmets, and all, except the driver, had a rifle, the butt on the floor between their feet, each holding onto the barrel so as not to lose it as they bumped along the unlit lane.

The black Mercedes turned into open gates, followed by the Krupp-Protze truck, water splashing from a puddle at the entrance to the drive. The leaves and broken branches cracking and rustling as the wheels of the vehicles passed over them. Crows squawking at the disturbance of the vehicles passing by them, flew up into the moisture laden trees.

The cars travel for a couple of hundred metres further; as the trees thin out, the headlights of the leading car, fell onto the reason they were there: the mansion. The cream building; the pillars, facias and balustrade painted white, along with the white of the window frames and main door, the glass panes being small in a crisscross pattern. The front of the building had a Georgian arch with a half-moon window in the upper section. To the left- and right-hand side of the main door were two large windows either side downstairs and the same upstairs. Beyond the house was a single-storey extension to the main building, on the left and the right, keeping a balance to the symmetry, the roof to the main building and the extensions were of a black tile.

The black Mercedes pulled up at the steps in front of the main door, the Krupp-Protze pulling up behind it. The four soldiers quickly jump out of the truck, standing to attention at the steps between the vehicles and the house.

The driver of the Mercedes slowly emerged from the driver's door, making his way to the rear door, taking the handle, slowly opening it. A black calf-length boot stepped over the door's footplate, coming to rest on the leafy ground. The second boot followed, both boots turn towards the car; the first boot rises till it rests on the footplate. A white cloth wiping around the boot till it shines. As the first boot was lowered to the ground, the second boot followed to the footplate, till it shone equally. The boots back on the moist leafy driveway, they turn to face the mansion, only then to take a step forward. The driver shutting the rear door of the Mercedes. The boots take two paces till they reach the steps leading up to the main door of the mansion, a dark blue-grey trench coat just covering the tops of the high boots, then two more paces forward, up the steps.

The four soldiers from the Krupp-Protze truck stand two each side. One of the German soldiers moved forward quickly, towards the main white door of the building. The two shiny black boots face the door, the trench coat swaying slightly from side to side as the bitterly cold north wind blew through the roofed cover they were under. The soldier that had moved forward, stood in front of the door to the mansion, picked up the rifle he was carrying and with a slow and loud thud, he thumped the butt of his rifle against the door. Bang... Bang... Bang.

Inside, stood the owner of the mansion. He remained stationary, breathing deeply and slowly. The large hallway with elegant stairs opposite the main door, large internal doors to his left and right. He stood in the middle of the hallway, directly in front of the main door, looking straight at it.

The lights in the hallway were on, an attempt to keep out the darkness and oppression that lurked outside. The medium height businessman with a slight paunch, in his late fifties, greying hair and greying skin, stood upright and aloof. He wore brogue shoes, black trousers, a decorated maroon dressing gown with a silver cravat tucked into the front of the gown.

Bang... Bang... Bang as the rifle butt hit the door once more. He swallowed heavily, looked up at the grandfather clock in the corner, ten thirty-five in the morning.

He walked towards the door, lifted the lock, turned the handle and stepped back; the door opened as he retreated slowly back to his former position in the hall. The door crept open further, a few brown dried leaves blew into the mansions entrance as the four German soldiers moved quickly into the hallway. Two, stood to one side of the door, and two to the other, standing to attention, rifles diagonally across their bodies, right-hand fingers on the butt and trigger, left hand on the barrel.

The businessman standing in the warm room, suddenly shuddered at the coldness that invaded his skin.

Following the soldiers, the 181cm (five feet eleven inches) figure of an SS officer. Tall, broad shoulders and fit, dark hair and chiselled features, his polished black boots clicking against the tiles of the floor. His dark blue-grey trench coat buttoned up to the top, the dark green collar with an SS symbol on each side, a Nazi eagle on the right-hand breast and black leather gloves. The dark grey-blue peaked hat with the Nazi eagle and polished black rim pulled down low allowing his eyes to just be visible; he continued walking till he stood face-to-face with the businessman.

"Krzyztof D'browski, good morning to you... let me introduce myself. I am Wilhelm Schick. I am the commander of this area. I am so sorry I hadn't got around to seeing you earlier... but as you can imagine, we have been rather busy," said Commander Schick, in a smiling pleasant tone.

Schick looked around the hallway, seeing an ornate antique table to one side; started pulling off his gloves, turned to the soldier nearest the door.

"You may close it!" he ordered the soldier, pointing at the door.

The soldier pushed the door to, then returned to his position at attention. Warmth returning to the hallway as Schick turned back to the businessman.

"Still Mr D'browski, we are here now..." said Schick as he studied the room. He then asked quizzically, "And I assume you would have been expecting us?"

"Of course, I have Commander Schick... ever since you invaded our country!" said D'browski.

"That's good then, less of a shock when we discuss our issues."

"Issues?" enquired D'browski.

"Issues... yes Mr D'browski, issues, you know, we all have issues," said Schick, as he stopped, suddenly turning, looking directly into the businessman's eyes. "And my attention has been brought to 'issues' we may have here."

"I don't know of what 'issues' you may be referring to, Commander Schick."

"All in due time Mr D'browski," said Schick offhandedly, as he turned and strolled around the room, picking up ornaments, eyeing them up, then placing them back down. "But first things first, I understand you have a chef, as well as some staff present... is that correct Mr D'browski?"

"Cook is here today, that is correct."

"And other staff Mr D'browski?" Schick having picked up another ornament, turned his head to look at the businessman.

"I believe there may be a couple in today," said D'browski looking straight ahead, to avoid eye contact with the SS Commander.

"And how many will that be exactly?" said Schick walking back towards D'browski. "And I suggest you think very carefully about the answer... your move will be crucial to the game."

"There are four, if you include cook," answered,

D'browski nervously.

"Ah, yes," said Schick brightly with a smile on his face. "Cook… we have travelled up this morning from Wroclaw. How hospitable it would be of you to make breakfast for my men and myself."

"Would it?"

"Of course, Mr D'browski," said Schick smiling. "Then on a full stomach, you and I can get down to business."

"Business, I have no business with you."

"Oh, but you will have," smiled the Commander, his expression turning more forceful. "Now, breakfast, Mr D'browski."

"I'll see what she can do."

D'browski walked to one of the doors to the side of the hallway, opened the door, leaned in and pulled the cord, ringing a bell in the kitchen; letting the kitchen staff know that they were required in the main house. Schick turned to the four soldiers standing behind him.

"I want you to search the building and grounds. Everyone you find, bring them back to the front of the house. They are to stand on the driveway until I am ready to see them… you are looking for at least four, but I have a feeling you may find more, so as you find them, one is to keep guard over them, the others keep searching. Ah, but leave Cook till she has completed her task."

"Yes sir," the soldiers said, saluting.

Two go out of the front door to search the outer grounds and buildings, one went up the stairs, the other into one of the side rooms. D'browski returned to the hallway as the soldiers were leaving the room.

"Cook will be here shortly," said D'browski.

"Excellent," said Schick, brightly. "Now Mr D'browski, when I received a piece of certain information regarding you, back at the Headquarters, well, I have to say, I was very excited. I have been watching you for a long time, and by a long time, I mean, long before the war started..."

"Me?" said D'browski "Why me?"

Cook opened the door to the hallway and cautiously stepped in, her eyes looking sideways at the German commander, then back to the mansion's owner.

"Hello sir, can I be of any help?" said Cook.

"Yes Cook, could you do breakfast for the Commander and the soldiers he has with him?" instructed D'browski.

"Breakfast, sir?"

"Yes, bacon, eggs, bread, you know the type of thing."

"Would you like mushrooms with that as well sir?" she said to D'browski.

"No," interrupted Schick. "No mushrooms, don't trust them."

"Yes, sir," said Cook, as she turned and left the room.

The two men turned back to each other.

"Mr D'browski, please don't be so shy..." said Schick, continuing the earlier conversation. "You are a chess hero of mine!"

"Chess, but I haven't played chess for some time now."

"Well, I do understand you have a room specially set up for the game," enquired Schick. "Is that correct?"

"W... why yes," said D'browski stuttering. "I do have a chess room!"

"Good," said Schick. "I am dying to play against you, it has been an ambition of mine for such a long time... would you show me the room?"

"Y... y... yes, please would you follow me?"

D'browski went to a side door, opened it and walked through, Schick following, passing through this room to a second small door.

As he opened this door, Schick could see inside, medals and shields on the walls and shelves, as well as black and white photographs of the tournaments and champions he has faced in the past. To one side of the room was a large window that faced out onto the driveway. In the middle of the room, a baize-topped solid table, in the middle of the table a magnificent polished, light and dark wood chequered chessboard: the pieces in a box to the side of the board.

D'browski offered the chair nearest the window to Commander Schick. Schick took a deep breath in, then slowly out, unbuttoned his trench coat, removing one arm, then the other. D'browski gesturing to a coat stand behind the door, Schick hung the coat carefully, then his cap. He then turned and walked towards the chair offered by the businessman.

The Commander in his dark grey-blue officers' uniform, a belt around his middle, a strap diagonally from the belt going over his right-hand shoulder, an iron cross pinned to his upper left-hand pocket, above the pocket, the Nazi eagle, SS insignia on the dark green collars. On the right-hand side of the belt, a pistol holder, holding a Luger pistol.

"Would you like a drink, Commander?"

"Tea would be nice, Mr D'browski. I don't drink alcohol; I like to keep a clear head."

There was a knock against the open door. Cook had arrived with the breakfast on a tray for the Commander.

"What shall I do about the food for the others sir?" she said to D'browski.

Schick answered, "Have it ready on a table for them in the kitchen, then go and tell them from me, that they are to go down two at a time to eat, then the driver. And Cook, when you have finished that, I would like you to stand outside with the others."

"Outside sir, but sir, it is very cold… to stand out there!"

"*Yes,*" said Schick, offhandedly, his head looking down at the black king he had picked out of the box of chess pieces.

Cook placed the tray on a small table in the corner of the room, turned and left through the first door, then into the entrance hall. She opened the main door, took a step through, closing the door behind her.

D'browski looked past Schick, through the window.

Outside, he could see Cook walking over to the three soldiers standing on the driveway, three members of the mansion staff standing close to the soldiers.

After the cook had passed on the message from the Commander, she turned and walked back towards the main door. As she did, the fourth soldier appeared from around the corner of the building with two more people.

D'browski gulped as he realised, he had the number of staff wrong.

Two soldiers stayed guarding the staff, while the other two enter the building following the cook.

The soldiers enter the hallway, walk through the first door towards the Commander, stop in the doorway of the second.

Schick picking up the black knight from the box of chess pieces, running his fingers over it.

"Sir," said the soldier in the doorway.

"Yes?" said Schick calmly picking up the other knight.

"Sir, we have so far found six members of staff!"

"Six, no Private, there must be some mistake… there should only be four, we were told… there will only be four."

"But sir, there are!"

"THERE ARE FOUR?" interrupted Schick sternly. "Make it so there are only four, Private."

"Yes, sir!"

"Oh, and Private, make sure Cook is outside will you."

"Sir!"

The two soldiers turn from the doorway and head back to the hallway. One turned to go outside, the other to get cook.

Schick raising his head, D'browski looking into his face.

"I got it wrong," said D'browski. "I forgot cook had her two children here today helping her… they are not staff… just children… twelve and fourteen, that's all Commander, twelve and fourteen."

Cook walked past the open door to the hallway, the soldier behind as they walk towards the main door. The door opened, they both walk through. Schick and D'browski looking straight into each other's eyes, staring at one another across the chess board. Two shots fired as Cook screamed, bursting into tears, shouting and cursing at the soldiers standing over her.

"Four Mr D'browski, now, there are four!"

Schick looked down at the box of chess pieces, picked it up and gently poured the pieces out, onto the board in front of them. The black pieces made from dark rosewood, the white pieces of boxwood. Kings and queens, knights and bishops, the polished pieces rolled across the chequered surface.

"A game Mr D'browski, let us play a game," said Schick, enthusiastically. "And, as you said you had not played for a while, I think it only fitting that you should have the advantage of going first."

Schick pushed all the white pieces towards his opponent.

D'browski, drained of blood, his face pale, his hands shaking, picked up the pieces and placed them on the board, as does Schick.

Two of the soldiers enter the main door, on their

way to get their breakfast.

"Oh, Private," Schick called. "Could you just go out and see the driver. Ask him to bring the camera and equipment in!"

"Sir," answered the soldier.

One of the soldiers continued towards the kitchen, the other left the house to see the driver.

With the pieces now laid out ready to play, Schick rises from his chair, calmly walked over to the tray waiting for him on the small table. While standing, he cut a piece of the bacon, then a piece of the egg, scooping them onto the end of his fork, lifting the food towards his mouth.

The soldier returned through the main door, then turned towards the chess room.

"Driver is on his way in, sir," said the soldier.

"Good," replied Schick. "Oh, Private, when you have had your breakfast, I want you to wait here, next to the chess room door."

"Yes, sir!"

Schick returned to his seat. The driver entered the house carrying a camera and tripod, which he immediately started setting up in the doorway to the chess room.

"Mr D'browski," smiled Schick. "I hope you don't mind your photograph being taken... oh, of course you don't mind, just look at all of these wonderful images around the walls... it's just that... well, this is history Mr D'browski, we are making history, the German nation in the big picture, and in our own little way, you and I are making history too. You see, when Europe, the world even, is under Nazi control, this picture will be used to show our control, our strategy, our intellectual superiority."

"Ready sir," said the driver.

"Ah excellent," beamed Schick. "If you would be so kind as to look at the camera Mr D'browski?"

The Polish businessman reluctantly looked towards the driver... Flash!

"Thank you, sir," said the driver. "I have finished."

"Very good, driver," said Schick. "Once you have put the equipment away, you may go and get your breakfast in the kitchen."

"Very good, sir. Thank you, sir!"

As the driver was moving the camera, Schick turned back to D'browski.

"Right Mr D'browski, let us play, and, of course, as white, you go first!"

The mansion owner's hands shaking, his arms feeling like a lead weights, his fingers move to the first piece.

> ➢ White Pawn e2 to e4
> ➢ Black Pawn e7 to e5
> ➢ White Knight g1 to f3
> ➢ Black Knight b8 to c6
> ➢ White Bishop f1 to c4

The first two soldiers return from their breakfast, one exits the main door, returning to guard the staff still waiting in the cold outside, the other soldier stood by the door to the chess room.

"Now Mr D'browski," said Schick, in a relaxed way. "There is a war going on, and the fact that I am here, in the clothes I am wearing, I don't want you to feel that I have had anything to do with this war…, or the making of it!"

> Black Knight c6 to d4

"You see, I am just a businessman, just like you Mr D'browski."

> White Knight f3 to e5 taking Black Pawn.

"I am not anti-Jewish, or anti-Gypsy… I have no fight with the British, Americans or French. As far as I am concerned, they are all markets I can sell to."

> Black Queen d8 to g5
> White Knight e5 to f7 takes Black Pawn.

"A lot of my staff were Jewish," he continued. "I was sorry to see them go, they were good workers."

Two more moves made, the quietness of the room only being broken by the sobbing and wailing of the cook on the driveway, in front of the mansion house.

Inside, the game continues.

> Black Queen g2 a diagonal move to e4 taking White Pawn.

"Mr D'browski, are you sure you have played this game before… I certainly expected more of a challenge."

> White Bishop c4 to e2 blocking the view of his King.

> Black Knight d4 to f3 "CHECKMATE!"

"Well, Mr D'browski, that was not what I was expecting, over with far too soon. Now, let's play again, and, this time, I expect a proper game!"

Schick pushing the white pieces towards D'browski, then set up the black pieces in front of himself.

131

The grandfather clock strikes eleven-fifteen.

The Polish chess champion making the first move.

> ➢ White Pawn e2 to e4.
> ➢ Black Pawn c7 to c5.
> ➢ White Pawn h2 to h4.

"If I may continue Mr D'browski?"

> ➢ Black Knight b8 to c6.

"Whatever a person's lifestyle, religion, makes no difference to me, I have looked at the situation in this way…"

> ➢ White Bishop f1 to b5.

"I didn't make this war happen, neither did I want it, but I am here, as are you Mr D'browski, and because of being thrown into this position, we have to make a choice."

> ➢ Black Knight c6 to d4.

The game continues.

"You see, I know that one day the war will be over, and believe me Mr D'browski, I look forward to that day immensely. But you see, being an officer… in an army, any army, doesn't give you the chance to make money… and money Mr D'browski, is what it is all about, money and power!"

The clock strikes eleven-thirty.

"Money and power, yes, it is what I am here for, the party requires I find it, and, of course, my percentage as a nest egg for once the war is over."

> ➢ White Pawn g2 to g4
> ➢ Black Pawn d7 to d5
> ➢ White Bishop c4 to b5 (Black in CHECK)
> ➢ Black Bishop c8 to d7 (Blocks the CHECK)

> White Pawn a2 to a4 covering his Bishop at b5

> Black Pawn a7 to a6 ready to take Bishop at b5

> White Bishop b5 to d7 takes Black Bishop (Black in CHECK)

> Black Queen d8 to d7 takes White Bishop

Schick looked up from the chessboard as D'browski continued with his move.

"May we return to 'Issues' Mr D'browski?" said Schick leisurely.

"As I said, Commander Schick," said the businessman, calmly. "I have no issues!"

"Games, Mr D'browski!" insisted Schick. "Games, that is all this is... games can sometimes be fun, enjoyable... but sometimes painful!"

Schick turned to the soldier standing in the doorway.

"Private, go outside and make four become three!"

"Sir," said the soldier.

The soldier turned, walked back into the hallway, out of the main door. D'browski looking at Schick; he cannot understand the mentality of this person. Two seconds later, a shot, and Cook stopped screaming.

"Now, where were we?" smiled Schick "Ah yes!"

> Black Pawn b7 to b6 (Challenging Bishop)
> White Bishop c5 to d6
> Black Rook a8 to c8
> White Rook a1 to c1 (Stopping Black Rook)

> Black Rook c8 to c1 (Taking White Rook)
> White Rook e1 to c1 (Takes Black Rook)
> Black King f8 to g8
> White Rook c1 to c7

The game speeds up as the tensions rise.

> Black Knight e7 to g5

The white pieces almost entirely surround the Black of Schick, only two White pieces back with the White King, the Black pieces trapped in the left-hand corner at the Black end of the board. D'browski putting all his effort, all his anger, into finishing Schick off, even if only on the chess board.

The clock strikes eleven forty-five.

"Where is the gold, Mr D'browski?" demanded Schick.

"Gold, I know nothing of any gold!" insisted the businessman.

"Mr D'browski, this can be an easy game, or a hard one. It is your choice."

D'browski's hand shaking violently, he moved the next piece.

> White Bishop e5 to f6 (Takes Pawn)
> Black Knight f5 to e7
> White Bishop f6 to e7 (Takes Black Knight)

"You see, Mr D'browski, we found a certain business friend of yours... Jacub Kaplan..."

Schick stopped to see the reaction of D'browski. D'browski felt sick with fear.

"Ah," continued Schick. "So, you do know Mr Kaplan."

> Black Queen d7 to e7 (Takes White Bishop)
> White Rook c8 to c7

➢ Black Queen e7 to f6

"We found Mr Kaplan on his way towards Russia. Seems he, with his family, were trying to escape the inevitable; the takeover of Poland. Unfortunately, his family got through the net, still, we have a high-ranking piece... and as you can imagine, he is old, not very strong, and, to be honest, Mr D'browski, it didn't take much persuasion for him to talk, and he talked, and talked... He is no longer with us, I am sorry to say, but, of course... he talked about you!"

"I do know Jacub." D'browski hesitated.

"Good, we are getting somewhere at last," said Schick, calmly. "Now Mr D'browski, let me come straight to the point... where have you hidden the gold? Oh, and it's your turn to play."

➢ White Queen c2 to c6 (An all-out attack by White)

"Commander Schick... please!" pleaded the businessman.

Schick turned to the soldier, having returned to the doorway.

"Private," called Schick.

"Okay," D'browski interrupts. "...It's hidden in the woods behind the house!"

"Three is to become two in two minutes," said Schick, looking at D'browski but talking to the soldier. "Unless I notify you otherwise!"

"Sir!" said the soldier as he walked towards the hall.

"Okay, Mr D'browski, tell me more," demanded Schick.

"At the back of the house, there is a path to the right-hand side, it leads down to a pond. On the other side of the pond is a woodman's cottage. You will find a hatch in the floor; it is all hidden under the floor."

"Mr Kaplan's gold?"

"No, there were many people who left their belongings with me, hoping to get it back once the war was over."

"How much do you believe to be there, Mr D'browski?"

"Some of it is in bullion, some in gold coins and pieces. I would estimate at about two million dollars."

"Ah, there. It's just a game, Mr D'browski," Schick calmly said.

Schick got up from the chair he was sitting in, walked towards the door as if to talk to the waiting soldier, suddenly stopped and looked over at the breakfast, he moved away from the doorway, towards the tray, cut another piece of egg and bacon, eating the forkful, then returned to his chair.

"The game, Mr D'browski, we must finish the game," laughed Schick.

➢ Black Queen f6 to f3
➢ White King g1 to f1
➢ Black Rook h4 to h1 (CHECKMATE to Black)

"Checkmate!" grinned Schick. "Oh, and congratulate your cook for that magnificent breakfast, would you please?"

"Cook, but you shot..." gulped the businessman.

"Yes," smiled Schick. "It's just a game!"

One bullet from the Luger into D'browski's forehead.

The clock struck twelve.

# Late Spring Present-day

## Lincoln, England

## Chapter 7
## Goodbye My Friend
## Late Spring Present-day

"Great is the man and greatly too he will be missed, and his greatness is unsearchable..."

The Reverend Bratby had sashayed his way across the room, taking one step up to the podium, his arms waving and gesturing as he spoke the words.

"My mouth will speak only the praise of this great man, and let all flesh bless his name for ever and ever."

The room was full, overly full. There were people standing at the back of the room, as well as all the way down the sides.

"The man, a good man, a stronghold in the day of trouble; he knows those who take refuge in him."

The Reverend's voice booming, but as everyone there had thought, if it wasn't for the picture above the podium, nobody would have been really sure at that moment, that they were at the correct funeral.

"Let not your hearts be troubled; believe in... HUMANITY... In this Earth, there are many rooms; if it were not so, would we have told you that there will be a place for you? And when it is time to go to that place, HUMANITY will come again and will take you as one of its own. That is where you are, all will, one day be with you also.

And you know the way, where you are going."

The Reverend, knowing the room was full of different, if not all religions, was desperately trying to not seem too Christian. In his efforts to make this happen, sharply and over-enthusiastically using the word "humanity".

The Reverend suddenly stopped waving his arms, his hands coming to rest on the top of the pulpit. He lowered his head and the volume of his voice dropping as he read the words from the stand.

"We gather here today, to remember a good friend and colleague... Professor Aluisius Wise," said the Reverend, solemnly. "And as can be seen by the gathering here today, a much-loved man."

Lincoln Crematorium would normally hold about 100 people, seated, but today, there was easily three times that amount.

"Professor Wise may not have had any children but leaves behind his sister and many friends... but, everyone who came into contact with him, knew he was a genuinely wonderful man; caring, compassionate and thoughtful, not just to those he knew, but everyone... Professor Wise was born and raised in Lincoln, he studied Politics and History, writing several books and becoming an authority on the subject before becoming a lecturer at Newcastle University."

The Professor was a committed humanitarian and humanist, the crematorium reflecting this, as it was filled with an array of people from all over the world: Africa, the Americas, Europe and Asia. Religions of Islam, Christian, Sikh, Buddhist,

Judaism and Hindu, and many, many more.

There were others who he had worked at university with, as well as his charity work.

"Professor Wise," the Reverend continued, "knocked down in a hit and run at sixty-two years of age, far too young to be leaving the great work he was doing for the community... and the world."

Tom was sitting in the front row, to the left-hand side, the podium directly in front of him.

He was dressed in black jeans, a black collarless shirt with white buttons and a long baggy thick knitted cardigan, which was black with red noughts and crosses around the middle.

Sitting next to Tom was the Professor's older sister and her family. Tom didn't know her, apart from the times she had come up in conversation with the Professor.

"It's a lovely service," she whispered to Tom. Tom nodded back to her.

"But," said the preacher. "Today is not a day for mourning, today is a day for memories, and today will be remembered for many reasons, but mainly I hope it will be remembered by you all; as a very special day, a special day in which you shared some time with others; in order to pay your last respects; and to say both mentally and physically; a sad and fond farewell to a wonderful man... a man whom many of you were privileged to have known..."

The Reverend looked up at the gathering.

"The Professor's family have today asked that we sing *Jerusalem*... please stand."

' 🎵🎵 *And did those feet, in ancient times* 🎵🎵🎵...'

At the end of the song, everyone who could, sat.

"And last of all," said Reverend Bratby. "As you will know, the Professor had two people he greatly admired, and it would be an enormous pleasure to read quotes from these two great intellectuals… firstly Shakespeare, from the play *Hamlet*."

Cmm… cm as he cleared his throat and putting on his best theatrical performance, in his most superior Shakespearian voice.

"*'thou know'st 'tis common, all that lives must die, passing through nature, to eternity'*" He looked up, hoping for an applause… he got none.

The disappointment showed on his face.

"The other man the Professor hugely admired being Bertrand Russell, I would like to give you this extract… *'An individual human existence should be like a river — small at first, narrowly contained within its banks, and rushing passionately past boulders and over waterfalls. Gradually the river grows wider, the banks recede, the waters flow more quietly, and in the end — without any visible break, they become merged in the sea, and painlessly lose their individual being.'*"

Reverend Bratby stood upright at the podium in quiet thought for a second, on opening his eyes, he looked down at Tom and nodded.

"Would you like to lead the congregation out of the door to the left please?"

Tom looked towards the door. There was an usher already there waiting to open it, the ushers head bowed as he waited for mourners to move in his direction.

Tom stood and walked towards the usher,

followed by the Professor's sister and her family.

As they reached the light outside, the exit pathway was covered in flowers and tributes to the Professor.

Tom wandered up and down the mass of colour; he didn't know anyone at the funeral so kept himself to himself. Kristina, still in Columbia, couldn't make the funeral, but had sent flowers, which Tom had just spotted.

As the gathering still filed out of the crematorium, the exit walkway became more and more packed. The first leavers now moving out to the main path around the building.

"Oops sorry!" said a tall slim gentleman in his mid-fifties, smart but shabbily dressed, a shaggy beard on his chin, as he bumped into Tom. "Well, this certainly was a good send-off wasn't it. I think it would have surprised the old bugger just how many turned up. Oh, my name's Jim, by the way."

"Yes, mm, hello, Jim," said Tom

"And you knew the Prof?" asked Jim.

"I worked with him," said Tom. "At the charity... in London."

"Of course, where he died?"

"Yes... it was right outside the office. I was there at the time, you know, when he left us."

"Yes, yes, yes," said the tall man, with too much body movement when he talked. "I worked with the Prof at Newcastle, the university, that is. I am the painting specialist... as you can imagine, with the Prof and I working together, well, it was nothing but fun... all the way... I am sorry to see him gone."

"Yes, me too. I don't know where this is going to leave me, or the work we are doing. I mean, will the charity close as there is no one to run it, you know?"

"I'm sure something will come of it."

"Do you mind if I ask you something?" Tom said sheepishly.

"Mind, no, go ahead," said Jim.

"When the Professor died, I was working on a painting that had been uncovered in Italy… had the name Leonardo di ser Piero on the back of the painting. If I could tie-up with you for some advice, that would be great?"

"Not a problem at all young man. Listen, as we are going back to the wake, well I assume you are going back, we will talk more about it there, what say you?"

"Love to… see you there."

***

The big hall was filled with ornate paintings, decorative masks and figurine heads, mahogany wood and large arched windows.

Lincoln University had organised a room and the charity sponsors had laid on the food. One side of the room had tables laid out with various hors d'oeuvres and sandwiches. There were drinks of squash, carbonated drink, beer and wine.

There were several photographs on easels dotted around the room, mostly showing scenes of the Professor in his younger days, studying at university or teaching in his later years. The pictures showing that, even when he was younger, he felt no need to dress in any way, other than to make himself feel comfortable — mostly corduroy trousers and jacket, the occasional tie or bow tie. His crazy flyaway hair in all directions.

Tom had spoken to several people by now, some he had recognised, but most he hadn't. Friends and colleagues of the Professor, knowing Tom was with him at the end, asked what happened, how could this be.

Tom was happy to talk about it but felt tortured every time he had to recollect the event.

The Professor's old Uni friends talked about the past, the charity friends wanting to know what is happening about the future.

"Hello," said a sexy, sultry voice that had come up alongside him.

"Hi," said Tom, munching on a vol-au-vent, a beer in his left hand.

"My name is Samantha... friends call me Sammie. I believe your name is Tom?"

"Yesh," said Tom, bits of vol-au-vent spraying out of his mouth.

"It's a very sad time, is it not Tom?" she said.

"You knew the Professor?" Tom quizzed, as Samantha seemed a bit too young to know him from university.

"Not personally, Tom, but I had spoken on the phone to him a few times." Samantha looked around the room, then back at Tom. "We made contact with the Professor as he deals with the charity... so I guess you could say... I am a charity worker"

Tom was more than a little confused.

If one was to look around the room full of charity workers, university lecturers and ex-students, he mused, it was clear to see that none of these jobs came with a large pay packet, their suits and clothing being of a cheaper brand and more worn out.

Unlike Samantha — she stood out, her black perfectly ironed trousers and waistcoat, on a crimson shirt, a perfect fitting jacket, somehow seemed out of place.

Samantha was medium height, 162cm (five feet four inches) tall, she had straight shoulder-length blonde hair, combed over from the parting on the right to the left side of her face. Her dark eyebrows on her pale skin accentuated her beautiful large dark piercing eyes. Her lightly blushed cheeks and perfectly formed red lips, hinted at a smile.

"A charity worker," said Tom. "You are very smartly dressed for a charity worker."

"Charity workers come in all types," she replied. "I will assume you work in an untidy little office?"

"Well… yes," hesitated Tom.

"But some charity offices will be smart and modern, will they not?"

"I guess so," he mused.

"The sponsorship that your charity gets," she said, smoothly, "has to come from somewhere…"

"Yes… I guess so," said Tom.

"Wealthy businesses… that then, is where I come in."

Tom tried to guess where Samantha was from; it was very hard to say. She looked like she could be English, well, or Scottish, or European… American maybe.

He could definitely make out a slight accent but could not pinpoint it.

"So, you are a businesswoman?"

"Yes, well, let's say… I make things happen," said Samantha, offhandedly.

"And, so, what is it you want with the charity… that you should be speaking to the Professor about?"

"Yes… the Professor." She looked into Tom's face "We must move on… We will make sure the charity keeps running, Tom. We need you to carry on with what you are doing… do you understand?"

"Er… I think so!"

"Go back to work tomorrow, Tom. The charity will keep running; we will make sure of that. But we need you to keep working on the task you have in your office."

"Okay," he said, getting excited at the thought.

"I will be leaving now," she smiled. "I trust you to do your work well… it was nice to have met you Tom, but we will never meet again. So, I will say farewell!"

"Oh… okay, sure, it was nice to have met you too!"

Tom watched her as she oozed sex appeal walking down the main hall, past the tables of food… He continued to watch as she exited the, already open, large oak wood doors. As she went through, two big men in dark suits, shaven heads and sunglasses — one either side of the doorway, turned and followed her out.

'Well, you don't see that every day,' thought Tom.

# Chapter 8
## Leonardo
## Late Spring Present-day

The morning following the funeral, Tom was back in the office, buoyed up by the chance conversation he had with the businesswoman Samantha.

And so, he set about getting on with the task, to carry on the work of the much-loved Professor.

He now knew he had to right the world of the wrongs that had been done, take over the mantle set out by the great man.

First things first, he switched on the old computer sitting on his desk. It seemed to take longer than normal to start up, *'maybe'* he thought to himself *'if there is now a sponsor for the charity, I could ask them, if they had an old computer they are getting rid of, could I have it?'* But for the time being he would use the old one, after all, it was still going.

He sat looking at the screen, still dark, one or two flicks of light. Then, a few seconds, his face lit up with the blue tint radiating from the screen, his eyes reflecting the rectangular shape of the monitor.

*Now, what is this about Leonardo di ser Piero that I have missed?*

He opened up his emails and started to read through them.

First, there were authenticity checks, the frame details along with an X-ray of the canvas.

There was a photograph with the details; it looked to be an early work, a landscape.

Later that day, he contacted Jim, the tall art expert he had met at the Professor's funeral. Jim then emailing back the things Tom should be questioning; has it been touched up by 'painting surgeons?', Its provenance: has the painting been made with walnut oil? Jim spoke about technique, composition and style.

As much as Tom thought about this painting, he could still not see what was so special that it required Samantha to insist he kept going at it; but keep going he did.

He had, after two days, exhausted all the avenues that he could, he had arranged all of the certificates, the paintings history and feedback from experts, there was no more he could do.

He had found its owners at the time the painting was stolen by the Nazis and had let the heirs know of the find, and the possibility it could be returned to them. That is, of course, after all checks had been completed.

By the third day, Tom had finished work on the Leonardo return, which was a stroke of luck; as mid-morning that day, his computer went 'pop!' A puff of smoke rose from the back of the machine, Tom quickly diving under the table, unplugging the device in case it burst into flames.

It was coming up to lunchtime, so trying to forget the problem with his computer, he set off for the post office, then getting himself a sandwich from the local Co-op.

Back in the office, he made himself a cup of coffee, sipped it while he opened the sandwich box. Pulling out one half of the meal, his thoughts returning to the Professor.

He stood up, walked over to the window, looked down into the street and took a bite out of the bread.

Still chewing, he turned and looked around the room. 'What will become of all of this?' he wondered, looking at hundreds of books, papers and documents.

Tom looking at his old broken computer then over to his mentor's empty chair, the black screen of the other computer, around the Professor's desk; he pushed the last of the sandwich into his mouth.

The package had sat there on the desk, still unopened since the day it had been delivered by the postman. Tom felt an unease at looking inside. This was a project of the Professor's; it didn't seem right that he should take it over.

Tom, taking a deep breath, picked up some scissors, cut the black plastic wrapper that surrounded the parcel, pulling out the package inside; brown paper with string tied around the wrapping paper.

The string cut, Tom peeled back the paper one section at a time, the back then the left side, then the right; Tom now had a partial view of the cardboard box, blackened with smoke.

With the final section of brown paper pulled down, it now revealed the whole damage to the box; the outside singed, a hole burnt away at one end, a few blackened bits of paper poking through the hole.

Tom grabbed a couple of new file envelopes and a plastic tray from the shelves. He would, he thought, at least sort out the good from the bad, what he could use, and what was beyond help.

Tom tentatively lifted the lid, the Professor's words ringing in his ears: *"I have a feeling Tom, that this is what I opened this place for in the first place... I feel it, Tom, I feel that this is the one that will put us on the map."*

Tom turning the lid over, slowly lowered it onto the table top; looking down into the remains of the chard contents: a picture. He lifted the picture from the box. It was in a reasonable condition, the black and white photograph showed two men sitting in front of a chess board, the pieces laid out ready to play a game. The man on the left was older, greying hair, pale skin. He was wearing a dark dressing gown with a light-coloured cravat.

To the right of the picture, an SS officer, smiling, confident and upright. He wore a dark uniform; visible above the table were the Nazi eagle and iron cross on his upper jacket pocket, SS symbols on the collar.

He had dark hair combed to one side, menacing eyes and a narrow chin.

In the background of the picture were plaques on shelves along with photographs on the wall.

Tom turned the picture over. On the back was a very faint pencil handwriting. He was not sure if it was 'X' or 'K' 'Dbra...', the other name 'W' 'Smick'... 'Shok'. The box may have the answer, and he would certainly need a magnifying glass. He laid the photograph in the box lid.

Tom pulled out documents, papers, envelopes, the damage caused by the fire getting worse as he got further down the box.

A commendation, a military campaign, a letter giving instructions to visit a mansion in Poland.

Tom was about half-way down the box, lunchtime now drifting into afternoon. The box contents were all in German but Tom having a degree in German this is a simple translation.

So far, Tom had only skimmed over the documents, arranging them in files or trays, prioritising the contents into what he believed to be most important.

As most of the letters had been sent to a Wilhelm Schick, Tom guessed that the SS officer in the photograph would be Schick.

At the end of the day, Tom was no wiser about the box other than that it was a record of the officer's military service.

He would continue tomorrow.

The next morning Tom woke, after a very bad night's sleep. He tossed and turned, his mind full of ifs and buts. What had he missed? Was there something he should have done? It was not clear in his mind; the Leonardo painting kept popping into his brain.

He hoped that when he reached the office today, not having a computer, something would arrive in the post that he could follow up on.

At the office, of course, the post doesn't arrive till later in the morning, so he would carry on looking at the box's contents.

He pulled out a blackened parchment. He could just make out a signature; it looked like 'Kaplan'. Of the words on the rest of the paper, he could see 'mansion', 'Krzyztof D'br...', 'Petrykozy' and 'Jewish'.

Tom put this into the to 'look into' file and picked up another paper. This time a newspaper cutting with a photograph, the same person as in the first picture, with a name D'browski. Into the pile to be looked at. Next, a payment to a blacksmith in Poland. 'Strange' thought Tom, he obviously needed something to be fixed... but he is a Nazi commander. This is occupied Poland in the middle of a war, you just tell a blacksmith what to do, not pay them. That is definitely going into the 'look into' folder.

Below that was a contract, burnt, charred and blackened. It was difficult to read anything on it, it was handwritten in English, but Tom could just make out some words... it read:

A CONTRACT between

Samuel Plant and Wilhelm Schick

The boxes contain ingots that belong to the names printed above, the financial gain from the Ingots.

The rest was burnt away, but the next piece to be pulled out looked like it was the bottom of the same sheet.

Samuel Plant Wilhe

uary 1945

What Tom could make of the rest was not in a

language that he knew, but he believed to be Arabic.

عائلة بن دي وعدتأنتعتني بألسناديق و تحافظ عليهم آمنة في قبو
منزلها حتى يتم جمعها
كما أن الله هو شهادتي
سيلستين بورغوان
مصطفى بن دي

The Professor, thought Tom, was getting excited about this box. Why? What did the Professor know before the box arrived? He must have known something. It can't have been a guess that there was something about this box.

What was on the Professors emails, letters, phone messages?

He must find out.

Tom turned away from the box and with a huge sense of guilt, sat in the Professor's chair, leaned forward and switched his computer on.

While he waited for the machine to warm up, he opened the drawers to the desk, pulling out scraps of paper and notepads, thumbing through each one, trying to find anything related to what he had just seen in the box.

The monitor screen came on as he looked up and down at the icons, would anything help.

Emails, that would be it, he must have had emails….

Tom clicked on the Internet Explorer, then emails….

Two seconds passed and a password was required.

"Argh," growled Tom

Again, Tom went through the drawers, into the notepads, the shelves above the computer. Finally, he found a slip of paper with the password, under the computer body on the desk.

Tom punched in the password and immediately... Bing; 'You have mail!' Most of what came up on the screen was junk, Tom immediately disposed of it. What was he looking for? he thought. A name. A contact?

He decided to clear everything to new folders on the screen, keeping only that that would be of possible interest, and to watch for the few names he now knew existed... Kaplan... Schick... Plant and D'browski. And what have all of these names got in common?

After an hour of looking for more clues about the box, he had found nothing. The day was getting late and he knew he would have to leave soon. So, leaving the emails, which he knew he would go back to the next day; there still being hundreds of emails to check, he decided to spend the rest of the day searching for the names. Starting with D'browski; he knew D'browski was a chess player, he was featured in a newspaper article, so he had to be known... surely?

Forty-five minutes later, Tom had found an article: *'Krzyztof D'browski, Polish chess champion and businessman, found dead in his chess room, along with the rest of his staff after what was believed to be a gun battle with German troops.'*

The following day, Tom was straight onto the Professor's computer. With a renewed determination, he set about reading each of the emails, sure that this would give him the information he needed.

Later that morning he found Jennifer Pinski, studying to be a doctor at Stanford University on the West Coast of America.

The Professor had been in touch with this young woman, but in no great detail. Clearly, at the time of the email, he was just checking he had the correct person and no more.

The vague emails asked Ms Pinski about her family history, as he (the Professor) was seeking information about the movement of families and individuals at the time of the war.

Ms Pinski had written back telling the Professor of her father and mother who had left Russia after the Cold War and settled in England.

When she was ten years old, they had moved again to America, her mother and father working in medical research, with Ms Pinski moving to San Francisco after her father's sudden death.

She didn't know a great deal about the family before Russia, except that her great grandfather Joseph Kaplan was a Polish businessman, who died while being held by the Germans, the rest of the family escaping to the Baltic States.

"So, Ms Pinski, I think I need to get in touch with you and let you know what has happened to the Professor," Tom said to himself. "I think we need to talk."

Tom drafted up an email to Jennifer, explaining all that had happened over the last few weeks, that he was sorry about the delay in getting back to her and that now, he will be taking over the task of following the family trail. He hoped this was not an inconvenience, as the charity was trying to right an historical wrong and that they had to check all details thoroughly.

Tom switching off the computer, thinking to himself, *'Oh dear... poor Leonardo, he is going to have to wait.'*

# Summer 1943

## Lodz District, Poland

# Chapter 9
## The Next Move
## Summer 1943

Commander Wilhelm Schick hadn't returned to the mansion since the events surrounding the death of the businessman Krzyztof D'browski.

Today, though, he had planned to retrieve his stake in the spoils of war, having eighteen months earlier cleared out half of the gold, cash and jewellery. This had been recorded, catalogued and shipped out to fund the Nazi war machine.

The rest was still hidden in the woodman's hut, waiting to be moved to a place where Schick could keep a closer eye on it. A place closer to his home in Dresden.

As Schick would normally do in situations like this, he had planned in great detail just how this was all going to happen, the date, the timing, the fine details. Planning was all crucial to winning a successful game.

Plan several moves ahead, think clearly and calmly, his gambit so far in this long game, was the shooting of two of his soldiers the last time he had visited the mansion.

While two had stood guard at the house, he took the other two to load the hoard into crates ready to be moved out, the crates then loaded onto the Krupp-Protze truck waiting on the driveway in front of the mansion. Once the Truck had half of the hoard on board, the Commander ordered the driver of the truck to return to the headquarters, telling him that he would follow on later.

The remaining items in the basement of the woodman's hut were then crated up and put to one side, Schick telling the soldiers to return to the front of the mansion, ordering them to fire several rounds at the front door and windows.

The soldiers followed Schick to the driveway, standing at the edge of the steps that lead up to the front door, Schick standing behind them.

"Okay," ordered Schick. "You may fire when you are ready!"

The soldiers lifted their rifles ready to follow out the order.

Each soldier firing several rounds, smashing the windows, wood splintering from the door.

Schick standing watching the scene of destruction, lifted his head, took a deep breath of the cold Autumn air, raised his pistol and shot them both in the back of their heads.

Schick's driver and confidante, Horst, had been working for the Commander for many years. He was Wilhelm Schick's driver before the war. Schick, knowing he could trust him implicitly, kept him as his personal driver when military service was introduced.

Horst had seen many things and knew not to talk about them.

Schick had a week before, sent Horst back to Petrykozy to find a blacksmith who could be trusted.

With this organised, the move today will go smoothly.

The Mercedes-Benz swept along the narrow country lanes of the Lodz district of Central Poland; the sun rising in the Summer sky, the trees and bushes full of life, wild flowers blooming, birds, insects and flying creatures filling the air.

"This is a good day to be alive," Schick said to Horst as they drove through the woods and fields.

"It certainly is sir!" Horst replied.

"How much longer to get there, Horst?" asked Commander Schick.

"About fifteen minutes sir!" answered the driver.

"Good... good!"

Behind the Mercedes, Schick had arranged for a Tatra 111 heavy truck to follow them along.

Two soldiers on board the truck, young recruits, straight from the Nazi training camp; tall, slim, blond hair, pale Aryan complexions and very eager to help the Nazi cause.

They both wore reddish-brown trousers, khaki shirts with buttoned-down epaulettes, a belt carrying a holster and Luger. Diagonal straps from the belt, which went through the epaulette on the right-hand shoulder, a black neckerchief held in place with a red neckerchief slide.

On their upper left arms, they wore red and white armbands having a black swastika facing the side. On their heads, loose fitting khaki caps.

One of the youth soldiers driving, the other sitting in the passenger seat.

Schick looked out of the rear window of the Mercedes at the Tatra truck, then turned his head back to the front.

"The timing is looking good Horst," said Schick.

"Yes sir, the journey has been much easier than the last time we came this way."

"Nine-thirty to the mansion, load the trucks and on our way by early afternoon."

"The blacksmith is expecting us, sir!"

"Good, will he have everything ready that we need?"

"He promised he would sir… and he understood the consequences, should he not be ready."

"Good work, Horst, very good work!" said the Commander, a slight smile on his lips.

The Nazi staff car and the truck pulled into the gates leading to the mansion, the dry hard ground making both vehicles roll from side to side.

The once smooth and well-maintained track to the mansion becoming overgrown and rough.

The car of Schick pulled up at the steps to the main house, the truck behind them.

Leaves and broken branches littered the front of the once orderly house. Bushes and borders overgrown and thriving with weeds, rambling plants climbing the walls and pillars.

The truck driver and passenger, sat, engine running, waiting for their instructions.

Schick's driver, Horst, stepped out of the Mercedes and made his way to the truck.

"Take the truck around the back of the house," said Horst, pointing to the side of the building. "Stop on the lawn, but leave the engine running and we will be around shortly to give you further instructions."

"Yes, sir... Heil Hitler!" said the two young enthusiastic troopers as they raised their right arms to salute, their palms facing the front.

"Yes... heil," acknowledged Horst.

The truck's engine's revs rose, as it clunked into first gear, pulling out and around the staff car, disappearing around the corner of the building towards the gardens.

Horst made his way back to the staff car, opened the rear door, Commander Schick stepped out, the rustling of leaves and stones underfoot.

Schick stretched, took a deep breath and placed his officers cap onto his head.

"Okay Horst, let's get this done as quickly as we can."

"Sir!"

They both took the route down the side of the house taken by the Tatra 111 truck moments earlier, the truck now sitting in the middle of the overgrown lawn, engine still ticking over.

"Okay, you two," Horst called up to the soldiers. "The path is over there; I want you to pull up with the back of the truck as near to the trees as you can. Once there, lower the tailgate, we will then head down to the hut, we will show you the items we need to move... Is that understood?"

"Yes, sir!"

The soldier in the passenger seat suddenly and enthusiastically opening his door, jumping down to the ground as he quickly ran over the area that Horst was pointing at.

The driver pulled forward, then hard on the steering wheel, until the truck was facing the back of the mansion.

The sound of gears grinding as it jumped into reverse, handbrake off, the truck moved backwards. The young passenger waving his arms to guide the driver, it pulled onto the path, reaching the walkway into the trees.

The passenger putting both his hands up, indicating to the driver to stop… The truck stopped, the handbrake pulled up, the engine off.

The driver's door swung open as the young, tall, slim soldier jumped down from the cab.

Horst standing in the middle of the lawn watching their every move. Schick standing two steps behind Horst, his hands held together behind his back, his mind going through every conceivable combination of possibilities, calculating the next move.

"Okay, Bund Deutscher Arbeiterjungend," called Horst, as he started to make his way down the path. "Follow me, it isn't far!"

Horst headed into the undergrowth, towards the hut, closely followed by the two young workers, behind them not saying a word, but watching every movement and every sound, walked Commander Schick; his hands still together behind his back.

Around the pond, the hut came into sight. The weeds and brambles having grown thicker since the last visit, the path not having been used, had become difficult to walk.

Horst opened the door; nothing had changed since the last time they had been there.

"You two," he said to the youths. "Go back to the truck, there will be an axe and spade in there somewhere... bring them down here and clear some of that path. It will make our lives a bit easier!"

"Sir." They both turned and ran back towards the truck.

"All going to plan Horst?" smiled Schick.

"Like clockwork, sir!" replied Horst.

Horst took the keys from his pocket, bending down, he pulled at the large heavy rug that was covering the floor.

Below the rug was a metre square hinged hatch.

Horst bending to his haunches, put the key into the slot and turned. A click as the lock flicked open.

Horst put his fingers under the edge of the hatchway and lifted; as the trapdoor rose, he lifted it out of the lugs at the other end. Lifting the whole lid, he put it to one side.

Taking an oil lamp from the cupboard in the corner of the hut, along with a can of lamp oil, he poured the oil into the lamps base.

The youths had returned and were hacking at the vegetation, clearing a way that would make the removal of the stored items easier.

Horst having lit the lamp, took a step onto the ladder, descending to the basement below.

About thirty minutes later, the two jugends ran into the hut.

They quickly looked around for Horst, but he

was not in sight. Schick sitting on a wooden chair looking out of the window.

"We have finished, sir," said one of the youths to Schick but not knowing if he should speak to the officer. "What would you like us to do now?"

Schick remained looking out of the window.

"Ah," said a voice from down below. "You have finished then... good... can you make your way down here? We have these things to get up to the truck."

"Okay, sir," called the youth, heading for the hole in the floor.

As the two young soldiers stepped onto the floor of the basement, they could see the size of the bunker. It was two or three times bigger than the woodman's hut. It stretched back into the darkness, shelves and units filled most of the area, from floor to ceiling.

The shelves themselves were mostly empty, except for bags that had already been packed waiting to go. At the bottom of the steps were boxes and cases ready to be taken up.

"This is it jugend," said Horst. "There is some rope over there in the corner. Now, everything must go... as soon as possible, onto the back of the truck... Now get to it!"

As soon as Horst had finished his instructions, one of the young soldiers bounced over to the rope. The other shimmied up the ladder, waiting for the rope to be thrown up.

By one p.m. the truck was full and waiting to go. Schick had returned to the staff car waiting for

Horst. When Horst arrived back at the car, it would be time for them to make their way to the blacksmiths.

"Drive around to the front of the house and follow me!" he told the youths.

They arrived at the blacksmiths at two p.m.

The young soldiers unloaded the boxes, crates and bags. Clonking and banging, they carried the heavy loads to the shed and furnace.

Sitting next to the furnace were two crucibles and several rectangular iron moulds.

The young soldiers, having finished unloading the truck by three-thirty p.m., headed back to the truck, waiting for further orders.

Horst had opened the rear door of the Mercedes, Schick emerged from the back of the black saloon.

Schick and Horst then walked back down to the shed, they could feel the heat already emerging from its doorway. The blacksmith had started his work as soon as the first pieces had arrived. Gold was hard to melt; it needed a high temperature, and time was not on his side.

Horst walking into the shed; Schick stood in the doorway looking on.

"Blacksmith!" Horst called out over the sound of the furnace.

"Sir, yes, sir?" acknowledged the blacksmith, lowering his eyes.

"You have now seen what we have here... we need a realistic time that you will finish the work we have asked you to do... So, how long?"

"T-t-tomorrow, sir," the blacksmith stammered.

"Would that be okay with you, sir? I really don't think it will be any sooner. I will work on it all night, sir."

"That's fine, blacksmith. I did say a realistic time, did I not?" said Horst.

"Yes, sir… definitely tomorrow afternoon."

"Don't worry blacksmith…" called out Commander Schick from the doorway. "All we ask is the job is done correctly, efficiently and on time… you will be paid handsomely for any work we have asked you to do."

"Sir… thank you very much, sir," said the blacksmith, looking down towards Schick's feet.

Schick turned from the doorway and walked back up the path to the staff car, closely followed by Horst.

Schick climbing into the back of the Mercedes whilst Horst told the youth they will be driving back to the mansion where they will billet for the night.

***

Three p.m. the following day, the staff car followed by the Tatra 111 truck pulled up outside the blacksmith's shed. True to his word, sitting in the yard were sixteen wooden crates ten inches wide, four inches high and twenty inches long, each containing four gold ingots; painted a dark military green, the words in German down the side reading 'For Military Use'.

On top of the crates were three hessian bags containing the remaining jewels.

"Jugend," called Horst standing next to the crates.

"Sir!" they came running.

"Put these crates on the back of the truck and await further orders!"

"Yes, sir!"

The young soldiers quickly ran to the cases, grabbing the rope handle attached to each end of the case, they immediately race back to the truck with the weighty load.

Schick, remaining on the back seat of the staff car, watching on as the work was done. The blacksmith, exhausted, looked on as the young soldiers ran back for the second crate.

"Thank you for your efforts, blacksmith," said Horst.

"You are welcome sir!" replied the blacksmith.

"Now, as I said, blacksmith," Horst said, sternly. "A good job done, and you will receive a handsome reward."

Horst pulled out of his pocket a large number of notes, taking a random amount, he placed them into the blacksmith's hand.

"There you are blacksmith," continued Horst. "I think you will find that that will be more than reasonable for the work you have done."

"Why thank you, sir," said the blacksmith. "Are you sure, sir? That is rather a lot you have giving me."

The youths pick up another case.

"Blacksmith, as I am sure you are aware," said Horst, looking the blacksmith directly in the eyes. "The payment is not just for the work you have just done, but for your silence as well... and should we hear that silence has not been kept, the consequences will be swift and harsh. Not just to you, but for your family as well... am I making myself clear?"

"More than clear, sir," said the blacksmith, starting to shake. "Yes sir, not a word to anybody sir... I give my word."

"Good," said Horst, standing upright and smiling. "I'm glad we have an amicable arrangement."

The young workers collect another crate and run off with it to the truck.

Horst opening one of the hessian bags, put his hand in and pulled out two gems.

"For you, blacksmith," he said dropping them onto the blacksmith's open palm.

The blacksmith nodded.

The final case loaded onto the Tatra 111, the hessian bag of gems put into the boot of the Mercedes staff car, the tailgate to the truck lifted; the two young soldiers jump up, ready for their next instructions.

"Okay, jugends," directed Horst as they sat in the cab of the truck. "We will be heading for Dresden. I would like you to follow me all the way there."

"Yes, sir, heil Hitler!" they replied together, their arms raising to a salute.

The staff car pulled slowly away, heading for Commander Schick's home on the outskirts of Dresden, closely followed by the truck.

The two 'jugends' not knowing that in the back of their truck was over a million dollars' worth of gold bullion; having just been cast into ingots.

# Summer Present-day

Sebastian's Flat
Stratford, London

# Chapter 10
## Name and Place
## Summer Present-day

Sebastian's curiosity had got the better of him. The German wording on the piece of paper he had found in his parents' loft, was still not really clear, but it had to be there for a reason.

He didn't want to tell anyone what he had found, thinking for the present time he would keep this to himself, but had now had several conversations with friends; in kind of general terms, would they know how to find information about old relatives, family history, military records and the like?

Most advice he had was online, family history sites or the National Archives.

He would return from work each day, throw his jacket onto the couch and immediately switch on the laptop; his coffee table becoming cluttered with notepads and printouts of the research he had done. The armchair filling up with birth, marriage and death certificates, that he had ordered and received from the Office of National Certificates.

With each document, each tiny bit of research, he grew more and more to know about the life and history of Samuel Plant.

But for all of this information, it was still not telling him about 'the contract', what it meant, who was the other name? Why was it in German at the time of war?

The German part of the contract itself had been the easy part to check, even though, without knowing what the contract was about, it was, to Sebastian, still meaningless.

The online German translator had read the text as:

Die Boxen enthalten Barren,
*(The boxes contain ingots,)*

die gehören zu den Namen oben gedruckt,
*(which belong to the names printed above,,)*

des finanziellen Gewinns aus den Blöcken zwischen den oben genannten Namen zu gleichen Teilen getragen.
*(of the financial gain from the blocks between the above names in equal parts.)*

Die Schachteln dürfen erst im Herbst 1947 angefasst werden
*(The boxes may not be touched until autumn 1947)*

wenn wir einender kontaktieren und der Erlös zwischen uns geteilt.
*(when we contact somebody and the proceeds are shared between us.)*

Bis zu diesem Zeitpunkt wird es in gehalten und von den Namen und Ort unten betreut.
*(Until that time, it is kept in and cared for by the name and place below.)*

The boxes contain ingots, he thought. Well what type of ingots, gold, aluminium? After all, it could be that he had shares somewhere, in a mine or something.

And the names above… who is the guy with the German name, is he German, or Dutch or Polish? And the name just sounds German; he needs to find this person. What had he to do with Great Grandad?

Boxes, cartons of what? The ingots? So, if it was shares in a mine for example, why would they want to hide the boxes away?

Whatever they had, thought Sebastian, to be shared equally, was it worth a lot of money then? And Great Grandad never went back for it… or did he? The death certificate showed he had died in September 1947, so maybe he never got to the boxes… if he had, after all, surely Dad would have known all about it. They talked about the family and the past, it was important to them.

What if Great Grandad had told someone else, a friend… who is the 'Somebody' it mentions? What if *they* have the boxes… or the German, did the German return for the boxes?

Autumn 1947, that's what it says, Autumn 1947… if Great Grandad didn't get the boxes, and the German didn't get the boxes… they may still be there… but where?

And as for the other writing, he hadn't a clue. Still not even sure what language it was.

But it was all clues to something, something he felt was in his interest to find.

'It is to be kept and cared for in the name and place below…'

"Well, name and place below," Sebastian said to himself looking at the unknown writing at the bottom of the contract "We are going to have to find out exactly who you are, and where you can be found... yes... we most certainly are!"

# Chapter 11
## Jennifer
## Summer Present-day

<Dear Ms Pinski, you will not know me. My name is Tom Paige. I work at the charity run by Professor Wise. I'm afraid I have some bad news about the Professor. A little over three weeks ago, he was killed in an accident.

I will be taking over the work he had already started. I will be picking up from where the Professor was at the time of his death. For this, I will be following your family trail. Please let me know that you are happy for me to do this. It would help me greatly if you could let me know you have received this email and are happy for me to continue the work already undertaken.>

Tom felt that with the woman Samantha telling him the charity would still be funded and the Leonardo investigation in limbo, he would keep himself busy carrying on with the case that the Professor was doing.

He had found the password to the Professor's email account; he should at least let the Professor's contact in America know what had happened to him.

If she was happy for him to continue with the project, he would carry on the work he had already started on the parcel from Germany?

Tom knew very little about Jennifer Pinski. He

had read a couple of emails between her and the Professor, but these were no more than just first contacts.

Was she even the correct person?

There were a few details about her family history, having come from Russia after escaping the Nazi invasion of Poland.

If the Professor was right, she had mentioned her great grandfather being Jacub Kaplan. Tom now had four names to follow: Krzyztof D'browski the chess player; Wilhelm Schick the German commander; Samuel Plant— the other name on the contract written in English; and Jacub Kaplan — a name mentioned by both Jennifer, as well as in the box that appears to have originated from Commander Schick. The Professor clearly believed she was the descendant of Kaplan. After all, the day the Professor died, he was very excited about what he had found.

Only the box would confirm his theory.

One thing Tom was curious about though, how did the Professor find the original lead?

Tom continued to search the box, most of it unusable, damaged over time. Smoke and fire leaving only scraps.

Of the usable but smoke damaged items he found, was a shopping list of jewels and precious stones: Diamant 275, Smaragd 199, Opale 105, Saphire 127, Rubin 152. The list went on, getting more damaged and harder to decipher the further down the note he went; next to the list of the precious stones was a separate blackened note with the words 'Bone'... ivory... maybe?

A letter — he put in the 'to-read' pile, a newspaper cutting from a German newspaper. A scrap of paper with what appears to be the name of a ship: *Suraat Allah*, just visible the words Captain Abou Nasir and Marseille.

Tom managed to check this vessel out in old shipping records. The ship was a cargo vessel registered in Algiers. During the war, it was used by the Allies to supply food, water and stocks around the Mediterranean.

Tom was now starting to piece some of the puzzle together.

Later that afternoon, he received an email.

<Good morning Mr Paige, how wonderful it is to hear from you. I am so sorry to hear about the Professor. I didn't know. It must be difficult for you, taking over his work. Was he a good friend? It has just gone 8 a.m. where I am. I am just checking my emails eating breakfast, the time delay is a bit of a nuisance, isn't it?>

<Hello Ms Pinski, yes, I sent the email earlier in the day, well that is earlier in the day to me. It's coming up to 4:10 p.m. here. I have been working for the Professor for around three years. As you can imagine, in that amount of time, and that there were only the two us working in the office, we did get to know each other very well. Please call me Tom.>

<OK Tom, then you can call me Jennifer.>

<Wonderful. So, Jennifer, I don't know exactly how far the Professor was with his investigation, how much was in his head. He had told me, on the day of his death, that he was following up on a lead;

one that he thought would be worthwhile, and that a box that was coming to us would have the answers. I now have the box, but, give me a couple of days to get up to speed with it.>

<That's fine Tom, I look forward to hearing from you in a couple of days.>

The following day, Tom delved deeper into the histories of Kaplan and D'browski; Kaplan was, prior to the war, known to be a businessman and philanthropist. He owned several factories and was well respected in the community, sponsoring schools and Universities. He believed education was the way to a better future for all humanity. He was a leading member of the Jewish peoples in the Lodz area of Poland.

D'browski was a businessman, having several shops and small outlets. He had, for a while managed two of Kaplan's factories, and stepped in to help deal with problems in the other business concerns.

D'browski was not Jewish by faith, Tom could not find that he was of any religious faith at all; anything written about Krzyztof D'browski considered him to be a humanitarian, a humanist. When the talk was of a German invasion, he was asked by the Jewish leaders to look after the property and valuables of as many of the local faiths as he could handle, until after the troubles had passed, when they would be returned to their rightful owners.

Two days later…

<Hi Jennifer, hope you are well. I have now had

a couple of days to get my head around the issue. It would seem that your great grandfather, Jacub Kaplan was caught trying to escape from Poland. He was presumably tortured by the Germans to give details of who had helped them escape. As well as, who was now looking after all of their possessions. This I can tell you, was a man called Krzyztof D'browski. He worked with your great Grandfather at his factories; he was a manager there. Mr D'browski was also killed. Stories are saying: a gun battle at his mansion, well, could be. Get back to me and we can discuss the next path we have to go down.>

<Thank you, Tom, I have been so excited waiting to hear back from you. It will be great to find out what had happened to my great grandfather. Hopefully, put a name to his killer.>

<Not sure if giving the name of a killer is what I can do, my job is to find gold, jewellery, paintings and items of wealth and to see that they get back to their rightful heir. If the name of the possible killer crops up, I will give this to you in a final report, but you must remember, I am an investigator for theft, not murder.>

<Sorry, Tom, perhaps I got a bit carried away. Of course, I understand your view, and I am fully behind your work and your ethics.>

<Jennifer, as we are in contact, I will need some further information about you and your family. I will need to draft up the questions I need to ask you. As it is, I am still going through the box the Professor was sent, so am still not sure of the exact questions,

but they may come to you a bit at a time.>

<Tom, I'll tell you what I will do, I am due some leave from college coming up. I can be over to London in a few days. We can meet up, that way we can go through the box together. Ask the questions as we do so. Would that be easier?>

<Jennifer, that would be great. Are you sure that's not a problem? It's a long way to come.>

<Tom, not a problem at all, I will book a flight later today. I will contact you to let you know what time I am arriving, flight number, etc. How does that sound?>

<Sounds great. Once you know what time you will arrive here, I will make arrangements for you to be picked up. I will need to know who to look for, can you send some details.>

<Of course, Tom. I've attached a recent photograph, it is a picture of me with my friend. I am the one on the left.>

Tom opened up the attachment; a picture popped up on the screen.

The picture showed a room; plain walls, except for a couple of posters; one featuring a young nineteen-sixties Bob Dylan in a very grainy black and white; a head and shoulders shot, his collar up high on his jacket, covering his neck, black wavy hair, looking like it hadn't been combed, his head slightly tilted, pale skin and black sunglasses.

The other poster had a white background, featuring a large red circle in the middle, within the red circle was a black 'ban the bomb' symbol, below this in large red letters with black edging, the words

'BAN THE BOMB'.

Around the rest of the room were a couple of old, red easy chairs and a coffee table.

The woman on the right of the picture was good looking, in a plain 'girl next door' type of way. Wearing denim dungarees, a white T-shirt and a baggy cardigan, she had long fair to blonde hair and a shy look in her face.

The woman on the left was a little shorter, her hair a light brown, long with a slight wave.

Her beautiful cheeks narrowing down to her chin, a wonderful fair complexion, dark eyebrows and dark brown eyes.

She was wearing jeans and a red long-sleeved cotton shirt.

*'So, this is Jennifer.'*

*'Okay,'* Tom thought. *'I now have just a few days to work out where the clues lead us, so there is no time to waste. Let's get on. Next, I must find out more about Commander Wilhelm Schick and Samuel Plant.'*

# 18 February 1945

## Just North of
## Mulhouse, France

# Chapter 12
# Clearing Resistance
# 18 February 1945

There had been heavy losses on both sides, as the German troops tried to hold onto the remaining parts of France that they still occupied. Bodies littered the streets, the alleys and demolished buildings. The heavy bombardment had flattened most of the town of Mulhouse, but the allies were slowly pushing forward.

Rat-tat-tat as machine-gun fire rang out, bullets hitting the building as plaster exploded from the craters formed by the small projectile hitting the wall.

Two explosions in quick succession threw up dust and rock, which fell onto the four British soldiers held up in the ruin of the old house; two rooms, no windows and half a roof was all that remained after the shells fallen while taking back the town.

Stan Stupple, kneeling just below the window, quickly jumped to his feet. Rifle out of the window, letting off two rounds, aiming into the window of the derelict house across the road; immediately, two rounds came back at them.

Stan Stupple at the front window, Peter Kitchen at a hole in the side to the house to the left, and Barry Billingham in the room to the right; keeping the right-hand side clear of any attack.

Sergeant Samuel Plant zipping from room to room, assessing the way to move forward.

He moved quickly into the room of Billingham.

"Seems a bit quiet on this side," said Plant, pushing his body tight against the wall behind the window. "Keep your eyes peeled, Billingham. I guess they are planning something to happen over this side."

"Okay, Sarge!" he replied.

At that moment, Plant looking up the alley of the house opposite, saw a German soldier cross the gap, moving quickly from the house the British soldiers were shooting into, towards the house next to it.

"'Ere they go, Billingham," said Plant, nodding out of the window towards the alley opposite. "Get ready, I just saw one cross the gap, keep an eye for the next!"

"Sir!"

Plant could see just enough of the alley to get one or two quick shots off, with both of them shooting, there was a better chance of hitting the German trooper.

A head popped out from the building, then back again, the German soldier checking he was clear to run.

"Get ready Billingham, I've just seen a head poke out!"

Billingham, his rifle poised ready for action, his body waiting to spring to the window.

"Kitchen… Stupple," called Plant. "We are just about to start shooting, make sure you cover us by shooting at their windows as soon as we start firing!"

"Sir!" they called back in harmony.

The head reappears, followed this time by the body, the German soldier running as fast as he could between the gap.

Billingham and Plant sprang up, letting off two rounds each. From the window of the other room, gunshots from Kitchen and Stupple fired towards the open wall that used to be windows of the house on the other side of the street.

The German soldier didn't make the gap, his body crashing to the ground.

The top of his body falling behind the wall of the building that he was running towards, out of sight to Plant, but his legs were still visible, face down in the alley, until they were slowly pulled out of sight.

Billingham, looking up the alley as the legs were being pulled behind the building, quickly turned to Plant.

"Sarge," said Billingham as he looked over to Plant. "There's got to be someone at the back of that building. If I move quick, get across the road, I'll get a grenade up to where they are."

"Sounds good, Billingham," replied Plant. "Get y'self ready. we'll cover you as you move."

"On my way, Sarge!"

As Billingham turned, he quickly headed for the door to the side of the house they were using, Plant calling out to Stupple and Kitchen.

"You two, Billingham is going to try and make it across the road. I want you to shoot several rounds at the upper and lower windows as soon as I say NOW!"

"Will do!" called back Stupple

Plant waited a moment; Billingham called out.

"Ready."

Okay… NOW!" shouted Plant.

Gunfire ringing out from the two rooms of the three remaining British soldiers.

Billingham running as fast as he could across the road, towards the building next to the one occupied by the German shooters.

As he reached the building, quickly turning his back to the wall, getting as close to it as he could, slowly he moved towards the alley, the gap between the two houses.

Plant, Stupple and Kitchen stop firing at the windows.

Immediately, a return of fire as a volley of shots ricochet around the room of the British troops, followed swiftly by machine-gun fire from the upper room occupied by the Germans. Rat-tat-tat-tat-tat.

Billingham quickly looking around the corner and up the alley. He couldn't see people, but he could faintly hear voices. Pulling a grenade from his belt, quietly pulling the pin, he listened again to hear the voices. Letting the handle on the grenade go, he gently rolled the grenade up the alley, like a bowling ball.

The German soldier at the other end of the alley, behind the building, having pulled his friend and colleague away from the alley and any more shots was kneeling down. The soldier on the ground face down, hit twice in his side as he ran, his head twisted to one side, still alive and in great pain. The kneeling friend comforting him, telling him they will get medical help as soon as they can.

Suddenly, realising he could hear a metallic sound on concrete, he looked up. *'What's that?'* he thought, as the grenade, slowly rolled towards the feet of the fallen soldier. The kneeling soldier watching as the grenade stopped. He lowered his head, but too late, they both died instantly.

Billingham rushing up the alley, his pistol ready for action.

A grenade flew from the upper room of the German building. Bouncing once in the road, it came to rest against the wall below the window of Stupple and Kitchen. They hear the thud as the grenade stopped, both dropping facedown to the floor, hands over their heads as the grenade went off, showering the area with shrapnel; the wall that Stupple and Kitchen were behind collapsing in, rock, dust and brick flying everywhere.

As the dust settled, machine-gun fire started once more, rat-tat-tat-tat, the bullets hitting the bricks and debris from the wrecked wall, Stupple and Kitchen hoping none hit them.

Plant, firing into the upper room, where the machine-gun fire was coming from. He couldn't see the shooter but hoped a lucky bullet may bring him to a halt.

As the machine-gun fire stopped, Stupple and Kitchen quickly jumping up from their prone positions in the rubble, their khaki uniforms, steel helmets and faces covered in a grey dust. Moving to either side of the room, out of direct firing line from the house opposite.

As Billingham reached the end of the alley, moving his body to the wall of the house the shooters were in, carefully checking the grenade had done its job, the two soldiers behind the second house both covered in blood.

He crept to the end of the shooters house, then turning the corner, he could see the back door, from here he could hear two German voices, one in the upper part of the house, one in the lower; creeping quietly in through the backdoor, one step at a time, he stood in the doorway between the front and back of the house.

In front of him a German soldier, his gun to the window as he let off two rounds towards the British house.

Billingham being careful not to get caught in the crossfire.

Rat-tat-tat-tat, from the upper part of the house.

Billingham looking around the lower room with the German firing out of the window, checking that the soldier in front of him was the only one there.

Satisfied that he was, Billingham lifted his pistol, aimed and shot the German soldier in the back. The German soldier's gun falling silent as his body collapsed to the floor with a crumpled thud.

The German soldier upstairs hearing the shot from below; he knew this was not his colleague's gun. He was now on his own; he had one last hope of getting the British troops in the house opposite, and he knew he only had a few minutes to do it before the British soldier downstairs made his way up.

The German soldier shutting the door to the bedroom he was in, barricading it with a table, went back to the machine-gun and aimed out of the window, towards the enemy in front of him.

Rat-tat-tat-tat-tat. Plant and his two fighters held up, clinging to the walls of the building as the bullets riddled the two rooms, they were in.

"Ahh," screamed Stupple.

"What's happened?" called Plant.

"Stupple's been hit," shouted Kitchen. "looks like it's in the shoulder."

"It's okay, Sarge," called Stupple. "looks worse than it is"

Billingham was creeping up the stairs towards the sound of the machine-gun.

Rat-tat-tat as the gun continued to spray lead into the rooms of the British troops opposite.

Billingham having reached the door, pulled the handle down slowly and went to push. The door did not budge, but the sound drew the attention of the German trooper. He spun around from the machine-gun, lifted his pistol, firing several shots at the door, Billingham falling back as he avoided the bullets and splinters zipping past him from the German's gun. The lone German turning his attention back to the machinegun.

Rat-tat... Click, click... click.

"Sounds like he is out of ammo," smiled Kitchen.

"Take no chances lads," called Plant. "It could be just a trick. We still don't know how many there are!"

"Will do, Sarge," replied Kitchen.

Stupple lying on the floor holding his right shoulder, blood running down his arm. Kitchen carefully looking around the edge of the blown-out window.

Plant, in the other room, eased towards the window, his rifle ready to his shoulder. Resting it against the remains of the window, he looked toward the now quiet house opposite.

The silence suddenly broken by a German voice, then a heavy metallic object hitting wooden floorboards. Out from the shadows of the upper room of the house opposite, the lone figure of a German soldier appeared at what remained of the upstairs window. His field grey uniform covered in dirt and dust, black belt with gun holster, eagle badge above the pocket on the upper chest. On his head he wore a green Stahlhelm.

He had both hands in the air.

As he came into view, stopping at the window ready to surrender.

Plant took one shot, the body of the German trooper toppled forward, out of the window; crashing from the upper room of the house to the cold, frozen ground below.

# Chapter 13
## Pulling Rank
### 19 February 1945

Allied headquarters was about ten miles south of Mulhouse, a farmhouse, the grounds taken over in an effort to make strategic gains against the Nazi invaders.

Captain Johnson sat in his makeshift office, a desk, a table with papers and files and an old chair, on which the captain was now sitting.

Those and a second chair under the window were the only things in the room.

Captain Andrew Johnson had, like a lot of officers fighting in the war, been put into the position of commanding a group of men that he felt completely out of his depth with.

Johnson had, before the war, been working as the manager of a department for the civil service; bowler hats, dark suits and black umbrellas.

Staff that followed orders, did as you told them; the consequences for not following Mr Johnson's rules were to be out on the street.

With Johnson's air of middle-class superiority, he believed he could win over the troops. If you talk like you are in charge, the lower classes will follow.

He was signing the bottom of a document when the door to his office was suddenly knocked. It was his secretary, waiting in the doorway for the captain to acknowledge her.

"Yes?" called Captain Johnson, exasperatedly.

"Captain Johnson," said the secretary. "You asked me to let you know as soon as I could, Sergeant Plant has arrived."

"Ah good," said the captain. "Send him in…"

Plant walked straight past the secretary.

Captain Johnson still pushing around several bits of paper in front of him as Sergeant Plant grabbed the back of the chair that was close to the window, putting it down in front of the captain's desk, and sat.

Johnson continued to scrutinise his paperwork; however, he was aware of the presence of Plant.

"Ah, Plant," said the captain in his middle-class accent and still looking down. "Stand at ease."

Plant crossed his legs.

"Now Plant," the captain continued. "I have had some feedback… you and your men did some grand work yesterday pushing back the enemy."

"We certainly did, Johnson!" replied Plant.

The captain looked up from the papers on his desk and directly at Sergeant Plant.

"Is there any more news on the injury to Stupple?" the captain enquired.

"The bullet broke the bone at the top of his arm. He's in the field hospital right now. They will be taking him home next week. He will be fine but has lost a lot of blood."

"Good… good," said the captain. "And the others, they came out of it okay?"

"Kitchen had some cuts after the grenade blew

out the wall. Billingham is fine."

"Ah, Billingham... yes... I hear he risked his life to get around, behind the enemy that is... is this correct?"

"It is," said Plant.

"Then I would like to put him forward for a bravery award. How would you feel about that?"

"I would say that it was well deserved."

"Ah, good... good," said the captain. "I have already started the paperwork for it."

Plant put his arm over the back of the chair.

A short silence as Captain Johnson looked down at the papers in front of him, then, a little more nervously, back up to Plant.

"Ah, now, Sergeant, the powers above me have asked me to speak to you."

Plant took his arm from the back of the chair, uncrossed his legs and leaned forward.

"I have had some news from my informants!" said Plant.

"They have said I am to tell you, to have more respect for your superiors and that you must follow orders!"

"My informant has told me of something I need to deal with behind enemy lines."

"And if you don't do as I ask, I am to reprimand you!"

"I am told that a command centre has been set up on the outskirts of Neuenburg," said Plant, staring at the captain.

"That you are to take your men to Northern France."

"Just the other side of the Rhine," Plant continued.

"You will report to Warrant Officer Bootes," said Johnson, trying to be more forceful.

"I will be taking Billingham with me; we will wipe out the command centre... we will be making our way over the Rhine at midnight."

"Plant... are you listening to me?" snapped Johnson, angrily.

"No... are you listening to me?" said Plant, calmly.

"For crying out loud, Plant. They warned me you were difficult to work with, but you are exasperating!" fumed Johnson.

"Just getting a job done... you know I didn't ask to come here, I was told, so get used to it."

"Bloody hell, Plant, you are infuriating," blurted Johnson, his face red with anger. "Now just piss off and don't get yourself killed!"

"Killed Johnson... No, I don't ever intend getting myself killed... But if you hadn't noticed, there is a war going on out there. The only way we will win that war is by killing more of them than they do of us. So, if you don't want someone killed, don't have a war."

"Aargh!" snarled Johnson.

Plant stood up, pushing the chair back with his legs; making a screeching sound as the chair's feet scraped on the floorboards.

He turned and left.

# Chapter 14
## The Maverick
## 20 February 1945

At midnight, Sergeant Samuel Plant and Private Barry Billingham quietly made their way through Petit-Landau, towards the banks of the Grand Canal d'Alsace.

They found a small boat and rowed to the opposite bank.

Reaching the causeway, they carried the small craft across the narrow piece of land, making their way towards the banks of the Rhine.

It was a cold night, the temperature around two degrees Celsius. The ground was hard, a ground frost had frozen the earth. The small wooden boat was heavy and painful on the hands.

"Okay, Billingham," whispered Plant. "You take the first stint at the oars, then I'll take over."

"Okay, Sarge," whispered Billingham.

"The river's current is flowing to the north; we should land on the other bank just north of Bad Bellingen," said Plant. "We are heading towards Auggen, which we should reach by the morning."

They carried the rowing boat to the water's edge, one either side.

"Are we going to find resistance, Sarge?"

"Don't know, the message I got was a bit uncertain. I think we will have to see when we get there."

"No problem, Sarge."

They lowered the little boat down the slope until they reached the edge of the water, pushing the craft as silently as they could into the cold flowing water.

Billingham stepping into the craft, picked up the oars and placed them into the rowlocks either side of the boat, he sat, taking hold of the oars grip, he was ready to start rowing.

Sergeant Plant pushing the boat around until it faced the opposite side of the river, stepping onto the stern of the craft, he sat. Billingham took the first quiet stroke towards enemy ground.

They rowed in a straight line, first Billingham, then Plant, aiming the boat towards the bank on the German side of the river.

The river, from the point they were crossing, was about one hundred metres across. The flow of the river taking them down stream and past Bad Bellingen. After a short while, in the low light, they could see trees.

Pulling into the bank, Billingham jumping out holding onto a rope attached to the front of the boat. Grabbing hold of a tree, he quickly threw the cold, wet rope around the trunk, bringing the vessel to a halt.

"Well done, Billingham," whispered Plant. "Now up here should be a road, the Rheinstraße. My source said, 'Head north to Auggen, then to the east of the village'… So, let's go and get this war over."

"I'm right with you, Sarge."

They climbed over a fence to reach the road, then

turned left, the road stretching out into the distance before them.

Their heads low and their eyes and ears picking up each sight and sound that might stop them in their tracks. But all was quiet, all except for the sounds and flashes from fighting in a distant town.

By six a.m. the light, faint on the horizon, was starting to creep into the February sky. The frost in the early morning making them feel cold, despite the walk heating their bodies, keeping them from feeling the worst of frosty night.

They were about one mile from Auggen.

Just before the village was a turning to the right. 'Head east' the message said, so this was the road Plant and Billingham took.

As they turned into the small lane, they could hear the sound of vehicles coming towards them; ducking down behind some trees, two German troop carriers passed them by, heading for the front line; extra troops to bolster the bridges over the Rhine.

Plant and Billingham looking at each other, as the sound of the trucks grew quieter, happy they hadn't been spotted. They nodded to each other as they crept out from behind the trees, stood up and carried on their walk towards the sunrise.

Around a mile further down the road, a small farmhouse to the left-hand side, still at a little distance. Around the farmhouse were two or three outbuildings and a moderately sized barn. They moved to the left side of the road and laid their bodies into the bank, making sure not to be seen.

There were no signs of movement, or at least,

from what they could see, but what there was, was a Nazi troop carrier and motorcycle sitting close to the house.

As they watched, the door to the barn opened and a German soldier left the building, jumped onto the motorcycle; kicked over the engine, which roared into life. He spun it around, then made his way up the track to the road, turning left. The motorcycle headed away from them over the hill disappearing into the distance.

They waited for a minute, listening as the sound of the engine faded away.

"This must be it," said Plant.

"Certainly, looks that way," agreed Billingham.

"Okay, here's what we will do. We will head down to the rear of that first outbuilding. We should be hidden from sight there, then over to the side wall of the farmhouse. It doesn't have a window so should keep us out of their sight, then around to the house, once we are at the door we'll see if it's still quiet!"

"Okay, Sarge," said Billingham.

"Let's get going," ordered Plant.

Climbing up, over the small bank, keeping very low as they moved across the field, behind some small bushes and overgrown hedgerows. They moved closer to the rear of the outbuilding.

Over a small fence, keeping low, until they finally had both their backs firmly pressed up to the wall of the wooden building.

Plant crept closer to the edge of the building, carefully listening for any sound, but it was silent.

Looking around the corner of the building, nothing. He looked back at Billingham, put his finger to his lips, then gestured for Billingham to follow. Plant turning the corner of the building slowly and silently, making his way along the side of the farm shed. Billingham following his every footstep.

As they break from the cover of the outbuilding, they keep low and fast, moving quickly; they reach the wall of the farmhouse.

"So far, so good," whispered Plant nodding to Billingham.

They turned the corner of the farmhouse, their hearts racing as they move step by step closer to the main door.

Breathing in the cool still morning air.

Reaching the door to the Farmhouse, they stop. Plant put his head close to the door, listening for any sounds that might alert them to the possibility that there will be someone in the room.

But still silence, not a sound.

Plant lifting his head to the window, checking he was correct, there was no-one inside the room, it's clear.

Putting his fingers around the door handle, slowly turning the door knob. Steadily pushing the door open as he crept inside, Billingham following closely, looking behind for any enemy movement.

One quiet footstep after the next they slowly inched into the house.

Their rifles at the ready, they moved forward, crossing the kitchen, reaching a door that led into a hallway, they stop; they could hear the sound of an indistinct German voice.

Moving slowly into the hallway, following the voice which got louder the further they moved into the hall.

Suddenly, the German voice stopped.

Thinking they must have been heard, Plant and Billingham stood, quiet and still, holding their breaths, waiting to find out what will happen next. Their hearts thumping, expecting any second to be in the middle of a gun fight.

Then, suddenly, the silence was broken.

"Ah, Mr Plant," called a voice from the next room with a strong German accent. "You have finally arrived. I have been expecting you!"

Plant looked around at Billingham, confused that they knew he was there.

A second of hesitation from Plant and...

"How do you know who I am?" he called.

"Mr Plant," called the voice. "There is a lot I know about you!"

"H... How do you know a lot about me?"

"Mr Plant," the voice continued. "You are very famous in this part of the world"

"Famous, what do you mean... famous?"

"Please, let us not continue our conversation either side of a wall," said the voice. "Please come and join me for a drink... You have nothing to fear, I mean, I am sure you realise by now that, not only did I know you were in this house, I knew you were coming from up the road. I could have, if I wished, had you shot several times over!"

Plant again looking at Billingham; this is not how

it's supposed to be. He has now been in this war for nearly five years. It's been either, he shoots the enemy, or they try and shoot him. Never in that time has it been... let's sit down for a drink.

"What would you like Mr Plant, a cup of tea or something stronger maybe?"

"Why should I trust you?" called Plant.

"A good question Mr Plant... to that, at *this* moment in time, you shouldn't. But, if for the time being, we say... call a truce. I have something I want to put to you... Now, Mr Plant, I will assume it will be a cup of tea; in fact, it is already made, and on the table waiting for you. So, if you and Mr Billingham would like to make your way in, you will be made very welcome."

Billingham turned to Plant.

"He knows I'm here too!" Billingham mouthed at Plant.

"Oh yes," called the German voice. "I knew you were coming also Mr Billingham!"

Plant took a step forward till he reached the edge of the doorway, moving his head closer to the opening, he peered inside.

It was a square-looking room and from what he could see, had very little furniture and plain walls, a window to the left-hand side.

He could make out a part of a table. Sitting at the table, the arm of a German officer in a dark uniform. Standing behind the officer was a German soldier.

The soldier standing to attention, his rifle butt at his feet, the barrel in his right hand as he looked straight ahead over the officer's head. Plant took another step into the room, clearing the doorway, he could now see the whole room; the plain walls, the single table with a chair each side of the table.

The officer stood up, lifting back his chair, stepping to the side, he walked towards Samuel Plant.

The German SS officer, 181 cm (five feet eleven inches) tall, dark hair and chiselled features. His uniform dark blue-grey with a dark green collar, black belt with gun holster. Nazi eagle above the right pocket, polished calf-length boots that clicked when he walked.

"Good morning, Mr Plant, my name is Commander Schick, Wilhelm Schick," said Schick smiling, holding out his hand ready to shake the hand of Plant.

"Schick," said Plant, taking the hand that had just been offered to him. "Commander Schick, so... how do you know so much about me?"

"Ah, well, for a start, in these parts you are known as 'Einzelgänger', what in English I believe you would be known as, a bit of a maverick," said Schick. "Now, please come and sit. There is a cup of tea here waiting for you, two sugars I believe... if you would like to rest your rifle against the wall there, we have a lot to discuss, and very little time."

"Commander Schick," said Plant, having rested his rifle. He moved towards the chair, which he pulled away from the table, then sat. "I am, in a way, finding this difficult to grasp. Why we should be here... now?"

"All in good time, Mr Plant."

As Schick was about to sit in the chair opposite Plant, he turned to the soldier who was standing to attention behind him.

"*Soldat, komm und steh hier,*" said Schick as he pointed to the left-hand side of him.

The soldier lifting his gun by the barrel, moved to the left-hand side of Schick and the table, with his back to the wall. Lowering the rifle butt back to the floor, again standing to attention.

Billingham seeing this, moved to the opposite side of the table, to Plant's left-hand side, facing the German soldier.

Schick picking up his cup of tea, Plant followed.

"Now, what's this about?" said Plant.

"Oh, Mr Plant, I hope you don't mind me asking," said Schick as he opened the pocket of his Luger pistol, pulling it out by his index finger and thumb, then placing it gently on the table. "Would you mind doing the same please? I know it seems old fashioned, but I feel just a bit dirty carrying a gun while drinking tea."

Plant took the gun from his holster laying it on the table in front of him.

"Mr Plant, let me first tell you about me... you see, from the outside, the uniform tells you, I am a commander, and a commander in a Nazi uniform. But, that's not who I was... no, Mr Plant." Schick took another sip of tea. "I am a businessman, not a warmonger; this is not for me Mr Plant. Here, I kill because I am told to... or out of necessity, not because it's in my nature to."

"And you see me as someone who can help in

your business?" said Plant.

"Yes, Mr Plant, yes I do," said Schick, his eyes narrowing. "I need someone I can trust, someone I can see as an equal, as a business partner. And yes, Mr Plant, I have been watching you for some while now."

"But how did you know I would be here?"

"Chess, Mr Plant, chess... strategy and planning, understanding your opposition. Read them, know what they like and how they play the game... Be prepared to lose a piece or two, draw your opponent towards you and the game will be yours." Schick smiled. "You see, Mr Plant, I knew the thought of getting behind the German lines and knocking out a command post would be too much for you to let go. I knew you would be here. I just had to feed that information to you!"

"So, no command post?" said Plant.

"I'm afraid not, Mr Plant."

"And the business you wish to put to me?"

"Well, if you agree to join me in this venture, you will stand to gain a lot of money, and I mean a lot of money."

"And if I choose not to join you?"

"Then I will have to find another business partner, and as for you leaving here; well, Mr Plant, as I said, I am not a killer, just a businessman. I would, of course, say goodbye to you and Mr Billingham. No malice or revenge, business after all... and you can both make your way back to the Allies."

The room was quiet and peaceful, but in the

distance, the sounds of war could be heard. Big guns, small arms and explosions.

Plant and Schick looking directly into each other's eyes, Plant trying to work out what Schick was planning.

It was a small room, about three metres square. They were sitting at a small square table in the middle of the room, Plant on one side, Schick on the other side; to Plant's left, Billingham was standing to attention; to Schick's left was the German trooper. Billingham and the German soldier facing each other.

On the table sat two cups of tea and two hand guns.

"Now," said Schick. "What I have to offer…" he sipped the tea "Over the last few years of serving the German forces, I have had the opportunity to, shall we say, acquire some wealth: gold, jewellery, gems… I'm sure you get the idea. While acquiring these items, I, of course, have been storing them at my property in Dresden; waiting for the day that this awful war finishes, then to use the wealth gained during the war to further my business dealings… Things have changed Mr Plant… the Allies are pushing forward. And a week ago, my property only just missed the firebombing of my city. This has led me to take a new course."

"So, you need me to help you," said Plant.

"Oh, Mr Plant, like a good chess game, this has been part of my planning for a long time, this is no… 'What is it you say?'… knee-jerk reaction. What had to be right, was the timing… and the time is now perfect."

"So, what's in it for me?" asked Plant.

"Half a million dollars!"

"Oh, phew… well I wasn't expecting that!"

"This is, of course, a rough estimate… most of it is in the form of gold ingots, boxed and ready to move."

"Move?"

"Yes, it has to be moved, and this is where you come in Mr Plant. The Allies are moving forward… a few kilometres every day, eventually we will be overrun. Western forces from one side, the communist countries from the east. The timing is right to move the gold now!"

"And how do you expect me to help with this?"

Schick leaned towards Plant.

"The gold is at present in the back of a truck, a few kilometres from here. We would need to move it close to the line of fighting and store it in a place, where it could not be found… a barn, a shed… Then, as the Allies move forward, the gold will then be on the Western side of the military line. You and I will then pick the gold up with a British truck. Once on the truck, move it to a new safe place, where it can be stored until after the war is over."

"You and I pick the gold up on the British side?"

"Yes, you and I will have to work together for the next few weeks until it is safely stored somewhere."

"And, of course, you have thought about how this will happen?"

"All part of the game… I will dress as a British soldier… an escapee from Poland, fighting for the

Allies."

"And the share?"

"Fifty-fifty, Mr Plant. I think there is enough for the both of us not to worry about small percentages."

"Who else knows about this?" said Plant, hesitantly.

"So far, just you, me and my driver..." said Schick watching Plant's face. "My driver, Mr Plant, is a dedicated man. He has worked for me for many years. I have run most of my dealings through him. He is safe …. He is, at the moment, with the truck and the gold, waiting to hear from me."

"You say, just you and me, Commander Schick?"

"Yes, Mr Plant. I did just say, you and me."

Schick's eyes look down at the two guns laying on the table, they then shift to his left to look at the German soldier, then Billingham to his right.

Plant watching his eyes move from side to side, then back down to the guns.

Schick's head gives a small nod as they both pick up their weapons; Schick shoots the German trooper in the chest; Plant shoots Billingham in the head.

The two soldiers hit the ground together.

# Summer Present-day

The National Archives
Kew
West London

# Chapter 15
## The Archives
### Summer Present-day

Sebastian had parked his car, making his way towards the building adjacent to the car park. To his right, a large pond with three fountains close to the nearest building itself. In the pond, two swans floating, paddling; following the visitors, hoping for a treat, the odd piece of bread.

Walking close to the barrier, the swans paddled towards him. Below the swans were several carp, waiting to gobble up any bread that the swans had missed.

Through the revolving door, the sign above the door announcing that you are entering 'The National Archives'.

Once inside, to the left for a bag search then on towards the lower part of the building; to the left the café, to the right, the book shop and exhibition displays.

Sebastian continued to walk straight ahead, the stairs in front of him.

At the top of the stairs and through the main door to the research and record holding floor.

Sebastian had already been here twice, so was getting to know the routine.

On the upper floor, to the left and head for the big sign that read 'Start Here'.

Sebastian was finding this difficult. Research was hard; he had no idea of what he was looking for. The information on the contract vague, the writing at the bottom of the contract, still unknown. And to make matters worse, when he asked about certain bits of information he needed at the Archives, he was reluctant to give too much away.

But, he had, of course, in the last couple of visits taken note of what they had suggested to start his search: Samuel Plant's army military records from Military Service Records at the Ministry of Defence as well as Birth, Death and Marriage Certificates.

The information on Sgt. Samuel Plant's military record described a soldier who would be permanently in trouble for one thing or another, not obeying orders, disappearing for days or even weeks at a time; but always returned. Always seemed to have achieved things that no ordinary soldier would dare do, and his success rate was nigh on perfect; he always returned from the mission, with the exception of, the occasional loss of one of his troop.

The senior officers had, according to the records, found Samuel Plant very frustrating to work with. But would look over his indiscretions, knowing, whatever he was up to, would almost certainly benefit the progress of the war effort.

Today, Sebastian was finding information on the group Samuel Plant was with on the date of the contract. He had, during his prior research, found the Archives reference number, but not had time to deal with the contents. He had not even seen it, just the number, which the 'Start Here' assistants had suggested he look at on his next visit: today.

After he had arrived, he immediately requested the document and had given himself a lot of time to follow up on other lines of research while he waited. He had on previous visits been told that, sometimes it can take a long time for the document to be obtained from the storage area and brought to the requester.

An hour and a half had passed, Sebastian thought he would visit the main desk to see how much longer it would be.

There was a queue of two people in front of him, a woman asking about her mother who lived in Motherwell, and a tall, physically well-built man, with longish fair hair and a short beard. He wore baggy casual clothes.

The woman, dealing with her mother, finished with the assistant. She picked up her papers and moved off to the side.

"Good afternoon," said the assistant to the fair-haired man in front of Sebastian. "Can I help you?"

"Yes… I have pre-ordered the military documents on a Sergeant Samuel Plant," said the man with his back to Sebastian.

The assistant picked up the package from behind her, then laid it on the table ready to be picked up.

"Hang on!" interrupted Sebastian, suddenly.

The fair-haired man putting his hand down to pick up the folder, when Sebastian's hand came down on the same folder.

"I'm here to look at the file of Samuel Plant," said Sebastian as he moved to the side of the fair-haired man, standing in front of the desk next to him. "I've been here nearly two hours waiting for it... and what the hell do you want it for anyway?"

"I am so sorry," said the fair man. "I'm doing some research on a military campaign in France and his name has come up..." The fair man held his hand out towards Sebastian. "My name is Tom, Tom Paige."

"I don't care who the hell you are!" stormed Sebastian. "This is my research, not yours!"

Tom thanked the lady assistant at the desk, turned and followed Sebastian who had walked off tightly hanging onto the folder.

"Hang on one second," called Tom, walking quickly to catch up with Sebastian.

Sebastian keeping his back to Tom, reached his table.

He had been working at a computer and found some information about the end of the war and the medals that Samuel Plant had received.

As Sebastian sat, Tom pulled out a chair and sat next to him.

"So, are you really after information about Samuel Plant?" asked Tom.

"Yes... why shouldn't I? He's my great grandfather... And what is he to you?"

"Me?" said Tom. "Me, I'm a researcher for a charity, we have a lead and I was following it up."

"What charity?"

"Wise, Find and Return." answered Tom.

"Never heard of them!" said Sebastian abruptly.

"There are, I would guess, many charities you

have never heard of. But none the less, they exist, as does the one I work for."

"So, what does it do, and why the interest in my family?" said Sebastian, defensively.

"We find lost or stolen effects from the Second World War, that is gold, jewellery, paintings, you know, property taken by the Nazi party to fund its movement."

"And my great grandfather, what's he got to do with this?"

"Well, yes... that's the question... I don't know," admitted Tom. "We have fragments of information, but no direct line... What we do know though, is there are a few names that have come up. We don't know if they are part of the plot or not... that is why I am here. Samuel Plant may have had nothing to do with it, but until I can trace the route the plot went, that's when I will know the full story."

"And you are an expert in this sort of thing?"

"Yes, it's my job, researching lost and stolen items from the war."

Sebastian suddenly having a thought. He didn't know this person, Tom, and Tom didn't know him. So maybe, if Tom was an expert on finding this type of treasure, could *he* find the ingots mentioned in the contract? Sebastian felt he was getting nowhere, or if he was, it was very slow. With an expert in finding this type of stuff helping, possibility was, it could be found a lot sooner.

Sebastian thinking hard, going over the wording on the contract. As far as he could remember, there was no mention of stolen, or Nazi, or lost. To

Sebastian, it was legitimate, a business deal, shares, or for work his great grandfather had done for someone; not stolen, and definitely not from a Jewish source.

Does he let this man help or not, *'Come on Sebastian!'* he berates himself?

"So, what do you think you have found that you need to follow up on my great grandfather?"

"Ah, well," said Tom. "A box has turned up in the office from Germany. It had inside a bundle of papers, including photographs and newspaper cuttings. But the most interesting part of the papers was a part of a contract!"

"A part of a contract?" echoed Sebastian, realising that this man may have the same contract.

"Yes, there are only a few words, nothing meaningful, not even a full sentence... But what it did have, was a name... Samuel Plant!"

Tom felt that this stranger was warming to him. Feeling that, if he was doing family history on Samuel Plant, it may be worth gaining his trust. And maybe, he could help with the finding of the gold.

Tom's other thoughts telling him to be frugal with any information at the moment. He doesn't know this man, so for the time being, tell him only what he needs to know.

"So, what does the contract say?" asked Sebastian.

"Not a lot; the boxes contain ingots that belong to the names printed on the contract, then something about financial gain... signed by Samuel Plant and, I guess, Wilhelm Schick followed by a date... It just says 'uary 1945', then some foreign words that I haven't had translated yet… Have you come across this Wilhelm Schick while doing your research?"

"Vilhelm Schick, umm, not sure… who is he?"

"A German commander."

"So, the German commander wrote the contract?"

"No, Samuel Plant wrote the contract!"

"What… it's in English?" quizzed Sebastian.

"Yes, is that a problem?"

"Well yes! I have found a contract in German, with the same names… but it doesn't mean much to me!"

"Would it be okay, if I could see this contract?"

"Er, well… well if I let you see it, you are not to tell anyone else about it!" huffed Sebastian.

Sebastian looked around the Archives hall. The odd whisper or quiet question being asked, the banks of computers and desks filled with people deep in thought, having their own searches on their minds.

Sebastian opened his briefcase and pulled out an old, tatty, dusty piece of paper. Looking at Tom, still not sure whether to hand it over.

His arms hesitantly swing around, the contract in his palms.

Tom lifted the note from Sebastian's hands, slowly opening the folds.

"Oh, this is excellent!" enthused Tom. "This is just what we need."

"Is it?" said Sebastian.

"Why yes, it fills in all the parts of the contract that have been burnt away in my copy."

"But it's in German... do you understand it?"

"Of course, I do. I'm a language specialist, I speak fluent German."

"And, so!" urged Sebastian. "This says?"

"Okay, let's have a check."

Tom lifting the paper to his eye level, increasing the light falling onto the parchment.

"Okay, now let's see," said Tom "*Die Boxen enthalten Barren*. The boxes contain ingots. Umm... *die gehören zu den Namen oben gedruckt*. Which belong to the names printed above."

"So," said Sebastian, sharply. "You are only reading out what I already know."

"Wait one minute," said Tom, calmly studying. "*des finanziellen Gewinns aus den Blöcken zwischen den oben genannten Namen zu gleichen Teilen getragen*. Of the financial gain from the blocks between the above names in equal parts... uh ha"

"*Die Schachteln dürfen erst im Herbst 1947 angefasst warden...* The boxes may not be touched until autumn 1947," Tom continues.

"*Wenn wir. einender kontaktieren und der Erlös zwischen uns geteilt*. When we contact each other, and the proceeds are shared between us."

"Well," insisted Sebastian.

"Hang on," said Tom. "*Bis zu diesem Zeitpunkt wird es in gehalten und von den Namen und Ort unten betreut*. Until that time, it is kept in and cared for by the name and place below."

"So, what does it all mean?" said Sebastian

"Well, what I do know already is, your great grandfather didn't get the ingots, he died at the beginning of the autumn 1947!"

"How do you know that?" said Sebastian angrily.

"Well, it's not difficult when you research this type of thing for a living. You look up when someone has died, and Samuel Plant died in September 1947, just before the date they were due to meet up."

"Anything else?"

"Well, the ingots were probably made of gold, stolen gold. And at the time, I guess... a lot of money!"

"What... half a million, a million?"

"Could be!" said Tom calmly.

"So, if Great Grandfather was dead, would the gold still be hidden?"

"Not really sure, difficult to say... but what I can tell you is... I have been onto the German Archives and have done some finding out about Wilhelm Schick. The Deutsche Dienststelle managed to find a few things that will be of help."

"Such as?"

"Well, on the contract that I have, the English version, there is no date... it's been burnt away. Although, there is part of a date... which could have been January or February. Having seen your copy of the contract, I now know it to be February and that Commander Schick was in the area of Neuenburg am Rhein in February 1945. It was recorded by Samuel Plant's senior officer, a Captain Johnson, that Sergeant Plant was crossing the Rhine at Petit-Landau to Bad Bellingen on the night of the nineteenth of February that year. That would put them about five miles from each other…"

"So, you think they got together?"

"It's too much of a coincidence for it not to have been that day that they met up. But how, and where? And more to the point… what did they do after?"

"And you think the answer is here, at the Archives?" said Sebastian.

"A mixture, here, the German archives and the box… if we can work out where they went after they met up, it may lead us to the gold."

"And you think the troop movements may help find that?"

"Not sure, according to his senior officer, Sergeant Plant was ordered to go to the north of France. But, as we can see from his military records, it showed he disappeared. He was presumed dead for three weeks having gone off on one of his crusades behind the enemy lines again… missing in action! So, those three weeks are what we need to concentrate on." said Tom.

Tom opened the file relating to troop movements during the early part of 1945.

Tom and Sebastian looked for anything that may help with the whereabouts of Samuel Plant during that time. But nothing came to light.

Tom now knew the contract date was the end of February 1945, and the probability that he met Schick on the nineteenth or twentieth of February, which is when Plant's military record showed him as missing. The timeline from Plant meeting Schick, and where they might have gone? Would this be the trail they would have to follow?

As the closing time for the Archive grew closer, both Tom and Sebastian knew they needed each other to move this quest forward. They both had information that would and could be the only way to solve the puzzle.

Sebastian was still reluctant to let himself open up completely, his idea of finding the gold was to keep it all for himself. This was his great grandfather's gold, not for him to give away to others. And especially now, given to this scruffy bohemian, who worked for a charity, no! *I will get help from this man, but it will be my gold.*

Tom knew his only chance of solving this riddle was with the help of Sebastian, but what does Sebastian want from this hunt for the gold?

As far as Tom was concerned, Sebastian was not looking for any gold, well not at least until he had just told Sebastian about it.

Sebastian, he thought, was just researching his family history.

Tom knew he would have to play his cards close to his chest, at least for the time being, only give as much information away as he needed to.

"Well," said Tom as he started to get up from his chair "I am glad we met…" he hesitated. "I'm sorry, we have been sitting here trying to solve the riddle, I didn't catch your name…?"

"Sebastian Plant, but please call me Bastian, everyone does."

"Okay, *Bastian* it is…" said Tom. "I will follow up on the information we have found today and will get back to you as soon as I can, is that okay with you?"

"Yes, sure Tom, that's fine."

Before Tom left the National Archives building, they exchanged numbers.

Having a better understanding of the direction he needed to head, he now needed the words written at the bottom of the contract translated.

His next plan was to meet his Arabic-speaking friends. It was time to get to the bottom of the contract.

# Chapter 16
## Arrival from San Francisco
## Summer Present-day

Tom had borrowed a friend's car to pick Jennifer up from Heathrow Airport.

Jennifer had already texted him to say she was on the plane and ready to leave in the early hours of the California morning.

She would be on the British Airways flight from San Francisco flight time was 16:35 and all being well, will touch down at Heathrow at 11:00 this morning.

Tom having finished his breakfast, jumped on his scooter and was on his way to change his two wheels for four.

The flight checker on his phone, showed all okay, **British Airways flight BA284 from San Francisco International (SFO) to London Heathrow (LHR): on time**.

Tom had given himself plenty of time; there should be no rush.

The car was ready to go, and he already had the keys.

Tom's friend didn't use it very often. "It's a bit temperamental," she would say. Tom dreaded it would be temperamental today.

Sheila lived in Cobourg Road, Bermondsey, not far from Tom. They had met on a litter picking and tree maintenance day at Burgess Park; Sheila was one of those really helpful people, who would do anything for anybody.

Sheila had already left for work, so couldn't be at home when Tom arrived at her house for the car, which was sitting on the road outside.

The car, an 'F' registration Citroen Deux-Chevaux, with patches of rust, but still running. It had a black roof and upper windows, crimson red lower doors and bonnet, with black following the lower part of the door and over the front wheel arches.

It was the classic 2CV, even as late as nineteen eighty-eight, still having the flat screen and round headlights on stilts.

Tom loved this car; he was so pleased when Sheila had said he could use it.

The engine started, to Tom's amazement, first time... then stopped.

A pump of the pedal, a turn of the key and the engine burst back into life. Tom checked the time 9:30, perfect he thought. He hoped to arrive at Heathrow by the time Jennifer would be coming through customs; a quick check on his phone to see how the flight is doing, *'Yup!'* he thought to himself, *'All looking good.'*

He put the 2CV into first gear and was on his way.

The 2CV was just on the outskirts of Heathrow at 11:10 when Tom's phone received a message: <Have arrived, just picking up luggage, will see you shortly. Jennifer.>

The roads were a little heavy with traffic, but always moving. Tom had been this way many times and was convinced he would be at the terminal just as she arrived.

He found the car park, pulled up, turned the engine off. Jumped out, looking back at the car, shut and locked the door. Then gave it a pat on the roof.

The arrivals area was packed, a constant flow of people and suitcases. Taxi drivers and couriers waiting; boards with the customers' names held to their chest, or above the heads of those further behind the line.

Tom had looked on the information board, still okay. She had just picked up her bags and was heading for passport control. As much as everyone would like to make this quicker, Jennifer would have to wait.

Flights from Paris had brought people on British Airways and American Airways; New York was Iberia and Aer Lingus; Chicago had American Airways, Finnair, British Airways, Aer Lingus and Iberia; as well as San Francisco, having brought passengers on board Finnair, Aer Lingus, Iberia and Jennifer arriving on British Airways.

Each and every person was now making their way through customs.

Tom stood about half-way up the exit walkway.

Tom was tall enough at 180cm (five feet eleven inches), so stood behind the front row of cabbies.

Before he had left the office the day before, he had grabbed an old piece of card, which when he got home, he had scribbled the words 'Jennifer Pinski' on.

He now held this up, high above the group in front of him, waiting for Jennifer to walk through the exit door and into Britain.

Ten minutes had past when over the heads of the waiting couriers was, he believed, the face he recognised. The face of a beautiful woman, pushing a case trolley, with two large cases and a smaller hand luggage case.

She was in her early twenties; medium height with light brown, slightly wavy hair, but that's all Tom could see. Her head was down as she headed for the end of the driver's barrier.

If this was the Jennifer that Tom was waiting for, she had passed him.

He brought the board down quickly and raced to the end of the rope barrier.

Reaching the end, moments before the woman he was looking at reached the same point.

Tom, this time, holding the board against his chest, stood directly in her path.

"Oh, I'm ever so sorry," said the woman. "I had a million things on my mind."

She slowly looked up at Tom; it was a warm day, so Tom wore his best baggy shorts, odd socks, nearly white tennis shoes and a Greenpeace T-shirt.

Tom looked at the woman in front of him and knew it was her, her fair complexion, narrow chin and dark eyes. She wore a white loose-fitting cotton shirt and trousers, with a red belt. It was the woman in the picture.

"Ms Pinski?" said Tom, hesitantly.

"Tom?" said the woman. "Yes, of course... Jennifer, please call me Jennifer."

"Okay, thank you... may I push your trolley?"

"That would be wonderful if you could," said Jennifer.

Tom spun around the back of the trolley as Jennifer stepped to one side.

Jennifer lifted off the hand luggage case that sat on top, lowering it to the ground.

Tom grabbed the handles of the trolley and started to push.

"If you would like to follow me, Jennifer," said Tom. "I will take you through to the car."

"Thank you, Tom," said Jennifer half stretching "That was a long flight... you would think the number of times I come over here, that I would be used to it."

"I could see it was a long flight... you come to Britain often then?"

"When I can. I have family still over here," she said.

They exit the doors of the terminal and cross to the car park area, a short distance till they reach Tom's little 2CV.

He opened the passenger door then stood to one side, ready for Jennifer to get into the passenger seat.

Jennifer looked at Tom, then around the rest of the car park.

"Is this it?" she said, looking down at the seat that Tom had just offered. "Is it actually a car?"

"Why... yes... it's a classic!" insisted Tom.

"Er, no, a Pontiac Firebird or a '69 Chevrolet

Corvette, or even a '68 Mustang are 'Classics'. Believe me, Tom… this is no classic!"

While Jennifer sat uneasily in the passenger seat, Tom put her cases on the back seat and the hand luggage in the boot. He eased the boot down till it clicked shut, walked around to the driver's door, opened it and sat, ready to take them on their way.

"London Marriot County Hall, that's right isn't it?" asked Tom

"Yes," answered Jennifer. "Any idea how long it will take?"

"Well, the traffic was okay coming here, so should be about an hour."

"Hhhh," she sighed turning her head to look out of the side window. "Oh well… let's get going."

They pulled out of the carpark and made their way to the M4, heading for the city.

"So, how is the search going Tom?" Jennifer asked.

"Ah, yes, the search… I had, up until yesterday had a lot of success."

"Then something went wrong?" interrupted Jennifer

"No, quite the opposite," said Tom, smiling. "I met, completely by accident at the Archives, the person who held the other part of the contract written by Wilhelm Schick."

Jennifer turned to look at Tom.

"Schick," She said, "*Schick's contract*… and was the contract complete?"

"Yes! And written in German!"

"No!" exclaimed Jennifer "So *this* must be really

helpful to you?"

"It certainly is," agreed Tom. "I have now read the whole message; not just the burnt version in English!"

"Oh, that's great... But who is this person?"

"Sebastian Plant."

"Plant... *Plant*," Jennifer said hesitantly "Do I recognise that name?"

"Quite possibly, his great grandfather was Samuel Plant, the other name on the contract."

"Of course, Samuel Plant... so this is his great grandson?"

"Yes."

"So, what was he doing at the Archive?"

"Family history... or so he said," said Tom. "He had come across it while in his parents' loft, thought he would do a bit of research."

"But he had the German contract?" said Jennifer, her eyes narrowing.

"Oh," said Tom. "I never thought anything of it, he told me he was just doing family history, so I just took it that that was what he was doing!"

"Tom," said Jennifer, looking towards him as he was driving. "I think you are a bit too easy-going, don't you?"

Tom shrugged his shoulders and kept on driving. At the end of the M4, they turn onto the Great West Road, a little further, then onto Cromwell Road, passing the London Marriot Kensington.

At Knightsbridge, they turn right towards Belgravia, following the green and tree-lined Belgravia Square. Right at Grosvenor Place, as they head towards Westminster, onto Victoria Street, they pass Westminster Abbey. Around Parliament Square Gardens and onto St George Street, passing Big Ben and the Houses of Parliament. They cross Westminster Bridge, keeping to the left.

As they reach the end of the bridge, a left turn under the arch of County Hall that would lead them to the Marriot Hotel. Tom slowed the 2CV as he reached the end of the arch, pulling the car into a parking space.

Jennifer turning to Tom.

"Were you planning on driving me around in this again?" said Jennifer pointing at the 2CV.

"Well, I was, if that's okay?"

"Mmm," she said. "I think I will hire a car for a few days."

"Oh, okay," he said.

"Now Tom, can you bring my bags in please?"

"No problem," said Tom.

As Jennifer walked towards the entrance, the hotel doorman opening the door for her. He was about to help Tom with the bags when:

"Leave him," Jennifer told the doorman. "He will manage it."

"Yes mam," replied the doorman.

Tom retrieved the bags from the back seat and the boot of the car, then followed her in to the hotel.

He entered the main doors, out of the warm summer sunlight. Jennifer was just signing the register as he pulled up alongside her, bags in tow.

The desk clerk handed Jennifer a card to her room, pointing in the direction she needed to go.

"Come on Tom," she said turning, walking in the direction she had just been told by the desk. "Follow me!"

Jennifer called for the lift, which took them up to the second floor.

She headed for the rooms on the north side of the building, overlooking the Thames and the London Eye, St Paul's Cathedral in the distance.

She placed the card in the slot of a door, then pushing the door open, she stepped inside.

The room plush, elegant and grand. The décor tasteful and the bedding luxurious.

"Thank you, Tom," she said, throwing the door card on the table, then slipping off her shoes. "Put the bags down somewhere and close the door, would you?"

Tom pushed the door with his foot; it closed with a hush. Jennifer walking towards the bathroom, undoing the buttons on her cotton shirt as she crossed the room. Tom carried the cases to the other side of the room, putting them down just below the window. As he turned around, he watched as Jennifer threw her shirt onto the bed, her bare, braless back disappearing into the bathroom. Tom continued looking at the open door of the bathroom as a pair of white cotton trousers drop into the doorway.

"Make yourself at home for a minute Tom," she called from the bathroom "It's been a long journey... I'm going to have a quick shower."

"Okay," a nervous Tom called back.

Tom heard the shower start. A few seconds later,

the sploshing and burbling of running water hitting a human body; turning the tinkling, pitter-patter, into a flow of water heavily hitting the showers base and sides.

Tom made himself comfortable on one of the chairs next to the table.

He only had to wait a short while when the running water stopped, the shower door opened, and a wet foot came to rest on the tiled floor.

Within a minute, Jennifer walked back through the bathroom door, into the bedroom where Tom was now sitting.

She had her hair tied up above her head and was wearing a thick white cotton dressing gown.

She walked in with a small towel, wiping the back of her neck.

"Now Tom," she said walking towards him "Tell me more about this Sebastian Plant?"

"I really don't know what else to say," said Tom "He seemed like a nice guy, genuine, you know?"

"Hm, go on!"

"Well, just talking to him for the time I did, the research will be much better."

"So, he was helpful?"

"Yes, very much."

"And you think we would benefit from having him along?"

"Yes, I would say yes," agreed Tom. "He has a lot of family information that we don't have."

"Does he know about me?"

"Oh no, that's personal information," said Tom. "That's not for me to tell him."

"Thank you for that Tom," said Jennifer smiling. "I'll tell you what then Tom, let me go and have a chat with him… if your research is correct, and we find the gold with the help of Mr Plant, it will come to me anyway, as the bloodline of Jacub Kaplan will it not?"

"There's a lot of 'ifs' there."

"All help will be greatly appreciated, and, I think… rewarded," said Jennifer, her eyes looking up at Tom, with an even bigger smile. "And your plans, Tom. What else is needed to find the missing gold?"

"Well, I have arranged with some Arabic friends to meet up for coffee and a chat about the wording on the bottom of the contract."

"Good, okay, and I would like *you* to give Mr Plant a call, find out where he will be at lunchtime tomorrow, would you?"

"Y-yes of course, not a problem," Tom stammered.

"You carry on the research… I will help find out what I can from Mr Plant, okay… Text me to keep me up to date, and we will meet again in a couple of days. How does that sound?"

"Sounds good."

Jennifer walked over to Tom who had stood up as she moved towards him.

"You're doing a great job, Tom," she took his hands in her hands. "I'm really pleased you contacted me. My family has been through a lot of bad times, and it's good to know, there are people like you in the world to put it right."

# Chapter 17
## Strong Black Coffee
## Summer Present-day

That evening, Tom had arranged to meet a couple of his old college friends. He had kept in touch with Jamil Najjar and Omar Tahan after leaving college but had not spoken to them for a little while. Jamil and Omar were part of the same languages department as Tom. They often met up while on Green demonstrations and environmental meetings. Tom didn't get to see them as much as he would have liked as they live in north London, Omar in Muswell Hill and Jamil in Finsbury Park, which is where Tom is heading this evening.

Tom had called Jamil a couple of days earlier and mentioned the project he was on, the German connection, the gold and the contract and the fact it has what appears to be Arabic writing. It would be wonderful to see his old friends, and this puzzle would give them a challenge.

Jamil contacted Omar, who would love to see Tom again; it will be like old times.

Tom left his houseboat for the fifteen-minute walk up to Surrey Quays' station, his head going over the earlier conversation with Jennifer. As soon as he was on the train, he must contact Sebastian, let him know that he was on his way to decipher the Arabic writing and to find out where he would be at midday the next day.

The train pulled up at the station, the doors open, Tom stepped on board, finding a seat, he pulled out his phone ready to make his call.

"Hello," said the voice answering the phone.

"Hi, Sebastian, it's Tom."

"Tom, good to hear from you. How is it all going?" said Sebastian.

"Good, it's all good," said Tom "Just to keep you up to speed with what is happening, I am, this evening, meeting up with a couple of old friends from college. They both have Arabic backgrounds., Hopefully, I'll get the wording on the bottom of the contract translated."

"Sounds good."

"Maybe, we could meet up, go over what I have found... say, tomorrow lunchtime?"

"Yes, tomorrow, lunch would be great... let's say, Amerigo Vespucci, it's Italian, is that okay with you?"

"Perfect!" agreed Tom.

"Okay, let's say 12:30. It's on Mackenzie Walk. It overlooks the dock."

"Fine, see you then," said Tom.

"Great, look forward to seeing what you have come up with... see you then!"

The phone hung up.

Tom lowered his mobile to his lap and texted Jennifer:

<Jennifer, I have been in touch with Sebastian, he will be at Amerigo Vespucci, Canary Wharf at 12:30 tomorrow. Tom.>

<Hi Tom, brilliant, I shall catch up with you later and let you know how it went.>

<Okay, he is tall, in his early thirties, dark hair combed back. He was wearing glasses when I met him.>

<All sorted, Tom. I have seen him on Facebook. I know what he looks like.>

<Okay, catch up with you soon.>

<Tom, make some excuse close to the time that you can't make it okay?>

<Okay!>

The train pulled into Highbury and Islington station. Tom jumping off the train, he made his way to the Victoria Line. Just one stop to Finsbury Park.

It was a pleasantly warm evening, the smell of cut grass and flowers blowing across from the park as Tom crossed Stroud Green Road and the ten-minute walk up Seven Sisters Road, finally reaching the house of Jamil.

Tom opened the gate to the thirty-foot front garden, nicely cut lawn, flowers and three or four bushes.

There were two steps up to the front door with a small archway over the steps, two children, a boy and a girl playing on the steps in the evening sunshine.

"Hello," said Tom to the children.

"Are you here to see our daddy?" said the young girl.

"Does your daddy live here?"

"Yes, he does, we all live here."

"Then, yes, I am here to see your daddy," said

Tom.

The young girl got up from the step and ran indoors, closely followed by the boy.

A minute later a beautiful woman came to the door. She was in her late twenties, perfect light brown skin and large clear eyes.

Her black hair hung long, down over the full length bright red dress. The dress having gold and yellow embroidery patterns from top to bottom.

"Hello," she said in a clear English accent "You must be Tom?"

"Yes." answered Tom.

"I am Jamil's wife, A'isha, please come in!" She stood to one side of the door as she gestured to Tom with her hand to enter the hallway.

"Thank you," said Tom "I believe we have met, a long time ago... I'm afraid, time just runs away. I have meant on many occasions to visit."

"Yes, Jamil and I have said the same, we all seem to lose track of our friends over time... and yes, we met before Jamil and I had children, a party at Omar's house."

A'isha walked Tom through to the back of the house, a large, three-story Victorian house overlooking the park. A'isha took him down a couple of steps, from where he could hear the sound of men's voices talking and laughing. Through the lounge and into the conservatory they went.

"Tom!" came a voice from the conservatory "How wonderful to see you!"

Jamil walked over to Tom, put his arms around him as they both gave a manly hug and slap on the back.

"Hi Jamil, well I have to say, you are looking very well."

Jamil stood back.

"It's the love of a good woman Tom, you can't beat it!"

Omar stood up and walked over to Tom.

"Hi Tom, it's great to see you," said Omar as he shook Tom's hand.

"And you too, Omar."

Both Jamil and Omar had been living in Britain since they were children, both still had slight Middle-Eastern accents.

They were about the same age as Tom; Jamil a little smaller than Tom and Omar a little shorter than Jamil, slim, wearing jeans and light-coloured shirts. Both having dark hair and beards.

Tom used to think, with Jamil's family coming from Tunisia and Omar's family coming from Egypt, how lucky he had been to meet them, how he learnt from them of other parts of the world, other cultures.

"Tom, sit, come and sit here." Jamil gestured to Tom to sit next to him.

Tom sat. As he looked up, the view of the back garden stretched out before him, the bushes, wild planting and at the far end a beehive.

"Oh, I love what you have done with the garden Jamil!"

"Yes Tom, a love of nature, it's a wonderful thing," said Jamil "We have to look after it!"

"Of course," said Tom.

The conservatory was a good size. There were

two double wicker chairs and three single; all set in a semi-circle around a low round glass-topped wicker table.

Tom heard the sound of footsteps coming into the conservatory behind him. As he looked around, A'isha was carrying a tray, followed by the two children carrying a tray each.

A'isha set her tray down in the middle of the glass-topped table. On the tray was a tall china coffee pot on a saucer, with the pot were three small cups each on a saucer, a small jug of milk and a bowl of sugar. As she moved over, the children placed their trays down.

The children's trays contained small plates, with the plates were larger dishes containing several types of cake and biscuits.

A'isha sat on the edge of one of the wicker chairs, leaned forward and picked up the coffee pot and one of the small cups, then looked up at Tom.

"Would you like a coffee Tom?" she said.

"Yes please," said Tom.

She started to pour the dark coffee into the cup. It was strong and black.

"Do you have sugar with that?"

"No thank you," said Tom. "But could I have a little milk please?"

"But of course," said A'isha.

A'isha poured the coffee, added the milk and handed the cup to Tom. She then turned to the other two men.

"The usual for you two?"

A'isha poured the black coffee into a cup and

handed it to Omar, then started to pour the same for Jamil. Jamil turned to Tom, putting his hand on Tom's arm.

"There you go Tom, the most beautiful woman in the whole world, and she is my wife, I am so lucky!"

"Oh, shut up you flirt," said A'isha. "Please help yourself to the food Tom."

She picked up the first bowl to show Tom.

"This is basbousa," she continued then moved to the next bowl. "This is baklava and the other is ghorayeba."

"Thank you," said Tom. "They look delicious!"

"Believe me, they are," said Omar. "She is a wonderful cook."

"And you can stop the flirting as well," said A'isha. "Like a couple of dirty old men, the pair of you!"

A'isha turned to leave the conservatory, smiling, she looked at Tom.

"You've got to love them really... haven't you?" she whispered.

As A'isha left the conservatory, Jamil and Omar lean across to pick up a plate, Jamil picking up a second, handing it to Tom.

"Help yourself, Tom!"

Tom picking up one piece of food from each of the plates and taking a bite of the first: the basbousa.

"Oh wow," exclaimed Tom. "This is delicious!"

"Told you so," said Omar.

"Okay," said Jamil. "You wanted our help... so what is it we can do for you?"

Tom laid his plate down on the table, then pulled from his pocket a couple of photocopies, having the full German contract, handing one each to Jamil and Omar.

"This is the case I am working on at the moment," said Tom. "There is a possibility that the items stolen during the war may still be where they were put at the time. Through Professor Wise, we have tracked down, what appears to be the only surviving relative of the stolen items... I am hoping that the Arabic writing on the contract will be the address, where the stolen items were put. If so, we can make sure, as much as we can, that justice will be done."

"Okay," said Jamil, looking down at the sheet "mmm."

Tom leaned back in his chair, looking at the two men, as they carefully study the documents he had just handed to them.

"Right Tom, have you a notepad?" said Jamil.

"Yes," said Tom pulling a pad out of his bag.

"Now, the first line is easy, do you agree Omar?"

عائلة بن دي وعدتأنتعتني بألسناديق و تحافظ عليهم

"The family of Ben Dee, promise..." said Jamil. "Yes?" he looked up at Omar who nodded back.

Tom noting every word onto his pad. Jamil continued:

"To look after the cases," he said. Then:

آمنة في قبو منزلها حتى يتم جمعها

"And to keep them safe in the basement of our house until they collect them," said Jamil. "Agree Omar?"

"So far," said Omar. "But I don't think Tom is going to have what he hopes for."

كما أن الله هو شهادتي

"God is my testimony, no, no... ah yes. As God is my witness, yes."

سيلستين بورغوان

"And this bit here," said Jamil pointing down to the lettering. "Has 'Silsitin'... not sure."

"Maybe Celestine or Celestin," interrupted Omar.

"Could be," said Jamil. "Then 'Bourgogne?'"

"Again," said Omar "Could be 'Borgon', 'Bourgoin'!"

"You see Tom," said Jamil as he turned to face him. "We just have the phonetics of the Arabic character, this may not have exactly the same sound in the Latin equivalent... let me explain! If you had the same word for something... *hand* for example... it would be easy. 'Hand', written in English, is a 'hand', 'hand' written in Arabic, is 'hand', and we all know what a hand is! But in this case, it is a name, possibly of someone. But also, it could be a thing or a place, and not an object... do you see?"

"Yes... yes of course," said Tom. "But anything that can help, anything to move this case forward, will be of value."

"Good," said Jamil. "And the last part is a name we recognise."

مصطفى بن دي

"Mustafa Ben Dee," Jamil and Omar said together.

Tom leaned forward, picked up a cake, put it in

his mouth. Then sipping the coffee, his thoughts running through his head. Leaning back on the chair again, looking at the notepad.

"So, we have something like: 'The family of Ben Dee promise', is that right?"

Jamil and Omar both agree.

"That they will look after the cases in their basement, and keep them safe, okay so far." Tom continued.

Jamil and Omar nod.

"That they are waiting for someone to return to get the boxes', and then a name you say, possibly Silsitin or Celestine, Bourgogne or Bourgoin"

"Yes," agreed Jamil.

"And then Mustafa Ben Dee," said Tom. "But no address, as you said Omar, the thing that I was really hoping for, the thing that would have made this a lot easier."

"Yes, Tom," said Omar. "It looks like we have helped a little, but not as much as you had wanted."

"This is true Omar," said Tom "No road, no house number, no town... and still not even a country!"

"Is there nothing in the papers you have received that has the possible place?"

"I think I am going to have to go back and look again... it could be possible there is something, but I just hadn't recognised it. I guess I was just hoping that the Arabic writing on the contract was the address."

"But the names!" said Jamil "Let's assume it's Celestine Bourgogne, it sounds French, does it not?

So, could it be in France?"

"But why then, the Arabic writing?" said Tom

"Okay, could she be a French woman living in a French Colony in say the Arabic part of the world... North Africa for example?"

"This could be... living with Mustafa Ben Dee." agreed Tom.

"And his family?" said Omar.

"Yes," said Tom looking down at his notes "The Ben Dee family promise, it says, this suggests Mustafa's family *all* know about the cases."

"And they also know about Celestine Bourgogne," said Omar.

"With a name like 'Celestine Bourgogne'," acknowledged Jamil "She sounds like a singer, or actress maybe?"

"She does," said Tom.

Tom joined Jamil and Omar in another couple of the delicious cakes and coffee, gave his thanks to his old friends, made arrangements to revisit; telling Jamil how lucky he was to have such a wonderful wife.

On the train back home, Tom picked up his notes and had a quick scan. Tomorrow, he would have to follow up on the information he had just received.

Celestine Bourgogne and Mustafa Ben Dee, these are the next people he must find.

## Chapter 18
## A Docklands Lunch
## Summer Present-day

Just after midday, Sebastian had left his office and was heading towards the bars and restaurants around the dock. It was a beautiful summer's day. The temperature in the mid-twenties, the sun was shining, a few fluffy clouds dotted the otherwise blue sky.

Sebastian's head was filled with the possibility of gold; he was already spending most of it before they had even found it, or, even its existence. Out of The Onyx Building and towards the skyscrapers of Canary Wharf, along South Colonnade.

Across the road and down the steps opposite 1 Canada Square, you will find the fast-food stalls; food and drink establishments, filled at this time of day, with the quickly grabbed lunches, strolling sandwich eaters and business deals over a steak or Chinese- along with a glass of wine.

At the bottom of the steps, Sebastian turned right, walking along the footpath that ran along the water's edge. A gentle breeze blowing the warm smell of food into his face.

Amerigo Vespucci in front of him. He crossed the footbridge, looking around for Tom, but no sign of him. *'Tom,'* Sebastian thought, *'does not seem the type to be late.'* Still, they did make the meeting time

12:30 and it is only just 12:20, so still time.

Sebastian continued looking, as he walked up to the bar.

"Can I help you, sir?" said the smartly dressed young man, white shirt and black trousers. The Italian accent not out of place at this well-respected Italian restaurant.

"Yes, could I have a lasagne and salad please" answered Sebastian

"And a drink sir?"

"A cranberry juice please."

"With ice?"

"Yes, please. I'll be sitting just outside."

"Okay, sir," said the barman politely smiling.

Sebastian, desperate to know the outcome of the meeting that Tom had had the evening before. What was the writing on the bottom of the contract? What did it say?

He sat on the red chair, laying his phone down on the black table; the table, next to a handrail overlooking the water; he looked around, still no Tom. Most of the tables on this lovely day were filled with customers. A large American man, with a slightly smaller woman were at the table in front of him. A Chinese family walked past looking up at the vast buildings. Two business men loudly chatting and laughing about a deal they were doing, sitting on the table next to the Americans.

12:30, just as the waiter came out of the restaurant, towards his table, lasagne and juice on a tray; a young woman in a white dress, carrying a glass of red wine sat at the table behind him.

His phone rang, Bm Ba Ba Bm, ♫, Bmm Bmm Bm, ♪♫♪.

"Hello," said Sebastian into his mobile.

"Sebastian, it's me, Tom, look, I'm very sorry... I'm not going to be able to make it."

"Any reason?" said Sebastian harshly.

"I went to see my Arabic friends last night."

"Uha!"

"It seems the wording isn't an address... it has a couple of names, but nothing that can immediately help. *So*, I want to see what I can find today before I come to see you with anything that will be helpful to us."

The waiter laid the lasagne onto the table in front of Sebastian, followed by a glass of cranberry juice, knife, fork and napkin.

Sebastian looked up at the waiter and smiled, with a small nod, the waiter turned and left.

"Names... what, *Arabic* names?" questioned Sebastian.

"Well, no!" said Tom. "One is Arabic, but the other is French."

Sebastian took a sip of his juice.

"French, a French name... could that be relevant to us?"

"Possibly, but this is why I needed to follow up on this today, coming for lunch would just take time... time I would rather spend finding the answers to who these people are."

Sebastian cut a piece of the lasagne with his fork and popped it into his mouth.

"Are the names obvious... I mean, do they mean

anything to you?"

"I haven't yet had time to go through them," said Tom. "There is someone definitely called Mustafa Ben Dee, but there was some uncertainty about the other name, they said it could be Silsitin or possibly Celestine, and the surname of Bourgogne or Bourgoin."

Sebastian cut the next piece of lasagne with force, his frustration with the lack of progress showing. He put the food into his mouth and followed with the drink.

"So, where do we go from here?" Sebastian said frustratedly.

"Leave it with me and I will see what I can come up within the next couple of days."

Sebastian taking the phone away from his ear, frustratedly lowered it to the table.

"Argh," he barked as he pressed the off button angrily.

Taking two more mouthfuls of the lasagne, tipped the glass up to finish the cranberry juice, forces the chair away with the back of his legs, turned away from the table and... crash, straight into the woman with the white dress, red wine all down her front.

"Oh my God!" she fumed. "Look what you've done!"

"Oh, I am so, so sorry," spluttered Sebastian.

"What a stupid man, just like the rest of them!" the woman glowered.

Sebastian looked at the woman in the white and thought, what a beautiful woman, if she wasn't so angry, that is.

"No, I didn't see you!"

"And that doesn't surprise me… I could hear you, just like everyone here could hear you; getting angry on the phone, banging and crashing with your mobile."

"But…"

"Oh, do shut up, bloody men, absolutely useless."

Everyone sitting at the tables and passing by now looking at the spectacle.

Sebastian pleading for forgiveness, cursing himself for getting so frustrated with Tom on the phone. After all, it wasn't Tom's fault the Arabic writing was not as rewarding as he had hoped.

The woman in the white dress, the red wine stain all down the front; the barman rushed over with a clean damp tea towel and started to pat at the ruby red mark.

The crowd of onlookers now growing.

"So," said the woman. "What are you going to do about it?"

"Wha…" blurted Sebastian.

"What… are… you… going… to… do… a… bout… it?" she said slowly, emphasizing every word.

"I…"

"Stop keep blurting… spit it out!"

"I… I don't know…" said a tongue-tied Sebastian. "Oh… yes, I know, I don't live far from here, come back to my place and I could wash the dress."

"How dare you…" she said angrily. "Do you think I am some type of slut… I'm not going back to your place and taking my clothes off… if that's what you are suggesting?"

Sebastian wishing the ground would open up.

The crowd growing even bigger, him feeling even smaller.

He felt like it was one of those street-shows, that they put on at Covent Garden.

"Okay," said the woman. "I'll tell you what we will do… first, I will go back to my hotel and get changed into something less stained, with me so far?"

"Yes," Sebastian nodded.

"Then, I will come over to your place later where *you* can wash my dress… right?"

"Mmmm."

"And, while the dress is washing, you can take me out for dinner… got it?"

"Okay." Sebastian felt relieved there was a conclusion to what had just happened.

The crowd, also satisfied the spectacle was over, started to move away. The diners went back to their dinners and chat.

The woman looked up at Sebastian; *well,* he thought, *she is gorgeous, I think I have done well out of this accident.*

"So, come on," she said, picking her phone up and opening the contacts' page. "Give me your name and address or I won't be able to get to you?"

"Oh, yes of course…" He said looking down at her phone while she is writing "Sebastian Plant… I live in Stratosphere Tower."

"Hmm, well... you say that like I am supposed to know where that is. London is a big place, you know, I will need more than that!"

Sebastian felt enormously attracted to this woman, she was strong, determined, knew what she wanted. She reminded him of his ex-wife, Amelia, and the brilliant Suki.

Once he had finished giving her all the details that he hoped she needed, he picked his phone up.

"Can I have your details?" he said nervously

"You must be joking," she said. "I wouldn't trust you not to lose it in the next six hours... no, I will contact you. Now, expect me at six-thirty, have a restaurant booked for seven-thirty, and I don't want cheap... okay?"

"Ye... yes!" he spluttered.

"So, where were you just off to when you walked into me?" she said.

"The office, I was just going back to the office."

"Okay then, Sebastian, you had better get back to the office, don't you think?"

"Ah... yes," he spluttered. "But I don't know..."

"My name's Jennifer... okay?"

# Chapter 19
## Soho, so Good
## Summer Present-day

Sebastian had spent the afternoon readying himself for the evening. *'Jennifer'* she said her name was.

Six-thirty was getting closer; the time she said she would be at his flat.

His nerves jangling, he felt overwhelmed by her presence.

He had booked the restaurant, one of London's top establishments; Sebastian had been lucky, he just managed to get a cancellation, which allowed him the opportunity to book the table for two.

Six twenty-five, he is hoping she doesn't 'stand him up', or turn up 'fashionably late'.

Pacing the room, stopping occasionally to look out of the window. Looking down at the pavement many storeys below, seeing if he could catch a glimpse of her as she entered the building, but not a sign.

He started pacing once more.

Six-thirty, bing-bong was the sound of his doorbell.

Sebastian rushed towards the door, grabbing the handle as quickly as he could, not wasting any time, turning the latch and then, slowly opening the door, as if there were no rush at all.

His eyes opening wide, his heart skipped a beat,

the wonderful sight at the entrance to his flat, drawing in a sudden sharp breath, as there in front of him, Jennifer. Her long brown hair tumbling over her lightly tanned shoulders, her beautiful face smiling in recognition. But, thought Sebastian, that dress, a red mini dress, tightly fitting and showing every curve of her body.

The neck having a silvery-white neck strap in a lace design, the red silky material of the dress, with a lacy swirling pattern going down either side of her breasts leaving her arms and shoulders bare. It neatly fitted the shape of her bosom, showing her perfect shape. It narrowed in at the waist to another silvery-white lace band. Below that, the red lacy swirl continued to follow her flowing figure, as it stopped half way up her thigh.

Her legs, a light brown, down to her silvery-white strapped high heel shoes.

Sebastian's emotions surged in his groin, as a twitch of sensation ran through his penis, giving a slight erection. Only then, to be tamed, as Jennifer brought both her hands forward; draped across her hands, the white dress with the red wine stain.

"Good evening Sebastian," she said. "I have a little gift for you."

Jennifer held the dress towards Sebastian.

"Oh, oh yes," stammered Sebastian, taking the dress from her hands. "Please come in... can I get you a drink?"

Jennifer walked into the hallway following Sebastian, then through the door into the lounge.

"A glass of water will do fine for now please,"

she answered as she dropped her bag on the settee.

As she entered the lounge, looking around the room, the white walls and furniture, the wood flooring and then over to the painting of the masturbating woman.

She stood at the bottom of the painting and studied it carefully.

Sebastian walked back to Jennifer from the kitchen carrying two glasses of water.

Turning to Sebastian as he moved towards her.

"This is interesting," she said.

"It's a friend of mine," said Sebastian. "A long time ago, that is."

"You no longer see her?"

"No, unfortunately... she married some rich businessman. The painting wasn't on show anywhere, so she contacted me and asked if I would like it... good memories... of course, I said yes."

"It is good," continued Jennifer. "Very good, I might see if I can contact the artist, see what he can do for me."

Sebastian's penis twitched and swelled a little again.

Jennifer continued her tour of the lounge, looking out of the window at the London skyline.

"How are you getting on with that dress?"

"I have put it in the washing machine with something that is meant to get wine stains out."

"And if it doesn't?" asserted Jennifer.

"Er... I'll take it to a professional, they'll know what to do to get it out."

"Mmmm," she hesitated. "We'll see... What

about dinner, did you do as I asked?"

"Yes," said Sebastian, feeling he had at least got this right. "It's in Soho, taxis booked for seven, so we will have to be down in the reception for the pick-up soon."

"I'm ready when you are," she said.

Sebastian threw his jacket over his shoulder, he was wearing a light navy-blue herringbone suit, a white shirt with a thin tie, the colour matching the suit. Light brown leather shoes.

"Ready?" he said as he looked at Jennifer.

"Lead the way!" she replied.

***

The taxi drove into Soho, following the narrow one-way streets that crisscrossed their way around the district.

Into Beak Street, it pulled up outside the restaurant of Bob Bob Ricard.

As Jennifer jumped out, the sky was still light and the evening warm in the early summer evening.

Sebastian leaned over to the driver.

"Driver," he said.

"Yes sir?" replied the driver.

"When I have finished here, I will call you. I want you outside of here within ten minutes of me calling. Have you got that?"

"Yes sir!"

"I will pay you when you have returned me and my guest back home, and you will get a bonus by making sure you are back here on time."

"Thank you, sir," said the driver.

Sebastian stepped out of the taxi, the sounds of distant cars, motorcycles and horns tooting. The driver getting onto his taxi controller, updating them on the situation and that he will need to return later.

Sebastian stepping onto the pavement as Jennifer put her hand through his arm.

Looking up at him, she smiled.

"You are looking very handsome," said Jennifer in a half-whisper. "Might just have been a lucky glass of wine."

"Very lucky," replied Sebastian, as he admired this beautiful woman on his arm.

They are greeted as they walk through the door.

"Good evening, sir, and how may I help you?" said the waiter with a French accent.

"Good evening," replied Sebastian. "I have a reservation for two... in the name of Plant... Sebastian Plant."

"Ah, *oui*, yes sir," acknowledged the waiter. "This afternoon, you were very lucky sir, to have called just after a cancellation."

"We," interrupted Jennifer, "will be the judge of how lucky we were, after the meal... so please don't disappoint us."

"*Oui*, madame. We have a first-class reputation, we make sure that in every way, we maintain that first-class reputation."

"I'm sure you will."

"Sir, madame... would you like to follow me to your table?"

Jennifer and Sebastian follow the waiter as he

leads them through the restaurant.

"Monsieur, madame… your table," the waiter said politely, gesturing with his hand to the table in front of him.

Jennifer slid her way onto the blue bench seat, making herself comfortable in front of the immaculately laid out table. Sebastian sliding in on the opposite side of the table. The waiter bowed slightly as he held the menus in their direction.

"Monsieur, madame, someone will be with you shortly to take your orders."

"Thank you," said Sebastian, looking up at the waiter.

"Well," said Jennifer, looking down at the menu. "Looks like you might have chosen well."

Sebastian looking up, a little smile on his face, the thought that he had got this evening right giving him a warm glow inside.

"Any thoughts on what you are going to have?" asked Sebastian.

"Oh, yes," said Jennifer. "I know exactly what we are going to have."

Sebastian gave an unsure smile and nodded over to the waiter.

"Good evening," said the waiter. "Are we ready to order?"

Jennifer looked up at the waiter.

"Yes," she said. "I would like for starters the Salmon Tartar Imperial… and for my friend," she continued, "he will have the Crab with Chilli and Avocado."

"Thank you, madame," said the waiter, as he

jotted it into his notebook.

"Hope you didn't mind," Jennifer said to Sebastian. "I didn't know which one to have, so, I thought, if I have one, and you have the other, I can try both…" she said with a sexy half smile on her face. "I knew you wouldn't mind."

"And the main course?" asked the waiter.

"Oh, well," continued Jennifer. "It's got to be the Beef Wellington for Two."

"Thank you, madame," said the waiter, taking the menus. "The wine waiter will see you shortly."

The waiter nodding slightly as he turned, making his way back to the serving counter. As he left, the wine waiter appeared.

"Madame, monsieur," smiled the second waiter. "I believe you have ordered your starter and main course… would you like any wine to go with the meal?"

"What do you suggest?" asked Jennifer.

"Well, madame, as you will be having seafood for starters, could I recommend a white wine… we have at the restaurant a particularly good Blanc Châteauneuf du Pape?"

"Okay," agreed Jennifer. "And what about with the beef?"

"Madame," smiled the waiter. "May I suggest the Volnay 1er Cru 'Santenots' Burgundy?"

"Mmm," hesitated Jennifer. "Is that the 2005?"

"I'm sorry, madame," apologised the waiter. "This will be the 2013."

"Well, okay then, but if they are not right, we don't pay for them."

"Madame," said the wine waiter, nervously. "These wines have never failed to please our clientele... I am sure you will find them to your satisfaction."

The wine waiter turning, still making notes, walked back to the bar, wiping his brow as he moved away from the table of Jennifer and Sebastian.

"You do know what you want, don't you?" said Sebastian.

"And I get what I want!" smiled Jennifer.

"Mmmm, and... am I included in 'What you want'?" asked Sebastian, half questioning.

"If you play your cards right... you might be!"

Jennifer having slipped her foot out of her shoe, started rubbing it against the inside of Sebastian's calf; looking straight into his eyes as her toes stroke the inside of his thigh, coming to rest at his crouch, where her big toe rubbed against the bulge that was starting to rise in his trousers.

Her toes stroking his balls, massaging his cock, the manhood inside Sebastian's trousers; trapped by his underpants, adding pressure to the swelling between his legs.

Her big toe making a circle around the helmet as Sebastian's breathing got deeper.

"Your Châteauneuf du Pape, madame," interrupted the wine waiter.

"Wonderful," said Jennifer. "My friend will sample it."

Sebastian was really not ready to sample wine, his head spinning, his heart racing.

"Oh... oh yes, of course," said Sebastian, jerking

himself back into the real world, Jennifer's foot still stroking up and down his cock. "Yes please... in here," Sebastian croaked, as he pushed his glass towards the wine waiter.

The waiter removing the cork, poured a sample amount into Sebastian's glass, Sebastian, his hands shaking, his head in a spin, raised the glass to his lips as Jennifer's foot rubbed harder into his crotch.

Sebastian's mouthful almost ending back in the glass as he fought to keep some sort of control.

Nodding up at the waiter, he splutters...

"Okay."

But the reality was, at that moment, his emotions were so high, he really wasn't thinking about wine. It could have been lemonade and he would still have said it was good.

The wine waiter poured two glasses of wine for Sebastian and Jennifer, then placed the bottle in an ice bucket at the end of the table.

The waiter moving away, Jennifer lowers her foot, putting it back into her shoe.

"So," said Jennifer to Sebastian. "Tell me about yourself."

"Well, first, my name is Sebastian... Sebastian Plant, close friends call me Bastian."

"Am I your close friend?"

"I hope so."

"Then, I shall call you Bastian?"

"It sounds good when *you* say it!"

"Bastian, Bastian," Jennifer teased "And your job... I mean, it doesn't look like you do things by halves... your flat, this restaurant?"

"Well, as you saw earlier, I work down at Canary Wharf. I'm a hedge fund manager."

"And that means?"

"I look after business interests, buying, selling shares… making money."

"And you are good at it?"

"I like to think so," said Sebastian, puffing out his chest.

"What about interests?" Jennifer asked.

"Not a lot really, making lots of money… that's about it really. Well, I do go to the gym a lot, like to keep myself fit. Oh, of course, I go to the boxing club, sparring in the ring, you know?"

"Sounds a bit dangerous to me," said Jennifer, looking slightly sideways.

"No, not at all, I just do it to keep myself fit; punch bags, medicine balls, a trainer with punching gloves on. You know, that sort of thing."

"I wouldn't like to see you get hurt."

The waiter walked towards the table with the starters.

"Madame, monsieur… we have salmon for you madame and the crab for you, monsieur."

"Thank you," said Sebastian.

Jennifer taking a forkful of the salmon, raised it to her mouth, her eyes closed as she enjoys the wonderful tastes, her head giving a little nod of pleasure. She took a second mouthful.

Sebastian too, finding the food really good.

Jennifer picked up her glass of wine, raised it to her lips, sipping a small amount into her mouth.

"Mmmm, that's nice," she said.

Sebastian agreed.

"Okay," said Jennifer. "Let's try the crab now."

Picking her plate up, she rested it on Sebastian's side of the table, then picking up Sebastian's plate, she placed it in front of herself.

"Do you do this sort of thing with all your dinner dates?" asked Sebastian

"No… only the ones I want to get to know better," she winked.

Sebastian's knob twitched again.

"And what about you," coughed Sebastian. "What do you do?"

"Me? not a lot really," said Jennifer, offhandedly. "My name is Jennifer Pinski. I live just outside of San Francisco, study at Stanford University. I aim to be a doctor."

"That's not a strong American accent though," enquired Sebastian.

"No, I was born in England," she said. "My family moved to America a few years ago… so I guess I still have a few of my British roots in me."

"So why are you in London right now?"

"Just visiting, catching up with some old friends and family."

Jennifer took a couple more mouthfuls of the crab and avocado, one more sip of the wine and put her knife and fork together on her plate, she had finished.

Jennifer's glass was still almost full, the bottle only half empty.

Sebastian wasn't going to waste it, so finished his glass as the waiter came over to their table.

"Was everything okay for you, madame?" said the waiter, as he was picking up their plates from the table.

"It was fine," said Jennifer.

"The main course will follow along shortly," the waiter assured.

Jennifer turned her attention back to Sebastian.

"So come on you," she said jovially. "It can't just be work and the gym, what else do you have going in your life... wife, family... what about them?"

"Well, I did once have a wife... a long time ago. We had a son, Samuel. I have parents who live a few miles from here."

"Do Mum and Dad have a name?"

"Oh, yes, Russell and Elizabeth."

"Will I get to meet them?"

"Maybe, one day, would be nice."

The waiter arrived with the main course.

# Chapter 20
## Shaking the Tower
### Summer Present-day

By the end of the meal, Sebastian had had several glasses of wine, Jennifer several sips.

Sebastian a satisfying amount of food, Jennifer, several mouthfuls. Sebastian had already notified the taxi that they would be leaving shortly and to be waiting. They eased their way out of the seats.

Jennifer took Sebastian by the arm as they walked over to the bar to pay the bill. They continued to walk arm in arm to the door. Sebastian, stood to one side as Jennifer walked through.

The sky now a deep blue, with some of the brighter stars twinkling. A few orange tints where the sun continued to beam the last of its rays into the upper atmosphere.

Still warm, with wonderful smells coming from the restaurant they had just left, mingling with the fast food and pub restaurants. The streets thronging with party and theatre-goers; the happy atmosphere, the smells of food and the sounds of distant music filling the air.

Sebastian content with the evening so far, stepped out of Bob Bob's, looking over to where the taxi had dropped them off earlier, and there he was. The taxi waiting to pick them both up. The driver seeing them heading towards his cab, jumped out of the driver's door, ran around to the rear passenger door, opening it as Jennifer arrived at the vehicle.

"Was everything good for you sir?" the driver enquired to Sebastian.

"Yes, wonderful," said Sebastian, as he jumped in the door on the opposite side of the cab.

"Is it home now, sir?" asked the driver.

Sebastian looking at Jennifer for the answer. She nodded.

"Yes, thank you, driver, back to Stratosphere Tower."

"Okay, sir, I will have you there as quickly as I can."

The driver did the best he could to get them back to Sebastian's flat. The roads in London, at that time of the evening, with the theatres finishing, the crowds starting to mingle on the streets, the cars, taxis and coaches stopping to pick up their passengers.

Sebastian sitting in the back of the taxi, looking out of the window, the sights of London passing by.

Jennifer, sitting close to Sebastian, her head laying against his shoulder. Her arm tucked through his arm.

The taxi turned left into Regent Street, heading towards Piccadilly, the sounds of music as buskers played on street corners.

Trafalgar Square, Charing Cross and the Strand, Temple and Fleet Street, the journey taking on the sound of a Monopoly board.

Bank, Bow, Cannon Street and Fenchurch Street as they headed home.

Sebastian's emotions making him flushed with excitement, Jennifer content in the way the night had gone, just as she had hoped.

Stratosphere Tower came into view, as darkness descended on the East End of London.

The taxi drove up Stratford High Street, left into Great Eastern Road, right, the taxi stopping outside the towering structure.

The driver jumping out of his seat, quickly around the back of the vehicle as he opened the door for Jennifer.

Sebastian sliding over as Jennifer stepped out of the car, reaching the path, she stood waiting for him to finish with the taxi driver.

He paid the cab fare, then handed the driver another twenty pounds, thanking him for the journey.

The taxi pulling away, Jennifer took Sebastian's arm once more as they head towards the entrance of the building.

Through the doors, they walked toward the lift, a nod from the concierge as they pass his desk. Sebastian pressing the lift call button. Jennifer and Sebastian stood quietly waiting for the lift to arrive. Another nod over to the concierge as the lift dings, the lift doors open.

Sebastian smiles once again to the concierge as he and Jennifer calmly enter the lift, the doors shut...

The lift doors open on the floor for Sebastian's flat. Sebastian staggering out, Jennifer's legs wrapped around his waist, grunting and moaning as their mouths tightly locked together in a passionate kiss. Her arms around his neck, her knickers stuffed into his jacket pocket.

Losing his footing, he stumbled sideways, their bodies crashing into the wall on the opposite side of the lift doors, their mouths still not parting.

Sebastian's arms under Jennifer's bottom, his hands holding her up, her legs clinging tightly to his hips.

The feel of her bare skin on his fingers as he stroked the soft tissue, the crease of her vagina.

The lift doors shut as Sebastian regained his balance, two steps towards his flat, then staggered once more into the wall on the other side of the passageway, his eyes half-closed, he made his way up the corridor.

Stopping outside the entrance to his flat, their lips not parting, he leaned Jennifer's back against the door.

Lifting her slightly, attempting to get a better hold of her with his left arm, his right-hand stroked gently across her smooth flesh, running across the crevice of her fanny, his right hand then dropping to the pocket of his trousers.

Jennifer's eyes tightly shut, enjoying the passionate embrace.

Sebastian pulling the door key from his pocket, partially opened an eye as he felt for the lock.

The key entering the hole, he turned the lock and with a jerk, they stagger forward, the door suddenly flinging open, being helped by the weight of them both leaning against it. Inside the room, Sebastian once again regained his footing.

Jennifer moving her head as she kissed Sebastian from another angle, her tongue darting into his mouth. He bursting with emotions; he felt his cock alone could have held her up it was so stiff.

Her legs still entwined around his middle; putting his foot around the back of the door, kicked it gently with his heel, the door shutting with a clunk.

One foot at a time he headed for the bedroom.

Jennifer desperately pulling the jacket from Sebastian's shoulders, he stuck an arm out as she pulled at the sleeve until it came off. Then the other sleeve, she tossed the jacket into the air to land... anywhere.

Through the bedroom door she had his tie off, then started to unbutton his shirt.

Finally, at the bed, releasing the grip of her legs, she slid her feet to the floor.

Quickly unbuttoning the rest of the shirt, roughly pulling the bottom of the shirt out of his trousers.

She kissed his chest as she slid the shirt from his shoulders and down his arms.

Her kisses lower from his chest to his stomach as she pulled at the zip of his trousers, unbuttoning the waist button, pulling his pants open, she sank her mouth over his hardened cock, taking as much of the phallus in as she could.

She sucked and twisted her head, up and down several times, then released the object from her mouth. Turned Sebastian into a position she could sit him on the bed, kissing him on the lips as she lowered him backwards until he sat.

She knelt, undid his shoes pulling them and his socks off one at a time and hurling them across the room.

Lifted him slightly as she pulled his trousers all the way off.

Jennifer stood up and looked down at Sebastian, naked, sitting on the bed.

"Okay," she said. "Go and get my bag... it's on the settee."

Sebastian duly obliged, got up from the bed, walked naked from the bedroom and into the lounge.

Jennifer's bag sitting on the settee, he picked it up and headed back into the bedroom.

The sight took his breath away.

Jennifer stood at the bottom of the bed, completely naked. Her beautiful face now being matched by a perfect body. The curves of her hips, the slightly erect nipples, a Californian tan on her body; just a thin lighter area around the bottom, hips and crouch from a skimpy bikini.

Sebastian stood in the doorway, mesmerised, without a stitch on, Jennifer's bag held in two hands, dangling in front of his erect manhood. His mouth half open.

"*Well?*" said Jennifer in a sexy come-hither voice, her head slightly leaning to one side. "Come here then, I want to suck that cock of yours again."

Sebastian, lost for words. He by this time could only mumble Neanderthal sentences.

He looked around the room. Was this really happening? he thought. He took a couple of steps forward; Jennifer taking the bag from him, laid it on the floor at the bottom of the bed, took both his hands, leading him to the side of the bed, turned him around then sat him down.

"Put your feet up on the bed," she said, "I can't do everything for you."

Sebastian did as ordered, lifted his feet onto the bed then laid back with his head on the pillow.

Jennifer moved to the bottom of the bed, her back to Sebastian, she bent down from the waist, her hands feeling for something in the bag, Sebastian's eyes almost popped, he could see her beautifully rounded buttocks, her close-shaven vagina, with its moist lips.

She stood back up, holding several pieces of pink ribbon; turning back to Sebastian, she smiled.

"We are going to play a game!"

Jennifer walked up one side of the bed, took Sebastian's arm, tied the pink ribbon around his wrist, lowered the arm to the bed, to the top corner of the mattress. She then tied the other end of the ribbon to the bed frame.

Having tied the first arm, she slowly walked to the other side of the bed, her eyes looking into his face the whole time, picked up the other arm, tied another ribbon to the wrist and to the bed frame.

She bent her head forward, kissing him on the lips, letting her fanny stroke across his fingers. As he tried to stroke her vagina, she teasingly moved away.

Looking into his eyes, she slowly moved to the bottom of the bed, a pink ribbon for each ankle and tied them to the bed frame.

"Okay Bastian," she smiled. "Let the games

begin!"

"Mmm," babbled Sebastian, in his best Neandertal talk.

"Oh, and remember... you only cum, when I want you to cum... clear?"

Sebastian nodded, and hoped he could oblige.

Jennifer moved to the side of the bed, knelt to the floor, leaned over and sucked his nipples, Sebastian was bursting with pleasure. This was so overwhelming; he couldn't ever remember sex being this good; even at Queenie's.

Jennifer lifted her head, her hair tumbling down over her face as she moved her head over Sebastian's crouch. Moving her head from side to side, her hair brushing over his cock, the swelling growing bigger and bigger.

Her mouth lowering onto his gamba, making sure she didn't get him to a point of over-excitement, she released her mouth.

Climbing onto the bed, she kneeled, with one leg either side of his torso, she faced him. Looking down into his eyes as her hand reaching behind, grabbing the base of his shaft, she lowered her vagina closer to Sebastian's swollen erection.

Her labia lips parting as his cock slid into the moist and inviting hole.

Slowly down and down till her bottom came to rest on his balls, her body leaning slightly forward, her hands either side of his chest.

"Now, Bastian," she said. "The game, let me tell you about this game..."

She raised her body, then slowly slid back down

the shaft.

"Oh, it is a simple game."

Up and down.

"I am going to ask you questions about your life... and you are going to answer them."

Up and down.

"Now the game is, if I think you are telling the truth..."

Up and down.

"I will swallow your cum... and if I think you are lying..."

Up and down.

"You will have to swallow your cum... have you got that?"

"Mmmm," said Sebastian, straining to control himself.

"Okay, let's start with simple... where do you work?"

"Ohh, Milstone-Hanks Finance."

"Good."

Up and down.

"You have a friend there?"

"Harry... Harry Chang," breathed Sebastian.

"Oh, I like this game... don't you Bastian? Now let's see... oh yes... tell me about the last couple of weeks?"

Up and down.

"Queenie's party, Mum and Dad's with Samuel."

"Bastian, just two things, surely a man like you will be doing more than two things in the last fortnight... and may I remind you... I swallow... or you swallow!"

"My family history... yes, I went to the National Archives."

"Now, that sounds more like it!"

"And what were you looking for at the Archives?"

"My great grandfather... oh, I was looking for information from the war."

"And what information was that?"

Up and down.

"I found a contract, my great grandfather and someone with a German name, something had been hidden."

"Hidden... hidden where?" continued Jennifer.

"I don't know, I am looking for it with someone else."

"And when you find... whatever it is you are looking for, will you be sharing it with this other person?"

"Oh, no, I have the contract... it's my contract... if we find whatever it is, it will be for me... not him."

Jennifer lifted her bottom up and away from Sebastian's cock.

On her hands and knees, she worked her way up the bed, kissed him on the lips, her body raised as she got higher on the bed, her knees now above Sebastian's arms.

She lowered her quim onto his face, slowly working her vagina up and down over his chin, nose and lips, the moistness of her fanny getting wetter and wetter by the moisture of his tongue as it darted in and out.

"Make me cum!" she urged "Make me cum!"

Her hands going down to her labia, pulling the slit apart to reveal her clitoris.

"Suck it," she cried "Make me cum!"

Jennifer moving her body to and fro, the urgency of the pressure building up in her groin.

Forcing her clitoris into Sebastian's mouth as he enthusiastically sucked at the love button. His tongue lapping across the sensitive organ, then darting up into her vaginal hole.

Her fingers rubbing over her clitoris, Sebastian's tongue flicking and teasing the vaginal lips.

Faster and faster her body movements, her bottom and legs thrashing forwards and backwards.

Sebastian grabbing a breath at every opportunity.

Wetter and wetter Sebastian became.

Jennifer's body oozing pleasure liquid, running over Sebastian's face.

"I'm cuming," she squeaked. "Ohh, I'm cuming!"

Her head went back.

Sebastian looking up, he could see her writhing body, her shaven pussy wriggling on his face, a slim tanned body, beautiful breasts and the underside of a chin all shaking and juddering as he lay tied up to his bed.

Her body lurched forward.

"Erggh!" she cried. "Oh my god, *yes!*"

Her hair covering her face, her eyes shut.

Her body shuddering as she pushed her clitoris into Sebastian's face, writhing as the orgasm floods her body, the excitement, the sheer joy of the sensations in the lower part of her body.

Her hands coming forward, grabbing the back of Sebastian's head, pulling it forward. She slowly and gently urged his mouth to keep teasing her clitoris, which he happily did.

For several minutes, she sat like this, the occasional shudder as a mini orgasm engulfed her being.

Her body drooped, limp, enjoying the last of the sensations... until, she slowly sat upright.

"Okay," she oozed. "Now, it's time for your challenge."

She lifted her backside away from Sebastian's face, stood up on the bed, her legs either side of his chest. Sebastian looked up at her, her shaven pudendum, her clit slightly protruding through her vaginal lips, moist, glistening and swollen. She, turning on the bed, her backside now facing Sebastian, lowered herself till her bottom was close to his face.

Her mouth kissing the top of his cock as she flicked it with her tongue; she moved slightly forward, her tongue and lips running down the underside of his penis. She nibbled her way back to the top, her mouth opening as she took his manhood as far in as it would go, then flicked her tongue around the head.

Slowly moving her mouth back to the top of the shaft. She could feel Sebastian's excitement. She knew he was not far away from cuming.

Keeping her mouth on the top of the shaft, she

moved her body around until she knelt between his legs. Her eyes looking up at Sebastian's face, his eyes closed, a little movement side to side of his head; she knew he would soon cum.

"Okay, Bastian," she said, flicking the piece of skin under the head of the shaft with her tongue. "Let's see if I think you are telling the truth or not."

Jennifer's palm cupped under his balls, her index finger and thumb around the bottom of the shaft, her mouth slowly moving up and down over the head of the gamba, her hand moving up and down his balls and shaft.

The rhythm slow, to keep the sensation lasting longer, the throbbing in the shaft, she knew it was on its way.

Sebastian's head moving from side to side, he had never had pleasure like this... ever.

Jennifer could taste the first signs of liquid as it seeped into her mouth, then... whoosh, the back of Sebastian's head buried itself into the pillow, his torso pushing up as the cum rushed into Jennifer's mouth; she sucked and sucked. The white liquid surging in, she continued to keep Sebastian's cock in her mouth.

Sebastian's body dropping back down to the bed, his eyes shut, the sensations overwhelming.

Jennifer keeping her mouth over his cock for a few seconds longer, waiting for Sebastian's full senses to return.

She then slowly pulling her mouth of cum away from the top of his cock, closing her lips tightly, she crawled slowly up the bed. Millimetre by millimetre, her breasts and body sliding across Sebastian's cock until her head became level with Sebastian's head, her mouth level with Sebastian's mouth.

Sebastian looking up at her, her mouth full of cum, getting closer to his mouth.

Her tight lips about to join with his lips, to transfer Sebastian's cum into his mouth should she not believe what he had to say.

"It's true," Sebastian pleaded "It's true, there's lots more, if you want to know, I can tell you more."

Jennifer's mouth got closer and closer... their lips just about to meet when...

"It's okay," she whispered, showing she had already swallowed it. "Now, there's more you say, well, I would love to hear more... it sounds like a fascinating story."

"Yes," agreed Sebastian. "I just hope it has a happy ending."

"Happy ending... oh yes, I'm sure there will be a happy ending... and we still have the night ahead for many more happy endings... now." Said Jennifer looking down at Sebastian's penis. "Oh, look, we have a bit of spillage... we can't have that now, can we?"

She moved down the bed, until she could rest her head on Sebastian's stomach.

Slowly moving her mouth towards his now semi limp cock, cum slowly oozing from the top as the erection seeped away.

She put her fingers around the drooping shaft, lifted it a little and popped it into her mouth.

The warmth of her mouth making his cock twitch,

she sucked until the last of the cum had gone from his body.

***

Jennifer woke the next morning as the bedroom curtains were partially opened, her eyes, just open enough to make out the silhouette of Sebastian's naked body at the window as he pulled back the cord to the shade.

The brightness blurring Jennifer's eyes as the silhouette walked toward the bed, laid a cup on the small table beside her, the smell of fresh coffee suddenly hitting her senses.

Sebastian strode around to the other side of the bed, lifted the cover and gently laid back on the mattress.

Jennifer felt the warmth of his body, as he slid across to her side of the bed. His body forming the same shape as her body, as the front of his body came into contact with the back of hers, his arm came across her front, his hand coming to rest against her chest, his head nestled in her hair.

She closed her eyes as a warm glow ran through her.

Her eyes opened wider once more, the light from outside beginning to focus more clearly, the London city skyline spread across her view; the skyscrapers, the river. An aircraft just taking off from City Airport, diagonally crossing the window; jetting business men, women and holidaymakers off to other places. Places to find fun, happiness and pleasure.

But none of them could have had the pleasure that Jennifer and Sebastian had had last night.

Her hand moved from the side of her, she settled it on the hand of Sebastian, his hand laying on top of her breast.

"Good morning," she sighed.

"Good morning to you too," he breathed gently.

They both settled back down to the pleasure of lying in each other's arms. Jennifer and Sebastian lying close, their eyes closed, enjoying the moment.

"Have you been up long?" she whispered.

"Long enough to go to the shops and get breakfast."

"Oh, you are good... you'll make someone a wonderful husband one day, if you keep that up."

"One day... you never know," he whispered into her hair, kissing the back of her head.

Jennifer stretched as she started to turn over, pushing him back on the bed till he was lying on his back.

She tucked his arm nearest to her under her head, then laid on her side facing him.

Sebastian's other arm going behind his head as Jennifer stroked his chest, running her fingers around his nipples, down across his stomach and side.

"How was your night?" she uttered, her head laying on his arm.

"One of the best nights of my life!" he sighed. "And you?"

"I don't think I have ever cum so much!"

"It was okay then?" he mocked.

"Okay is an understatement," she said.

"I got fresh fruit, natural yoghurt, honey, Scotch pancakes... how does that sound?"

"Mmmm... mouth-watering."

"Shall I go and get it ready?"

"No... don't you dare leave this bed... you are far too comfortable."

"I was hoping you were going to say that."

Jennifer's head snuggled into Sebastian's chest.

"Tell me more about your family," she murmured. "That was fascinating... what you said last night."

"Well... there's not really a lot, well at least, not a lot so far."

"You said about your great grandfather?"

"Yes, I was trying to find some information on him... he was killed in a shooting in an East End pub... 1947, I think it was, well around about then."

"Was he a criminal or something then?"

"Well, according to the stories my father has told me, he did tend to mix with the criminal types... gangs, and that sort of thing... At the time that was, well, at least as far as I am aware, before the war. Of course, during the war he was a soldier, he was decorated with a few medals for the campaigns he had been on."

"Gangs... what, East End type gangs... They didn't have a good reputation?"

"Don't know, I guess so... dad himself has been... well, at least from a distance, involved a little with the London gangs."

"Is your dad violent then?"

"No, not at all, gentle as a lamb."

"And your mum, what's she like?"

"She's lovely really... besotted with her grandson... my boy Samuel."

"You have a son Samuel?"

"Yes, Samuel... named after his great grandfather... you know, the one from the war."

"Ah, yes... Samuel Plant... your great grandfather... who died in 1947," she said, thoughtfully. "And you said you were researching him?"

"Yes, well, at least trying, I am now starting to realise that to do that sort of thing takes a lot of time... unless you are an expert... at that sort of thing... you know!"

"And you didn't want to ask an expert to help?"

"Well, no, not really."

"Why not?"

"Well, it was me... the contract, you know, I found the contract, it had my great grandfather's name on the contract... well, as well as the German name... and well, it was down to me to find."

"And you think there is something worthwhile finding?" said Jennifer, going up on her elbow to look him in the face.

"I don't know. I met this guy, he seems to think it is all related to stolen gold," said Sebastian looking over at her.

"And is it?"

"We aren't going to know, well at least until we find it, wherever it may be, and of course, if it's still there."

"So, is he the expert you talk about?" she said.

"Yes, yes, I believe he is, he does this sort of thing as a job... you know... for a living."

"So, does he need *you* to find this?"

"Well, the clues to its whereabouts seem to be either in my great grandfather's history or the German's history... I think we need each other!"

"How far has he got with it?"

"I'll find out later this afternoon... I've got to meet up with him... Tom's his name... Tom Paige. I'll tell you what, why don't you come along with me, meet up with him?"

"Tom Paige... yes, I think I would like that."

# Chapter 21
# Burgundy
# Summer Present-day

Tom had received, as a gift to the office, a brand-new computer to replace the broken one he used to work at. So, he was back in his old chair, behind the door, with his back to the window.

His desk was covered with papers, now relating to his new project.

The table under the window having the box from Germany, the important burnt scraps retrieved and sorted into useful and less useful piles.

Pinned on the wall, a large map of Europe, including North Africa.

Tom was convinced the clues either led him to the Dijon region of France, Southern France or North Africa; he had yet to narrow it down.

The parts of the Arabic that Jamil and Omar were unable to correctly translate, Silsitin or Celestine, along with the word Bourgogne. 'Does that relate to France?' thought Tom. After all, the date on the contract being 24 February, and Samuel Plant going missing from the 19 February. He was bordering on the Burgundy region at the time. But it's a big area, Yonne, Nièvre, Saône-et-Loire, Jura, Haute-Saône, Côte D'Or and more.

And then what? Written in Arabic, could it have been Arabic people living in the Bourgogne region, unlikely in an area of France just reclaimed from German occupation.

Arabic soldiers maybe, but this too seemed too farfetched to be the case. He could find no evidence of Arabic fighters in France called Mustafa Ben Dee, or, how he could have promised that his family would look after the boxes.

How the word Silsitin or Celestine could be found there, but then, as much as he searched, nothing was coming to light.

Southern France could also be the area to search, there was a ship's captain's name, Abou Nasir. Could he have a place, friends maybe in the Marseille area?

But, he thought, the ship. There was a ship's name... but no dates on the half-burnt document from the box.

Tom was meeting up with Sebastian later that day. He knew he must come up with an answer to the problem, and hopefully, before they meet.

# 20 February 1945

## A Farmhouse
## East of Auggen, Germany

# Chapter 22
## On the Move
## 20 February 1945

Samuel Plant and Wilhelm Schick had taken all the necessary things off the two dead soldiers as they lay lifeless on the floor.

Rifles, pistols, belts and ammo.

Helmets from both soldiers as well as ID from the dead German soldier.

Schick, in his best next move strategy, had a German uniform ready for Plant to change into, as well as a British uniform for himself, to use later, along with civilian clothes, should they need them.

"Once we have taken everything useful to us. We will take these two out to the barn."

"Okay, so what's the next step?" asked Plant.

"Well, first we hide the bodies. My driver will be here shortly with the truck and the gold, he will leave it with us... it will then be down to us to get it across the border, then hide it away until the time is safe to retrieve our interests."

"And you think it will be successful?"

"But of course, Mr Plant, plan well... and I have a plan. But of course, like chess, make sure your plan is flexible enough to change, but will still work. It will work... now, these two to the barn before my driver arrives."

Having removed everything they needed, from

the prostrate servicemen, they each dragged their countrymen out of the room, up the corridor and through the house till they reached the main farmyard.

Across the cold, frosty, hard ground till they arrived at the barn.

Plant dropped Billingham's shoulders, his body slumped to the ground. He turned, opened the big barn doors, picking up the soldier by his shoulders again, he continued to drag the lifeless body across the dusty soil, closely followed by Schick with the German soldier.

Both bodies dropped into a corner of the barn, boxes piled on top of them, then covered with straw. It will be a while before the bodies are found.

The fighting now only a few kilometres away, and just the other side of the Rhine, any farmers and civilians have moved far away.

"Okay," said Plant. "What next?"

"My driver should be here any moment now. If you would kindly get changed into the German uniform. While we are the German side, we must be seen to be working together," said Schick.

"What if I am spoken to?"

"Don't worry, no one will speak to you, while I am the senior officer. They would only speak to me."

Back in the house, Plant changed into the German uniform, putting on the belt and picking up the rifle; the sound of a heavy truck pulling up outside.

"Ah," said Schick. "That sounds like Horst now!"

Schick walked from the room, picking up the gun, rifle and belt that were once worn by Billingham.

Plant following close behind.

At the front of the farmhouse between the main building and the barn stood a Tatra 111 Heavy Truck, the driver opening the door to the truck and jumping down.

"*Guten tag*, Horst," called Schick as he and Plant walked through the door from the house and into the yard.

"*Guten tag mein Herr*," replied the driver.

"Now Horst, meet Mr Plant," said Schick, gesturing towards Samuel Plant.

"Mr Plant," said Horst. "How good it is to meet you... the Commander has many times spoken about you. I know for quite a while now, he has wished to meet you."

"Why thank you," exclaimed Plant. "But I have to say... that is the last thing I would have expected a German, especially Germans in military uniform to be saying to me."

"And speaking of German uniforms, sir," said Horst to Samuel Plant. "Seeing you dressed as a German soldier, you wouldn't know the difference whose side you were on."

"Now," interrupted Schick. "We do have a lack of time, the window of opportunity is getting lesser by the day. We must move now, and move quickly!"

"Yes sir," said Horst.

Schick put Billingham's gun and rifle, as well as a couple of shovels, in the back of the truck, along with spare uniforms and suits.

"Horst," said Schick. "The car is in the far barn," he said pointing about two hundred metres down the track. "Make your way back to Dresden, I will contact you as soon as I return."

"Yes sir!"

"Mr Plant, can you drive this truck...? only it wouldn't look good, for a commanding officer to be seen driving with an ordinary soldier sitting in the passenger seat."

"But of course," said Plant. "It can't be any different from any other truck... can it? and I have driven many of them over the last few years."

"Good," said Schick. "Okay then, let's get going."

Plant jumped up into the driver's seat, feeling a bit out of place in a Nazi uniform, having been on the opposite side for the past four years.

Schick stepped up, into the passenger door and sat, ready to be driven, his head going through the next few moves, weighing up the odds, ready to alter the plan at any moment.

The truck moved off. Horst standing behind the truck, he watched, as it disappeared up the old road, the Commander going over the plan with Horst in the days earlier. Horst knew what the Commander had in mind, but he also knew it was tricky. One wrong move, one word out of place and the whole thing would go terribly wrong.

At the main road, Plant turned the truck right, heading towards the local village of Auggen, deserted but for a few soldiers having been injured on the front line, being treated in this, the nearest place of safety.

Plant taking a quick look down at the soldiers lying on stretchers outside of a makeshift medical centre. Schick continued to look straight ahead.

Two and a half kilometres past Auggen, they reached the village of Müllheim, then a further half a kilometre to the junction. They turn left towards the battle lines, the guns and shells. The noise of the war getting louder the closer they got to the Rhine.

At Neuenburg-am-Rhein, they could see the river; the bridge still intact, ready for them to cross. As they reached the bridge, two German soldiers on the German side of the border stood in front of the vehicle, bringing the Tatra 111 to a halt.

Seeing the German officer Schick in the passenger seat, one of the German soldiers moved up the side of the truck to speak to him.

Schick opened the window and in German called down to him.

"I am Commander Schick; I have urgent supplies to get to our troops."

"Can I see your papers, sir?" asked the guard.

Schick putting his hand to his inside pocket, pulled out his credentials, handing them down to the soldier, who looked down at the papers.

The guard then looking back up at Schick who was now unbuttoning the clip on his Luger's holster.

The guard still looking up, studying Schick's face for a second, then back down to the papers.

Schick silently sliding the Luger from its holster, moving it to just below the window, his eyes looking at the guard the whole time.

"That's okay, sir," said the guard. "Sorry to have kept you."

Schick turning to Plant and without saying a word, nods his head, they move on.

Plant putting the truck into first gear, let out the clutch and over the bridge they head.

The French side of the bridge still had pockets of German troops holding ground around the bridges of Chalampé and Breisach to the north.

At Chalampé, they head south, taking the river road past the railway lines, until they are just outside the village of Ottmarsheim.

Schick knew of a barn he had planned to use, it was as close to the fighting, as he dared to go.

As they drove closer to the barn, an Allied shell dropped close to them, they swerved to miss the explosion.

Pulling up close the barn, jumping down from the truck, they ran towards a wall next to the barn doors, not knowing who, if anyone, would be inside.

Their backs to the barn wall, they slowly made their way to the main doors. The door slightly open, Plant looked through the crack, then turned back to Schick.

"There are three German soldiers inside, all on the opposite side, their guns pointing through gaps in the barn walls," Plant whispered to Schick.

Schick nodded to Plant.

"Follow me and do what I do," asserted Schick.

Schick stepped around Plant, opened the barn door. The three German soldiers jumped back quickly; their guns ready to fire at the intruders.

"It's okay," said Schick in German. "Just checking how we are getting on. So, tell me, how far is the enemy from here now?"

"Sorry sir, we weren't expecting you."

"That's okay," said Schick. "I'm here to assess the situation, to see what we could do next."

"Okay, sir," said the soldier. "The allied troops are working their way through the village... about half a kilometre."

"Okay you three, you had better get back to your observations, just in case the Allies head this way now."

"Yes sir," said the soldier.

The three soldiers turned back to the wall, their guns back through the holes and cracks in the barn wall and continued their watch for any Allied troops coming towards the barn.

Bang... Bang... Bang rang out of Schick's Luger as the three German soldiers fell to the ground, each with a hole in their back.

"Right," said Schick. "Quickly go and get the British uniforms from the truck. We have to get changed, unload the cases from the truck, and ditch the truck as soon as we can."

"Yes, Commander," said Plant.

"Well, that's the last time you will call me Commander, once I am in the British uniform, I will be a Polish fighter having joined the British forces."

"So, what do I call you then?"

"Then, you will be the senior officer, you will be back to Sergeant Plant and I will be Private Wiktor

Symanski."

"Private Symanski it is," agreed Plant.

Plant got the uniforms from the cab of the truck, along with an empty metal box that Schick had asked him to get, then took them back into the barn.

Changed into the British uniforms, they started work on their next tasks.

Plant backed the truck into the barn, they started unloading the cases. Putting them to one side, then covering with tarpaulin, hay and soil, camouflage, to hide the haul.

On the other side of the barn, Schick had retrieved the shovels and was digging a hole, having taken off his uniform, he folded it neatly into the metal case, along with his guns and documentation. This was lowered into the hole he had been digging.

On his return, the plan was for him to collect his uniform, make his way back over the border, to re-join with German troops, to then carry on as if nothing had happened.

Having finished the work, they needed to do in the barn, they jumped into the truck and drove it back towards the bridge at Chalampé, taking it off the road about half a kilometre from the bridge on the river side.

Taking their rifles and heading back to the barn. Reaching the barn about an hour later. In the distance, the Allied troops had cleared the village and were heading in the direction of the barn.

Two British soldiers crept through the long grass and divots caused by exploding shells, cautiously they moved towards the barn, expecting a hail of bullets to be fired at them at any moment; once the Germans troops defending the barn had caught sight of them.

But nothing, it was quiet, too quiet. Had the German troops fled already?

"It's okay, lads," called a voice from behind the barn. "We've cleared it already."

Plant leaning up against the side of the barn smoking a cigarette, Schick standing talking to him.

The two British soldiers, half-stand, uncertain if what they were being told was just to flush them out. Half-raised from their crawling positions on the ground, they moved forward.

"Are you sure?" one of them called out.

"Of course, I'm sure," called back the voice. "Come over, we are just having a little break"

The two soldiers, still not sure this was safe, crouch their bodies slightly. Their rifles out in front of them, wary that this could be a hoax, a way of getting them into the open, then to shoot them.

Slowly they eased forward, slightly protected by the edge of the barn wall, they made their way toward the front of the building.

"Want a cigarette?" called the voice.

"Are you British?" questioned the soldier.

"Well, I am," replied the voice. "The private, here working with me is Polish."

The soldiers reach the edge of the barn, the leading soldier putting his head close to the corner of the barn, with one eye he could see two soldiers in British uniforms, one a sergeant.

The sergeant leaning up against the edge of the

barn, the private a couple of paces away from him.

Both standing relaxed.

As the head of first British soldiers appeared around the side of the barn, the sergeant turned to look at him.

"What are you doing here?" asked the head.

"What are any of us doing here?" replied the sergeant.

"Well, we are here fighting a war, you seem to be standing in the middle of a war zone, smoking a cigarette."

Just then, a second head appeared, just above the first one.

"I know you," said the second head, in a cockney accent. "You're that Sergeant Plant!"

"Plant," said the first head.

"I'm Plant. This is Symanski."

"Oh, wow," said the second head. "We have heard so much about you."

"Nothing bad I hope," said Plant.

"No sir, they say you have a way of getting behind enemy lines and clearing a way for us to move forward," said the first head.

"Well, hopefully, you will find exactly the same now. This barn has been cleared of German fighters. And although I can't be sure as you get down towards the railway lines, I think there is a clear run almost to the bridge."

The two heads come out from behind the edge of the barn, walk over to Plant and shake him and Schick, now known as Symanski, by the hand.

"Are the troops far behind you?" asked Plant.

"About two hundred yards sir," said the first soldier.

"Okay," said Plant. "Tell you what to do, go back to your troop, let them know you have seen me, tell them that the barn is safe and to keep moving forward. But be aware of the buildings by the railway line."

"Yes, sir," they said together, in awe that they had met Sergeant Plant.

"And," continued Plant. "*Where* can I get a British truck?"

# Chapter 23
# Drive Time
# 21 February 1945

The early hours of the next day, Plant and Schick; now having the name of Wiktor Symanski, were on their way back to the barn.

Sergeant Plant having returned to the Allied side the day before, along with Schick posing as a Polish fighter, having joined the British Army.

They had managed acquire a truck later that day, a Fordson W.O.T 6.

Reaching the barn in the early hours, they uncover the cases, stacking them on the back of the truck.

As part of the Schick plan, the cases had been repainted with the words 'For Military Use' now in English.

Plant taking the first shift driving the vehicle as they head west and away from the war zone.

Plant driving the heavy truck for two hours, into the region of Burgundy, through Belfort, Montbéliard and on into the Boubs district, passing Bessançon, they journey west.

The biting February cold night air only just bearable in the cold and draughty cab, by the heat given off by the V8 3621cc engine of the Fordson truck.

Schick sleeping in the passenger seat, they

continued their journey.

Into Jura district passing Dole and on towards Beaune in the district of Côte D'or.

The road now turning south, Plant stopping the truck, taking an opportunity to jump out and stretch his legs.

Schick taking over the driving for the next couple of hours, Plant now in the passenger seat, grabbing the chance of some shut-eye for a while.

Heading south, into the district of Saône-et-Loire, they pass the towns of Chalon-sur-Saône and then Mâcon, before they finally leave the Burgundy region. They continued south.

Schick had a plan, a plan conceived in the months leading up to February 1945.

Schick knew the war was turning, the tide of control by the grip of the Nazi regime on Europe had been stretched too far.

Schick's game plan had had to take a new path.

The pieces on the board needed repositioning.

This was part of Schick's new plan.

He had guessed that the invasion tactics of the Allies would, of course, lead to a heavy bombardment of the cities of Germany, but the devastation of Dresden almost took his house and his family.

It was too close for comfort, he thought.

The time was now right to move the gold, find a new and very safe hideaway, somewhere it could not be found. There would be no heavy bombardment — no mass destruction.

The gold would then be looked after, until a time

of his convenience. A time that was right, the war over, the world a much calmer and safer place.

After a few hours, the truck had arrived at Lyon. The sun just starting to rise in the east as they saw a French café, French troops and trucks at the front of the small building, soldiers standing around the entrance smoking, while more were inside grabbing breakfast before their troop movement north, towards the push into Germany.

Plant and Schick jumped down from the truck, making their way into the café. Schick did all the talking, French with a Polish accent.

"Hey British, how can I help you?" said the middle-aged woman in French, standing behind the counter.

She wore a black knee-length dress, with long sleeves, belling out at the end, a white cotton shirt under the dress. Her hair had a red tint, she wore a red with white polka dot headscarf, tied into a knot at her forehead.

"Good morning, madame," said Schick "Two breakfasts please… and a large amount of coffee?"

"We don't have a lot, the troops here moving north have cleared out of most of the stock… but I can do you bacon and bread," she said, politely.

"That will be fine, madame," replied Schick.

"Go and find yourself somewhere to sit, I'll bring the coffee over straight away… it looks like you need it."

"That will be very kind of you, madame."

Schick looked around the café as two French soldiers were just getting up; having spotted the table becoming vacant, he pointed, saying to Plant, to sit there.

As they sat, the waitress arrived with two cups and a pot of coffee.

"There should be plenty in there," she said. "But there'll be more if you want it."

"Many thanks, madame," said Schick.

Plant nodded to the waitress.

Schick picked up the coffee pot and poured a cup, pushing it towards Plant, followed by the jug of milk.

"Well, Mr Plant," said Schick. "This is, I believe, the first time we have been able to sit and talk properly, no business, no war, no what side are we on... so tell me something about yourself."

"Me?" said Plant, taken aback. "Not a lot to say."

"Well, okay," Schick continued. "What do you do..."

"Didn't really do a lot before the war... my life... well, a quarter of it has been at war... I guess, I haven't known much else — apart from war."

"You didn't work before the war?"

"No, not really. Me and a friend would hang around, make a bit of money betting... times were hard in the East End slums then."

"Surely, you couldn't have made enough money to live on just betting?"

"Well, no, I guess there was more to it than that... I did do a bit of roughing up... for some of the local gangs... if you get my drift?"

"I'm afraid I don't, Mr Plant," said Schick, curiously. "Please explain?"

"Well, I guess I was known as a bit of a hard man... the local gangs didn't challenge me, nor was I involved with them. Mum wouldn't have liked me being involved with the local gangs..." said Plant as he looked up at Schick. "But if they wanted someone beaten up, they would come to me. For a small price, I would give someone a beating for them."

"Well, Mr Plant," said Schick, his eyes narrowing. "Should you be looking for work after the war, perhaps you could come and work for me?"

"You, Mr Schick?" said Plant, suspiciously. "But I thought you were a businessman?"

"Mmmm," said Schick, taking a sip of coffee. "There are business men... and there are business men."

The waitress laid a basket of sliced bread on the table.

"I don't understand," said Plant. "How can there be two types of businessmen?"

"Of course, Mr Plant," said Schick, with a smile on his face. "In the East End, you would only know them as the gangs... But the gangs... well, just did the dirty work... go up the ladder, at the top, there will be a legitimate business. Someone with a nice home and car... a nice family and a nice lifestyle. On the surface, they are running a successful import and export company. They go to work in the morning, they come home in the evening. But dig deeper and you find, the imports are not just tea from China, not just wood from Brazil or spices from the Middle East, but people! Arriving as imports, guns arriving as imports, opium... the list goes on."

"And this is your business?" enquired Plant.

"Why, of course, Mr Plant,"

The waitress walked towards their table as Schick stopped talking. She laid on the table two plates with two slabs of thick bacon.

"Thank you, madame," Schick said in French to the waitress, then continued talking to Plant.

"I, before the war, was a businessman. I had factories, I had houses. But to fill those houses, and cheap labour for the factories, I would import people."

"And it was successful you say?"

"Ah, very... before the war, of course, the war ended all that..." Schick's eyes narrowed. "As much as I love my country, Mr Plant, they took a lot of my workers and put them into concentration camps... so for me now... Well, I use the system to continue making money... it's what I do best Mr Plant... it's what I do best!"

"And you have a plan... a plan now, making money, with the hoard we are carrying?"

"I do... but, strategy does not come from just having one plan, of course. There is a preferred plan. But this may alter at any moment."

"But we are going south?" said Plant.

"South... yes, south Mr Plant... somewhere warm... well, at least, that is the plan!"

# Chapter 24
## A Warmer Climate
## 21 February 1945

Leaving Lyon, after refuelling the truck at a nearby depot, they stopped on the outskirts of Lyon and caught up on some sleep for a couple of hours.

Continuing their journey south later that day, taking two-hour stretches at the wheel.

Past Valence and towards Montélimar. The climate warmer the further south they went, the more comfortable the journey became.

But for both of them, the thought of a million dollars' worth of gold in the back of the truck, they could put up with a little cold.

A little after midnight, they had reached their destination, Marseille harbour.

They pulled into the dock area, turned the engine off and jumped down from the truck.

In the darkness, it was difficult to see anything, but Schick had something in mind. He knew the plan; he knew exactly what they needed to achieve.

He glared into the darkness, looking down the dock. He knew what he wanted so started to walk.

Plant was right there with him.

"What's on your mind?" said Plant.

"A ship," said Schick. "We need a ship."

"Well, there's plenty here."

"A particular ship, Mr Plant. I will let you know

when I see it!"

They continued walking. Around the old brick buildings and wooden storage warehouses, up and down the dock, in and out of the jetties. Schick searching for the missing piece, a piece that he knew should be there, and then...

"Ah," announced Schick, excited at what he had just found. "Here we are, exactly what we need!"

"A ship?" said Plant.

"Not just any ship Mr Plant... this is *our* ship!"

"Our ship?"

"Yes, our ship... now we have found it, we will return in the morning and seek out the captain. We need to know who is in charge of this vessel," said Schick

"Yes..." agreed Plant, not fully aware of Schick's plan.

# Chapter 25
## Suraat Allah
## 22 February 1945

Seven a.m. and a glimmer of light was appearing in the February sky. Schick and Plant stir, as the first light brightens the inside of the Fordson's cab. By 7:30, the sun was just starting to break the horizon, beams of early morning sunlight streaming up into the sky, orange glows on the underside of the high, frosty clouds.

"Okay," said Schick. "Let's go and find the captain."

Leaving the truck on the end of the dock, they made their way back to the ship that Schick had seen the night before.

"There it is," said Schick, pointing up at the mid-sized merchant vessel sitting quietly in a bay waiting to be loaded.

"How do you know that is the one?" asked Plant.

"Because it's going to the place we need to head for!"

"And that is?

"Algeria!"

The rusty hulk of a vessel looked barely sea worthy. Not a big ship, but ideal for carrying the loads that needed going to and fro the ports of the Mediterranean.

Schick knew this vessel had a good chance of

going to where he needed to be going, the countries to the east of Algeria, still being occupied by German troops.

It was a safe bet that Algeria or Morocco, were going to be the destination of this one.

Algeria was, after all, a French colony.

French troops, as well as Allies, would have been defending the country, pushing back the Nazi invaders who were fighting their way across Libya and Tunisia.

Merchant ships like this would have carried goods to the North African countries, food and shelters, such as tents and blankets, guns, ammunition and supplies.

The ship was registered in Algiers with the name *Suraat Allah*... Gods Path.

Schick and Plant walk up the gangplank, a wooden board with worn-out battens crossing the boards all the way to the top, ropes either side to use as handrails; an aid to the journey to the top.

As they reached the top, their first steps onto the ship, Schick in a British soldier's uniform, using the name of Symanski and Plant the sergeant, heard the sound of people talking in Arabic.

"*Bonjour?*" called Schick. The Arabic talking stopped.

"*Bonjour?*" he called again.

Two ship hands walk around the corner from the far-side of the bridge, carrying a broom each, they walk towards Schick and Plant. The seamen dressed in tatty worn-out, off-white, light cotton trousers, ripped in places. Sandals on their feet and off-white thin shirts with patches of grease.

Their hair tatty, dark and unclean, along with their dark olive skin. Both had greying beards.

"Good morning," said Schick in French. "We are looking to speak with the captain?"

"I'm sorry sir," said one of the seamen, bowing his head slightly. "The captain is not on board the ship at the moment."

"So," continued Schick. "Where can we find him?"

"At the moment, sir, he is best not to be disturbed," said the seaman, looking worried. "The captain stays in the town overnight, while we are in a French port."

"Is there any particular place that may be?"

"I wouldn't like to say, sir," said the seaman, looking at the other seaman. "We could be in trouble, so we don't ask."

"Of course, I understand," said Schick. "What time will he be back?"

"Nine a.m., sir… he should be back by nine a.m. The ship is due to be loaded at that time and I know he will like to be here to oversee the loading."

"And what is his name?"

"Abou Nasir sir… Captain Abou Nasir."

Schick thanked the seamen for their help as he and Plant made their way back down the gangplank.

Finding a bar, they had breakfast while they awaited the return of the captain.

\*\*\*

8:50 a.m. Schick and Plant were back on the dock, overlooking the gangplank to the *Suraat Allah*.

8:55 a.m. they see a man of an Arabian complexion walking towards the ship. He was medium height, wearing dark trousers and a dark blue, thick worn-out woollen roll-neck jumper, old and tatty around the bottom of the sleeves and neck.

On his head he wore a captain's hat, tatty and torn. It had a stained white upper flat top, a black peak, a black ring all the way around below the white top; a worn-out badge in the centre above the peak, in the shape of an anchor.

As he walked towards the gangplank, Schick and Plant reaching the wooden platform at the same time.

"Mr Nasir?" Schick asked him, in French.

"Yes," he replied. "And how can I help you?"

Nasir looked like a man of the world, strong and confident. He had seen many things and had lived through many more.

He had a short dark beard and dark eyes.

"Can we have a word with you? We are in need of moving something to Algeria."

"And, is there paperwork for what you need to move?"

"No, there is no paperwork, but we need to move it urgently!"

"No paperwork, then I am sorry… it cannot be done," said Nasir, as he turned to walk away.

"We would pay you handsomely!"

Nasir stopped and turned back towards Schick and Plant.

"Follow me," said Nasir, with a sideways movement of his head.

As Nasir stepped onto the gangplank, five seamen jumped to attention on the ship at the far end of the gangplank.

Since the crack of dawn, the dock had started to become alive with workers toing and froing. Goods, bags of food, boxes of all shapes and sizes running up and down the dock's jetty, some being delivered to the ship of Captain Nasir.

Nasir stepped onto the ship's deck, ordering the waiting seamen in Arabic to get on with their jobs. Two of the seamen running down the ship to steps that led to a lower deck, the other three heading off down the gangplank as they start loading items ready to be brought aboard the *Suraat Allah*.

"Follow me, gentlemen," Nasir said in French.

Nasir turned and walked toward the large rusty door to the bridge, stepping over the raised metal lip, the threshold of the door.

"This way please," he said.

Plant not being able to speak French, followed close behind Schick.

Plant having stepped onto the bridge, closed the door they had all just walked through as he continued to follow Schick. The back wall of the bridge had another door; a wooden door.

This was Nasir's quarters, a narrow bed in the corner, a wooden table to one side; clean and tidy.

Charts showing the Mediterranean on one wall. To the sides of the cabin were four portholes, with the early morning sunshine shining through to one side.

Below the portholes, rust followed the track where water had once run, leaking through the worn-out seals of the windows.

"Excuse my room, gentlemen," said Nasir. "Mine is a simple life and, I am afraid, I do not have many visitors to my ship."

"Mr Nasir, Mr Plant and I, in the last few years, have seen things many times worse than this," said Schick.

Nasir looked around the room, then turned to Schick.

"If you would excuse me one moment, I will get one of the ship's hands to fetch more chairs."

Schick nodded as Nasir stepped through the door to the bridge.

A few moments later, he returned, followed by one of the seamen carrying two battered and dirty wooden chairs.

"Gentlemen," said Nasir. "This is all I have in way of furniture."

"This will be fine," said Schick.

Nasir pulled the table into the middle of the room allowing the chairs to be sat on each side.

Schick placing his chair on the longer side of the table. Plant, the other side of the table, Nasir to the end.

"Now, gentlemen," said Nasir, putting the palms of his hands gently onto the table top. "You have something you need moving... and I take it, it is for your personal use?"

"This is correct, Mr Nasir," said Schick. "We

have a few little items, that, well, are not safe in Europe."

"And you feel Algeria would be a safer place to leave them… until after the war, maybe?"

"This is exactly what we are thinking," agreed Schick.

"Well, gentlemen," smiled Nasir. "I can say, I could deal with this for you. I'm afraid to say though, this isn't a ship built to carry passengers, our sleeping arrangements are simple… you would have to stay in the cargo hold… I can get one of the crew to set up a couple of hammocks for the journey."

"And the journey time?" asked Schick.

"Around about thirty hours," answered Nasir. "But we won't be able to enter the harbour until the following morning… it will be too dark to see and too dangerous."

"This will be fine."

"And there are no luxuries," continued Nasir. "I'm afraid, if you should need the toilet, it will be over the side of the ship."

"This, too, is okay."

"Now, the payment," said Nasir, sitting up and crossing his arms.

Schick put his hand inside the jacket of his coat, pulling out a hessian bag and handing it to Nasir.

"I think, Mr Nasir," said Schick, grinning. "This will be more than adequate for what we are asking you to do."

Nasir took the bag that Schick was holding in his direction, opening the string at the top, he poured the contents onto the table.

From the bag rolled around twenty gems of various types; mostly diamonds, emeralds and sapphires, with a couple of rubies and opals.

Nasir stood up and walked over to the bed, bending down, he pulled a wooden box from under the bed. In the box was a magnifying glass, which he carried back to the table.

He picked up the first, second and third of the gems, holding them close to his face. Looking through the magnifying glass, he studied the gems closely.

Picking up the fourth, fifth and sixth gems, studying these, a wry smile starting to appear on his face, his eyes raising from the gem, he looked over the magnifying glass, his eyes moving from Schick to Plant, then back to Schick.

Without checking the rest of the gems, Nasir picked up the precious stones one by one, placing them back into the hessian bag.

"Gentlemen," said Nasir, holding out his hand to Schick. "I think we have a deal"

Having shaken the hand of Schick and Plant, the captain went back about his duties of organising his crew as they load the ship.

Schick and Plant going back to get the truck, driving it to the *Suraat Allah*. They pulled up at the bottom of the gangplank.

Two of the crew jump up onto the back of the truck and start to move the boxes to the drop-down flap at the rear of the truck.

Jumping down from the truck, with one either end of the heavy cases, they walk them up the gangplank, then down into the hold.

The British Army truck empty of its contents, Schick and Plant drive the truck around to the railway yard at the back of the dock, parking it with other army trucks already there.

The truck will be fine left there for the next few days Schick told Plant. Once they had completed their task, they would return for the truck.

In the back of the truck, they change into the civilian clothes that Schick had arranged for them to use.

Schick wearing a dark blue-grey suit, baggy trousers with turn-ups, white shirt with a dark blue tie.

Plant in a beige suit, baggy trousers, white shirt and a red tie. Both wearing trilbies, Schick's matching his suit and Plant's a sandy colour.

Back at the ship, they walk up the gangplank to be greeted by Captain Nasir.

"Good afternoon, gentlemen," he said, smiling. "If you would make yourself comfortable in my quarters, we have nearly finished loading. Once complete, I will finish the paperwork with the authorities... We will be leaving port at about five p.m."

"Very good," said Schick.

The sun was starting to get lower in the sky as the day wore on, the ship fully loaded, the canvas sheet pulled over the hold for its trip to French Algeria.

The air in the ship was chilly, as around 4:30 p.m. the ship's engines fire into life.

The rusty hulk shudders and shakes, as the motion of the engines build to a vibrating tick over, the sound more even and rhythmic.

The seamen still running around the ship readying it for the sea, still wearing the light cotton trousers and tops, seemingly oblivious to the cold February late afternoon chill.

At five p.m., the vessel released its ropes, the captain at the helm as the hulk moved away from its berth, slowly easing its way along the harbour wall, *Suraat Allah* passing the harbour entrance, it made its way out to the open sea.

The Merchant vessel picking up speed as Marseille and a war-torn Europe grew dim against the early evening dusk; the ship moving further into open water, the French coast disappearing into the distance, the sun setting for the night. A cold mist on the surface of the sea as the ship headed into the dark night sky.

On board, Wilhelm Schick, Samuel Plant and sixteen cases filled with a million dollars' worth of gold ingots, destined for their temporary home.

# Chapter 26
## Death Any Second
## 23 February 1945

The next morning, Plant and Schick awoke to the droning of the vessel's relentlessly chugging engine.

The journey so far had been about thirteen hours. This led them to believe they were somewhere around the middle of the Mediterranean.

By the light of a small oil lamp, they made their way onto the deck, the sky still dark. But with the first hint in the east that the sun was on its way up.

Schick and Plant stood on deck looking out over the sea, watching the low light in the eastern sky.

The captain still in his bunk, where he will be until the day breaks, relying on the crew to look after the safe keeping of the ship overnight.

A swell had formed in the sea, a sign that the weather may be on the change. But for now, Schick and Plant felt the less calm sea was an advantage in waters known for sudden attacks from underneath. Later that day, Nasir had arranged for his two guests and himself to have evening dinner in his quarters.

\*\*\*

Schick and Plant had entered the bridge and knocked on the wooden door to Captain Nasir's quarters. After a moment or two, the door opened.

"Good evening," said Nasir in French. "Do come in!"

They stepped over the bulkhead wall and into Nasir's cabin.

"If you would like to take a seat?" Nasir continued.

The sun, hidden all day by the heavy clouds, now in the west. The long day at sea, it had been raining and a moderate breeze had blown up.

Samuel Plant not understanding the French language, followed what Schick did.

Guided by Schick's knowledge of French, it was easier for Plant to just drift along with what others did.

"Thank you," said Schick in French.

"Thank you," said Plant in English as they sat.

Captain Nasir shut the door, he then followed Schick and Plant to the table, pulled out his chair and sat at the end. Schick to his right and Plant to his left.

The table was laid out ready for dinner, including a bottle of red wine.

"The crew will be bringing dinner through shortly," said Nasir, looking at Schick. "Would you like a glass of wine?"

"That would be much appreciated," said Schick.

Nasir picked up the bottle and filled Schick's glass, he then turned his attention to Plant, Nasir held up the bottle in the direction of Plant and nodded.

Plant understood this to mean, would he like a glass. He nodded back and said, "Yes please."

Nasir lifted the bottle and poured the deep red

liquid into the glass of Plant. He lowered the bottle back to the table, picked up a decanter of water and poured this into his own glass.

"Will you not be joining us in a glass of wine?" said Schick, looking at the glass of water.

"I am afraid not, my friend," said Nasir. "My faith does not allow me to partake in alcohol"

"Ah, a man of Islam," smiled Schick.

"I am, sir!"

"And your faith is dear to your heart then, Captain Nasir?"

"It most certainly is, Mr Symanski," said the captain, using the Polish name that Schick was travelling under.

There was a knock at the door of the cabin.

"Excuse me one-second gentlemen... this must be our dinner."

Nasir stood up and walked over to the door, turning the handle, he pulled the door towards him. Standing the other side of the door stood two of the crew, shabbily dressed, dark hair, unshaven and thin. They carried trays, one with a large tureen of stew, the other tray filled with a pot carrying boiled potatoes.

"*Sayidi taeamik,*" said the seaman carrying the tureen. "Your food, sir!"

"*Jayid, aihdarah,*" replied the captain. "Good, bring it in."

The two crewmen stepped over the lip of the door, their heads and eyes held down, fearing to look up.

They moved across the room towards the table

as the captain shut the door.

The light fading outside, the room now filled with the light of two oil lamps, one on either side of the room, hanging from a hook between the portholes.

The curtains shut, covering the porthole, not allowing light to escape.

The seamen walk around the table, the first lifting a ladle of the stew from the tureen and gently letting it flow into the dish of Schick.

As the tureen tray moved onto Plant, the second crew member took three potatoes from his pot and added them to the dish of Schick, then following the first tray onto Sergeant Plant.

A smaller tray of bread was placed in the middle of the table.

As the two crewmen finished, they stood beside Nasir for instructions.

"*Qad tadhhab al'an*," Nasir instructed them. "You may go now."

"*Sayidi*," the crewmen said in unison. "Sir!"

They turned and left the cabin.

"Eat up, gentlemen," said Nasir, raising his glass of water to them both.

Schick and Plant raised their glasses to the captain.

"It is a real pleasure to have company," Nasir continued. "Oh, the food, by the way, is a lamb stew. The crew slow cook it on the engine… I'm sure you will find it to your taste."

"Mmm, this is excellent," agreed Schick. "My compliments to the crew then!"

"This is…" Nasir hesitated. "Not a very safe journey, I'm sure you are aware of that?"

"Not safe?" questioned Schick.

"Yes, Mr Symanski, merchant ships in the middle of the Mediterranean. This is not a safe place to be. Merchant vessels are a common target for U-boats or attacked from the sky. It's all a matter of luck, right place at the wrong time, if you get my meaning?"

Plant sat eating his dinner, listening to the conversation but not understanding what was being said.

"Have you been doing this trip long?" asked Schick.

"Since 1942, as France was taken over by the Nazi forces, so French Algeria got drawn into the war, the Allied forces came to North Africa. I already owned this vessel, so I started moving… well, anything that was needed."

"So," said Schick. "You feel you have been lucky?"

"In war, my friend," said the captain. "Death could happen at any second… it would only take one torpedo to hit us now, and it is all over!"

"You must live in constant fear?" said Schick.

"I keep my trust in God, Mr Symanski. Allah will keep me and my crew safe," said Nasir. *"in sha' Allah,* if God is willing."

Schick and Plant finish their glasses of wine. The captain pouring two more for them.

"Please drink, my friends," he said. "This can be a long and arduous journey. If it pleases you, I will make the most of having you as my guests onboard."

"We, too, are pleased to have the company," said Schick. "What do you see yourself doing after the war?"

"Oh, the war," the captain sighed. "Things have got to change, this is not a good way to do business. The constant fear of death... not good. And you people, the Europeans, British, German, Dutch, Spanish, can't keep just walking into countries just because you feel like it! Africa, South America and Asia... carrying your guns and your weapons, taking over other lands by force. Telling the local population what to do, how to act, even when the native people don't want it that way... it's forced upon them."

"You sound very angry about that!"

"You ask what I will be doing after the war," said Nasir as he sat upright "None of us know the future, we do not know what will happen in five years' time. But in five years' time, we will know what has happened now. We can know the past, but we cannot know the future... but we can plan, we can dream."

"And your dream, Mr Nasir," said Schick. "What is your dream?"

"Like most people of my land, I dream of independence!"

"Independence?"

"Yes, Mr Symanski, for it to no longer be French Algeria... for it just to be Algeria... El Djazair!"

"And you feel this dream will be beneficial for your people?"

"It will... once the war is over. It will be seen that

it is not good for a bigger, more powerful nation to walk into a country and just take it over... we will want our nationality back, we will be a country in our own right... we wish to be the masters of our own destiny."

The captain stood up and walked over to the porthole, pulling back the curtain. He peered through the hazy glass.

The darkness of the night had now engulfed the ship, the sea still having a swell, but not enough to cause the merchant vessel any problems.

He turned back to Plant and Schick, sitting at the table.

"It will be around three to four hours before we reach land," said the captain.

"We are grateful for what you have done for us," acknowledged Schick.

"Grateful," said the captain. "There is no need to be grateful. This, gentleman, is just business!"

"But, of course."

"And, as business goes," continued Nasir. "I feel you may need some help when you reach our destination?"

"This is correct," said Schick. "One way or another, we need to deal with our cases."

"And, presumably, you will be needing to store the boxes?"

"Until after the war," said Schick.

"Ah, we are back to the future, a time scale, we do not know."

"It is not difficult to see, the tide is turning, the Nazi invasion of Europe and North Africa is coming to a close," acknowledged Schick.

"But time, we still do not have!" said Nasir.

"We would want these cases to be out of Europe, for a while... a time, of possibly two years."

"So, if I could find someone to look after the boxes for this amount of time, you would be pleased with that?"

Schick stopped and thought for a moment, then nodded.

"Yes."

"Okay," said the captain. "I will arrange for someone to look after your boxes for a couple of years... But this will be business, there will have to be a payment."

"I would not expect anything less, Captain Nasir."

"And the payment will be in gems?"

"Gems will be fine with us," agreed Schick.

"And you have them with you?"

"The gems, Captain Nasir," said Schick, leaning forward. "Are safe, I do not carry them with me, they are hidden away... but, as I have already shown you... I will pay generously for any help in achieving my final goal."

"So, the payment will be?" asked Nasir.

"You deliver us to a place we can keep the cases safe, unseen and unspoken about for the next two years... we will pay you in gems, a generous number of gems... Enough to see you out, for the rest of your life. But to do this, we would need you to take us on the return trip to France. There we will see to it that you get half the full amount now, the remaining, we will give to you in two years when we return for our cases…"

"This sounds like an offer I cannot refuse," said the captain.

"I have tried to make it that way… we need to trust you, you need to trust us… Captain Nasir… this is a good business deal!"

"Yes… I believe it is Mr Symanski."

Both Schick and the Captain took a deep breath and leaned back into their chairs.

Schick explained to Plant what the deal was going to be. He listened, nodded and asked a few questions, but he, too, could see that this was a great deal… for both parties.

Captain Nasir will have enough wealth to last many years. Once the war was over, Schick and Plant would return to pick up the cases, the wealth for their future.

"So, Captain Nasir," asked Schick. "What is the next move?"

"We are about three hours from the French Algerian coast… we won't be able to dock tonight. It will be far too dangerous. The docks and town have taken a lot of heavy bombardment since we became involved in the war." The captain leant forward. "We will move quietly towards the coastline, keeping to shallow waters, it is less likely to be hit by a torpedo there. It will be night-time, so we will drop anchor offshore till the morning. We will make our way into port at the break of day… around 08:00 hours, docking should be about 08:30."

"And our cases?" asked Schick.

"Once we have docked," the captain said, "I will

get a couple of boys to wheel the boxes to my friend's house, there they will put them into the basement of their house... I guarantee they will be safe there!"

"How will he know we are coming?"

"I will send a boy on in front, while the cases are being taken from the ship... I will send my friend a note, explaining what we have spoken about."

"Can we trust him?" said Schick, as his eyes narrowed.

"But of course," said Nasir, smiling. "You will find, as French Algerians, we are friendly, generous... and very honest... You will have nothing to worry about... your boxes will be extremely safe with us."

"Then, Captain Nasir... I think we have a deal!"

Schick stood up and held his hand out for the captain to shake. The captain immediately responded by getting to his feet. Sergeant Plant followed as he realised the deal had been done.

The captain firmly shook the hand of Schick, then turned to Samuel Plant and vigorously shook his hand also, as they smiled and laughed at the good work. After a moment, they sat back down.

"I feel we have achieved a successful end to our deal Mr Plant," Schick said to his partner.

"So where is the gold going to be held?" Plant said to Schick.

Schick turned to the captain.

"So, what is the town we are going to then, Captain Nasir?" Schick asked the captain in French.

"Bône, gentlemen..." The captain said, "We are going to Bône!"

# Summer Present-day

## The South Bank, London

# Chapter 27
## South Bank
## Summer Present-day

Tom had turned up early for lunch, frustrated with his lack of progress.

He sat on a round bench overlooking the Thames. The bench encircling a tree in the middle of the footpath.

It was late morning, the path full of tourists admiring the views of Big Ben, Saint Paul's Cathedral and The Shard.

Tom could think of none of these, his mind preoccupied.

Tom had felt he had a lot to be grateful for. Kristina had been a big influence on his life; her love of people, the planet, the wildlife.

She would take on challenges, determined to make each and every one a success.

He sat, remembering what she looked like; her dark skin, her long wavy auburn hair, smooth complexion, determined eyes.

When she was home, he would remember how they would mould together.

But the loss of his friend Professor Wise had made him realise the frailty of life. The way it could suddenly end, the way things could just suddenly change from huge excitement, as the Professor was that final morning, to... well, gone.

And why, why him… wrong place, wrong time?

And did the police ever find the driver, the car that did it?

He hoped they were getting closer to catching the culprit, people like that should not be driving, should not be on the road. People drive too fast, too impatiently and don't look where they are going, in their own little world; no care for others.

"Tom!" he suddenly heard a man's voice call his name, snapping him out of his dream.

"Tom!" his name was called again as he looked up.

Walking towards him, mixed up in the crowd of tourists was Sebastian, a woman at his side, her arm through his arm, they walked together.

Tom standing as Sebastian and the woman walked up to him.

"Hi Bastian," said Tom.

"Good to see you, buddy," said Sebastian with a smile.

"Sorry about that," said Tom, half shaking his head. "I was deep in thought."

"That's okay," said Sebastian happily. "I would like you to meet my friend."

Tom looked at the woman

"Tom, this is Jennifer," said Sebastian as he turned to Jennifer. "And Jen, this is my friend Tom… Tom is the brains here… certainly with this sort of thing, following trails and puzzles."

"Tom," said Jennifer, like she had never seen him before. "How wonderful it is to meet you… Bastian has spoken about you with such enthusiasm!"

"Jennifer," said Tom. "It is lovely to meet you too!"

"Now, Tom... Jennifer," said Sebastian. "Lunch?"

Sebastian turned, with Jennifer still holding onto his arm.

Tom picked up the felt bag he had put down on the bench, then followed where Sebastian led.

Walking past the National Theatre, they headed west along the footpath following the river. A woman in silver standing on a small box, standing perfectly still, statuesque, suddenly she changes position.

A group of six Jamaican acrobats in bright coloured shorts and T-shirts perform their act, as the three, walk past.

Under Waterloo Bridge, they head in the direction of Jennifer's hotel.

A train rumbling over Hungerford Bridge. Just passed Festival Pier, they take a seat on the walkway of one of the many restaurants dotted along the Queen's Walk overlooking the Thames.

The sun was shining; it was a beautiful day. A gentle breeze blew the smell of wonderful cooking in their direction.

"So, Tom," said Sebastian. "What have you found?"

"Well," said Tom, sheepishly. "There's some good... and some not so good!"

"Umm," questioned Sebastian. "Good? not so good? What's that supposed to mean?"

Sebastian looked around at Jennifer, then back to

Tom.

"Oh, Tom, you can talk openly, I have told Jennifer everything that I know, she will be with me," continued Sebastian.

"Oh, okay," said Tom, pulling his notepad out of his bag. "Ah... well, the German wording, well, that's kind of self-explanatory. I mean, it's German, easy to translate."

"But is it still there?" interrupted Sebastian. "The gold?"

"Don't know... and I don't think we are ever going to know... unless we find it,"

"And finding it?"

"Well, we have a limited number of clues to go by... and a hell of a lot of time has passed since the cases were put there!"

"So," sighed Jennifer to Tom. "You don't think we will ever find the gold?"

"Well, never say never," smiled Tom. "We will never be absolutely sure... until we see for ourselves."

A waiter stopped beside the table, dressed in a black shirt, and black trousers, thin but with a round smiling face.

"Would you like something to drink, madam, gentlemen?"

"Sex on the beach please," instructed, Jennifer.

Sebastian's cock twitched.

"And gentlemen?" asked the waiter.

"I'll have a house white wine," said Sebastian. "And you, Tom?"

"Orange juice and lemonade please."

"Very good," said the waiter. "And will you be eating?"

"I think so," said Sebastian.

"Then I will fetch over the menus for you."

Sebastian stretched back in his chair, leaning back, putting his hands behind his head, looking at all the people walking up and down the footpath: tourists, office workers, police officers and shop workers.

*I want that gold*, he told himself, the wealth… the power… *I want to be rich, really rich, enough to get out of this rat race.*

Sebastian knew deep down inside, there was only one option… the cases had to be found.

"And what about the Arabic writing then, Tom?" said Sebastian. "Any news on that front?"

"This, I am afraid to say," said Tom, partly frustrated, "was not as clear as I would have hoped."

"Why is that?" asked Jennifer.

"My two good friends, Omar and Jamil, spent some time going over it."

"You didn't tell them what it was about?" Sebastian jumped in, making it clear he didn't want other people to know about the contract.

"No, of course not… they know my job is researching this sort of stuff. To them, it's just another job."

"Oh, okay then," said Sebastian relaxing again.

"So, what *did* they tell you then Tom?" asked Jennifer.

"Well, it would seem that, that is, from what they said, if a word has a direct equivalent word in the

English language, for example, 'Hand'" Tom said, as he held up his hand "The Arabic word for hand is 'yd', so, as you see… words with an exact translation, will be easy to go from one language to the other."

Tom picked up his notepad and opened the page with some Arabic writing, he points at a symbol:

يد

"To use this as an example," Tom continued "This is how you would write Arabic for 'hand'. Omar and Jamil found the translation of this type of word easy. But when it came to obscure words or 'names', this became the difficulty."

"So, they were completely no help?" asked Jennifer.

"Well, shall we say partially," Tom carried on. "Some of the information from them was perfect, other stuff, *well,* will need more time to follow up."

"What do you mean… follow up?"

The waiter arrived with the drinks on a round tray. He laid three paper doilies on the table, then the three drinks on each doily. Beside each glass, he laid a napkin. Finally, he put down the menus.

"Thank you," said Sebastian.

"You are very welcome sir," said the waiter, partially bowing. "I shall return in a few minutes to take your order… sir, madam."

The waiter turned and walked away from the table.

"What Jamil and Omar had said for definite were," Tom read from his notes "'The family of Ben Dee promise'," he hesitated, looking up, then back down at the notebook. "'To look after the cases'…

'and to keep them safe in the basement of our house'."

"Basement... house?" said Jennifer "They are in the basement of a house," she said excitedly, looking up at Sebastian.

"'Until they collect them'," Tom went on.

"They?" interrupted Sebastian "Who the hell are 'they'?"

"I don't know," said Tom. "That confused me too... it is suggesting there is a third party, more people involved than just the two signatures on the contract."

"No," said Sebastian, sharply. "There can't be, no, no, there can't be!"

"Well," said Tom. "As we said before, there is only one way to make sure."

The waiter came and took their order.

"So, what else did they say?" Jennifer asked Tom.

"Apart from God is their witness... that's when it got really confusing."

"More confusing," huffed Sebastian. "Can it get more confusing?"

"Well, yes... it seems that below that is the name of someone... or maybe a place."

"And that is?" asked Jennifer.

"Silsitin, or Celestine," said Tom. "Then Bourgogne, or Borgon, or maybe Bourgoin, the translation wasn't exactly clear."

Tom put his hands out to the side and shrugged his shoulders.

"I don't... well at least at the moment, know the

answer to this one," Tom continued. "But we do have a name... the Arabic name at the bottom of the Contract is: Mustafa Ben Dee."

"So, you're saying," said Jennifer, looking for confirmation. "We have a name Mustafa Ben Dee, we also have that it's in a house, that it's in a basement?"

"Yes," said Tom.

"But what we don't have is a street, a town, a city, or even a country," she said.

"That is exactly where we are," Tom agreed.

"And we still don't even know if it's still there!" sighed Sebastian.

"Mmm," said Tom. "Not sounding good... so far, is it?"

They went into a quiet thoughtful moment, then Jennifer interrupted.

"So, Tom... what's your gut feeling, where do you think we should go from here?"

"Well, let's assume it hasn't been touched," Tom answered. "We now have the date that both Samuel Plant and Wilhelm Schick were together, it's on the contract... and that both of them were close to the Rhine at Mulhouse in France."

"And then?" said Jennifer.

"I have a piece of paper from the box I was sent, that has Marseille, and a boat, which mean nothing on their own. But, as a theory, it could be at Marseille, or somewhere between Mulhouse and Marseille is where we need to look."

"So, you think we should head there?" asked Jennifer.

"I would say... that if all of us are up for it... let's

go to Mulhouse and try and work out what was in their thinking. Head towards Marseille..."

The waiter arrived with three steel dishes, a wire handle at each side of the dish. The dishes were filled with paella. They ate as they continued to talk about the possible trip.

"So," said Jennifer to Tom. "You think we should make our way towards the Med, via eastern France?"

"Yes."

"Are you really sure about this?" interrupted Sebastian. "What if it's a wild goose chase, a complete waste of money?"

"Oh, come on!" mocked Jennifer, rubbing her hand up and down his thigh... aren't you just a bit curious?"

"Well..." exclaimed Sebastian.

"If we don't go... we will never know," smiled Jennifer. "And if we do go and find the boxes, we could be sitting on untold wealth!"

Jennifer and Tom both looking at Sebastian waiting for an answer.

"Oh, go on then," Sebastian said, narrowing his lips and huffing as he thought about the expense. "Looks like we are going to France!"

"Right choice," said Jennifer. "Now Tom, can you get everything together before tomorrow morning... Bastian and I will pick you up at about 8:00 a.m., is that okay?"

"Yes, perfectly okay, and yes, I will head back to the office and get everything together that I think we might need!"

"Bastian..." said Jennifer, turning towards

Sebastian. "You will be picking me up from my hotel in the morning... we are going on an adventure."

After lunch, Jennifer and Sebastian headed off to pack, Sebastian back to Stratosphere Tower and Jennifer to the County Hall Hotel, just a couple of hundred metres from where they were having lunch.

Tom went back to the office to organise everything he might need for the trip to the South of France.

Then to go home and pack... *a clean pair of shorts, a T-shirt and flip-flops*, yes, he thinks... *that's all I should need.*

# Chapter 28
## Pack up, Pick up
### Summer Present-day

Just before eight a.m. the next morning, Tom was in his houseboat, clearing things away, readying himself for the journey to France. Into a felt holdall went his shorts, T-shirt, sandals, hat and passport.

Tom liked to travel light.

A separate hessian bag held the information from the German box, now in a new unburnt cardboard box file.

Tom's phone rang, Sebastian and Jennifer were on their way and would be at the South Dock in a few minutes. Tom picked up his things, slinging the two bags over his shoulder, had a last look around, then made his way out of the door, locking up the houseboat, knowing he would be away for at least a few days.

Along the walkway, towards the parking area just as Sebastian's car turned up, into the dock road, turning into a parking space.

Sebastian's car stopped and out he jumped.

An Aston Martin DB11 Volante, bright orange and gleaming.

The number plate caught Tom's attention as he walked towards the car of Sebastian, BA57IAN.

"C'mon, hurry up!" urged Sebastian, as he stood beside his car.

The door wide open.

Sebastian leaned in, pulling the driver's seat forward ready to let Tom get into the rear seats.

Tom leaned forward into the car, threw his two bags onto the far side of the rear seat, then to see Jennifer on the front passenger seat.

"Hi Jennifer," said Tom. "Sleep well?"

"On and off," replied Jennifer. "Excited about today!"

"Just get in!" urged Sebastian. "Let's get going!"

Tom stepped into the car, making himself comfortable on the white leather rear seats, clicking in his seat belt.

Sebastian's seat clicked back into position as he jumped into the driver's seat, slipping on his seat belt, he hit the start button, the engine bursting into life with a roar, before settling into a throaty rumble.

Sebastian looking back over his shoulder, past Tom as he reverses back.

Into gear and away they go.

Tom looking back out of the side window, as his houseboat disappeared behind the houses and flats that surround the dock.

"Did you find anything new yesterday Tom?" said Jennifer as she looked back at him.

"'Fraid not," replied Tom. "I'm hoping now, that with all the information we have… something will jump out at us as we travel."

Sebastian's Aston Martin speeding away from Rotherhithe, it headed towards Deptford.

"What's your guess then Tom," asked Sebastian. "Where do you think it is most likely to be?"

"Mmm," Tom thought. "I'd say, mmm, if I were a gambling man, I think we will find it at Marseille... what with the note from the captain in Marseille. But even that is hard to tell, could be, they might have dropped it off before, and had just carried on to Marseille."

At Deptford, the car turned south towards Deptford Bridge Station, then on past Brookmill Park, picking up the A20 at Lewisham. From here, Sebastian could pick up a little more speed.

Onto the Sidcup Road, then the by-pass as they made their way towards the M25.

Under the M25, the A20 turning into the M20.

Soon to pass Maidstone, Leeds Castle and Ashford. At just under an hour and a half, they pull into the Folkstone Le Shuttle.

Getting out of the car, stretching their legs, they wait to board the train.

***

The thirty-five-minute journey under the English Channel bringing the three of them into France. The train pulling up in Calais.

Off of Le Shuttle, leaving Calais just before midday, making their way onto the A26 towards Lens, reaching Reims, they stop for lunch at a local bar.

Back onto the A26, they pass Châlons-en-Champagne, Saint-Dizier and Nancy on the N4.

Following the route to Colmar, they reach Kintzheim, where they turn south, reaching

Mulhouse at just after seven p.m. that evening.

Dropping Tom off at the Camping de I'ill on the Rue Pierre de Coubertin, Sebastian and Jennifer making their way over the Canal du Rhône au Rhin, past the Gare du Mulhouse as they head for Avenue de la 1ére Division Blindée and the Villa Eden.

The next morning, Tom left the Camping de I'ill, making his way the two and a quarter kilometres over the canal, heading for the Villa Eden. Joining Jennifer and Sebastian for breakfast, chatting about Mulhouse, and that all those years ago, this is where, at least for them, it all began.

Breakfast over, back into the Aston and they're off. From Mulhouse, they find the A36 and head for the Bourgogne region of France. Having now dismissed the thought that the Arabic writing and it's mentioning of Bourgogne could have meant the Burgundy region. They concluded that: the possibility that there could have been an Arabic connection in that area at the time of the war was very unlikely, it had to be further south. So, further south they are heading.

Passing Belfort, Montbéliard then Besançon, they reach Dole. Just past Dole they turn south onto the A39, making their way towards Lons-le-Saunier and Bourg-en-Bresse reaching Lyon at lunchtime.

After the break, the A7 taking them the rest of the journey to Marseille. The whole of the journey from Mulhouse to Marseille was filled with speculation, could the boxes be here, or there?

Tom thumbing through the papers seeing if any signs or local names would mean anything to help the search, but no joy.

Jennifer had rung ahead of arriving in Marseille. She had booked for her and Sebastian to stay at the Hotel Sofitel Vieux Port on the Boulevard Charles Livon, next to the harbour. Tom booked a bed for the night at the Vertigo Hostel Vieux Port on the Rue Fort Notre Dame.

The two-day journey had been long, and it was starting to feel that it was all going to be fruitless. Were they doing all of this for no reason? Had too much time passed, had the boxes already been taken? Could, the reconstruction of towns and villages along the way, after the devastation of the war, mean that the boxes would now be buried under some building construction somewhere? Made into a housing estate or an office block?

They all felt like they needed rest, to recoup and start afresh; tomorrow, the search would continue in Marseille.

# Chapter 29
## A Place of Learning
## Summer Present-day

Tom had had a bad night's sleep; the hostel was good. But a mixture of strange surroundings, noise and his thoughts had kept his brain too active, it would not shut off to sleep properly.

Sebastian and Jennifer were also tired; in their case, their bodies had been too active.

Having got up early, Tom made his way to the Sofitel Marseille on foot, at eight a.m., meeting Jennifer and Sebastian for breakfast and to work out what they would do next.

"Good morning, Tom" called Jennifer as Tom walked into the breakfast room.

"Good morning Jennifer, Bastian," replied Tom.

Sebastian nodded as he drank his coffee.

"Have a seat, Tom," said Jennifer. "Have you eaten?"

"No, not yet."

"I'll get the waiter to get you a breakfast then."

Jennifer turned to the waiter standing close to the wall.

Having seen Jennifer grabbing his attention, he walked over.

"Waiter, could you get a full English breakfast for our friend please?"

"Certainly, madame," replied the waiter, who

promptly turned and walked towards the kitchen.

"Are you all right Tom?" asked Jennifer, as he looked a bit bleary.

"Didn't sleep very well... just a bit tired."

"What, still thinking about our challenge?"

"Yes," said Tom. "I feel we have to work this out today... I mean, we can't keep at this for ever."

"Do you think we are getting close then, Tom?" asked Sebastian.

"I certainly think Marseille has the answer, but what that answer is and how we will find it...? Well, let's see how the day goes," Tom said, yawning.

Tom's breakfast arrived. Jennifer took a sip of her coffee.

"So... what is the plan?" said Sebastian.

"Well," said Tom enjoying egg and hash browns "I am going to start at the Archives. I want to see why, in the box, there was a reference to a ship, and the ship's captain. I am hoping he may have a residence here in Marseille; the Archives might help."

"And us?" asked Jennifer.

"I would like you two to go to the Town Hall," Tom continued. "Find anything you can about... well, an Arab quarter, an Arabic community in Marseille during the war... you know the sort of thing!"

"But neither of us speak French!" Sebastian pointed out.

"I can only suggest that you find someone, someone who works in the Municipal building. I mean, surely there's someone who should speak

English!"

Sebastian looked at Jennifer.

"Okay," he said. "I guess we can try!"

"And what if we don't find anything?" said Jennifer.

"We have to," said Tom. "It's here, something is here."

"So, where is the Town Hall?" asked Sebastian.

"Here," said Tom picking up a napkin. "This is the address… Avenue Roger Salengro. If you get a taxi, they should know where it is!"

"Let's hope we come up with something." smiled Jennifer.

"Yes… let's," sighed Sebastian.

Having all finished breakfast, the three headed for the entrance to the Hotel Sofitel, waiting outside were two taxis.

Jennifer and Sebastian jumping into one, ready to make the short journey to the other side of the Vieux Port, and a visit to the council buildings, hoping that any lead here will be helpful.

Tom was on his way to the Archive de l'Etat Civil de Marseille.

"Rue Clovis Hugues!" Tom told the driver and he was on his way.

From the hotel, the taxi almost immediately went into the tunnel under the Vieux Port, the tunnel popping up into the light, then back into the tunnel once more.

Right and right again, up a slip road, the taxi emerged into the light. Tom's cab heading down the Boulevard de Paris.

Tom's exhaustion from lack of sleep trying to catch up with him. As the taxi bounced along the road, Tom's head bouncing along with it.

At the end of the long road, they turn left, la Gare de Marseille Saint Charles in front of them. Down the Rue Honnorat, as it ran parallel with the station, its heavily graffitied walls and buildings. Another left and there was the Archives.

Tom got out of the taxi and paid the driver, walked across the road and into the entrance of the Archives. He had a sudden unease; a feeling that this was not the right place.

The building itself was lovely, the architecture inside was wonderful, the wood, the design. Tom had a love of these things, but for now, it looked too small, would it hold the information he needed? The timespan was a long time ago.

He decided he would give himself an hour, if he felt he wasn't on the right track, he would try somewhere else.

\*\*\*

Jennifer and Sebastian had arrived at the Avenue Roger Salengro.

The taxi drove away as they spun around to look at the place they needed to go.

"Reminds me of Rhubarb and Custard?" commented Sebastian.

"Mmmm," exclaimed Jennifer.

Through the, what appeared to be high security gates, Sebastian and Jennifer felt a bit out of place, convinced this was not working for them. But they had to play their part in the search, so continue they did.

Through the doors and to the desk.

"Hello," said Sebastian to the smartly dressed woman sitting behind the counter. "We need some help. Do you speak English?"

The woman behind the counter smiled at Sebastian.

"Pardon, *monsieur*, I speak not *Anglais*," she said.

"Is there anyone here who speaks English?" asked Jennifer.

"*Je suis désolé, madame.*"

Sebastian turned to Jennifer.

"So, what do we do now?" he said.

"I think wherever we go, not speaking French, with the questions we need to ask, it's going to be difficult..." said Jennifer, shrugging her shoulders. "Now listen, Tom's the expert here, if anyone is going to work this out, it's *not* going to be us, we are just wasting our time trying to do the things that Tom can do."

"So," said Sebastian. "What do you suggest?"

"I suggest, we relax, get a taxi back into town, do a bit of shopping... and let Tom get on with what he does best."

\*\*\*

Tom had spent an hour at the Archive de l'Etat, and it was proving fruitless, his tiredness not helping. He had difficulty concentrating; it was hard to keep his eyes open while reading lots of words in French.

Talking to the receptionists behind the desk of the Archive, they had mentioned the 'new' Archive... and that might be more helpful, they had suggested.

A taxi ride later, Tom was on his way down Boulevard de Paris, right into Rue Mirès and left into Rue Peyssonnel to stop outside the Archive et Bibliothéque Departmental Aston Defferre.

*'This looks a bit more like it,'* Tom said to himself. *'Maybe now we will get somewhere.'*

\*\*\*

By lunchtime, Jennifer and Sebastian were sitting, looking out over the sea, enjoying a glass of wine and a snack at Les Terrasses du Port.

They hadn't been in the centre long, but Jennifer knew she needed to see more.

"Did you see those shops?" she said to Sebastian.

"Yeh, Hugo Boss... I must go there!"

"Zara, Bershka... American Vintage!"

"Well, let's face it..." said Sebastian leaning back on his chair. "There is no rush... until we hear back from Tom... we are stuck."

"How do you think he is doing?"

"Don't know, I just hope he has a lead," Sebastian said, leaning forward again. "But I'm starting to think it would be a miracle if we found a lead to it now."

"Mmmm," sighed Jennifer. "I just hope you are not right... I trust Tom, he is good at what he does...

Oh, I know he will do his best, but it may be that this is the one that *cannot* be found!"

"It's only a little after midday, there are several more hours."

"Oh, but this morning," laughed Jennifer, "I thought he was going to go to sleep over the table… just hope we are not sitting here waiting for him to come back with some news… and he has fallen asleep on some bench somewhere."

\*\*\*

By mid-afternoon, Tom had found some information relating to the *Suraat Allah* and the captain, Captain Abou Nasir. But nothing that would help the search, brief mentions on logs, or some documents retrieved from the harbour after the war.

Tom was hoping that Abou Nasir had a residence in Marseille, a home and a family. That Nasir may have had a friend, someone he would have trusted, someone in Marseille who would look after the boxes. Tom stretched and turned his head to see the people around him. The quiet of the reading room, lots of faces, men and women; old and young, all searching for the information that they needed.

Books, posters, pictures, paintings and charts filled the walls, computers on the desks and tables; two women, one standing and one sitting behind the reception counter, chatting quietly to people just leaving.

Tom needed a breakthrough… and it wasn't coming!

Sebastian had bought a new pair of deck shoes and a white Fred Perry T-shirt. Jennifer had by mid-afternoon been in most shops, Sebastian carrying several bags and the tally so far at around seven hundred euros.

There were bags filled with shoes; silver high heels and a pair of flats, white with a lace tie up around the ankles. Dresses and skirts including: a long-sleeved maxi dress of indigo blue and grey flecks, a mini dress of a lacy, see-through white material, cut low to the chest with thin lacy straps over the shoulders. Another bag contained a silk semi-opaque blouse, a pale blue and pale pink pattern, the baggy sleeves coming just below the elbow. In the same bag was a mini dress, of light cotton. It was multicoloured, as if paintbrush strokes of every colour imaginable, had been splashed all over.

By late afternoon, Jennifer and Sebastian were getting concerned that they hadn't heard back from Tom yet.

***

It was coming up to five p.m. at the Archive et Bibliothéque Departmental Aston Defferre.

Tom was thinking his tiredness and concentration weren't helping with his lack of progress. He had been at the computer, the papers, logs and files all day and he was exhausted. Tom had been doing this job, tracking people and items from the war, for several years now. Working with the Professor, being shown the best ways to trace, to follow a route that may have been taken by the perpetrators of the crime, to follow a lead; to research.

In that time, he had also learnt, that, over time, information had not been kept, not been added to an archive; that sometimes a trail would just dry up and could be followed no longer.

Maybe this would be the case with this trail, but he was not prepared to give up just yet. He knew that there was a possibility that the information he was after, may not be in the Archives. It may have been lost in time. But there was always the possibility that, somewhere down the line of history, there could have been a typo error, or a logbook filled in with a name spelt incorrectly, or a house or street having the wrong number, or the wrong information being transferred to the computer system.

He looked around at the people sitting either side of him, deep in study on their computers. Behind him, people having finished work at their factories and offices, were coming in to carry out their own research.

The quietness of the room being broken only by the odd beep of a computer or the turning of a page from a book. Tom leaned back in his chair. His head going back, his hands joined together behind his lower back as his arms stretched out straight.

He thought to himself, should he carry on for a while longer, or leave it till tomorrow? Would he have a better night's sleep and arrive at the Archive a little more alert?

His hands parted from behind his back as he stretched them out to the side, then re-joined behind his head. His mind wandered as he sat there contemplating his next move.

His head back, he went into a dream world, sleep he needed, his eyes blurred as his body slid down the chair.

The pleasure of the relaxed state, a smile on his face as he looked up blearily at the wall above the computer he was working on.

He looked through his blurry, out-of-focus eyes. Looking up at the wall, a map, about a metre high and one and a half metres wide, the centre of the map being filled with the Mediterranean Sea. Tom could just make out the words *'Mer Méditerranée'*, below the map a sign saying *'Aujourd'hui'*. *'The Present Day,'* he thought.

His eyes in a haze, the map came in and out of focus.

"Marseille," he quietly said to himself. "Come on, where are you?"

His eyes wearily drifted from Marseille to Montpellier, Barcelona to Valencia then onto Malaga and Gibraltar.

His eyes, looking, but not seeing as they circled the Mediterranean.

Tangier, Oran, his eyes continued to circle the sea.

Alger, Annaba, Tunis.

The Islands of Corsica, Sardinia somewhere here had to have the answer.

Around the map with the label *'Mer Méditéranée Aujourd'hui'*, were photographs of modern-day France, Spain and North Africa, with hotels, clothes shops and fast-food restaurants. The ports with several huge passenger liners.

A semi-sleep had taken over Tom in the quiet room as his eyes moved away from the map.

They settled on the next map.

It was similar to the first map, one by one and a half metres. It was older, with a sepia colour to the land area and a faded blue to the sea. The words *'Mer Méditerranée'* in a darker blue.

Around the map were old black and white photographs of fishing villages, pictures of men and women mending fishing nets, vast merchant ships; their funnels smoking with dirty coal.

Under the second map was a label with the words *'La Méditéranée 1923'*.

Tom's head swirling with his need for sleep, his eyes wandering in and out of focus, they again followed the land around the sea.

Marseille, his thoughts still convinced had the answer.

Montpelier, come on, he thought, come on... Tangier, his eyes now nearly closed, Oran, Alger, Bône, Tunis, Corsica.

"What?" he, half-sleeping, thought something was wrong... something was different.

He, still not clear in his head, looked at the first map... Annaba, then back to the second map Bône, Annaba, Bône.

He suddenly sat up, opened the box file with the

contents from the burnt German box, He flicked through, piece of paper, after piece of paper.

Then, he pulled out the piece he was after, a dirty smoke-stained scrap with the words 'Bone'.

He looked closer, was it his imagination, the sudden realisation… it wasn't Bone, it was Bône. The ship, the *Suraat Allah*, had sailed to Bône.

Tom was suddenly wide awake with the thrill that he had just found the answer to the problem.

He jumped up, his arms in the air as he burst out.

"YES, YES, YES, I have found it!"

With a sudden realisation of where he was, he slowly looked around to see everyone in the room staring at him.

He slowly sat back down putting his hand up to everyone there.

"Sorry, pardon, sorry, pardon," he mumbled, embarrassed.

Tom, finally seated, the room went back to normal. He knew he had the next destination; he knew Annaba was the place they had to head to.

He packed up the papers and information he had achieved so far.

As he left, he bought a map of the Mediterranean and a map of Algeria.

He called ahead to Jennifer and Sebastian to let them know he was on his way to see them.

And that he had some good news.

# Chapter 30
## Water, Water, Everywhere
## Summer Present-day

'Knock knock', came the sound on the bedroom door.

Jennifer getting up from her chair, she had while waiting, been sitting on the balcony overlooking the old town and Vieux Port.

Having had a shower, she went to the door in a long bathrobe.

She opened the door and Tom stepped in.

"Hi Tom," she said. "What's the news? You sounded excited?"

"Hi Jen," Tom replied. "It was a long day, but I finally made a breakthrough!"

Tom could hear the shower running.

"Bastian in the shower?" asked Tom.

"Yes," said Jennifer. "He shouldn't be long."

Jennifer turned to face the bathroom.

"Bastian... Tom's here darling!" she called.

"Okay," came a voice from the shower. "Be there shortly."

"Want a coffee?" Jennifer asked Tom.

"Love one please."

The sound of the shower stopped, shortly followed by the sound of the shower door opening.

"Did you get very far with your research?" Tom asked Jennifer.

"Sorry Tom, no we didn't, the language barrier

became too great, we gave up at almost the first hurdle."

"That was kind of what I thought might happen. Speaking French in conversation is one thing, but when you need to use technical words, it is so much harder."

"Yes," she answered.

Sebastian walked in from the bathroom.

"So," he said all buoyed up. "Do we carry on, or do we all go home?"

"Ah, well," said Tom. "That depends."

"Depends, depends on what?" asked Sebastian.

"Well, it kind of depends on... do we want to make our way across the Med or back across the English Channel?"

"Across the Med," said Sebastian. "What have you found then?"

"Well, I didn't get anywhere at the first Archive, so went to another... there I found fragments of information, but nothing that would really help us with our search now."

"Mmmm, and?"

"Having spotted two maps, of different eras at the second Archives, it came to me, that the boxes must have been put on the ship, *Suraat Allah*. I know it's a merchant ship, probably moving freight, stocks. You know, to and from France and North Africa during the war."

"So, you think the boxes may have gone to North Africa on this ship?" asked Jennifer.

"There was a piece of paper in the burnt German box that had what I thought said 'Bone', you know,

Ivory?"

Tom opened his bag and pulled out the map of Algeria, he opened it up and laid it out on the table. He sat one side and Jennifer the other, Sebastian still drying his hair stood to the other side of Tom.

"What I didn't know," Tom continued "Was that at the time of the war, the city of Annaba, was called Bône"

"So, you mistook Bône for Bone?" said Jennifer.

"In a nutshell, yes," said Tom.

"So, where does that leave us now?" said Sebastian chucking his towel on the bottom of the bed, then walking over to the bureaux and picking up a comb.

"Ah, this will depend on you two." Tom's face was half screwed up.

"On us?" Sebastian's head turning away from the mirror to look at Tom.

"Yes," Tom sighed. "This is where it may be a little more complicated."

"Why?" said, Jennifer.

"Mm, well one, we all need a visa to enter Algeria… two, we have to *get* to Algeria and three, my funds won't take the strain of going to Algeria."

"Okay," said Jennifer. "Here goes, what do we need to get a visa? The world is a small place now Tom, moving from one country to another, really isn't that difficult any longer. And as for finances… well, let's say for you to not worry about it… I'm sure between Bastian and myself, you shouldn't have to worry… What do you say to that Bastian?"

"Mmmm, visas, can we get them?"

"Yes," said Tom. "There is an Algerian consulate in Marseille."

"Okay," continued Sebastian. "Well, Tom, let's hope we find something in this Bône, and this whole journey will be worth it."

"Thank you for that," said Tom. "Bône is the old name. It is now called Annaba"

Tom pointed at the city of Annaba on the map.

"And as for transport," continued Sebastian. "I have just the thing."

Tom and Jennifer looked up from the map and over to Sebastian.

"What do you mean?" said Jennifer. "What thing?"

"Ah," said Sebastian, his grin, now becoming a smile. "My company have a boat that they keep for very special guests in Marseille Harbour!"

"A boat, what, big enough to get us to North Africa?" asked Jennifer.

"Well, we may have to go the long way around, but there is no reason it shouldn't get us there."

"Will your company give you the okay to do that?" asked Tom.

"Sure, why not? After all, they owe me, and I have already been out on it several times… taken clients on it, you know the sort of thing."

"So, you can use it, no problem?" said Jennifer.

"Absolutely," smiled Sebastian. "Piece of cake!"

Jennifer turned to look at Tom.

"Okay Tom," she said. "That's all three problems solved, what do we do next?"

"Tomorrow, we will get the visas. Bastian, if you

can make sure we can get the boat."

"Sure, will do, I will email them straight away." answered Sebastian.

"Now, a good night's sleep, I think is required," said Tom "There's a lot of water out there… and that water, we have to cross!"

# Chapter 31
## Sunseeker
## Summer Present-day

Tom, Jennifer and Sebastian had visited the Algerian consulate, as early as they could. They needed to make sure that everything they might need was dealt with, and any problems sorted as quickly as they could be.

Sebastian had had a reply from Milstone-Hanks; it would be okay for him to use the boat. But it would be required back in Marseille Harbour in twelve days, as the management were having a meeting with some prospective clients.

Sebastian had acknowledged his company and agreed that the boat would be back, long before the twelve days were up.

They had all packed up and left the hotel and hostel by midday. Sebastian picked Tom up as they passed by the hostel.

They didn't have far to travel, the boat of Milstone-Hanks was docked in the Old Town Port, just a stone's throw from the Sofitel Hotel.

The Aston made its way down to the Old Town and parked up.

Tom, Jennifer and Sebastian headed to the harbour.

Jennifer and Tom waiting to see this 'boat'.

Tom knew no more of 'boats' than the one he

lived on, and that of his neighbours. And he could not picture how such a vessel would get them all the way to North Africa.

Sebastian leading the way as Jennifer and Tom follow behind.

Sebastian's arms filled with the bags of new clothes that Jennifer had recently bought.

Going through customs, he registers with the Port Authorities that he will be taking the boat for a few days.

All clear and onto the quay they go, down this walkway and round another.

Tom admiring every boat that he passed, 'How the other half live' he thought to himself.

Eventually, Sebastian stopped, announcing.

"Here we are!"

Backed up to the walkway, was a gleaming Sunseeker Yacht. Sixteen and a half metres long and four and a half metres wide. It was huge. The white hull down the side with a black frame around the windows, allowing light into the lower deck.

The upper deck having a cockpit deck, surrounded by windows. Further to the rear was the lower cockpit. Behind that, the swim platform, which was at sea level.

"This is nice," said Tom.

"It should be okay for the next few days… to get us to Annaba and back," said Sebastian.

"And how long do you think it should take us then Sebastian?" asked Jennifer.

"Three, possibly four days, depends on the weather. If it holds okay, we'll be fine!"

"So, what is this?" asked Tom.

"It's a Sunseeker Predator 50."

"It's nice!" exclaimed Tom.

As Tom made his way onto the swim deck, Jennifer was already taking the steps up to the lower cockpit.

Across the rear transom, Tom read the words *Gold Rush To*, and below that 'London'.

As Tom reached the main cockpit, in front of him, to the right-hand side of the boat was the helm; a series of buttons, knobs, steering wheel and handles, as well as monitors. Looking to Tom, more like something out of Star Trek's *Enterprise*.

Out of the front screen, he could see a bow railing that went the whole way around the top of the white deck.

"Can't wait to be lying out there in the sun!" Jennifer said to Tom as she looked around the vessel.

To the left of the helm, were stairs that led to the lower deck.

"Down here," Sebastian called. "Tom, you will be sleeping in the bow, Jennifer and I will have the midship's bedroom."

Sebastian made his way down the stairs, stopped and waited for Jennifer and Tom to make their way down.

"This is the lower lounge and galley," welcomed Sebastian. "Through there, Tom, are your quarters. It has its own en-suite. Jen, we are in here."

As Sebastian showed Jennifer into the midship bedroom, Tom carried his small bag of clothes into the bedroom that Sebastian had pointed to.

The room had more space than he had expected. A carpeted floor, white walls-with dark wood inlaid and two beds. One each side of the room, set in a 'V' shape, at about forty-five degrees, to fit the hull of the boat as it narrowed to the bow. Above each bed, a narrow window within a black surround.

Tom took his shoes off and laid on the bed, very comfortable, I'm going to like this, he thought.

Jennifer laid out on the bed of the main bedroom, manoeuvring her body around all the bags that Sebastian had just dropped there.

She slowly rubbed her hands across the cream silk sheets that covered the bed, twisting her body from side to side as she squirmed her bottom into the soft mattress.

I'm going to like this, she thought.

The room had a cream carpet and walls, with a mixture of light and dark woods for the cupboards and furniture.

A long narrow window each side of the boat, having a black frame, looking out onto Marseille Harbour.

"Like it?" Sebastian asked Jennifer.

"Can't wait to be trying it out properly!" she replied.

"And me!" grinned Sebastian.

"You never know." Jennifer gave him a smile and half wink. "We might even have a threesome in it!"

Sebastian took a step back, as the shock of the words came out of her mouth. He thought it was the two of them together, not that she would want to be thinking about sex games so soon after they had got together.

"Oh," said Sebastian.

"I'm sorry, did I shock you?" she smiled, her head slightly down and big eyes looking up at him.

"N-no," he stammered. "No, sounds like fun."

"Anyway," she said. "For now, shouldn't we be going?"

"Of course, yes, it's time we set off... I will go up and get everything ready to leave."

"Good, you do that, and I will put the clothes away... Be with you soon."

Sebastian looked back at her lying on the bed as he left the bedroom, up the steps to the bridge, turning, he slid onto the seat at the helm.

Having set the controls, he started the engine.

As Tom heard the engine start, he left his bedroom and headed up to the cockpit, seeing if he could help Sebastian with anything as he prepared the ship to leave the harbour.

"Hi Bastian... anything I can help with?"

"Sure Tom, just setting up the navigation and we can leave."

"What's the plan to get there?"

"Well, we will have to do the journey in several steps... First, we will be heading for St Tropez, we will have dinner, refuel and then head off for the next refuelling stop."

"It won't make the journey in one go?"

"I'm afraid not, Tom. Marseille to Annaba is around seven hundred and fifty kilometres. This Sunseeker has a fuel tank, that has a range of about two hundred and thirty nautical miles, that's around four hundred and twenty-five kilometres, well short of getting us there!"

"So, island hoping?"

"Just the one island… Sardinia."

"So, Italian?"

"Yeah, should be some great eating when we get there… and the sooner we start, the sooner that will be!"

Sebastian looking back to the navigation screen while Tom looked over his shoulder, interested in how to use one of these big vessels.

"When we are out at sea," said Sebastian, still looking down at the navigation screen, "I will show you how to use all of this, you can then be in charge of the boat while I have a break."

"Sounds good to me," Tom said happily.

"I am just about ready here Tom… can you jump down onto the walkway, untie the rope from the mooring. When we are a little clear of the walkway, pull in the fenders and rope? There is a box at the back there, they will go into that."

"Sure, will do," answered Tom, enthusiastically.

Tom turned and walked from the main cockpit to the lower cockpit, down the steps to the swim platform. Stepping onto the walkway, he untied the mooring rope, then, still holding the rope, stepped back on board the Sunseeker.

"All done Bastian!" Tom called.

"Okay," replied Sebastian. "Hang on, just going to pull away."

"Will do!"

The Sunseeker's revs rose as it slowly eased away from its berth. Tom bent down and pulled at the rope attached to the fender, pulling it onboard.

Then the second fender rose from the rim of the swim platform.

"All finished!"

"Good," Sebastian called back. "Now come up here and I will show you what we have to do!"

Tom was soon up, watching Sebastian manoeuvring the vessel away from Le Vieux Port.

It slowly eased away from the boats berthed either side, as Sebastian manoeuvred the Sunseeker into the middle of the harbour.

The harbour entrance in front of them. The Cathedral de Notre Dame de la Garde on the hill, looking down towards them as they gently made their way towards the sea.

Through the Old Port Wall, they passed St Jean Castle and the Pointe du Pharo, as they leave the serenity of the harbour and start their journey on the vast open sea.

The vessel heading towards Les Îles, passing sailing ships and motor launches, the odd windsurfer, venturing off-shore.

Tom still watching Sebastian as Jennifer emerges from the lower deck; her legs, shoulders and arms bare, wearing only a pair of Flip-Flops and a white towel wrapped around her upper body, covering her breasts down to her mid-thighs. A pillow and sun cream in her hand.

"Hi Tom," she said, "Bastian, how long till we get to St Tropez?"

"Should be about three hours."

"Great... I'm going to sunbathe on deck for a while, let me know when we have about an hour to go, I will need to go and get showered... okay?"

"Will do," said Sebastian, still not happy about the idea of a threesome with Tom.

Sebastian slowed the boat from about 25 knots, down to five or six, as Jennifer made her way along the side of the boat, hanging onto the bow railing until she reached the deck in front of the main cockpit.

As Jennifer reached the top deck at the front of the vessel, Sebastian at the helm, Tom standing behind him, taking in his lesson on how to control the ship, Sebastian pointing out of the window at hazards they will have to be aware of.

Jennifer laid the pillow down on the deck, removing the towel from her body, laying it out flat in front of the pillow.

Tom looking up to realise that Jennifer was standing in front of him, her body facing the direction they were travelling; stretching her arms straight up into the air, her legs open, her feet either side of the towel and completely naked.

Sebastian started to bring the speed back up.

Jennifer bringing her hands down to her hips, her head tilting back as the wind from the forward movement blew through her hair.

The Sunseeker, back up to 25 knots, Jennifer lay down on the towel, spread out on the deck; her legs facing forward as the vessel rode smoothly over the calm sea.

Before reaching Les Îles, the Predator 50 turned south, sailing between the islands of Île d'If and Île d'Endoume.

Working its way in, and around, many small craft, yachts and fishing boats.

A speed boat passed close by, being followed by a water skier.

Keeping the Mainland of France to their left, they turned south-east at Île Maïre. The temperature in the high twenties.

Jennifer turning onto her front, rested her arms on the pillow as she lifted her head to look through the window… into the cockpit.

"Bastian," she called.

"Yes?" he called back, through the front glass window.

"Can you bring me a cold drink?"

"What do you want?"

"Orange juice please."

"Okay, I'll be right there."

Bastian turning to Tom.

"Okay Tom, it's your turn to take the helm… do you feel confident?"

"I think so… if I'm not sure, I'll just slow down and wait for you to get back!"

"Okay, sounds good," said Sebastian, slowing the speed, letting go of the steering wheel and getting up from the helmsman's seat. "Just follow the navigation directions and all should be fine."

"Will do."

Tom sat at the helm, taking the wheel, as Sebastian went down the stairs to the galley.

Tom looked around, taking in the coast to one side and Mediterranean Sea to the other. In front, the naked body of Jennifer, her skin glistening and brown in the mid-afternoon sunshine. Her bare arms, back and beautiful round bottom constantly in Tom's view. But he concentrated on his task, as he controlled the vessel.

Sebastian returned from the galley, stepped out onto the gunwale and made his way to the front of the boat. Orange juice in one hand.

"Put it down there darling," said Jennifer pointing beside her.

Sebastian lowered the glass to the side of Jennifer as she stretched her arms and legs.

"Bastian darling, do me a favour?"

"What's that?"

"Put this sun cream on me please?"

Jennifer reached out in front of her, picked up the bottle of sun cream, handing it to Sebastian.

Jennifer, still lying on her front, brought her hands up behind her neck, parting her hair into two. Pulling it away from her shoulders and around to her face, carefully leaving a gap, so that she could still look forwards.

Sebastian squirted the cream into his hand and started rubbing it into her shoulders. Tom at the helm, looking left, right, at the navigation equipment; anywhere he could without looking out of the front, Jennifer lying naked and having sun cream rubbed into her smooth body.

More cream into Bastian's hand as he smoothed it into the sides of her chest, feeling the roundness of her bosom, his hands massaged the cream down her body to her hips.

"Do my legs now Bastian."

Sebastian dribbled the cream from the bottle down the back of each leg. Jennifer pushed her torso up onto her elbows, pushing her hair away from her face at the same time.

Sebastian slowly put his palms around the thigh of her right leg and gently stroked towards her feet. When at her feet, his hands returned to the thigh on the outside of her leg, he then rubbed towards her feet again. She closed her eyes, her legs parting a little further as Sebastian's fingers rubbed the cream from her right foot up to the inside of her right thigh, passing millimetres away from her vagina.

She shuddered with pleasure; his fingers continued their travels, as they eased the cream into the rounded cheeks of her bottom.

Sebastian moving to Jennifer's left side, he started to rub the cream into her left leg, as he had done on the right side.

Coming up the inner thigh of the left leg, Jennifer whispered.

"Rub it into my Pussy."

Sebastian poured a little more cream onto his fingers and rested his hand on the crack between the cheeks of her arse, slowly easing his finger into the crack, his hand moved downwards towards her vagina.

Tom, trying not to look at what was happening right in front of him, but cannot avoid it. Catching Jennifer's eye, she smiled as she slowly winked.

Fingers now penetrating the inside of her body, she closed her eyes again as her head returned to the pillow. The sun shining on her body, her legs open and her bottom twisted up. The fingers working in and out, occasionally gently flicking her clitoris.

Jennifer's bottom slowly working up and down as Sebastian's fingers gently rubbed, her fanny pushing into the deck of the boat, as an orgasm swelled in her groin.

Her eyes half-open looking at Tom.

Then with one last giant shudder, her head buried itself into the pillow, liquid oozing from her vulva in an explosion of pleasure.

Sebastian's head lifting to see Tom looking out of the front window, at Jennifer; still writhing with the thrill of the orgasm, Sebastian's fingers still inside her.

Jennifer's arm squeezing under her body, as her fingers rub her clitoris, keeping the height of emotions and the thrill of the orgasm going for as long as she can.

Sebastian's expression sour as Tom caught his glare.

Tom turning his head, embarrassed, quickly looking out of the side window to the sea.

\*\*\*

Sebastian took back the helm from Tom just before they had reached the Îles d'Hyères, steering the boat between the north of the island and the mainland. Continuing on, in silence until they had passed between Île du Lavant and Cap Bénat.

Sebastian leaned forward and knocked on the windscreen in front of him, getting the attention of Jennifer.

"Jen," he called through the glass. "About an hour to go!"

"Thanks, Bastian" she called back, slightly lifting her head to smile at him.

Jennifer got up from the deck, her naked body looking wonderful in the late afternoon sunshine.

Tom and Sebastian, watching every move she made.

Bending over to pick up her towel, her legs straight, her arms straight down.

The cheeks of her bottom almost touching the windscreen, her shaven pudendum flushed with colour from the earlier pleasure.

Having grabbed the towel, Sebastian slowed the boat to a crawl, allowing Jennifer to make her way along the gunwale, back to the main cockpit.

The boat, moving slowly, Sebastian getting up from the helm to help the naked Jennifer back onto the main deck.

"Here Tom," said Sebastian as he turned towards the aft of the vessel "Take the helm and I'll help Jen back onto the deck."

"Sure," said Tom grabbing the steering wheel.

"Once she is on board properly, you can put the speed back up, keep the navigation on track, I will take over when we get to the outskirts of St Tropez," Sebastian said, looking over his shoulder at Tom.

"Okay" Tom replied.

Tom watching Jennifer's naked body through the glass side windows of the boat as she made her way down the gunwale.

Having reached the open end of the cockpit, she chucked her towel onto one of the seats at the stern of the boat then took Sebastian's hand.

"Thanks, Bastian," she said gratefully.

"My pleasure." he replied.

She stepped off of the gunwale and onto the lower cockpit.

"How far to go?" she said.

"About 25 miles." Sebastian replied.

"Good, I'll go and get a shower and slip into something nice for the evening."

"It looks nice... what you have on already!" Sebastian smiled.

"Umm, well, we don't intend going to Tahiti Plage, just the town. So, I think clothes may be called for!"

Jennifer turned to look at Tom at the helm.

"Are you getting the hang of that yet Tom?" she said walking towards him.

"Well, I like to think so... so far, it's just look-out, at where we are going, look at the screen to check it's the right way... and steer."

"Sebastian, pick up the towel for me, there's a darling." Jennifer said as she headed towards Tom.

She walked to the front of the cockpit, standing next to the helm seat; putting her hand on the back of the seat, she looked down at the navigation screen.

"I haven't seen how this all works yet," she said. "Come on Tom, shove over, let's see what this all does!"

Jennifer sitting her naked body next to Tom, pushing him to one side with her bare hip.

"Okay Tom, I guess we can speed up again now. What's the throttle control, is it that one there?" she said leaning over Tom "Yes, this must be it!"

Jennifer pressing her bare body against Tom, pushed at the throttle lever, the boat sped up. Behind the two of them, Sebastian picked up the thrown towel, walking up the main cockpit, not happy to see Jennifer sitting naked next to someone else, and definitely not him.

"Um, thanks for that Tom," she beamed "We will have to do this again."

"Okay, um, yeah!"

"I'm going to get myself ready now. I'll see you boys shortly."

At that, she slid off the helm's chair, taking the towel from Sebastian, made her way down the stairs, towards her bedroom.

Sebastian glared at the back of Tom's head... *'Hang on though,'* he suddenly thought... She must be teasing, after all, he had spent the last hour on the top deck with her, masturbating her. Of course, there was nothing at all to get annoyed about, she was just playing.

Sebastian took three deep breaths, relaxed, and stood next to Tom.

"Is everything okay?" Sebastian asked Tom.

"I think so."

"Okay then, I am going downstairs for a while to get a drink, if you have any problems, give me a shout. Other than that, I will take over soon."

"I'm happy with that."

"Good, won't be long."

With that, Sebastian stepped onto the stairs, heading for the galley.

***

Having rounded the Pointe de Rabiou, Sebastian returned to the cockpit deck.

"Okay Tom, I'll take over from here!"

"All yours."

Tom getting up from the helm, as Sebastian took the controls.

St Tropez harbour in sight, Sebastian called into the Port de St Tropez, letting them know the *Gold Rush To* was coming in for refuel and dock for the night.

Rounding the harbour wall at Phare de St Tropez; the Sunseeker reversing back while Tom stood ready with the fenders on the swim platform.

Slowly, the vessel moving towards the pontoon, slowly, closer. Coming to a halt at the pontoon's wooden walkway.

The engine off.

Jennifer emerging from the stairs onto the main cockpit carrying three glasses and a bottle.

"Who's for a glass of red wine?" she said.

# Chapter 32
## Au Revoir
## Summer Present-day

The next day, refuelled and ready to leave. At eight a.m. they pull out of St Tropez harbour. A beautiful Mediterranean summer day, a gentle breeze, calm sea and the sun, even at this time of the morning, comfortably warm. The navigation set, today's journey is going to be long, two hundred miles.

The next destination: the island of Sardinia, they were heading for the port of Porto Torres on the north coast.

After an eight-hour journey, it will be rest and sleep in the evening.

Having pulled out of St Tropez, they headed for the open sea. Taking turns at the helm, Jennifer suggesting they took one-hour stints at the wheel each.

She wore a white mini dress, Sebastian thought it showed off her wonderful tan beautifully, her long brown hair tied back away from her face.

Sebastian was wearing white tennis shorts and deck shoes.

Tom was in his usual baggy sandy-coloured shorts and flip flops.

Sebastian took the first hour as he was pulling the Sunseeker Predator 50 out of the harbour. He continued at the helm until it was time to be relieved.

Jennifer sat in the main cockpit watching the coast of France disappear across the horizon. The early morning coolness in the air, she decided to stay in the shelter of the main cockpit's roof and windows, until later in the morning, when the sun would be higher and the sea air a bit warmer.

Tom had made himself comfortable in the lower lounge. With a big TV on the wall, he could put a film on.

Beside the TV was a cupboard, it had a little nameplate on the front, with the letters, DVDs.

Tom opened the cupboard door to see at least a hundred DVDs; the vast majority were porn. But he did manage to find the odd serious film, settling on Steve McQueen and *The Great Escape*.

The first hour passed quickly.

"Tom," Sebastian called down. "It's your turn."

"Be right there."

Tom turned off the DVD and the TV, sure that he would be back to watch the rest of the film once his stint at the helm was over.

"Just on my way up," Tom called to Sebastian.

Into the second hour of the journey from St Tropez to Sardinia, Jennifer had removed her dress and was now lying naked in the sun of the lower cockpit.

As Tom got to the top of the steps, he could see Jennifer's legs at the step down from the main cockpit as he looked towards the lower cockpit.

Her upper body being hidden by the transom wall.

She was laid out on a settee seat cushion. On top

of the cushion was a towel. She lay face up, with her legs either side of the cushion, her feet on the floor, her legs open.

"Here you go Tom," Sebastian said. "Nothing to report, just lots of water!"

"Cheers Bastian," Tom said, taking the helm. "I've been watching a film"

"What, the skin flicks?"

"Oh… no, a Steve McQueen film."

"Oh, do we have proper films down there… I didn't know that!"

"How are we doing for time?"

"Good," said Sebastian. "On time, we should be in at Porto Torres late this afternoon."

Sebastian went to the galley, got a bottle of water from the fridge, back up the steps; passing Tom, who was at the helm looking out of the front window.

Sebastian stepped down from the main cockpit to the lower cockpit, looked down at Jennifer lying naked on the cushion.

He moved alongside her; lifting one of his legs across her, he stood above her, one foot either side of her hips, slowly bending down, he kissed her on the lips.

She responded, slightly opening her mouth and nibbling his bottom lip.

Sebastian then slowly lowered the cold-water bottle onto her stomach, her body tensed, as a cold shudder went through her.

Still gripping his lip with her teeth, she relaxed, let go of his lip and whispered.

"You bastard!"

"I know," he replied.

"I want to suck your cock!"

"I want to suck your clit!"

"Well, *you* are going to have to wait," whispered Jennifer.

"Oh, and why is that?"

"You will have to wait and see!"

"Umm, this sounds interesting?"

"Yes, and you will be really hard!" she teased. "Now, sit on the seat there and enjoy the journey."

Sebastian sat as told by Jennifer on the seat, next to where she lay.

The day was warming up, approaching mid-morning, it was reaching the mid-twenties.

Tom's duties were simple; watch for boats, ships and obstructions in the water, keep on track with the navigation and steer, nothing to it.

After an hour, the helm changed. Jennifer took the wheel. Just to make sure she was okay with the controls, for the first few minutes Sebastian looked over her shoulder to check she was comfortable with such a large vessel.

She seemed fine; in fact, he could see she already had an idea of how to use a ship of this size.

Tom went back down to the lounge and continued with the film.

Sebastian got another bottle of water for himself and one for Jennifer, laying the bottle on the control panel as he passed, then made his way to the seats on the port side of the boat.

Sebastian sat on the white leather seats of the main cockpit, opened the bottle of water. Taking a swig, he looked over to Jennifer sitting at the helm, how beautiful he thought she was, how talented and strong. She sat there in control of the boat, not a care in the world; nothing seemed to phase her.

Sebastian was smitten.

# Chapter 33
## Ciao
### Summer Present-day

The Sunseeker Predator 50 finally pulled into Porto Torres late that afternoon.

Spaghetti Bolognaise at a portside restaurant and a couple of glasses of red wine.

The boat refuelled and watered.

An early night was needed as, the following day, they had another early start and long journey.

They set off at eight a.m., leaving Porto Torres in the north of Sardinia, for the capital, Cagliari, the south of the island.

Sebastian hoped for good weather, calm seas; the trip from Porto Torres to Cagliari would take the Sunseeker to its fuel capacity. It should make it okay, as long as the sea remains calm and they take the shortest route.

Although the day looked good, Sebastian kept having a nagging thought. Would the *Gold Rush To* make the distance? He had never had to take it this far before.

They rounded the northern tip of the island, the Parco Nazionale dell'Asinara, turning south and following the western coastline. Travelling at a steady 25 to 30 knots.

Tom at the helm as they pass the western point of Argentiera.

Sebastian called Jennifer and Tom to the navigation screen.

"Okay," announced Sebastian. "I am going to make a slight detour. I am not sure the ship will make the whole journey, so we are going to pull in at Marina di Portoscuso."

"Okay, Bastian," said Jennifer. "Is it going to add more time to the journey?"

"Probably about an hour."

"Which means Cagliari in the early evening?"

"Yes, we will still get there, but I am not going to chance running out of fuel"

"I'm happy with that," Tom said. "The end result will be worth the inconvenience."

"You're right Tom," said Jennifer. "A minor inconvenience."

Sebastian reset the navigation for the direction change, the vessel still heading south, the setting would have taken them close to Marina di Portoscuso, but now they would be visiting the Marina for more fuel.

After each hour, the three travellers changed at the helm, the ship following the coastline until they reached the Marina.

Stop, refuel and off, as quickly as they could.

Leaving the Marina di Portoscuso, they headed south-west, passing the town of Carloforte on the Isola di San Pietro. Navigating the straits between the Isola and Calasetta.

Once past the headland they turned east. Now on the southerly part of Sardinia, they could see an end to this long and tiring journey.

The sun getting low, but the sky still blue by the time their ship was pulling into Cagliari Marina.

Sebastian organised the refuelling.

Tom waited on the ship. Jennifer was getting dressed, ready for the evening in Cagliari town. Tom relaxing on the white leather seats in the cockpit deck of the Sunseeker.

Jennifer getting ready below, left her bedroom, making her way up the stairs to the main deck.

"Hello Tom," she said. "Bastian not back yet?"

"Not yet," he said. "When he returns, we will have to visit the Autorità Portuale to let them know we are here."

"I thought we might!" she smiled. "Tom, can you do me a favour?"

"What's that?"

Jennifer turned around. She was wearing a full length, figure-hugging maxi dress in bright yellow.

As she turned, Tom could see the zipper, which started in the middle of her bottom, went right up to the neckline, was undone.

Jennifer put her hands underneath her hair and lifted it up to reveal her beautiful, smooth tanned skin beneath the dress.

"Could you do my dress up?" she sighed, half looking back at him over her shoulder.

"Of course," Tom said, innocently as he stood up.

Tom reached down with his left hand trying to take hold of the material of the dress below the zip, the tight fabric clinging to her body shape perfectly.

Tom, trying to get hold of the material without

his hands rubbing against her.

Jennifer took one of her hands out from under her hair, lowered it and placed it on top of Tom's left hand; pushing it hard against the cheeks of her backside.

"It's okay Tom," she whispered "You can put your hand there... I promise I won't complain."

Tom looked down, his hand now pressed hard against her derrière, his right hand feeling for the zip.

Jennifer's wonderful crena, golden brown against the bright yellow dress.

He took the zipper, slowly pulling it upwards, reaching her neckline.

"There you are." Tom smiled, nervously.

Jennifer suddenly turning, dropping her hair, she put her arms around Tom's neck, kissing him on the lips.

"Hey, what are you doing?" came a voice from the quayside.

Sebastian was walking back to the Sunseeker.

"Just chatting," Jennifer called back, her arms still around Tom's neck.

"Well, that didn't look like chatting to me!"

"Oh Bastian," Jennifer pouted. "I'll kiss the end of your cock later... so don't get all uppity about a thank-you kiss to Tom... he helped me do my dress up... Now come on, let's get a move on and get out for dinner."

Sebastian stepped on board the *Gold Rush To*, staring at Tom.

*'She is getting too close to Tom,'* thought Sebastian. *'I will have to keep a close eye on what is happening.'*

"Bastian, hurry up!" insisted Jennifer, sitting on the white leather seats of the main deck, putting her shoes on. "Are you going as you are, Tom?"

"As always," said Tom in his sandy-coloured shorts and washed-out orange T-shirt. "These are comfortable!"

Sebastian looked back at Jennifer and Tom sitting on the cockpit seats as he went down the stairs to the bedroom.

Quickly getting changed into Bermuda shorts, a light blue short sleeved shirt with a darker blue checked pattern. On his feet he wore white tennis shoes.

Having dressed as quickly as he could, he rushed back up the stairs to see Jennifer and Tom still sitting on the seats, chatting and laughing.

"What's so funny?" huffed Sebastian

"Oh Bastian," laughed Jennifer. "Tom was just telling me some stories of playing rugby"

"I do play, but weekends only!" Tom said looking at Sebastian.

"Well, I'm ready..." announced Sebastian abruptly. "Shall we get going? We can talk more about it when we get to the restaurant!"

Jennifer was up from the white seat, making her way down to the swim platform finally stepping onto the quay, followed by Sebastian and Tom.

As they walked along the quay towards the Autorità Portuale, Jennifer took Sebastian's arm.

Tom walked along beside them.

Heading up into the old town, narrow streets crammed with cars, Jennifer saw the place she wanted, basic and Italian.

From the outside, of plain walls and shutters, looking more like the entrance to a garage, the Hostaria Via Aemilia in the Vico Rigina Margherita.

Inside, it had a relaxed, laid-back Italian easy-going atmosphere. The white walls were set against the dark wood of the wall units, chairs and tables.

They had a dinner of pasta, meat and sauce, washed down with a couple of glasses of red wine, along with the chilled feeling that comes from a mixture of an Italian and Mediterranean island.

"That was good," said Jennifer.

"Very good," agreed Tom, not used to eating in such restaurants.

Jennifer sat at the small round table, Tom one side of her, Sebastian the other.

"So, what next Bastian?" she said.

"They are refuelling the ship this evening. We should be able to be off first thing tomorrow. I think an eight a.m. start again. We should reach Annaba by mid-afternoon."

"It's an Arabic country, isn't it Tom?" asked Jennifer.

"It is, but as it was once a French colony, French is its second language… so most people speak French there… it should be okay."

"That's good to hear," said Sebastian, smiling. "We don't want to get to, what is hopefully the last hurdle, and find we can't communicate!"

"I will get by," smiled Tom. "It will be okay. After all, we have got this far. I'm sure it will all fall into place, as we work our way around"

"I am sure you will work it all out Tom," said Jennifer, taking his hand and gently squeezing it.

She then took Sebastian's hand on the other side of her, holding both hands and gently squeezing both.

"I am so pleased to be on this journey with my two favourite men!"

Sebastian looked at Tom's hand being squeezed by Jennifer.

His smile dropping and his eyes narrowing as he looked up at Tom's face, a hatred welling up inside him.

Walking back along the quay, Sebastian and Jennifer walked ahead.

Tom was hanging back; he wanted to stretch his legs, get a bit of air. He would be back at the boat soon, he had said.

As Sebastian and Jennifer reached *Gold Rush To*, Sebastian said he was just going to check the fuel and water had been done. He would be back as soon as he could.

Jennifer stepped on board the Sunseeker, up onto the white leather couch and poured another glass of wine, looking out onto the Cagliari evening; the lights across the town. She took a deep breath and relaxed.

Tom still walking, had just reached the entrance to the quay when Sebastian walked towards him.

Suddenly Sebastian grabbed Tom by the neck, forcing him back to the harbour wall.

Tom's hands going up, his palms out and facing Sebastian.

Sebastian's hand around Tom's throat, pushing his head backwards, into the wall behind him.

"Woah," said Tom, finding it hard to breathe. "What's the problem?"

"You are the problem, my friend."

"In what way?"

"Keep your fucking hands, off Jennifer."

"But I haven't put my hands 'on' Jennifer!" he choked.

"Don't give me that fucking shit, do you think I am blind... now, fucking leave her, or there will be some serious fucking trouble!"

"I don't think you understand Bastian," wheezed Tom, struggling for breath. "I am happy with my partner, Kristina. I am not looking for anyone else in my life!"

"Then keep your distance, okay, just keep your fucking distance!"

Sebastian let go of Tom's throat, turning, he walked at pace back towards Jennifer and the Sunseeker.

Tom stood dazed, holding his neck and wondering what that was all about.

He slowly continued to walk back to the vessel, telling himself he must keep away from any problems that happen on the ship. Clearly, Sebastian is jealous of Jennifer.

Tom reached their boat and stepped on board.

Sebastian was sitting, smiling next to Jennifer.

Tom carried on, as though nothing had happened.

"Want a glass of wine Tom?" asked Jennifer.

"That would be nice Jen, yes please," Tom replied.

Jennifer poured a glass for Tom.

"There you go Tom," she said handing up the glass to him. "Are you all right?" her expression changing to concern.

"Y... yes, fine." he stuttered. "Just wondering what we will find in Algeria."

"Don't worry Tom," Jennifer continued. "You have done brilliantly so far, I... we?" she said looking at Sebastian next to her, then back up to Tom. "We have all the faith in you, you will do it. If it's there, you will find it!"

"Thank you, Jen, Bastian, I will do my best... now if you don't mind... I will be taking my glass to my room, get an early night."

"That's okay Tom..." smiled Jennifer. "Good night... see you in the morning!"

"Night!"

Tom turned and headed for the stairs, then to his bedroom.

# Chapter 34
## Water Pressure
## Summer Present-day

After four days at sea, the pressure was starting to tell, especially on Sebastian.

His jealousy for Jennifer growing daily.

He had nothing else to think about while travelling from one place to another. Spending many hours at sea, his mind preoccupied with Jennifer, and not in the office making money.

Watching Jennifer's every move, her naked body as she walked around the vessel. The occasions she would brush against Tom, as well as the smiles she gave him.

Sebastian would be more than pleased for this journey to be over, back in London, back to his office in Canary Wharf; back with his friend Harry.

How nice it would be though, to be back home. Jennifer by his side and millions of pounds richer.

It was worth the wait, worth the pressure, even though he was finding the strain very difficult.

Tom had now run out of films.

He didn't mind watching porn, but if he was going to do that, he would rather be watching with Kristina.

And, after all, if it was naked bodies he wanted to see, all he had to do was go up to the upper deck. He would nearly always see Jennifer sprawled out, wearing nothing but sun cream.

Jennifer was the least stressed, lying out on the deck, sunning herself. Good food whenever they reached a port, fresh air and sunshine.

As well, of course, the reason they were travelling to Algeria, the contract, the history, the gold.

Sebastian, still had no knowledge of Jennifer flying in from San Francisco, meeting Tom and secretly arranging to meet him, to get him on her side.

Sebastian, from the first moment he and Jennifer met, was smitten by her looks, her charm, her power and confidence. And, of course, her blow jobs.

An hour and they would reach the Algerian port town of Annaba, Jennifer leaving the deck, making her way down to shower, readying herself to reach their destination.

Tom was at the helm when he first spotted the Algerian coastline.

"I can see the coast," Tom called to Bastian and Jennifer.

Sebastian looking down at the navigation screen.

"About fifteen miles," he said.

The hills of nearly 500 metres dominate the landscape of this part of the North African coast.

The hills of Djebel Bou Kanta and Djebel Edough, to the west of Annaba, green and lush. Dark against the blue sky. Sea and the odd vessel, the only things they had seen in the past seven hours.

As they get nearer, the rocky coastline coming into view, the sheer faces of the cliffs. The hard, dark grey rocks.

The top of the rocks, covered in green vegetation.

Soon, they see the El Manar lighthouse, the most northern district of Annaba, their journey to North Africa nearly over.

Will they be successful in their quest? Will it all have been worth it? Or would the thought of coming all this way and finding it had all been a waste of time, finally make Sebastian crack?

The strain of leaving his job back in London to search for something that may have already been long gone.

They pass the El Manar lighthouse to their right as the port of Annaba came into view in the distance, a little over four miles and they would enter the harbour.

The rocky face of the cliffs, guarded by the lighthouse, pass. Now to reveal the low-level ground of Annaba. The land gently sloping up towards the hills of Bou Kanta, green and lush, they seem to hold the town of Annaba, protecting it from the desert further to the south.

Sebastian had taken over the helm as they made their way south and towards the port.

Passing the beaches of Ain Achir, Bouna, Plage du Belvédère, Tôche, Plage Le Caroube, Rizzi Amore, Plage Saint-Cloud and Plage des Juifs.

They pass new hotels being built, and those that are newly built, Hôtel Chem-Les-Bains, Hôtel El Djamil and Hôtel Sabri.

As the three of them stood on the Sunseeker, looking at the passing coastline, the beaches and hotels; all thronging with people and guests, this could have been the coastline of California, they thought, instead of North African Algeria.

The Predator 50 now slowing to a crawl as it turned into the harbour, inching its way between the harbour wall and the dock to its left.

It continued into the long stretch of harbour; they found a berth.

Tom went with Sebastian to find the refuelling station, Jennifer staying on board until they had returned.

Tom's use of French, they thought, may be needed while in the dock.

Sebastian wearing his dark blue trousers and white trainers. Tom was in his old shorts and a T-shirt.

Having organised the refuelling, Tom and Sebastian returned to the *Gold Rush To*.

Jennifer sitting on the white seats of the main cockpit deck.

"Are you ready Jen?" Sebastian called from the quayside.

"Just coming!" she replied.

She stood up from the seat and rounded the transom, stepped down onto the lower cockpit.

She looked stunning in a sky-blue abaya, in a light cotton material, open at the front.

Below the abaya, she wore white calf-length cotton trousers, white thin-strapped sandals and a white loose-fitting top.

She glided down the steps to the swim platform, Sebastian put his arm out to steady her as she stepped onto the quay.

"Where now?" she said.

"Tom?" said Sebastian.

"Up there, at the end of the quay, the passenger terminal."

"Great, it's been a long and exhausting journey, let's hope it will be all worth it... now Tom." Sebastian looked at Tom with a serious face. "I know you like to tell the truth, find it difficult lying. But think when you are here. If you let the wrong person know what we are here for, well, we definitely won't find the gold. And we will be sent off, without stepping onto a pavement!"

"So, what do you suggest?" asked Tom.

"Oh, I don't know, let's say, I was doing some family history and found my great grandfather had been here during the war. And we are hoping to meet the family he was friends with here, at that time."

"Okay," said Tom. "I can do that."

Between the end of the dock, the Quai ouest and the main road, the Route d'el Kala was the newly build arched roof and glass building. A triumph of modern design, a hope of a better future.

The old dock, with its merchant vessels still filling most of the harbour, the rusty old hulks, starting to look out of place in this new world.

Jennifer, Tom and Sebastian strolled towards the new terminal, walked through the door and entered modern Algeria.

# 24 February 1945

*Suraat Allah*
Arrives at Bône

# Chapter 35
## A Place to Hide
## 24 February 1945

As the *Suraat Allah* finally pulled into the harbour at Bône, the devastation of bombing raids became clear. The ship steering its way past the blown-out dock walls, the harbour full of craters and burnt-out buildings.

They made their way into Grand Basin, pulling over to Quai Nord.

Wilhelm Schick and Samuel Plant leaning against the side rail, as Captain Nasir's ship *Gods Path* drew up to the quay. Ropes thrown down being tied up to cleats.

Captain Nasir stepping over the raised threshold of the bridge door, checking he was safely in position, before returning to the bridge.

Schick and Plant feeling a lot more comfortable in their cotton suits, now they had reached the warmth of the North African coast.

The blue sky and temperature of seventeen degrees Celsius, much better than the freezing weather they had come from, only a few days earlier.

The *Suraat Allah* pulled tight into the dock and all movement stopped.

A few minutes later and the engines stop turning.

The quietness of the vessel, now being overtaken

by the sounds of shouting and banging, the Dockyard workers of Bône, rebuilding the harbour and local houses; damage caused from recent bombing raids.

Captain Abou Nasir stepping out of the bridge once more, happy that the ship was safe where it was, if only temporarily.

Of course, with the war raging in Europe. The Mediterranean would still be full of danger; the ship could be shot at by a passing fighter plane, or a sudden torpedo attack. It could, during the conflict, never truly be safe.

But for now, the captain was happy to be in the dock… and in his home town.

"Mr Symanski, Mr Plant," the captain called in French, as he walked towards them.

"Good morning, from myself and Mr Plant," Schick replied.

Samuel Plant, not understanding what was being said, listened and smiled.

"I trust you had a good night's sleep… no engines, no lights on the ship, just the lapping of the waves… Ah, that's the best of this job. When I retire Mr Symanski, I hope, it is to somewhere I can just listen to the lapping of the waves."

"I hope you get your wish, Mr Nasir."

Dockworkers pulling the gangplank into position, throwing up two ropes to the deckhands, the walkway pulled into place.

"Now Mr Symanski, Mr Plant, what I shall do is; unload your goods and have them put onto a barrow. I will send one of the boys to my friend in the old part of town. He is a good man, I know he will be more than pleased to help you."

"Is it far, Mr Nasir?" said Schick.

"No, not that far, it should not take too long… there will be boys waiting on the dock to push the barrow… but of course, the barrow will be heavy, so it may be a slow walk."

"And they will know where to go with the note? Your friend will know we are coming with our boxes?"

"The boy with the note will know the streets, he will find it. My friend will definitely know what to expect when you arrive."

"If you say it will be a slow walk, will you be here when we return?" asked Schick.

"Most certainly, Mr Symanski. It will take a couple of hours to unload the ship now. We then have to load for the journey north and back across the sea. The *Suraat Allah* will still be here."

"I would like to thank you for your help, in what we are doing Mr Nasir."

"It is a pleasure, but it is just business. I am sure you will gain out of this little venture of yours, as I have gained from helping your… business."

"But of course, and if we can all make a little profit from the business… well… that, is that retirement by the sea, listening to the waves!"

They both laughed.

Realising the conversation was humorous, Plant laughed along with them.

The gangplank fitted into place, the ship's crew started running up and down, organising what they needed to empty the ship.

Their clothing was of off-white and dirty cotton tops and trousers, as well as sandals, more at home in the pleasant temperatures of North Africa than the colder temperatures of Europe.

Captain Abou Nasir walked down the plank.

Schick and Plant looking down at him from the side of the boat.

He walked over to two boys of about ten years of age, sitting on a barrow and waiting for a job.

Nasir talked to them for a couple of minutes. He then turned and looked up towards Schick and Plant. The two boys looking up to see who Nasir was talking about.

One of the boys suddenly ran off up the dock, the other waited while the captain took a piece of paper from his jacket pocket and started writing a note.

The boy taking the note from Nasir, half bowed, turned and ran up the road as quickly as he could.

In the meantime, the first boy had arrived back with a third boy of about the same age. All boys were dressed in off-white cotton tops and trousers held up by string. Worn-out leather sandals on their feet.

Nasir's crew having carried the green boxes down the gangplank, were staking them onto the barrow.

Schick and Plant watching from the deck of the ship, the boys waiting at the barrow.

The captain walked back up the gangplank, at the top he continued over to Schick and Plant.

"I have given the boys all the instructions they need. The first boy has taken a note up to my friend.

He will be waiting at his house for you to arrive."

"Thank you, captain," said Schick.

"And gentlemen, your journey will be slow, there is a lot of weight for the boys to pull... I hope it will give you time to look around my beautiful city. And after the war, when you return, and the devastation caused by bombs and guns is a distant memory, it will be even better!" The captain smiled.

"I'm sure it will be," said Schick.

"You will be heading for the district of St Anne; it is not that far."

One of the Algerian crew members called up to the captain, that all the green boxes were now on the barrow and it is ready to go.

"That is it, gentleman," Nasir said, turning to face Plant and Schick. "The barrow is ready for you."

Schick nodded and shook the hand of the captain, then started to walk towards the gangplank. Samuel Plant, too, shook the captain's hand and followed Schick down the gangplank.

At the bottom, they walked over to the barrow. The two boys, taking a handle each, started to push the heavy load.

From the Grand Basin, they dog-legged right into the Small Basin.

The buildings running along the opposite side of the road to the Basin were grand and majestic. Three and four-storey, small balconies, surrounded by attractive iron railings. The tops of the houses having reddish-brown roof tiles.

French colonialist influencing the design of the buildings.

The boys turn the borrow into the main road of Bône. The road, full of banks and hotels, theatres and shops.

The buildings on one side of the road, to the buildings on the other, were about fifty metres apart, running the four hundred metre length of the Boulevard.

In the middle was a park, running the length of the road, filled with grass, footpaths, trees and plants. It was called the Cour Jérôme Bertagna, after the former mayor of Bône, of French/Italian descent. Bertagna growing very rich from his businesses in Algeria.

As the boys, pushing the barrow, followed closely by Schick and Plant, reached the end of Cour Jérôme Bertagna, in front of them the magnificent Cathedral of St Augustine.

At the Cathedral, they turned left into Allees Guynemer.

With the French-named roads and colonial-style buildings, Schick thought, it could almost be that they were still in Marseille.

Past the Square Rondon, one of the boys turning to Schick said,

"It is not much further now, sir."

Schick nodded to the boy.

The road at this point, on a slight uphill gradient, with the weight of the cart, the boys started to slow.

Plant getting between the two boys as they pushed against the handles of the barrow.

He putting his weight into the flat bed, it picked up speed. At the same time, the boy that had left the dock earlier, taking the note to Ben Dee, had returned. Taking a rope from the barrow, hooked it onto the front of the cart, pulled while the others pushed.

About fifteen minutes later, passing fields of orange and jujube trees, the barrow working its way up the long straight road.

Passing the Eglise St Anne.

Both Plant and Schick looking up at the beautiful old church, a landmark they will have to remember when returning to collect the gold in two years' time.

A little further up the road were two young girls, about ten years old, playing in the street. One of the boys calling to the girls in Arabic.

"We have the cart for Ben Dee?"

"That is my father," one of the girls called back. "I will get him, this house here."

The boys and Plant eased the barrow toward the house. Stopping the cart at the doorway.

Ben Dee's daughter ran into the house followed by the other girl.

A few seconds later, a man came to the door. Behind him stood the two girls.

"Hello gentlemen," said the man in French, as he stood in the doorway. "My name is Mustafa Ben Dee. I am the friend of Abou Nasir. He sent the note saying you require something to be kept for a while. Is that correct?"

Mustafa Ben Dee was a short man in his early sixties.

He wore a white round cotton taqiyah cap on his head, a thawb tunic and leather sandals.

His face a light tan, filled with wrinkles. His hair grey, along with long stubble and beard.

"Yes," replied Schick in French. "We have some boxes that we were hoping you could keep safe for us, until after the war."

"But of course, it would be my pleasure," said Ben Dee. "Would you like to come in and we can discuss what you will require?"

# Chapter 36
## Out of Sight, Always in Mind
## 24 February 1945

"Come this way." Ben Dee gestured. "Follow me... Oh, don't worry about your boxes. Those lads don't look strong enough to carry that load. My children are a lot older. I will get them to move your things!"

Schick started to follow Ben Dee into the house, when he suddenly turned and looked at the three boys waiting by the cart.

"Have you got any French francs on you, Sergeant Plant?" Schick asked.

"Yes, I have a few."

"Good, can you give the boys one each please!"

"Yes, of course."

Samuel Plant took some money out of his pocket and found three francs, giving the boys one franc each. The boys, shocked to have this much money, looked at each other, then to Samuel Plant.

"*Monsieur, merci, merci!*" the three boys all said as they bowed, with great elation, showing their gratefulness.

Plant turning, he followed Schick into the house.

The house was a little over half-way up the street, in the old part of town. The house too was very old, the windows dirty and the walls had flaking paint.

Inside was clean and well kept. No windows to

the back of the house, there were shutters; they were open on this pleasant day.

Ben Dee called through to his wife in Arabic, then turned, looking at the two Europeans.

"If you would like to sit, my wife will bring through something to eat."

The table was low, there were no chairs. On the floor was a long cushion; the cushion a little longer than the table; shorter ones ran up each end.

Ben Dee sat cross-legged on the cushion, Plant and Schick followed.

"Gentlemen, forgive me," said Ben Dee. "Would you like a drink? I have a very good Scotch whisky."

"Whisky," said Schick. He turned to Plant. "Would you like a whisky?"

"I wouldn't say no."

"Yes, please then, Mr Ben Dee," said Schick.

"Please call me Mustafa, and I am afraid, I do not know your names?"

"Oh, I am sorry, I haven't introduced us!" said Schick. "This is Samuel Plant," he said as he held his hand towards Plant. "And my name is Symanski."

"Mr Plant and Mr Symanski, it is a pleasure to meet you, and it will be a pleasure to do business with you."

Ben Dee's daughter, who had been playing out in the street, came in carrying two plates. One filled with dates, the other grapes.

The girl following Ben Dee's daughter was a friend from the same road. She was carrying a dish full of homemade biscuits, as well as three empty plates, one for each of the men.

As the girls left the room, Ben Dee stood up and went to a cupboard in the corner the room. He pulled out three glasses, a bottle of whisky and poured three shots.

Returning to the table, he laid a glass in front of Schick and Plant, then one for himself.

"Please, eat, drink… Now, what is it you exactly require from me?"

Schick pulled from his pocket a hessian bag, untied the string at the top of the bag, then poured out a series of random jewels: diamonds, opals, amethysts.

"Are these real?" asked Ben Dee.

"If you check with Captain Nasir, we made the same deal with him. He checked his out and was more than pleased with the offer we made. And Mr Ben Dee, I believe you too, will be pleased with the offer we can make you… I will leave these with you for now, there will be more when we return!"

"If Abou is happy, then I too will be happy!"

"Good," said Schick. "Then, what we require is to store our boxes safely, in this house."

"Would the basement be okay?"

"Perfectly okay. Mr Plant and I will write a contract to each other, stating our agreement. What we get from the deal, as well as a time that we will collect the boxes."

"And collecting the boxes will be?"

"Not exactly sure about this, but I am suggesting about two years after the war has ended. The Germans look like they are retreating, so the war could be over soon. If that is the case, we will be looking at two years... September 1947, I would think."

"Two years, that will be fine."

"On the contract, that Mr Plant and I sign, I would be grateful if you could write your agreement to the deal, as well as where we are?"

"But of course, out of sight is one thing. But it's no good, not knowing where you left it... is it not Mr Symanski?"

"These are true words, Mr Ben Dee," said Schick "So we have a deal?"

"We have a deal!" Ben Dee smiled and picked up his glass. "To the future!"

Schick and Plant picked up their glasses.

"To the future," Schick said.

Plant just raised his glass and finished the whisky.

Ben Dee got up from the cushion and made his way out into the garden, shouting in Arabic.

Soon his two sons, in their late twenties, came into the room with Schick and Plant, closely followed by Ben Dee.

They looked at their father, who told them to go to the cart that was out in the street. To bring the boxes in, then take them to the basement below the house, to store them neatly. Once they were all there, to get some canvas and cover the boxes up.

Ben Dee's sons quickly got about their duties, out to the boxes, down into the basement.

As soon as they were finished, they told their father they were done, then went back to their duties in the garden.

"Okay gentlemen, if you would like to follow me

to the basement, I will show you how my boys have stored your goods. And I can promise you, that is exactly how you will find them, when you return."

Schick and Plant followed Ben Dee down the rickety steps to the small cellar below the house. A dirty window to one side, letting enough light in to see that the boxes were neatly piled into the corner of the room. Then covered with a dark green tarpaulin.

Once back up into the main room, Schick got two pieces of paper from his jacket pocket, laid them on the table, then a pen.

"Sergeant Plant, this is for each of us to write the contract. I will be writing the contract for you, and you will be writing the contract for me. If I could suggest, I will write mine first, then you can write the same words, that way we will be equal partners. Does that sound good to you?"

"Yes," said Plant "That sounds good."

Schick laid the paper on the table and started to write in German…

'The contract between', then their names, that the ingots in the boxes are to be split evenly; that they would collect the boxes in the autumn of 1947. He then signed, Plant then signed, then dated.

Plant then wrote his contract to Schick, as Schick read out what he had written on the first contract, Plant wrote the words in English.

He signed, Schick signed, then dated.

Schick then handed the two contracts to Ben Dee, who wrote at the bottom of each contract, that he would look after and keep safe the boxes until they were collected.

His name and his address.

# Summer Present-day

Annaba, Algeria

# Chapter 37
# Citronnade
# Summer Present-day

Passing through the newly built passenger terminal, Jennifer, Tom and Sebastian step out onto Algerian soil and the heat of the day. In front of them, the bustling traffic of the Route d'El Kala. Behind the huge palm trees lay the Gare Ferroviaire, the cream-coloured building featuring five large windows above the entrance. Each having a white and grey surround and an Arabic-style pattern.

To the left of the station, but part of the same building, the cream-patterned wall of the clock tower with grey corners. Above the clock face, on the roof of the clock tower, a white futuristic-looking spire.

It was getting late in the afternoon. So, having the Arabic copy of the contract, they thought they would try and meet up with some of the local Annaba townspeople, hopefully to see if they would know what the names Mustafa Ben Dee and Celestine or Silsitin Bourgogne may mean.

As they stood at front of the passenger terminal, to their right they could see trees and a wide-open area, a park or boulevard.

This may be a good place to start their search.

They crossed the busy road, until they reached the tree-lined concourse of Cours de la Révolution.

The four hundred metre length avenue, lined

with banks, shops and theatres.

In the centre of the concourse lay the forty-metre-wide meeting place for friends, business people and families.

The walkway filled with trees, plants, pavement cafés and entertainment.

They found a free table and chairs to one of the many open-air seating spots, a parasol over the table, covering customers from the hot midday Algerian sun.

It was now late afternoon and the sun had dipped below the banks and buildings to the south side of the walkway.

A waiter in his early twenties, wearing a black apron around his waist, walked towards their table.

"Good afternoon, sir, madame," he said in French. "Would you like a menu?"

"Yes please," Tom answered.

The waiter laid three menus on the table.

"Is there anything you would recommend?" Tom asked the waiter.

"The citronnade is very good on a hot day, and very popular."

"Thank you," said Tom. "I will keep that in mind."

Jennifer and Sebastian had already opened their menus and were busily flicking through the pages.

"It's all in French and Arabic," said Sebastian.

The menu, with a small picture showing the ingredients used to make the drink or dish.

"Well, the waiter had recommended the citronnade," said Tom. "So that's what I am going for."

Jennifer had already found that drink in the menu, so pointed it out to Sebastian.

"Citronnade, citron naturel," she said.

"Okay," said Sebastian "Three citronnades."

Tom turned in his chair and caught the eye of the waiter, who immediately walked over to their table.

Drinks ordered, the waiter left their table, towards a dark wooden hut, where drinks and dishes were being prepared.

A few minutes later, he returned with three citronnades, in tall glasses and straws.

As the waiter laid the glasses on the table, Tom took the opportunity to ask a question.

"We are visiting Annaba. This is our first visit. I wonder if I can ask you something?"

"Yes sir, I will help if I can."

"We are doing some family history and have found the name of someone we would like to meet."

"Yes sir," said the waiter

"The person we would like to know about lived during the war; he was Mustafa Ben Dee. But we also have a name of Silsitin or Celestine Bourgogne, or something like that!"

"I am sorry sir," apologised the waiter. "Annaba is a big city, there are many people here. I am afraid I do not know these names at all."

"Okay, well thank you anyway. We will keep trying."

"But if I can help in any way, sir?"

"Yes!"

"I have a friend, Hussan. He is a taxi driver. He

knows a lot of people. He may know how to get the information you need."

"Hussan, and how do we meet Hussan?"

"Where are you staying sir?"

"We are on a boat in the harbour."

"I could arrange for him to meet you nine a.m. tomorrow morning at the terminal. Would that be helpful to you sir?"

"That would be wonderful." Tom smiled.

Tom turned back to Jennifer and Sebastian, who were both enjoying the real lemon sorbet drink that they had received.

"Oh, this is good," Sebastian said to Jennifer.

"What did you find out?" Jennifer asked Tom.

"The waiter has a taxi driver friend, Hussan. He is very knowledgeable about Annaba. The waiter thinks he may be able to help us."

"What tomorrow?"

"Nine o'clock in the morning."

That evening, Tom, Jennifer and Sebastian relaxed in the warm Annaba evening air, dining on pizza and more Citronnade.

# Chapter 38
## Yellow Cab
## Summer Present-day

Nine o'clock the next morning.

Tom, Jennifer and Sebastian stood outside the passenger terminal, waiting for their taxi to turn up, with the driver called Hussan.

Tom in his usual T-shirt and shorts, on his head an old straw trilby hat.

Sebastian in beige trousers and a blue short-sleeved shirt. Jennifer looking stunning, in white calf-length trousers, a white and blue silk blouse, a light white cotton abaya with the image of a light blue bird. Its wings starting at the back, a long neck on either side of the abaya, around to its head at the front.

Around her neck, Jennifer wore a silk scarf, the same colour blue as the bird on the abaya.

The three of them standing in front of the modern glass building, watching every taxi that passed.

Taxis in Algeria, as here in Annaba, were once blue and white.

A former president of Algeria, having visited New York, deciding he liked the yellow cab so much, deemed all taxis in Algeria should from that moment be yellow.

The stream of cars now passing the port

entrance; every other car was a taxi, a yellow cab.

But just pulling into the port entrance, right on nine o'clock, a yellow cab pulled up in front of them.

Out of the cab jumped a fit-looking man, in his early forties. He had nicely cut, short black hair. He wore dark trousers, a white shirt and dark blue tie.

Smiling, he walked around the cab and towards Tom, Jennifer and Sebastian.

"Good morning," he said in French. "Are you the people that my friend Khalil the waiter said I was to pick up this morning?"

"Yes," Tom said in English, then, suddenly realising, said "*Oui.*"

Hussan's expression instantly beamed into a huge smile as his hands went out.

"Are you English?" he said in English with a slight Arabic accent.

"Yes," said Tom.

Jennifer and Sebastian becoming aware that here is someone who speaks English.

"Oh, that's wonderful," enthused Hussan, starting each sentence with an Arabic accent and finishing it with Cockney. "I lived in London for eleven years. I loved it there. I have lots of friends still in Lunden *(London)*."

Hussan greeted Tom with a kiss on each cheek, then to Sebastian, who felt a bit uncomfortable being kissed on the cheek by a man.

Hussan then shook Jennifer's hand.

"Please, please, get into my cab," Hussan said, excitedly. "Khalil said you were looking for something, but you don't know what it is, or where it is?"

Jennifer and Sebastian getting into the rear of the cab as Tom jumped into the front. As Tom sat, Hussan was closing the rear door.

"Yes, Hussan," said Tom. "As strange as it may sound, your friend has got that about right, and this was all over seventy-five years ago."

"Okay," said Hussan getting into the driver's side. "Let me have the details. We will see where we have to start looking."

Tom got from his pocket the copy of the Arabic part of the contract.

He gave it to Hussan who read the message, after a few seconds he turned to Tom.

"Mustafa Ben Dee... don't know... and what is this bit?" asked Hussan to Tom.

"Well, we are not sure either, Celestine, Silsitin, Bourgogne... we need to find someone who will know."

"Umm," exclaimed Hussan. "Difficult init?" finishing the sentence in Cockney.

"Any ideas? your friend at the café thought you would be good at this sort of thing!"

"I'll tell you what," Hussan grinned. "This is going to be a good day... this type of job beats picking up old ladies from the market and dropping them at home any day... now... Where do we start?"

Hussan thought for a moment, then announced.

"Right, if we start the search at the Basilica, we can see if anyone can help there!"

"It's a start," said Tom, as he looked around at Jennifer and Sebastian who both nodded.

"And I *know*," continued Hussan, "that behind the Basilica is an old people's home. If you say this happened over seventy-five years ago, well, they may have the answer to your question!"

The yellow cab pulled away slowly from the port, onto the Route d'El Kala, and into the flow of traffic.

No one was driving fast in Annaba, a mixture of speed bumps and large potholes. The traffic driving at a reasonable speed, a need to constantly watch for obstacles in the road.

Tom, Jennifer and Sebastian looking from the windows of the cab, see a city in transition. Half the buildings, gleaming glass and modern designs. The other half, tired, unpainted and unloved. Beautiful buildings, from an age of French colonial rule. Three and four-storey buildings, with large windows, small balconies and wrought iron balustrades.

Hussan's cab turning at the junction, took the Avenue de L'A.L.N. south-west and towards the main road of N44.

The cab slowly passing the railway station to their left.

Through the railings, they could see the bright shiny polished steel trains, ready for their journey to Tunisia and Algiers.

The slow-moving traffic thinning as they get further out of town.

As they made their way up the Avenue de L'A.L.N.; through the front window of the cab, about a mile in front of them, they could see the Basilica.

The magnificent white and sky-blue building,

with its two towers and majestic centre dome, sitting high upon the hill overlooking the city.

Reaching the roundabout at the end of the Avenue de L'A.L.N., Hussan following signs towards St Augustin's Abbey and Hippone, then the road for Chemin de la Basilique St Augustin. The road winding up the steep hill, passing wild goats eating grass at the side of the road.

The yellow cab pulling into the car park, up to the wall of the Abbey where it stopped.

"The entrance to the Abbey is just around the corner," Hussan said. "If you have no luck, we will see what we can try next!"

# Chapter 39
## No Photography
### Summer Present-day

Jennifer, Sebastian and Tom all exit the taxi. Hussan sat, waiting for their return.

Tom closing the cabs door, placing his straw hat on his head; they turned the corner, heading towards the steps to the Basilica's main door.

Standing at the bottom of the steps, they looked up at the monument.

Its white marbled walls, blue inlay and the two towers. One either side of the main entrance, high into the sky. Each featuring a small dome, topped with a cross.

In front of the main large door were four red pillars. Behind the pillars, a wrought iron gate. Looking to the left of the pillars, they could see a smaller door which was open.

Climbing the steps, they made their way towards the smaller door.

As they entered: the magnificent scene, as the inside of the Basilica opened up before them.

To their left was a table. On the table were books and pamphlets telling the story of St Augustin's Abbey, the history of Annaba and famous visitors.

Beside the table, sat a shabbily dressed man, of African descent.

Seeing someone to ask, Tom headed towards the

man at the table. But before Tom could say a word, the man of African descent spoke first.

"Can you take your hat off, sir?" he politely said in French, with an African accent.

"Oh, sorry, yes… of course," Tom stuttered, as he removed his straw trilby

Jennifer picking up that Tom had been asked to remove his hat. She tactfully and slowly pulled her scarf up, over her head.

"Now, how may I help you, sir?" said the man at the table.

"I was hoping to speak to someone… someone in charge, a priest, the bishop, someone like that."

"I am afraid you are out of luck with that, sir," the man at the table said quietly, slowly and calmly "The ministers…"

A flash from a visitor's camera flashed in the church.

The man at the table calmly said to Tom,

"Excuse me one second, sir."

He picked up a megaphone and shouted in French.

"NO PHOTOGRAPHY!"

He then laid the megaphone back down on the table and continued calmly talking to Tom.

"As I was saying, sir, we have no ministers here today, but we do have the administrator of the Abbey. Would that help?"

"It would very much, thank you," answered Tom.

"He is out at the moment," the man at the desk calmly said, Tom suddenly feeling deflated. "But he should be back in a short while… why don't you look around God's wonderful building while you wait?"

"That is very kind of you, if we may!"

"I will let him know that you wish to speak with him, when he returns."

"Thank you," said Tom.

Tom turned to Jennifer and Sebastian.

"The person we need to speak to is out at the moment, but will be back shortly. We can look around till he arrives."

Sebastian and Jennifer nod as they all walk into the Abbey.

It was a beautiful building. Amazing to think that the workers who built such a monument did so without any of the modern-day cutters, diggers or cranes. A marvellous achievement.

They walked up the first aisle admiring the stained glass and statues.

Then 'Flash'… "NO PHOTOGRAPHY!"

They had just reached the far end of the Abbey, turned the corner into the next aisle, just about to pass the lying statue of Augustine in a glass box, when a man's voice called out to Tom.

"Excuse me," the man said in French. "Joules at the desk had said you want to speak with me?"

Tom turned to see the old frail man, slightly hunched back, a long grey beard, his hair grey, straggly and thinning.

He wore a tatty black suit and a white shirt, done up to the collar, but with no tie.

"We are looking for some information," said Tom. "We have found a piece of paper in my friend's family history, and we are trying to trace the details of what it means."

"May I see it?"

"Yes of course."

Tom took the copy of the Arabic wording and gave it to the administrator.

"Oh, it's in Arabic. I'm afraid I don't speak Arabic."

"And neither do I sir, but I have friends, who have told me that there is a name, maybe two. We have Mustafa Ben Dee and Celestine or Silsitin Bourgogne, or something like that."

"I am afraid, that means nothing to me," the administrator admitted "Although I have been here for many years, I tend not to travel far."

"Still, I would like to thank you... and, do you know of anyone who may be able to help us?" Tom smiled.

"You may like to try Sister Josephine, in the old people's home behind the Abbey. She has many residents of Annaba come and go through the home. Someone at some time may have mentioned the names you seek. She has a good memory. She may be able to help you."

"Thank you once again," said Tom.

Tom turned to Jennifer and Sebastian.

"The administrator cannot help, but he has suggested seeing one of the nuns from the home behind the Abbey"

"Okay," they both whispered.

They all walked down the aisle towards the exit.

"Good luck with your quest!" called the administrator.

'Flash'... "NO PHOTOGRAPHY!"

# Chapter 40
## Lots of White Teeth
## Summer Present-day

They left the coolness of the Abbey stepping back into the heat of the sunshine outside. Down the steps and back towards the yellow cab.

Hussan seeing them coming, called out of his window as they walked towards him.

"Did you have any luck, my friends?"

"No," answered Tom. "There were none of the priests or ministers in today, but the administrator gave us a name of someone to see in the old people's home."

"Ah, yes," said Hussan. "Up that alley at the back of the church, there is a black gate. Pull the handle beside it. It will ring a bell."

"Thank you, Hussan."

Tom, Sebastian and Jennifer walked past the taxi, making their way towards the home, following the direction of Hussan's finger.

As they reached the far end wall of the Abbey, the passageway was about three metres long, from here they could see the black gate.

The wall to the old peoples' home was painted white. The gate was inset into the wall. To the right of the gate, a round metal bar painted black stuck through the wall, rounded off at the end to make a handle.

"Well," said Sebastian. "This looks like it, shall I pull it?"

"Go on," said Jennifer, Tom nodded.

Sebastian pulled the handle and a bell rang; the rod sprung back to the wall.

Sebastian pulled again as the bell rang for a second time.

They waited for what seemed to be a long time.

Thinking no one was going to come, then suddenly there was a click and the gate slowly opened.

Stood before them, was a short, rotund, but not fat man. His back was bent into a slight hunch.

He was not old, but he did not look healthy.

The gate was not fully open, just enough for his body.

"Good morning," said Tom in French. "We were hoping to see one of the nuns here today, a Sister Josephine?"

The hunched man nodded and shut the gate, leaving them outside and not sure if he understood what they wanted.

A few minutes passed. They wondered whether to pull the bell again, then the gate clicked and slowly opened once more.

This time, the gate fully opened as the short rotund man stood to one side and gestured for them to come through.

"Thank you," said Tom, Sebastian and Jennifer.

Inside the gate, they could now see the grounds to the old people's home.

There was a rectangular grass centre courtyard,

with paths set into the grass for the residents to walk. The building was about thirty metres long by twenty metres wide with white walls.

It was set on two floors, the ground floor having a tiled area, to a resident's door. On the far side, there was a nun in a white tunic sweeping the tiles.

Above the tiled walkway, an upper walkway ran down the width and length of the upper floor, giving the residents on the upper floor access to their rooms.

A wooden handrail followed the walkway all the way around.

Half-way down the upper floor, sat several residents in wheelchairs, looking through the wooden balustrade at Tom, Sebastian and Jennifer as they walked through the main gate.

Directly in front of them, on a footpath between the grass and the tiled floor, and in the direction the short, hunched man's hand was pointing, stood a nun. She was short and thin, her face pale with a few lines, giving a clue to her age.

She stood in her brilliantly white tunic, scapular, cowl and veil. She had a slim body and her head was upright with an air of superiority, of being in charge. Her arms were in front of her, her hands clasped together. There was a serene smile on her face. She had a lot of perfect teeth, which, if possible, were even whiter than her tunic.

Tom, Sebastian and Jennifer slowly edged towards the nun.

Jennifer having taken the scarf off of her head, pulled it back on.

"Good morning," said the nun in English as if

she knew.

"Good morning," replied Tom. "Are you, Sister Josephine?"

"Yes, I am. I hear you wish to speak with me?" she beamed.

"You speak very good English," said Jennifer. "Are you from England?"

"Yes, I was," acknowledged Sister Josephine. "But my calling was to come and look after the poor, old and sick of this part of the world."

"That is very admirable," said Sebastian. "I don't believe I could ever do that!"

"No," said the Sister, offhandedly looking at Sebastian. "Anyway." She turned back to Tom. "You are not here to talk about me, so, what is it that you *do* require?"

"Well Sister Josephine," said Tom. "We have, during family research, found that my friend's great grandfather had been here during the war. We are looking for the place or, even better, the family he was with during that time?"

"During the war you say?"

"Yes, we know it was a long time ago, and that it is a long shot."

"And how do you think I may be able to help, with what you are asking?"

"That you may know, or even, during a conversation with your residents, that the names I have, might have been spoken about!"

"Mmm," she sighed. "And these names?"

"Mustafa Ben Dee and Celestine or Silsitin Bourgogne."

Sister Josephine put her hand to her chin and thought for a while, she shook her head.

"I am sorry, these names mean nothing to me… I have been here many years, and I am afraid, I have not known anybody by those names."

"As I said, Sister," Tom said, looking dejected. "It is a longshot, and it may well be we never find out about these people."

"I am sorry," said the Sister, looking sad for Tom.

"Is there anywhere else you think it might be worth looking?" asked Jennifer.

"Hmm," the Sister sighed slightly shaking her head towards Jennifer, then with a sudden thought she said, "Oh, wait one moment!" getting as excited as an old nun can get. "We have an imam from La Colonne, he visits a friend of his every month. He is not very old, late thirties, early forties, but a very clever man, very intelligent… he might be able to help."

"La Colonne, Sister," said Tom "Where will we find La Colonne?"

"It is an area, just west of the city."

"Okay."

"If he is there," Sister Josephine continued. "You will find him at the Masjid El Forkane… it's the mosque in Avenue Colonel Amirouche."

"And his name… do you have his name?" asked Jennifer.

"Salim Wasem," answered Sister Josephine.

# Chapter 41
## Green Flaking Paint
## Summer Present-day

Back at the yellow cab, Hussan excitedly waited to hear from Tom, Sebastian and Jennifer. Eager to hear how they got on with the answer to their quest.

He looked in the direction of the alley and could see them all walking towards his cab chatting.

He jumped out of the driver's door and ran around the cab, ready to open the doors.

"So, what have you found out?" he asked as the three reached the cab.

"We met Sister Josephine," said Tom "But with the same news that we are hearing from everyone else, no one has heard of the names that we need."

"But she did give us another place to try," said Jennifer.

"I must find out who her dentist is," said Sebastian.

"And so," Hussan continued. "Where do we go next?"

"Avenue Colonel Amirouche," said Jennifer.

"To the mosque, Masjid El Forkane," said Tom.

"I know where that is."

Hussan opened the passenger doors.

"Please jump in."

As Hussan pulled away from the Abbey car park, following the winding road down the hill, Tom looking back over his shoulder at Sebastian, who looked quiet and pensive in the rear seat.

"Well," said Tom. "What are you thinking?"

"I'm thinking, this isn't sounding good."

"But we still have another lead."

"Yes, but there is too much time that has passed, no one has heard of the people. And I'm starting to think, it's all too late. We have missed it. These people have long gone, along with what we are looking for."

"But we knew that in England," said Tom. "We said, there was no guarantee, that if we came on this journey, we would definitely know one way or another, once we had checked for ourselves."

"And this is turning out to be a complete waste of time," said Sebastian, getting angry.

"Hey Sebastian," interrupted Jennifer. "Let's look back on whether this has all been worth it, when we reach the end. All the time we have a lead, it is still possible."

Sebastian looked out of the window.

"And what do you think Tom?" asked Jennifer.

"Well, I haven't given up hope yet… but I have to admit, as we seem to get nothing like the answers we were hoping for, not even an inkling of a clue, it has left me feeling a little deflated."

The taxi took the same route back towards the city as it came, but half-way down Avenue De L'A.L.N it turned north onto Emir Abdelkader Street. The heavy traffic of the town slowing them down.

Annaba, they all thought looked like a town in transition, the old French colonial parts of town, now looking old and tired. The houses themselves beautiful, with their balconies, large windows and shutters.

The terracotta and brownish-orange roofs, as well as flat roofs with washing lines. The old painted buildings with flaking paint but sitting next to a modern building; a building of marble and stone, of glass and steel. The transition is taking place, and this can only be a good thing for the future.

Every house they passed seemed to now be a shop. There were no longer house fronts; every house sold something, fruit and veg, clothes, hats, ornaments and trinkets, jewellery and gold.

There was everything for sale somewhere in Annaba.

At the end of Emir Abdelkader Street was a park, the Square El-Houria, then onto the Rue Emir Abdelkader.

At the roundabout, the taxi turned onto Avenue Abdelhamid Ben Badis.

At the next main junction, left into Chemin Maateri Lakhdar dit Abbes, then immediately into Rue Abada Ahmed. At the next junction, straight across into Rue Ferhani Mohammed.

"This is it," Hussan said, pointing out of his window to the left.

They all looked out of the window to see a large green wall, the paint flaking in places. And like a lot of homes, buildings and shops, certainly in the older parts of Annaba, in need of a facelift.

Half-way down the road was a large gate.

A metal frame with a wrought iron inlay in a

decorative pattern, the gate shut at the moment, but opened when at prayers.

Hussan drove on until he reached the end of the road.

"In front of us is the Avenue Colonel Amirouche. The entrance to the mosque is just around the corner there."

He pulled the taxi over and stopped for them to get out of the cab.

Three doors opened, as Tom, Sebastian and Jennifer went to get out of the vehicle.

"Ah," said Hussan. "I don't think the lady will be able to go inside."

"Oh?" exclaimed Tom.

"That's okay," said Jennifer. "I will wait here till you come out and you can tell me what you have found out!"

"Sure, okay," said Tom.

Sebastian and Tom shut their car doors, walking the short distance around the corner until they reached the entrance to the mosque.

The green flaking walls ended before the entrance door. The wall turning to a brown, beige and cream mosaic. The doorway having a light brown metal frame of patterned wrought iron. Above the door, a large opening. This, too, filled with wrought iron pattern, painted black. Two steps took them up to the door, Tom led the way.

Sitting just inside the door, was a thin man. He wore tatty dark-coloured trousers and light blue T-shirt. He was in his mid-fifties, with dark hair, heavy moustache and unshaven face.

"Excuse me," Tom said in French.

"Yes," said the man suddenly jolting upright.

"We are hoping to see the imam. Would he be here?"

"There is an imam here," said the man.

"I am told his name is Salim Wasem. Is that correct?"

"Salim Wasem is here," he said, as he stood up.

"Would it be possible to meet the imam? We are on a quest and we are hoping he may be able to help us."

"I will see... if you would wait one moment."

The man turned and went through a gate that was behind him. A few seconds later, he returned through the gate.

"Would you like to follow me this way?" the thin man said.

Tom and Sebastian walked through the gate and into the courtyard of the mosque, which was tiled with a beige and light grey tile in a chequered pattern.

The walls painted white, the lower section and pillars cream. The building was two storeys; arched holes in the main wall looked through to another open courtyard the other side. There were square windows into rooms and offices on the ground floor.

The thin man walked to one of the doors. Beside the door was a square window to an office.

The man opened the door as he asked Tom and Sebastian to enter.

Behind the desk was a handsome, young-looking man, dressed in a mid-grey lightweight cotton collarless jacket and trousers.

He had straight dark hair combed back, neatly trimmed beard and moustache, his olive skin looked fresh and smooth.

"Hello, gentlemen. I am the Imam Salim Wasem," he said in French. "And how may I help you?"

"Hello," said Tom. "We have come from England on a mission to find some information about my friend's family history… His great grandfather was here during the war, and he wishes to visit the family that his great grandfather met while he was here."

"So, you are English?" the imam said in a rough, broken English.

"You speak English?" Tom said.

"It is very poor, but I will try, but … I may have to go back to French."

"That will be fine, thank you," smiled Tom.

"What is it you are looking for?"

"As it seems we are looking for information that may not exist any more, it is a person, or maybe two, who lived in Annaba in 1945."

"And these two names are?"

"Mustafa Ben Dee and Celestine or Silsitin Bourgogne."

"Hmm, it seems familiar," he now spoke in French. "But as you can imagine, there are a lot of people in Annaba. I cannot expect to know the name of every one of them, not even the name of every visitor to my mosque… as well as… It took place in 1945. My Friend, a lot has changed in that time, a lot of the people that may well have been able to help you are long gone."

"Yes, we are aware, and we were not sure if we were ever going to be able to achieve the task, but we felt we had to try."

"And for that alone, you have to be admired," the imam smiled. "Now, as I have said, I am too young to know any people you speak of. And, of course, there are no guarantees, that what I am about to suggest will help."

"We are here to try as much as we can, so anything?"

"Well, just up the road from here is a fantastic old lady. She has been one of the pillars of the community for as long as I can remember. And so much respected. But, as I say, she is now very old and frail, and it may be that her memory is fading with time… but, as you say, someone may be able to help, and it may be her."

"I thank you very much for your help and advice Monsieur Wasem, and what would be her name?"

"Madame Bouroubi!"

# Chapter 42
## Dinner Is Served
## Summer Present-day

The imam at the Masjid El Forkane mosque asked the thin man at the entrance to the mosque to show Tom and Sebastian up to the house of Bouroubi.

Having left the mosque, Tom had said to the thin man that they had to pick up a lady who was sitting in a taxi around the corner.

***

"How did you get on at the mosque?" asked Jennifer as Tom reached the cab.

"The imam was too young to know the people we need. So, he has suggested that there is a lady; an older lady up the road. So, let's see."

"Well," said Sebastian. "I am starting to think this is just a huge waste of time!"

"Do you want me to wait for you?" asked Hussan.

"If you would please Hussan," said Tom. "This may be another short visit. Let's see."

"Okay," said Hussan. "If you return and I am not here; just get in, and I will return shortly."

"Will do, Hussan."

Jennifer got out of the taxi and the three of them walked the short distance to the thin man, he stood waiting on the corner of Avenue Colonel Amirouche.

"We are all ready," Tom said in French to the thin man.

"This way please?" he replied.

They passed houses and more shops, as they walked the short distance up the road.

The imam was right, the house was not far away.

It was a busy road, not very wide, but with a lot of one-way traffic heading towards the city.

The amount of traffic though, had taken its toll on the buildings, looking grubby from the dust and fumes given off by the cars, lorries and busses.

"This is it, gentlemen, madame," said the thin man.

"Thank you for your help," Tom said.

The thin man turned and started walking back down Avenue Colonel Amirouche, back towards the mosque.

Tom, Jennifer and Sebastian stood in front of the very old-looking, single-floor house.

The once white face now covered with the dirt from exhaust fumes. The white frames of the large windows with layers of fine dust particles.

There were two windows, neither had glass, shutters filled the gap. A metal frame filled with a fine mesh, outside of the shutter.

A large door frame, with a solid looking wooden door; the windows on each side of the door. In the middle of the door was a knocker in the shape of a clenched fist hanging down.

Tom knocked.

A few moments later, a fresh-faced, attractive

young woman of about twenty years old appeared wearing large glasses, smartly dressed in jeans and a T-shirt.

On her head, she had a creamy-coloured hijab turban, with a bun at the back.

"Hello," she said, in French.

"Good afternoon," said Tom. "We are on a quest. We come from England. We have been told that Madame Bouroubi might be able to help us."

"I speak English, well, a little," said the young woman, now speaking English. "If you would like to wait one moment, I will see if I can find someone to help you!"

"Thank you," said Tom.

A moment later, a man in his mid-fifties came to the door, medium height, short hair. He wore pale pink trousers, a blue and white short-sleeved checked shirt, hanging over the top of his trousers.

He had a round face, with a big beaming smile. He was the sort of person who looked immediately welcoming.

"You are looking for Madame Bouroubi, my daughter tells me?" he said in French.

"Yes," said Tom. "We are looking for some information about someone who lived during the war... the imam at the local mosque thought she may be able to help."

The smiling man fully opened the door and said, "Please come in."

As Tom, Jennifer and Sebastian entered the house, the smiling man had already walked down the short hallway to the living room. Sebastian, as the last in, shut the door.

"Please come this way," said the smiling man in a broken English.

He stopped in the living room, the walls painted green, the room very minimal. There was a large free-standing cabinet of dark wood and glass, holding ornaments. A small two-drawer cabinet of dark wood, a television on the wall, a low rectangular table, a long cushion on the floor under the window, immediately behind the table; the cushion turning right angles and along the wall on the left-hand side of the room.

"My name is Beh'hee," said the smiling man, his daughter standing alongside him. "My mother is asleep at the moment; she will sleep for a short while longer."

"Oh, I am sorry," said Tom. "Shall we return in a while?"

"Return, you mean leave?" grinned Beh'hee. "No, no, no, you shall join us for lunch… the family are here. It would be our pleasure if you would join us?"

"We could not possibly impose on you!" Tom doubted.

"Sir," said Beh'hee. "What are your names?"

"I am Tom, this is Jennifer" gesturing towards her. "And this is Sebastian," turning to him.

"Well, Tom, Jennifer and Sebastian," insisted Beh'hee. "It would be an enormous pleasure for us, if you would join us for lunch!"

"Well, if you are sure," Tom said, hesitantly.

"Then, when Mother is up and joins us, you will

be here waiting!"

"Thank you, then we will be pleased to join you!"

Beh'hee turned towards the door to the right of the only window and walked through into the kitchen.

In the kitchen was Beh'Hee's sister Saba, wearing a light green thawb and having a white khimar covering her head, which came around under her chin, leaving her face open.

"*Salaam Alaikum*," greeted Saba as Tom, Jennifer and Sebastian followed Beh'hee through the kitchen and into the garden.

Tom greeted her with "*Bonjour*" while Jennifer and Sebastian both said "Hello".

The kitchen was basic, worktops, a large refrigerator.

On the cooker was a big pot with a wonderful smell of stew.

As they all walked into the garden, Beh'hee announced that there would be some guests having dinner with them.

Immediately, the family got up and started moving places to make room for the three strangers.

They walked up to the table, which were three long wooden tables end-to-end, a table cloth on each table.

"Please, please... sit down, make yourself at home," said Beh'hee.

As the three of them sat at the table, the family had gone quiet, waiting for them to settle. They were waiting to ask a question, to find out about these newcomers, and hear about them and their lives.

Beh'hee proceeded to walk around the table, putting his hands on the shoulders of the family member sitting there, introducing each one as he reached them.

"This is Mehdi, my brother." he said in French, as Mehdi greeted the strangers.

"Then we have Phaiza, Waheba," Beh'hee continued. "This is my wife, Sumya, and my son and daughter, Haosam and Malek."

Turning to the other side of the table, he continued.

"This is Haneifa and her husband Jaber, and their daughter Zena, the baby."

As he introduced Zena, he picked her up, holding her high above his head, face down towards him as he growled like a bear, the baby laughing.

"And, finally, next to you Tom, is our own British family, Phoola. She lives in England."

"You live in England?" said Tom to Phoola in English

"Yes," she replied in a pleasant, quiet voice. "I married an Englishman many years ago."

Beh'hee took his seat.

"Mother will be out to dinner shortly," Beh'hee said in a broken English to Tom, Jennifer and Sebastian, and then continued in French. "I am sure she will enjoy your company here, but you must remember, she is eighty-five, and may struggle to remember."

The table now burst into conversation, everyone wanting to find out about Tom, Jennifer and Sebastian.

Phaiza trying the odd words of English that she knew.

The younger ones, Malek and Haosam, talking fluent English, having learnt from the television and records.

The garden was about four metres wide, and sixty metres long, with a concrete and tiled area for the table. Further down the garden were trees of lemon, limes and oranges. A high wall ran the length of the garden either side.

A call from Saba in the kitchen doorway, Beh'hee and Phaiza getting up from the table as they went to help.

A few moments later and bowls of lamb stew were placed in front of the guests, then to the rest of the family.

Flatbread made by Waheba was laid in the middle of the table. Mehdi poured water from bottles into the glasses of the three guests, as they all settled down to eat.

"This is delicious," Tom said to Phoola.

"She is a very good cook, is Saba," she replied. "And so is Beh'hee; he owns restaurants."

"A talented family," said Tom.

"There are some very clever people."

After they had all finished the lamb stew, the conversation was flowing around the table. Everyone was interested in what Jennifer, Sebastian and Tom did, and where they lived.

Saba went in to organise the next dish.

Phaiza and Beh'hee cleared the table.

Waheba got up from the table and followed them

in.

As Beh'hee started to bring the next dishes of couscous and fried chicken out to the table, Waheba came through the kitchen door, with her, an old and frail-looking lady in a wheelchair.

Although she was old and frail, her face had a healthy glow to it, one that has seen a good life with a loving family.

She wore a white thawb and khimar.

Waheba wheeled her up to the table, a place laid for her beside Phoola, on the opposite side to Tom.

As she stopped at the table, she leaned forward, looking past Phoola and stared at the three guests, not saying a word for several seconds then,

"We have guests?" she announced in Arabic.

"Yes, mother," replied Phoola. "They have come from London. They are on a quest and want to ask you a question."

"A question," said Madame Bouroubi, taking a forkful of couscous.

"Yes mother," Phoola continued. "We don't know what it is yet. We are all waiting to hear the question that they want to ask you."

Phoola turned to Tom.

"Mother is asking what it is you want to know?"

"Yes," said Beh'hee. "We all want to know."

The whole table went quiet as they listened to Tom.

"Madame Bouroubi," Tom croaked. "My friend Sebastian," Tom said, as he pointed towards Sebastian sitting two seats to his side, "had been doing his family history and had come across a piece of paper, which gave details of his great grandfather, that he had been to Annaba during the war. And that he had met an Algerian man who he befriended. We were hoping to meet up with his family, to see them and speak to them... we have come a long way, to find them and to see them would mean a great deal to us."

Although Tom was speaking to Madame Bouroubi, Madame Bouroubi didn't speak French or English. So, Phoola was translating into Arabic, then Arabic back to English as her mother spoke, so that Jennifer and Sebastian could join the conversation.

"And what is the information you have already?" asked the old lady.

"We have a couple of names Madame Bouroubi," said Tom.

"And these names?"

"Mustafa Ben Dee and Celestine maybe Silsitin Bourgogne?"

Madame Bouroubi slowly ate another mouthful of couscous as she thought about the question. Her head upright, she looked forward, her eyes staring at nothing; blankly looking ahead of her.

Her head dropped as it swayed from side to side.

Tom realising this was another dead end. He thought at this moment in time, he had no idea of where to go next. What would be the next place they could try, on this journey that he, Jennifer and Sebastian were on?

And Sebastian, how would he take more bad news? He was on edge for most of the journey already. His jealousy and his anger boiling up on several occasions, how would he cope with travelling back to Europe, not having an answer to the question they were all hoping to achieve?

Madame Bouroubi's head came back to an upright position as she looked at Tom.

"Celestin Bourgoin?"

"Yes, Madame Bouroubi," said Tom. "That is the name on the piece of paper that we found."

"Celestin Bourgoin?" Madame Bouroubi repeated.

"Yes, madame," said Tom as Jennifer and Sebastian nodded.

"This is Celestin Bourgoin!"

"Mother," laughed Beh'hee. "They are looking for Celestine Bourgogne!"

Beh'hee turned to Tom, Jennifer and Sebastian.

"Please forgive my mother," he said. "She sometimes doesn't remember things like she used to."

"This is Celestin Bourgoin!" she insisted once more.

Madame Bouroubi turned once more to Tom.

"Did you say this happened during the war?"

"Yes, Madame Bouroubi, during the war, February 1945."

Madame Bouroubi stopped and looked forward again, her eyes staring into a void, she slowly picked up another mouthful of couscous.

The three tables went dead quiet as the old lady thought.

She then spoke quietly.

"I was playing in the street with my friend

Adilah," Madame Bouroubi said, as she looked straight ahead. "It was late morning and nearing the end of the war. Two foreign men came up the road, with some boys and a barrow. There were lots of boxes on the barrow. I must have been about ten, but I still remember. One of the men didn't speak a lot, the other spoke in French."

Tom, Jennifer and Sebastian suddenly sitting up as they realise, this is the story they wanted to hear.

"They went into Adilah's father's house," she said, speaking quietly and softly. "Adilah and I took them food on trays, I remember… that was a long time ago!"

"And Mustafa Ben Dee, Madame Bouroubi?" asked Tom.

"Oh, Monsieur Ben Dee, he died a long time ago… and Adilah, she got married and is now living a long way from here."

Tom, now waiting to hear the words, *'the house is now gone, no one lives there any more'*, and then, the thought of him having to be with Sebastian for the journey home.

"After the war," Madame Bouroubi continued, "the people of Algeria wanted a new start, an end to the French Colonial rule. The men took to the streets, during the revolution years, people were rounded up. Soldiers would go from house to house looking for plotters, they even came here, but luckily didn't take Monsieur Bouroubi. In the early 1960s, Algeria gained independence, everything changed. It was a new start for the country. Even here in Annaba, under the French, it had a French name 'Bône', and the old French street names, like the main square, this was once 'Cour Jérôme Bertagna', now Cour de la Révolution."

"And this Madame Bouroubi, you said '*This* is Celestin Bourgoin'," asked Tom. "What did you mean, *this* is Celestin Bourgoin?"

"Because the road you are in… Avenue Colonel Amirouche, was before 1963, Avenue Celestin Bourgoin!"

Sebastian, Jennifer and Tom, all looked at each other. The joy that, maybe, just maybe, they have found it.

"And… the Ben Dee family?" Tom hesitated to ask.

"Oh yes," smiled Madame Bouroubi "They still live up the road!"

"Was this the news you wanted?" asked Beh'hee.

"Yes," smiled Tom "Very much!"

"What we will do to help you," said Beh'hee "After dinner, we will get the address from mother, Mehdi can take you there."

"That would be wonderful," said Tom "We are enormously grateful for your hospitality and your help."

"Hey, we are Algerian," smiled Beh'hee. "It's what we do!"

# Chapter 43
## We Were Expecting You
### Summer Present-day

After dinner, they all left the Bouroubi house.

Mehdi, having got the address, had told the three of them that it was a little further up the road and away from Annaba city centre.

Jennifer had suggested that Sebastian go back to the taxi of Hussan, to let him know that they are still following a lead, and that he is to stay. They would be back at the taxi as soon as they can.

Jennifer, Tom and Mehdi waited by the Bouroubi house, while Sebastian went to see Hussan.

As he returned, the three of them followed Mehdi up the road.

The green hills of Djebel Bou Kanta in front of them as they walked away from the city and the port.

Mehdi leading them across the busy one-way road of Avenue Colonel Amirouche.

About two hundred metres from the Bouroubi house, Mehdi stopped.

"This is it," he said. "This is the house, that Mother had said the Ben Dee family lived."

"Thank you, Mehdi... oh well, this is it!" Tom said, nervously. "Now's the time we find out for sure."

Tom turned to Mehdi.

"We would like to thank you and your family for

all of your help. It has been an enormous pleasure to meet you all."

"For us, too," said Mehdi. "It is good to help others... is it not?"

With that, Mehdi turned and made his way home.

Tom stood, looking at the door, waiting for it to knock itself.

It didn't, so he took the knocker of the two-hundred-year-old house and banged.

After a few seconds, a young girl of about twelve years old answered the door.

She was wearing tatty worn-out, torn and dirty clothes, she looked like she hadn't eaten properly for several days.

"Yes?" she said in French.

"Hello," said Tom. "We are looking for the family of Ben Dee?"

"Wait one moment," said the young girl, then closed the door.

A moment later, the door opened once more. This time the girl was holding the hand of a man.

He was wearing a worn-out qamiis, grubby and soiled.

His face unwashed, he had a long greying beard and long uncombed hair. His eyes completely white.

"Can I help you?" he said, his voice weak.

"We are hoping you can," said Tom. "We have come from Britain. We are from London. My friend is looking for the family of Ben Dee?"

"The family of Ben Dee?" questioned the man in the doorway. "What do you want with the family of

461

Ben Dee?"

"Are you the family of Mustafa Ben Dee?"

"Mustafa was my great grandfather!"

"Then, it is you we seek!"

"May I ask why?" the man said, suspiciously.

"We believe, something may have been left for you to look after during the war... we were curious... does it still exist?"

The man stood in the doorway, still holding the girl's hand on one side and the door on the other, keeping himself steady.

"Come in... come in!"

He turned from the door, the girl still holding his hand as she guided him back to a low bench seat along the wall.

"Please sit down," he said, his arm gesturing towards the bench seat.

"Thank you," Tom replied.

The young girl ran into one of the side rooms, coming back with two large cushions; the cushions along with the long bench seat were all dirty.

Tom sat beside the man, Sebastian on one of the cushions. But Jennifer preferred to stand, so as not to get her white trousers and light blue abaya dirty.

"As you see," the man said. "I am not in the best of health. My wife died a few years ago, then I had an accident at work. It has left me blind, and weak; I can no longer work."

"I am very sorry to hear that," sympathised Tom.

"There is now only my daughter and myself left here."

"And your name... is it also Ben Dee?"

"Yes, this is my name," said the man. "And, can you tell me the reason you are here?"

"Yes, we have come across a contract, belonging to my friend's great grandfather. The contract, with a part on the contract written by your great grandfather, saying items will be held here until they are collected."

There was a short silence as Ben Dee thought.

"Yes, generation by generation, we were told," said Ben Dee, with feeling and frustration in his voice. "That it will be collected in 1947!"

"Yes, we are sorry about that, we believe that both parties who were to collect it had died before that date."

"So, what if I tell you that it is gone?"

"We would say, thank you for your time, and we will leave."

"Have you got the contract with you?" croaked Ben Dee.

"Yes, we have a copy."

While Tom got the copy of the contract out of his bag, Ben Dee called his daughter.

As she arrived, Tom handed the copy to her.

"The top part is in a language I don't understand father," she said. "But the bottom part says, 'The family of Ben Dee will look after the boxes, until their collection'."

"And is there a name?" insisted Ben Dee.

"Yes, Mustafa Ben Dee and Celestin Bourgogne."

"The last part is the address. As long as it is signed by Mustafa!"

"Yes, yes, it is," the young girl agreed.

"Then," coughed Ben Dee. "Can I say… we have been expecting you!"

Tom turning to Sebastian and Jennifer nodded, then quietly said.

"It looks like we may be in luck!"

"Great," said Jennifer.

Sebastian looking at Jennifer with a huge smile.

"And may we see the boxes, Mr Ben Dee?" asked Tom.

"I am going to tell you; my family have all through the generations passed down the story. The two men who arrived on the merchant ship, the *Suraat Allah*, both tall and smartly dressed, one English and the other Polish. And that my great grandfather agreed to look after the boxes, and that an agreement was made, that although the two Europeans gave Mustafa a down payment, it was agreed that the rest would be paid on collection."

"Thank you, Mr Ben Dee… I can promise you that you will be handsomely rewarded for looking after our boxes!"

"When? As you can see, my daughter and I are struggling. We need help now!"

"Mr Ben Dee, let us see the boxes, make sure that all is okay. I will arrange with my friends to make you an offer. We will then arrange collection. There will be a very good reward!"

"Thank you… thank you!" sobbed Ben Dee.

"May we see the boxes, Mr Ben Dee?"

"Yes… yes, indeed, I will get my daughter to show you where the basement is, then you can check that everything is to your satisfaction!"

Ben Dee's daughter showed Tom, Jennifer and Sebastian to the top of the basement steps, then pointed to where they had to go.

The door, about one metre (three feet) tall, creaked open; at every rasping sound, dust and flaking debris fell from the annexe that they all stood in.

The door open, Tom ducking as he entered the opening, followed by Sebastian and Jennifer as they made their way down the rickety steps to the dingy hole below the house.

The dirty window letting virtually no light into the room, but with the light there was, their eyes slowly grew accustomed.

They could see the green tarpaulin in the corner of the room.

Everything they touched was covered in dust, a layer of what seemed like a couple of millimetres every decade since 1945, the steps, the floor, the walls, as well as the tarpaulin.

As they walk towards the green cover, dust kicked up, covering their skin and clothes with a grimy orange taint.

Sebastian's excitement finally getting too much for him, he rushed towards the corner of the room flinging the tarpaulin into the air.

The room disappearing into a dirty smog as dust flew everywhere, Tom and Jennifer turning their faces away from the dust explosion.

Under the cover, lay the objects that Sebastian had been dreaming about for the last several weeks.

The green boxes.

"Hey, Sebastian," cried Jennifer "Be careful, this dust has gone everywhere, just calm down, there's plenty of time."

Bending down, he started to pull one of the cases out from under the cover.

Surprised at how heavy they were, he put his fingers under the lid and pulled at the top of the green box, but not the slightest movement.

He looked around the room, he needed something to prise it open.

"Sebastian, calm down," insisted Tom. "Just chill!"

Sebastian's face screwed up in his urgency to look inside the green box.

His body stooped as his head scanned from side to side looking for a means of opening the treasure.

Tom and Jennifer jumping back as he thrashed his way around the room, then down on his hands and knees, feeling under the several millimetres of dust that has settled on the floor.

To and fro his body swept, under shelves, around corners, under the stairs where he suddenly stopped. Pulling something out of the dirt, half standing, a menacing look on his face.

Banging the object on the steps, kicking up more dust.

Turning, he quickly rushed back to the tarpaulin, crashing back to the ground, onto his hands and knees, directly in front of the green box he was trying to open moments earlier.

Forcing the flat bar under the lid of the box. Grunting and groaning; pulling and tugging at the bar.

Tom and Jennifer stand well out of the way as Sebastian thrashed and mauled at the lid.

Sebastian's face, red with anger and frustration, until suddenly a squeak, a nail; the lid started to move.

Sebastian's fingers back under the small gap, the bar on the other side as he pulled and fought with the lid.

More squeaking of nails as the lid slowly started to rise... until, finally, with one last big effort, the contents were revealed.

Sebastian slowly stood, his feet in front of the box, his clothes, hair and face covered in dust, his hands dirty and bloodied.

Tom and Jennifer move towards the now calm Sebastian, Tom on one side and Jennifer on the other. All three looking down into the open green wooden chest.

Four gold ingots, shining... glowing in the murky cellar. Each ingot around twelve and a half kilograms, the boxes piled high up against the wall.

Tom thought how wonderful the human nature of the Ben Dee family.

The man upstairs, ill, blind and in poverty, and below him millions of dollars' worth of gold, and all he wanted to do was the right thing, to look after it until it was collected by the people on the contract.

Sebastian suddenly turning to Jennifer, grabbing her under her arms as he spun her around, shouting.

"Yes, yes, yes!"

As he stopped spinning, lowering her to the

ground, her clothes dirty, covered in an orange coating of dust from the basement, now smeared with black, Sebastian's handprints on her new abaya and white trousers, a round black smudge on her face where he had kissed her.

"Well done Tom," said Jennifer. "We couldn't have done this without you!"

Sebastian lifted one of the gold ingots from the crate, walking around the basement holding it to his face and kissing it.

"Okay," said Tom. "Now we have found it, we will have to put it back under the canvas. We will have to give Mr Ben Dee upstairs something for storing this for all these years, then make our way back home… get in touch with the correct authorities to get this all recovered."

"Recovered?" said Sebastian.

"Yes, we will let the correct people know we have found it. It will be collected by them."

"And what about us?" continued Sebastian.

"We will get a finder's reward."

"*Hmmm*," sulked Sebastian, not sure.

"Now, if you can put that ingot away, we can cover it all back up!"

"Er… *no!*" huffed Sebastian.

"Come on Bastian," insisted Tom.

"Umm… *no!*"

Jennifer stood back, Sebastian's face getting redder again, his features screwing up as if he was going to start snarling.

"If you put it away Bastian, we can get going back to the ship," insisted Tom.

"I fucking told you **NO!**"

Sebastian rushed towards Tom, with an angry scowl he came face to face with the slightly shorter fair-haired man.

Tom taking a step back as his hands came up, stopping Sebastian from walking directly into him.

Sebastian's dark combed back hair, grey with dust, his face smeared with orange and black marks from the basement's dirt and grime, along with his angry expression made him look like a Māori warrior about to go to war.

"Whoa!" said Tom. "It's okay Bastian... I'm sure one isn't going to matter... keep it!"

Sebastian turned quickly away from Tom.

Sebastian having seen a piece of hessian material, while he had been feeling around the floor, picked it up, then wrapped it around the ingot.

Tom put his foot on the case top, now with one less ingot, he pushed the lid of the box back down till it was closed. He then pushed the case back under the tarpaulin, pulled the cover back until it was again, hiding the boxes.

"I think it was time we were going," said Jennifer "I need to put some clean clothes on and shower!"

"I think you are right" agreed Tom.

"Are you ready Bastian?" Jennifer said, looking at Sebastian.

"Mmm," answered Sebastian.

"So, what's the problem?" asked Jennifer

"Are we leaving this lot here?" said Sebastian, pointing at the canvas hiding the boxes.

"We cannot take it now," insisted Tom. "It's got

to be dealt with properly!"

"And, in any case," said Jennifer, calmly. "We, on our own, will never get this back to the ship. The best thing we can do, is bide our time and organise this to be picked up... Properly, with a team of people... now... come on Bastian. It's time to go. Let's get going. The sooner we get back to home soil, the sooner we can get this organised and picked up... okay?"

"Okay Jen, I see your point," agreed Sebastian.

"Good, now, let's get back up to the next floor and arrange how we are going to deal with the pick-up with Mr Ben Dee."

Sebastian made his way up the steps, his hands tightly holding onto the ingot wrapped in hessian.

Jennifer went up next followed by Tom.

Mr Ben Dee was still sitting on the long cushion on the floor.

"Is it all to your satisfaction gentlemen, madame?" Mr Ben Dee said in French.

"It is," replied Tom. "We weren't sure it was still going to be here, so we have not arrived with any way of moving the boxes."

"This is fine," said Ben Dee. "As long as you can help me with my condition, I will make sure it is still here when you return."

"We would like to thank you very much Mr Ben Dee, for taking care of the boxes for all this time."

"It is my pleasure... my great grandfather's word... is my word too!"

Tom turning to Sebastian and Jennifer, explained the situation with Mr Ben Dee.

They were saying goodbye to Mr Ben Dee as he rose from the cushion.

"Okay, Bastian," said Jennifer. "Give Mr Ben Dee some money."

"Money," exclaimed Sebastian. "How much?" he sighed

"A couple of thousand," she replied.

"How much?" blasted Sebastian, looking directly at Jennifer.

"You heard, the man is sick, he needs treatment... and you, you, are standing there with a gold bar in your hands, worth tens of thousands... and if he dies, and someone else moves into this house, with no more Ben Dee's to look after the boxes, they could be gone... Now, give him a couple of thousand and let's get going!"

Ben Dee's daughter walked into the room as they prepared themselves ready to leave.

Sebastian pulled two thousand euros from his wallet, handing it to Mr Ben Dee, Tom explaining what Sebastian had just given him, telling him, they will return soon.

The young girl opening the front door, Tom, Jennifer and Sebastian, leave the house of Ben Dee.

They cross the busy road of Avenue Colonel Amirouche, known before the revolution of 1962 as Avenue Celestin Bourgoin.

Happy with the find, they jump into Hussan's taxi and head back to the port.

# Chapter 44
## Power Trip
## Summer Present-day

The next day at eight a.m.

The Sunseeker Predator 50, known as *Gold Rush To*, owned by Milstone-Hanks, the company of Sebastian Plant, was ready to set off from its berth in the harbour; to leave the Port of Annaba.

They had all showered the night before, their bodies and clothes covered in dust and dirt.

The morning came with a new start.

Tom wearing his usual orange T-shirt, camel-coloured baggy shorts and flip flops.

Sebastian at the helm's seat, wearing a white Fred Perry T-shirt, beige trousers and light brown deck shoes.

Jennifer emerging from the lower deck, up the stairs to the cockpit deck of the Sunseeker as it was just pulling away from its docked position.

Tom still down on the swim deck putting the ropes and fenders away.

"Hello, Bastian... ready for the journey?" she said, kissing him on the lips.

"Hmm, you smell good, and you look really good!" he replied.

Jennifer was wearing a cotton mini dress, thin and light. It was designed with a multitude of colours, looking like a paintbrush from every tin in a paint shop had made its own unique colour on the dress. It had a thin strap over the shoulders and was open down the front to her stomach, with a black lace that criss-crossed from each side across her bosom.

Tom stepped up from the swim platform onto the lower cockpit, as Jennifer walked down to greet him.

"Here comes my hero!" she smiled.

Putting her arms around Tom's neck she kissed him on the lips.

Sebastian looked back and shuddered.

They passed through the gap in the harbour wall, turned to the north and set the navigation for Cagliari, Sardinia.

All pleased with the outcome of the trip. The end result, finding the gold, worth all of the trouble of the journey to get there.

Annaba was now passing on their left-hand side; they all knew it was somewhere they would have to go back to. The rest of the gold, sitting in the dirty, dusty cellar since 1945, would have to be rescued for good.

The last sight of Annaba was the lighthouse of El Manar, off the northern coast of Algeria.

The Sunseeker heading for the open sea and seven hours till they reached the next land.

They settled to their tasks, or just chilled, waiting for their turn at the helm.

A beautiful day, the sun shining, the sea calm as they made their way back to the European Coastline.

Sebastian taking the first hour at the helm. Tom, having rummaged through the drawers, had managed to find a Dan Brown novel, *Origins*, which kept him busy reading.

About twenty-five miles off the North African coast and about an hour into the journey, Jennifer took over at the helm; nothing to report, Sebastian had said. A few merchant ships, a cruise liner and a couple of small naval vessels; all at a distance, and no cause for concern.

As Jennifer took charge of the Predator 50, Sebastian made his way down the stairs.

Tom was sitting in the lounge reading.

"How's it going?" asked Tom, looking up from his book.

"Oh, it's fine. It'll be great if it is like this all the way back to Marseille."

"Let's hope!"

Sebastian continued on into his bedroom, over to the gold bar sitting on the cupboard, picking it up, he turned then lay it on the bed; where he stroked it several times.

He stood up again, walked around the bed, not taking his eyes off his prize. Picking it, he continued to walk around the room. Sebastian laid on the carpet to one side of the bed, the gold bar still in his hands, he lowered it to the floor above the top of his head.

From here he did sit-ups, the bar going up and over him until it reached his feet. Then he would reverse, going back to a lying position, the bar back on the floor above the top of his head.

The second hour into the journey ended, Jennifer leaving the helm as Tom took over. Again, there was nothing to report, all quiet, a couple of naval ships and a couple of merchant ships, that's all.

Jennifer made her way down the stairs, grabbing a bottle of red wine and a couple of glasses before drifting into the bedroom.

Sebastian still lying on his back on the floor, the gold bar on his chest. His hands underneath each end of the gold bar, pushing it up to his arm's full length above his body, then back down to his chest.

Jennifer opened the wine while Sebastian repeated his push-ups several times.

"Glass of wine?" she asked.

"Love one," he replied.

"Good, because I have already poured it!"

Picking up both the glasses, she walked over to where Sebastian was lying on the carpet, the gold bar now at rest on his chest.

Lifting the ingot, he then lowered it to the floor above his head.

With a glass in each hand, she put one foot each side of his legs as he lay on the floor. She slowly walked towards his upper body.

From here, Sebastian could see she was not wearing any underwear under the brightly coloured mini dress.

"Now, stop playing with that gold bar, and start playing with me," she said sexily.

As her feet reached either side of his head, she started to bend her knees. A glass of wine carefully balanced in each hand, down she went. Her pudendum getting closer to Sebastian's mouth, her vaginal lips red and moist as they longed to get his tongue inside her.

Sebastian could feel the heat from her pussy as it got closer to his face.

Jennifer dropped to her knees as Sebastian's tongue darted in and out, flicking across her lips and twisting around her clitoris.

Desperately trying not to spill the wine as the thrill of her impending orgasm engulfed her body.

She found the concentration difficult. The glasses remaining still, while her hips and vagina moved forward and backwards, faster and faster; her head went back.

Holding onto the two glasses, she came over his face.

Her head dropping forward, her hair tumbling over her chest. She took several deep breaths.

"Now, you sex god, get up on this bed… and bring that ingot with you!" she purred.

Getting to her feet, she stepped off of him.

Sebastian after getting up from the floor, laid on the bed, placing the gold bar in the middle. Jennifer handed him his glass of wine.

"Here, let's have a toast," she said.

"To what?"

"To wealth… on a grand scale."

"Mmmm, yes, I'll drink to that!"

The glasses clinked, they drank the wine. Jennifer walked around to the other side of the bed, putting her glass on the bedside table, then lay on the bed beside Sebastian, the gold bar between them.

"And, what do you plan on doing with this when you get back home?" she said, patting the ingot.

"I don't know, I mean, you don't just walk into a

bank with a gold bar and say, 'Can I deposit this please'?"

"Maybe hacksaw bits off and pay for your shopping!"

They both laughed. Sebastian took another swig of the wine then turned, laying his glass on the shelf beside the bed.

Jennifer put her hand on the front of his trousers, feeling the hard lump of flesh below the material. She squeezed her fingers around the lump, her hand moving slowly up and down.

"And, what if it doesn't go the way you planned?"

"What do you mean?" quizzed Sebastian.

Jennifer stopped rubbing and slowly pulled down his zipper, undid the waist button of his trousers, putting her fingers into his underpants she pulled at his manhood; it sprang into the open.

"Well," she said, clenching his cock a bit too hard "let's say... when we are back in London,"

"Hmm."

She released the tight pressure on his cock and dug her fingernails in.

"Let's say, Tom, *as he will*, goes to the authorities."

Jennifer scraped her nails up and down Sebastian's cock. His face cringing with the pain, but not sure if this was part of her game, he continued to endure.

"He will be the hero, he will get the notoriety, but most of all..."

She said grabbing Sebastian's balls tightly as he

jumped with the pain.

"He will get the money... and you, my dear Bastian, will get none!"

Jennifer releasing his balls, grabbed his shaft putting his cock in her mouth.

Sebastian immediately relaxed.

"So, what do you suggest?" asked Sebastian.

The pain now turning to a thrill as her tongue encircled his manhood.

Keeping hold of the shaft of his cock, she raised her head until it was level with his.

"Kill him!"

"*Kill him*, no, I couldn't do that!"

"Kill him, Bastian. No one will know, we are at sea!"

"No, I couldn't kill, no!"

"Then you get no money," she said, letting go of his cock. "You get no glory... and you get no more of me!"

Sebastian looked at her.

"If you haven't got the balls, Bastian," she continued. "Then I would rather be with Tom!"

"You wouldn't?"

"Try me Bastian... now, kill him!"

"But!"

"No buts Bastian, just tell him... you have the contract, it's your right to have that gold. It was owned by your great grandfather, it is yours, yours by right... not for Tom to do with what he wants! Now go!"

"Kill him?"

"Yes... and if while you are chucking him

overboard, you hear me shouting to stop, take no notice. Just KILL him!"

"Kill him!"

Sebastian stepped down from the bed, picking up his glass of wine, taking a large swig, he headed for the bedroom door. Jennifer jumping off the bed quickly followed him, grabbing the bottle of wine, her glass and her mobile phone as she did.

Tom sitting at the helm, about three-quarters of the way through his shift at the wheel. The North African coast about sixty-five miles behind them.

Sebastian walked up the stairs to the main cockpit, Jennifer a few steps behind him, his face red with anger.

"Can I have a word, Tom!" Sebastian announced abruptly.

"Yeah, of course… what is it?" Tom continued looking ahead of the ship.

Sebastian stomped over to the white leather seats in the corner of the main cockpit, put his glass down on the table, remained standing as he turned to look at the back of Tom's head. Jennifer followed, putting her glass and the bottle down next to Sebastian's. Then sat on the white leather seats.

"A word, Tom!" Sebastian's voice getting louder.

"Yes, of course!"

"Over here, now, stop the boat while we sort this out!"

"Okay Bastian, no problem," Tom replied calmly.

Tom pulled the throttle back and the *Gold Rush To* slowed instantly.

Tom jumped down from the helm and walked back to the seats, Sebastian staring at him. Jennifer picked up her mobile phone.

"What is it, Bastian? You seem a bit stressed," Tom said.

"What will happen to the gold back in Annaba?" Sebastian growled.

"Well, when we get back to the UK, I will contact the correct authorities, who will organise its collection."

"And what will *I* get out of it?" insisted Sebastian.

"You will get a finder's fee... I'm sure you will!"

"Finder's fee... FINDER'S FEE," Sebastian shouted. "That treasure... is mine!"

"Well... no!"

"Fucking YES," screamed Sebastian as his face got redder still. "That is *my* contract, my great grandfather's hard graft... IT IS MINE!"

"Hang on...!"

Sebastian pushed Tom backwards as Jennifer switched the video to her mobile phone on.

"Stop it, stop it *now* you two!" Jennifer called.

"You bastard," slammed Sebastian, as he walked towards Tom. "You thought *you* were getting it!"

Sebastian punching Tom in the face. Tom reeled, staggered back onto the seat, holding his chin.

"What the hell are you doing?" said Tom.

Jennifer getting up from the seat, looking into her phone as she videoed the two men.

Tom was starting to get back to his feet as Sebastian rushed in, grabbing the top of his T-shirt, he punched Tom in the face twice more; on the chin and his eye.

Tom kicked out with his feet, sending Sebastian staggering backwards across the main cockpit.

Tom jumping quickly to his feet, raced towards Sebastian who hadn't yet found his feet. Tom, lowering his shoulder, catching Sebastian in the chest. They both crashed into the helm's chair.

Jennifer keeping out of the way of the violent clashes as she continued to video the scene.

"Bastian... Tom, stop it for crying out loud, before someone gets hurt!"

As Sebastian's body was thrust against the helms seat, he raised his feet into Tom's stomach, pushing back hard. Tom flying backwards, falling to the deck and sliding into the seat opposite.

Sebastian rushed towards the prone Tom, kicking him hard in the ribs. Tom's body jerking back further across the floor. Sebastian's foot moving back for a second kick as Tom reached for a fire extinguisher under the seat. Sebastian's foot coming in for a second blow to the ribs, Tom stopping it with the extinguisher; a clang as Sebastian's foot hit the metallic object. Tom quickly thrusting the extinguisher down onto Sebastian's foot with a dull thud.

"Aye, *you* FUCKER!" shouted Sebastian, hopping back.

Tom, quickly up on his feet, punching Sebastian, who staggered back further. Grabbing each other, they punch at close range.

As Tom pulled away, Sebastian hit Tom in the

middle of his face, sending him staggering back, his legs hitting the table. As he fell backwards, the bottle of red wine and the glasses smash, red wine and glass violently shattering over the table and floor.

Sebastian jumping on top of Tom, his hands around Tom's throat. Tom, with one hand pushing Sebastian's chin upwards. The other swinging, trying to hit the side of his head. Tom, not able to breathe; he could feel himself getting weaker.

Tom's hand, now too weak to hit, dropped to his side, feeling around the table for anything that could help his fight.

His hand coming into contact with a broken wine glass. Twisting the glass, until he had hold of the glasses base. With as much force as he could muster, he plunged the broken stem into Sebastian's side.

Sebastian's face cringed with the pain as his hands loosen their grip in Tom's throat. Tom pulling the glass away from Sebastian's body, he stabbed the man on top a second time.

Sebastian letting one hand go from Tom's neck, he started punching the man below.

Blood pouring out of the wounds to Sebastian's side, covering his white Fred Perry shirt and beige trousers with a mixture of blood and red wine.

"Fuck you! FUCK YOU!" Sebastian shouted angrily.

"Bastian, stop it, Bastian, you'll kill him, stop it!" Jennifer screamed.

Tom swung his hand around from the side, catching Sebastian in the ear. Sebastian falling to the side but was quickly onto his feet along with Tom.

Punch after punch they reeled around the deck of the boat.

Sebastian picking up the broken wine bottle by the neck, swinging and slashing it at Tom, who managed to keep clear of the jagged edge.

Tom turned, dodging the lethal weapon, when the bottom of the sharp bottle slashes across the top of his arm.

"Hey, what are you doing," shouted Tom. "Just stop, will you?"

Tom punching Sebastian twice in the face. He staggered back, giving Tom one chance, he kicked at the broken bottle that was in Sebastian's hand. The force of Tom's foot propelling the bottle from Sebastian's fingers, sending the deadly weapon flying over the side of the boat.

Jennifer had switched the phone's video off and was now setting it up on a phone stand above the navigation screen at the helm.

Tom and Sebastian punch and kick as they fell around the main cockpit.

"Bastian... Tom... stop it!" she cried, as she turned to see them crashing towards her at the helm.

Both holding onto each other's necks; Tom having Sebastian's hair from behind him they bounce off of the helm's chair, to fall against the side window of the main cockpit. Sebastian's arm pushing up between his and Tom's chest. His hand forcing Tom's head back aggressively, hitting the side window of the Predator 50, several times.

Tom twisting his body quickly making Sebastian lose his grip; still hanging on to each other, they fell into the lower cockpit, into the hot Mediterranean summer sun.

Jennifer jumping up onto the white leather seats, looking down at the two fighting men. Tom landing blow after blow onto Sebastian.

Sebastian falling back, hit the transom of the boat, then crashed to the floor.

As Tom got closer, Sebastian lashed out with his feet, catching Tom's legs, the force sending him off balance. Tom hitting the side of the craft, half-falling backwards. Managing to grab the side rail just enough to stop himself from falling into the sea. Sebastian jumped up and was quickly over to the flailing Tom, trying to push him the rest of the way; punching Tom in the stomach, he tried to heave him over the side and into the Mediterranean.

Tom's leg coming up quickly, his foot catching Sebastian in the groin.

Sebastian's body bending double with the pain.

"Stop it!" shouted Jennifer from the leather seats.

Tom pulling himself back onto the boat as Sebastian grabbed a lifebuoy. Swinging the lifebuoy at Tom's face, just missing. Then back the other way, giving Tom a chance to land a punch into Sebastian's face. The lifebuoy flying out of Sebastian's hand, over the side of the boat as he staggered back.

They rush at each other, Sebastian's hand around the back of Tom as he pulled Tom's hair, the other hand pushing up at Tom's chin. Tom pulling at Sebastian's hair from behind, his other hand pushing up at Sebastian's chin, both their heads forced backwards.

Red with anger, the two of them crashed around the lower cockpit deck.

Catching both their feet, they fell into the upper main cockpit, Tom landing on top, he punched down onto Sebastian beneath him.

Blow after blow Tom landed on Sebastian's face, trying to end what he thought was this madness.

"Whoa, whoa, whoa," Sebastian suddenly shouted.

Tom's fist up, ready to land the next blow. Sebastian, his face red and bloodied, had put his hands up to surrender.

Jennifer looking over to the video, not sure whether to turn it off now or keep it running.

Tom sensed a truce, so got up to his feet. Sebastian still lying on the deck. Tom bending down, offers Sebastian a hand to help him up. Sebastian taking the hand gratefully as Tom pulled Sebastian to his feet.

Still having their hands around each other's wrists, they stood facing each other. Eye to eye, bruised, bloodied and exhausted, heavily breathing, face to face.

Tom turning, he started to head for the white leather seats. He needed to rest.

Suddenly from behind, Sebastian hit Tom with a huge blow to the back of the head.

Tom falling heavily forward, landing in a heap on the leather chairs.

Sebastian's fingers broken from the blow; shaking his hand with the pain, he held it to his chest.

"You FUCKING stupid FUCKING moron!"

Sebastian shouted.

Jennifer jumping off of the chair as Tom landed beside her. Sebastian rushing in, grabbing the back of Tom's T-shirt and shorts, throwing him towards the back of the seat and over the transom.

Tom hit the rear wall, falling over the top, landing on his back on the lower cockpit below.

Sebastian jumping onto the leather seats and over the transom wall, just missing Tom as he landed.

Jennifer getting back onto the leather seats, looking over the transom at the sight below.

"Stop it… stop it now!" she cried.

As Tom lay on the deck, Sebastian quickly picking up an oar from the wall of the swim platform.

Lifting it high above him, Sebastian sent the oar crashing towards Tom's head.

Tom just managing to roll out of the way, the heavy wooden pole missing him by millimetres.

Tom quickly jumping to his feet, exhausted but ready to fight on, grabbed the second oar.

Sebastian lifting his oar, he chopped it down towards Tom's head. Tom quickly holding his oar with two hands over his head. Sebastian's oar slamming down between his hands, Tom staggered back.

Sebastian's oar going up for a second time as it slammed down towards Tom's head. Again, Tom's oar taking the blow, Tom getting knocked back further.

A third blow from Sebastian's oar, again stopped

by Tom; Tom's foot catching the steps to the swim platform. Losing his balance, he fell backwards onto the sea level deck.

Sebastian looking down into the swim platform, still holding his oar ready to finish Tom off.

Jennifer jumping off the seats in the main cockpit, rounds the transom wall, now looking over the swim platform wall, a better position to watch the two men fighting below. As she moved from upper to lower deck, she looked back at the video, checking it was still filming.

Tom on his feet as Sebastian landed on the swim platform, but with one final last blow from Sebastian, Tom hit the water.

"Bastian, no, Bastian, no!" shouted Jennifer.

Tom floating in the water close to the boat, the oar still above his head as Sebastian's oar hit the water, trying to finish Tom off once and for good.

Tom clinging to his oar, watching as Jennifer climbed down onto the swim platform, moving swiftly behind Sebastian.

Tom drifted further away from the boat as he heard Jennifer say,

"Go on Bastian... go and finish him!"

Pushing Sebastian from behind.

He hit the water with a splash, letting go of his oar, he swam towards Tom. Grabbing Tom's head, Sebastian pushed the exhausted charity worker under.

Jennifer turning, climbing the steps of the swim platform, up to the lower cockpit, then to the main cockpit.

She switched the mobile phone video off.

Sebastian pushing Tom under the water once more, Tom looking through the watery bubbles of his last breath.

The Sunseeker's engines revs rose, the boat pulling a little distance away from the fighting men.

Sebastian stopped pushing Tom's head under the water as he looked around, watching his boat, the Sunseeker Predator 50 moving away from him.

Tom again reaching the surface, his head upwards grabbing air. The turbulence of the boat's propeller pushing the lifebuoy in Tom's direction, he grabbed the red and white life-saver as it was passing him. Pulling it over his head, his arms through the hole, he floated in the sea while he caught his breath.

Sebastian, stunned at what had just happened, floating, he stared at the Sunseeker as it moved away from him. After a few seconds, the boat started to turn, going in a full circle. It started to head back towards the two of them in the sea.

'*Thank goodness,*' thought Sebastian, she's coming back.

The Sunseeker stopped about ten metres away from the two men in the water, sideways on to them.

Jennifer stepping down onto the lower cockpit, looking over the side of the boat, towards the two men, Tom clinging onto a lifebuoy, Sebastian having grabbed an oar.

"Boys," she called out. "Boys, you can stop fighting now… I have some bad news for you both, and… well, as neither of you are going to be in this world for much longer, I guess I can tell you my story. Tom... you would have met my sister, beautiful, isn't she? You know, Sammie... at the Professor's funeral? Oh, and sorry about the Professor. I am afraid he had to die; he knew too much. You see, I am not the person you thought I was... Jennifer, I am sad to say, had to die as well. I killed her. We were roommates for a while; she was the other girl in the picture I sent to you, Tom. And, of course, the Professor had contacted her and knew who she was, so they both had to go. But you, Tom. I said to Sammie, you would be the real thing. You would find the treasure. Sammie agreed to get you onboard, fund your project... but only for a while.

"Sebastian... well, you were a bonus. Well, for me, sex, sun and good eating. What more could a girl ask for? But, sorry to say, you are surplus to requirements. You are no longer needed, so, you have to go too... Oh, thanks for the video of the fight, by the way, boys. If the authorities ever find you, I will let them know how you ended up in the sea... and I did try and stop you... And, of course, thanks for the gold, I will spend it wisely... I promise... Ah, and one last thing... me. Don't think of me badly if we meet each other in the next life. After all, the other part of that contract, the burnt one sent to you Tom... is mine... I am Anna Schick. Wilhelm was my great grandfather!"

Leaving the lower deck, sitting back at the helm. The throttle pushed up, the boat pulled away... heading south, on its way back to Annaba.

# Gold War
## Epilogue

For those tricked into something they didn't want, life can be, well, a bit frustrating. When someone dies or is caused serious harm while being tricked, this can, in some instances, lead to revenge.

For an ex-wife, Amelia, whose lifestyle revolves around the wealth of her ex-husband, and the girlfriend, Kristina, who has stealth and worldliness, as well as the intelligence, knowledge and access to a vast information resource.

Revenge could be sweet.

# For more information

If you would like to find out more about the author, please visit Terry Dee's website.

## terrydee.com

There you will also find interesting facts, pictures, drawings and sketches used in the making of this book.

I hope you have enjoyed my story.